D0282470

Hawk O'Toole's Hostage

SANDRA BROWN

Hawk O'Toole's Hostage

BANTAM BOOKS

NEW YORK · TORONTO · LONDON · SYDNEY · AUCKLAND

Doubleday Direct Large Print Edition

This Large Print Edition, prepared especially for Doubleday Direct, Inc., contains the complete unabridged text of the original Publisher's Edition.

HAWK O'TOOLE'S HOSTAGE
A Bantam Book

PUBLISHING HISTORY
Bantam Loveswept edition published June 1988
Bantam hardcover edition / January 1997

ISBN 1–56865–247–X

Bantam Books are published by Bantam Books, a division of Bantam Doubleday Dell Publishing Group, Inc. Its trademark, consisting of the words "Bantam Books" and the portrayal of a rooster, is Registered in U.S. Patent and Trademark Office and in other countries. Marca Registrada. Bantam Books, 1540 Broadway, New York, New York 10036.

PRINTED IN THE UNITED STATES OF AMERICA

This Large Print Book carries the Seal of Approval of N.A.V.H.

Dear Reader,

You have my wholehearted thanks for the interest and enthusiasm you've shown for my Loveswept romances over the past decade. I'm enormously pleased that the enjoyment I derived from writing them was contagious. Obviously you share my fondness for love stories that always end happily and leave us with a warm, inner glow.

Nothing quite equals the excitement one experiences when falling in love. In each romance, I tried to capture that excitement. The settings and characters and plots changed, but that was the recurring theme.

Something in all of us delights in lovers and their uneven pursuit of mutual fulfillment and happiness. Indeed, the pursuit is half the fun! I became involved with each pair of lovers and their unique story. As though paying a visit to old friends for whom I played matchmaker, I often reread their stories myself.

I hope you enjoy this encore edition of one of my personal favorites.

—Sandra Brown

One

They certainly looked like authentic train robbers. From the dusty brims of their hats to the jingling spurs on their boots, they looked as real to Miranda as Butch Cassidy and The Sundance Kid.

To avoid crashing into the temporary barricade of timber piled up on the tracks, the engine had belched a cloud of steam and the train had screeched to a stop. The actors, playing their roles to the hilt, had thundered out of the dense forest lining both sides of the track. The pounding hooves of their horses had plowed up the turf before they reared to a halt beside the tracks. While the well-trained mounts stood at attention, the masked "robbers," with pistols drawn, boarded the train.

"I don't remember reading anything about this in the brochure," a woman passenger remarked uneasily.

" 'Course not, honey. That'd spoil the

surprise," her husband said around a chuckle. "Helluva show, isn't it?"

Miranda Price thought so. A helluva show. Worth every penny of the cost of the excursion ticket. The staged holdup had all the passengers enthralled, and none more than Miranda's six-year-old son, Scott. He was sitting beside her on the seat, thoroughly engrossed in the realistic performance. His bright eyes were fixed on the leader of the outlaw band, who was slowly making his way down the narrow aisle of the train while the other bandits stood guard at each end of the car.

"Everybody be calm, stay in your seats, and nobody will get hurt."

He was probably a temporarily unemployed Hollywood actor, or perhaps a stuntman, who had taken this summer job to supplement his fluctuating income. Whatever they were paying him for this job wasn't enough, Miranda thought. He was perfectly suited to the role.

A bandanna covered the lower half of his face, muffling his voice but allowing it to reach every person in the antique railroad car. He was convincingly costumed, wearing a black hat pulled low over his brows, a long white duster, and around his hips a tooled leather gun belt with a thong strapping the holster to his thigh. The holster was empty because he was holding a Colt pistol in his gloved right hand as he moved down the row of seats, carefully scanning each face. His spurs jangled musically with every step.

"Is he really gonna rob us, Mommy?" Scott whispered.

Miranda shook her head no, but didn't take her eyes off the train robber. "It's just make-believe. There's nothing to be afraid of."

But even as she said so, she wasn't certain. Because in that instant the actor's eyes came to rest on her. Sharply, she sucked in her breath. His eyes, white hot and laser bright, pierced straight through her. They were a startling shade of blue, but that alone hadn't taken her breath. If the hostile intensity behind his eyes were part of the act, then his thespian talents were being wasted on this tourist train.

That smoldering gaze remained on Miranda until the man sitting in front of her asked the bandit, "Want us to empty our pockets, gunman?" He was the same man who had reassured his wife earlier.

The robber jerked his stare away from Miranda and looked down at the man. He gave a laconic shrug. "Sure."

Laughing, the tourist stood up and dug into the pockets of his plaid Bermuda shorts. He withdrew a credit card and waved it in front of the masked face. "Never leave home without it," he said in a booming voice, then laughed.

The other tourists on the train laughed with him. Miranda did not. She was looking at the robber. His eyes reflected no humor. "Sit down, please," he said in a whispery voice.

"Aw, say, don't get upset. I've got another pocket." The tourist produced a handful of cash and thrust it at the robber. Without juggling the pistol, he caught the money with his left hand. "There." Smiling broadly, the vacationer looked around for approval and got it from the other passengers. All applauded; some whistled.

The bandit stuffed the cash into the pocket of his duster. "Thanks."

The man sat back down beside his wife, who looked both ill at ease and embarrassed. The man patted her hand. "It's all a gag. Play along, honey."

The robber dismissed them and looked down at Scott, who was sitting between Miranda and the window. He was staring up at the masked man with awe. "Hello."

"Hello," the boy replied.

"You want to help me make my get-away?"

Innocent eyes opened wider. He flashed the robber a gap-toothed smile. "Sure!"

"Sweetheart," Miranda said cautiously to her son. "I—"

"He'll be all right." The hard stare above the bandanna did nothing to alleviate Miranda's apprehension. If anything it increased it. The cold expression belied the bandit's reassuring words.

He extended his hand to Scott. The boy eagerly and trustingly grasped it. He clambered over his mother's legs and out into the aisle. With Scott preceding the man, they started walking toward the front of the railroad car. Other youngsters aboard the train gave Scott envious looks, while the grown-ups cheered him on.

"See?" the man sitting in front of Miranda

said to his wife. "Didn't I tell you it was all a game? They even get the kids involved."

When the outlaw and her son had gone halfway up the aisle, Miranda scrambled out of her seat and started after them. "Wait! Where are you taking him? I'd rather he not get off the train."

The robber spun around and, again, pierced her with his fierce blue eyes. "I told you that he would be all right."

"Where are you going?"

"On a horseback ride."

"Not without my permission, you're not."

"Please, Mommy?"

"Come on, lady, give the kid a break," the obnoxious tourist said. "It's part of the fun. Your kid'll love it."

She ignored him and started up the aisle behind the masked robber, who by now was propelling Scott through the opening at the front of the car. Miranda speeded up. "I asked you not to—"

"Sit down, madam, and keep quiet!"

Stunned by the harsh tone of voice, she spun around. The two robbers who had been guarding the rear entrance of the railroad car had closed in behind her. Above their masks their eyes were wary, nervous, almost fearful, as though she were about to foil a well-orchestrated plan. It was in that instant that Miranda knew this wasn't a game. Not by any means.

Whirling around, she ran up the aisle and launched herself through the door and onto the platform between the passenger car and the engine. Two men, already mounted, were anxiously surveying the area. The robber was hoisting Scott up onto the saddle of his horse.

Scott clutched the horse's thick mane and chattered excitedly, "Gee, he's a big horse. We're up so high."

"Hold on, Scott, and don't let go. That's very important," the bandit instructed him.

Scott!

He knew her son's name.

Acting from the pure maternal instinct to protect her child, Miranda threw herself down the steps. She landed on her hands and knees in the gravel railroad bed, scraping them painfully. The two robbers were beside her in an instant. They grabbed her arms and held her back when she would have run toward Scott.

"Leave her alone," their leader barked. "Mount up. We're getting the hell out of here." The two released her and ran toward their waiting horses. Holding the reins of his horse in one hand and the pistol in the other, the leader said to Miranda, "Get back on the train." He made a jutting motion with his chin.

"Take my son off that horse."

"I told you, he won't be hurt. But you might be if you don't do as I say and get back aboard the train."

"Do what he says, lady."

Miranda turned in the direction of the terrified voice. The engineer of the train was lying facedown in the gravel beside the track. His hands were stacked atop his head. Another of the robbers was keeping him there at gunpoint.

Miranda cried out with fear and anxiety. She ran toward her son, arms outstretched. "Scott, get down!"

"Why, Mommy?"

"Get down this instant!"

"I can't," he wailed. His mother's anxiety had been transmitted to him. His six-year-old mind had suddenly figured out that this was no longer playacting. The small fingers clutching the horse's mane tightened their grip. "Mommy!" he screamed.

The leader hissed a vile curse just as Miranda threw herself against his chest. "Stop anybody who steps off that train," he shouted to his men.

The other passengers, who were by now filling every window on that side of the train, were beginning to panic. Some were shouting advice to Miranda. Others were screaming in fear. Some were too shocked and afraid to say or do anything. Parents were gathering their own children close and holding on to them for dear life.

Miranda fought like a wildcat. Her carefully tended nails became talons, which she would have used to claw the robber's face had she been able to reach it. As it was, his fingers had locked around her wrists like handcuffs. She was no match for his superior strength. She kicked his shins, aimed for his crotch with her knee, and was rewarded with a grunt of pain and surprise when it landed close.

"Let my son go!"

The man in the mask gave her a mighty push that sent her reeling backward. She landed hard on her bottom, but sprang up immediately and tackled him while he had one boot in the stirrup. Catching him off balance, she dug her shoulder into his ribs. She reached for Scott. Scott dived toward her and landed against her chest hard enough to knock the breath out of her. But she held on to him and turned, running blindly. The other bandits were all mounted. Their horses had been made nervous by the shouting. They were prancing around, kicking up clouds of dust that obscured Miranda's vision and clogged her nose and throat.

A thousand pinpricks stabbed her scalp when the robber caught her by the hair and brought her to an abrupt standstill. "Damn you," he cursed behind his mask. "This could have been so easy." She risked letting go of Scott to reach for the bandit's mask. He caught her hand in midair and issued an order in a language she didn't understand. One of his men immediately materialized out of the clouds of swirling dust. "Take the boy. Let him ride with you."

"No!"

Scott was wrestled from Miranda's clutching hands. When the bandit's arm closed around her middle like pincers and he dragged her backward, she fought harder than ever. Digging her heels into the earth, she tried to keep sight of Scott, who was wailing in terror.

"I'll kill you if you hurt my son."

The bandit seemed unfazed by her threat as he mounted his horse and yanked her up with him. She was still dangling half on, half off the saddle when he spurred the horse. It danced in a tight circle before streaking off through the dense forest. The other riders followed.

The horses' hooves thundered through the otherwise serene woods. They sped through the thick pine forest so fast that Miranda became more afraid of falling off and being trampled than she was of the kidnapper. She clutched his waist in fear that he might let go of her as they began to climb.

Eventually the trees thinned out, but they continued to ride without breaking their speed. The terrain became more rocky. Horseshoes clattered on the rocks, which formed shelves over which they rode. Behind her she could hear Scott crying. If she, an adult, were afraid, what terror must her child be suffering?

After about half an hour they crested a peak, and the band of riders had to reduce their pace to begin their descent of the other side of the mountain. When they reached the first copse of pine along the timberline, the leader slowed his mount to a walk, then came to a full stop. He pressed Miranda's waist with his arm.

"Tell your son to stop crying."

"Go to hell."

"I swear, lady, I'll leave you here for the coyotes to eat," he said in a raspy voice. "You'll never be heard from again."

"I'm not afraid of you."

"You'll never see your son again."

Above the mask, his eyes were icy. Hating them, Miranda reached up and yanked down the bandanna. She had intended to disarm him, but it was she who took a gasping breath.

The rest of his face was as startling as his eyes. The angles were precise, as though each feature had been lined up with a ruler. His cheekbones were high and as sharp as blades, his jaw perfectly square. His lips were narrow and wide. Above them he had a long, straight nose. He continued to stare at her with open contempt.

"Tell your son to stop crying," he repeated.

The resolve in his voice, in his eyes, chilled her. She would fight him when it was possible to win. Now, her efforts would be futile. She wasn't a coward, but she wasn't a fool either. Swallowing her fear and her pride, she called out shakily, "Scott." When his crying didn't subside, she cleared her throat and tried again, louder this time. "Scott!"

"Mommy?" Scott lowered his grimy hands from his red, weeping eyes and searched her out.

"Don't cry anymore, okay, darling? These . . . these men aren't going to hurt us."

"I wanna go home now."

"I know. So do I. And we will. Shortly. But right now, don't cry, okay?"

The small fists wiped away the remaining tears. He hiccupped a sob. "Okay. But can I ride with you? I'm scared."

She glanced up at her captor. "May he—"

"No." The blunt reply was made before she even finished voicing the question. Ignoring her baleful stare, he addressed his men, giving them orders so that when they urged their mounts forward again, the horse Scott was on was second in the procession. Before nudging his horse, their captor asked her curtly, "Can you ride astride?"

"Who are you? What do you want with us? Why did you take Scott off that train?"

"Throw your right leg over. It'll be safer and more comfortable."

"You know who Scott is. I heard you call him by name. What do you—Oh!"

He slid his hand between her thighs and lifted the right one over the saddle. The leather was warm against her bare skin, but that sensation was mild compared to the feel of his gloved hand on her inner thigh. Before she could recover from that, he lifted her over the pommel and wedged her between it and his open thighs. He flattened his hand against her lower body and pulled her back even farther, until she was snugly pressed against him.

"Stop manhandling me."

"I'm only making it safer for you to ride."

"I don't want to ride."

"You can get down and walk anytime, madam. It wasn't in my plan to bring you along, so if you don't like the traveling accommodations, you've no one to blame but yourself."

"Did you think I would let you take off with my son without putting up a fight?"

His austere face revealed no emotion. "I didn't think about you at all, Mrs. Price."

He flexed his knees and the horse started forward, trailing the others by several yards. Miranda was stunned into silence, not only by the fact that he knew her name, but because while one of his hands was loosely holding the reins of the horse, the other was riding lightly on her hipbone.

"You know me?" She tried not to reveal her anxiety through her voice.

"I know who you are."

"Then you have me at a distinct disadvantage."

"That's right. I do."

She had hoped to weasel out his name, but he lapsed into stoic silence as the horse carefully picked its way down the steep incline. As hazardous as the race up the mountainside had been, traveling down the other side was more so. Miranda expected the horse's forelegs to buckle at any second and pitch them forward. They wouldn't stop rolling until they hit bottom several miles below. She was afraid for Scott. He was still crying, though not hysterically as before.

"That man my son is riding with, does he know how to ride well?"

"Ernie was practically born on a horse. He won't let anything happen to the boy. He's got several sons of his own."

"Then he must understand how I feel!" she cried. "Why have you taken us?"

"You'll know soon enough."

The ensuing silence was rife with hostility. She decided she would say nothing more, not wanting to give him the satisfaction of refusing to answer her.

Suddenly the horse lost its footing. Rocks began to shake loose around them. The frightened animal sought traction, but couldn't find it. He began to skid down the incline. Miranda almost somersaulted over his neck. To prevent that, she clutched the pommel with her left hand. Her right squeezed her captor's thigh. His arm formed a bar as hard as steel across her midriff while, with his other hand, he gradually pulled up on the reins. The muscles in his thighs bunched with the strain of keeping both of them in the saddle until, after what seemed like forever, the horse regained its footing.

Miranda could barely release her pent-up breath for the arm across her diaphragm. He didn't relax his hold until the animal was well under control again. She slumped forward, as if with relief, but all her senses were alert.

When she had reflexively laid her hand on his thigh, she had inadvertently touched his holster. The pistol was within her grasp! All she had to do was play it cool. If she could catch him off guard, she had a chance of whipping the pistol out of the holster and turning it on him. She could stave off the others while holding their leader at gunpoint long enough for Scott to get on the horse with her. Surely she could find her way back to the train where law enforcement agencies must already be organizing search parties. Their trail wouldn't be difficult to follow, for no efforts had been taken to cover it. They could still be found well before dark.

But in the meantime, she had to convince the outlaw that she was resigned to her plight and acquiescent to his will. Gradually, so as not to appear obvious, she let her body become more pliant against his chest. She ceased trying to maintain space between her thighs and his. She no longer kept her hip muscles contracted, but let them go soft against his lap, which grew perceptibly tighter and harder with each rocking motion of the saddle.

Eventually her head dropped backward onto his shoulder, as though she had dozed off. She made certain he could see that her eyes were closed. She knew he was looking down at her because she could feel his breath on her face and the side of her neck. Taking a deep breath, she intentionally lifted her breasts high, until they strained against her lightweight summer blouse. When they settled, they settled heavily on the arm he still held across her midriff.

But she didn't dare move her hand, not until she thought the moment was right. By then her heart had begun to pound so hard she was afraid he might feel it against his arm. Sweat had moistened her palms. She hoped her hand wouldn't be too slippery to grab the butt of the pistol. To avoid that, she knew she must act without further delay.

In one motion, she sat up straight and reached for the pistol.

He reacted quicker.

His fingers closed around her wrist like a vise and prized her hand off the gun. She grunted in pain and gave an anguished cry of defeat and frustration.

"Mommy?" Scott shouted from up ahead. "Mommy, what's the matter?"

Her teeth were clenched against the pain the outlaw was inflicting on the fragile bones of her wrist, but she managed to choke out, "Nothing, darling. Nothing. I'm fine." Her captor's grip relaxed, and she called to Scott, "How are you?"

"I'm thirsty and I have to go to the bathroom."

"Tell him it's not much farther."

She repeated the dictated message to her son. For the time being Scott seemed satisfied. Her captor let the others go on ahead until the last horse was almost out of sight before he placed one hand beneath her jaw and jerked her head around to face him.

"If you want to handle something hard and deadly, Mrs. Price, I'll be glad to direct your hand to something just as steely and fully loaded as the pistol. But then you already know how hard it is, don't you? You've been grinding your soft little tush against it for the last twenty minutes." His eye darkened. "Don't underestimate me again."

Miranda twisted her head free of his grasp and sat forward on the horse again, keeping her back as rigid and straight as a flagpole. The military posture took its toll quickly. Soon she began to notice a burning sensation between her shoulder blades. It had become almost intolerable by dusk, when they rode out of the woods and into a clearing at the floor of the mountain they had just descended.

Several pickup trucks were parked between a running stream and a burning campfire. There were men milling around, obviously waiting for their arrival. One called out a greeting in a language Miranda didn't recognize, but that was no surprise. She was unable to concentrate on anything except her discomfort. Fatigue had made her groggy. The situation had taken on a surreal aspect.

That was dispelled the moment the man dismounted and pulled her down to stand beside him. After the lengthy horseback ride, her thighs quivered under the effort of supporting her. Her feet were numb. Before she regained feeling in them, Scott hurled his small body at her shins and closed his arms around her thighs, burying his face in her lap.

She dropped to her knees in front of him and embraced him tightly, letting tears of relief roll down her cheeks. They had come this far and had escaped serious injury. She was grateful for that much. After a lengthy bear hug, she held Scott away from her and examined him. He seemed none the worse for wear, except for his eyes, which were red and puffy from crying. She drew him to her chest again and hugged him hard.

Too soon, a long shadow fell across them. Miranda looked up. Their kidnapper had taken off the white duster, his gloves, his gun belt, and his hat. His straight hair was as inky black as the darkness surrounding them. The firelight cast wavering shadows across his face that blunted its sharp angles but made it appear more sinister.

That didn't deter Scott. Before Miranda

realized what he was going to do, the child flung himself against the man. He kicked at the long shins with his tennis shoes and pounded the hard, lean thighs with his grubby fists.

"You hurt my mommy. I'm gonna beat you up. You're a bad man. I hate you. I'm gonna kill you. You leave my mommy alone."

His high, piping voice filled the still night air. Miranda reached out to pull Scott back, but the man held up his hand to forestall her. He endured Scott's ineffectual attack until the child's strength had been spent and the boy collapsed into another torrent of tears.

The man took the boy's shoulders between his hands. "You are very brave."

His low, resonant voice calmed Scott instantly. With solemn, tear-flooded eyes, Scott gazed up at the man. "Huh?"

"You are very brave to go up against an enemy so much stronger than yourself." The others in the outlaw band had clustered around them, but the boy had the man's attention. He squatted down, putting himself on eye level with Scott. "It's also a fine thing for a man to defend his mother the way you just did." From a scabbard attached to his belt, he withdrew a knife. Its blade was short, but sufficient. Miranda drew in a quick breath. The man tossed the knife into the air. It turned end over end until he deftly caught it by the tip of the blade. He extended the ivory handle toward Scott.

"Keep this with you. If I ever hurt your mother, you can stab me in the heart with it."

Wearing a serious expression, Scott took the knife. Ordinarily, accepting a gift from a stranger would have warranted parental permission. Scott, his eyes fixed on the man before him, didn't even glance at Miranda. For the second time that afternoon, her son had obeyed this man without consulting her first. That, almost as much as their perilous situation, bothered her.

Did this pseudo train robber possess supernatural powers? Granted, his manner and voice were seductive. His eyes were unusually blue, but were they truly mesmerizing? Were the men riding with him fellow outlaws or disciples?

She glanced around her. The men had removed their masks, making one thing readily apparent: They were all Native

Americans. The one referred to as Ernie, whom Scott had ridden with, had long gray hair that had been plaited into two braids, which up till now his hat had kept hidden. His eyes were small, dark, and deeply set; his face was lined and leathery, but there was nothing menacing about him.

In fact, Ernie smiled when her son politely informed his kidnapper, "My name is Scott Price."

"Pleased to meet you, Scott." The man and the boy shook hands. "My name is Hawk."

"Hawk? I never heard that name before. Are you a cowboy?"

Those encircling them snickered, but he answered the question seriously. "No, I'm not a cowboy."

"You're wearing cowboy clothes. You carry a gun."

"Not usually. Just for today. Actually, I'm an engineer."

Scott scratched his grimy cheek where tears had left muddy tracks. "Like on the train?"

"No, not that kind of engineer. A mining engineer."

"I don't know what that is."

"It's rather complicated."

"Hmm. Can I go to the bathroom now?"

"There is no bathroom here. The best we can offer is the woods."

"That's okay. Sometimes Mommy lets me go outside if we're on picnics and stuff." He sounded agreeable enough, but he glanced warily at the wall of darkness beyond the glow of the campfire.

"Ernie will go with you," Hawk reassured him, pressing his shoulder as he stood up. "When you come back, he'll get you something to drink."

"Okay. I'm kinda hungry, too."

Ernie stepped forward and extended his hand to the boy, who took it without hesitation. They turned and, with the other men, headed toward the campfire. Miranda made to follow. The man named Hawk stepped in front of her and barred her path. "Where do you think you're going?"

"To keep an eye on my son."

"Your son will be fine without you."

"Get out of my way."

Instead, he clasped her upper arms and walked her backward until she came up against the rough bark of a pine tree. Hawk kept moving forward until his body was pinning hers against the tree trunk. The brilliant blue eyes moved over her face, down her neck, and across her chest.

"Your son seems to think you're worth fighting for." His head lowered, coming closer to hers. "Are you?"

TWO

His lips were hard, but his tongue was soft. It made stroking motions against her compressed lips. When they didn't part, he pulled back and looked down into her eyes. Her defiance seemed to amuse rather than anger him.

"You won't get off that easy, Mrs. Price. You deliberately stoked this fire burning in my gut, so now you're going to put it out." He closed his hard fingers around her jaw and prized open her mouth for his questing tongue.

Miranda placed her fists against his muscled chest and put all her strength behind the push, but he wouldn't budge. She was subjected to the most thorough, intimate, rapacious kiss she'd ever had, and there was nothing she could do about it but submit. She was ever mindful of Scott. If their captor turned violent, she wanted him to take his wrath out on her, not her son.

But she didn't capitulate entirely. She squirmed against him, trying to put distance, no matter how slight, between their bodies. However, he seemed to know the softest, most vulnerable spots on her body and adjusted his accordingly while his tongue continued its swirling caress of her mouth.

Miranda finally succeeded in tearing her lips free. "Leave me alone," she said in a low, husky voice. She didn't want Scott to notice them and come charging across the clearing, wielding the knife this barbarian had given him.

"Or else what?" he taunted. He took a strand of her fair hair between his fingers and brushed it across his stern, but sexily damp, mouth.

"Or else I'll take that knife from Scott and stab you in the heart myself."

No smile relieved the austerity of his features, but a facsimile of a laugh rumbled inside his chest. "Because I stole a kiss? It was okay, but hardly worth dying for."

"I didn't ask for a grade."

"If you don't like my kisses, I'd advise you not to try and distract me with your feminine charms again." He slid his hand down her front, covered her breast with his hand, and gave it a gentle squeeze. "This is nice, but it's not nice enough to keep me from accomplishing what I set out to do."

She slapped his hand aside. He took a step back, but she knew it was because he chose to and not because she had warded him off. "What have you set out to do?"

"Force the government into reopening the Lone Puma Mine."

His reply was so far removed from what she had expected, she blinked rapidly and wet her lips misapprehensively. In the darkest recesses of her mind, it registered that her lips tasted like a kiss, like a man, like him. But her bewilderment overrode all other thoughts. "Reopening what?"

"The Lone Puma Mine. It's a silver mine. Ever heard of it?" She shook her head. "I'm not surprised. It doesn't seem to be important to anybody but the people who rely on it for their livelihoods. My people."

"*Your* people? The Indians?"

"Good guess," he said sarcastically. "What gave me away? My stupidity or my laziness?"

She had neither done nor said anything to suggest she was a bigot. His reverse snobbery was wholly unjustified, and it caused her temper to snap. "Your blue eyes," she retorted.

"A genetic slip."

"Look, Mr. Hawk, I—"

"Mr. O'Toole. Hawk O'Toole." Again, Miranda blinked at him in confusion. "Another quirk of fate," he said with a dismissive shrug.

"Who are you, Mr. O'Toole?" she asked in a soft voice. "What do you want with Scott and me?"

"My people have worked the Lone Puma Mine for several generations. The reservation is large. We have other means of income, but most of our economy depends on the operation of the mine. I won't bore you with the machinations that took place, but we were swindled out of our ownership."

"So who owns it now?"

"A group of investors. They decided that it wasn't economically feasible to keep it open, so they closed it. Just like that." He snapped his fingers inches in front of her nose. "Without any warning, hundreds of families have been left virtually destitute. And nobody gives a damn."

"What does all that have to do with me?"

"Not a damn thing."

"Then why am I here?"

"I told you before that you were brought along only because you raised such a ruckus."

"But you boarded that train to abduct Scott."

"Yes."

"Why?"

"Why do you think?"

"Obviously to hold him hostage."

He nodded brusquely. "We're holding him for ransom."

"For money?"

"Not exactly."

Enlightenment dawned. "Morton," she whispered.

"That's right. Your husband. He just might get his fellow legislators to listen to him if a band of wild Indians is holding his son hostage."

"He's not my husband any longer."

The blue eyes moved over her caustically. "Yes, I read about your messy divorce in the newspapers. Representative Price divorced you because you were unfaithful to him." He leaned forward again, pressing her against the tree and nudging her body suggestively. "From the way you were snuggling against my fly on our way here, I can see how he's well rid of a wife like you."

"Keep your filthy opinions of me to yourself."

"You know," he said, reaching up and running his index finger along her jaw, "for a hostage, you're awfully high and mighty."

She jerked her head away from his touch. "And you're a fool. Morton won't lift a finger to get me back."

"Undoubtedly. But we've got his son, too."

"Morton knows that Scott is safe as long as he's with me."

"Then maybe we ought to separate you. Or send you back and keep the boy." He carefully gauged her reaction. "Even in the firelight I can see how much that idea frightens you. Unless you want that to happen, you'd be smart to do as you're told."

"Please," she begged shakily, "don't hurt Scott. Don't keep us apart. He's just a little boy. He'll be afraid unless I'm in sight."

"I have no plans to injure either you or Scott. Yet," he added menacingly. "Just do as I say at all times. Do we have an understanding, Mrs. Price?"

As hateful as it was to comply, that was the safest tack to take for the time being. She nodded.

Hawk stepped aside and motioned with his head for her to precede him toward the campfire. Over her shoulder she asked him, "Aren't you afraid the fire will be spotted? They're bound to be looking for us by now."

"Since that is a likelihood, we've made provisions for it."

She followed the direction of his gaze. All the horses had been unsaddled and were being loaded into a long trailer.

"We'll erase their hoof marks and the trailer tire tracks. If anyone happens upon us tonight, they'll find a group of inebriated Indian fishermen who can't hold up their britches, much less a train full of tourists."

"Except that I'll be here screaming my lungs out for help," she said smugly.

"We've made provision for that, too."

"Like what?"

"Chloroform."

"You would chloroform us?"

"If the need arises," he said offhandedly,

before sauntering away and calling out an order for the men to speed up the loading process and get the trailer on its way.

Miranda fumed over how negligently he turned his back on her, obviously considering her nothing more than a nuisance, certainly not a threat. Stung by his casual disregard, she went in search of Scott and found him devouring a plate of canned beans and Spam. "This is good, Mommy."

"I'm glad you're enjoying it." Nervously, she glanced at Ernie, who was sitting cross-legged beside her son. She hesitantly lowered herself to a fallen log and sat down.

"Would you like some food?" the Indian asked her.

"No, thank you. I'm not hungry." He merely shrugged and kept on eating.

"Guess what, Mommy? Ernie said that tomorrow I can ride on the horse again, only this time by myself, if I'm careful to hold on. He said his little boy will teach me how. I'm going to visit their house. They don't have a VCR, but I said that's okay 'cause they have horses. And a goat, too. I'm not scared of goats, am I? Ernie said they don't hurt you, but sometimes they chew on your clothes."

She wanted to shout at him, to remind him of the danger they were in, but she caught herself just in time. Scott was only a child. His innocence of the gravity of their situation was his protection from it. Hawk O'Toole hadn't threatened either Scott or her with physical injury or death. He seemed certain that Morton would respond favorably to his demands. She dared not think of what would happen to Scott and her if he didn't.

Shortly afterward, the loaded horse trailer lumbered out of the clearing and disappeared down a dirt road. Using blankets, the men whisked away its tracks, until all that was left were the tire tracks of the pickup trucks parked nearby.

After taking several swigs apiece of cheap whiskey, they sprinkled it on their clothes. The clearing began to smell like a disreputable tavern. They jokingly practiced walking and talking drunk. After everyone had eaten, they sat around the campfire, chatting companionably, smoking, and preparing their bedrolls for the night. They hardly looked or acted like hardened criminals who just that afternoon had committed a federal offense.

When Hawk got around to noticing Scott and her again, the child was leaning heavily against her arm. "He's exhausted," she said haughtily. She disliked having to look up Hawk's tall, lean body in order to address him face-to face. "Where will we be sleeping?"

"In the back of that pickup." He pointed it out to her and reached for her arm to help her to her feet. She rudely refused his assistance and stood up on her own. He bent down and lifted Scott into his arms.

"I'll carry him," Miranda said quickly.

"*I'll* carry him."

His long stride covered the distance much faster than hers. He had already deposited the boy in a sleeping bag in the back of the pickup by the time she caught up with him.

"Can I say my prayers now?" Scott asked around a broad yawn.

"I think you're too sleepy tonight. Why don't you just say them in your heart?"

"Okay," he mumbled. "Gee, Mommy, look how many stars there are."

She looked above her and was startled

to see a velvet-black sky studded with brilliant stars. They looked enormous and close enough to touch. "They're beautiful, aren't they?"

"Uh-huh. I think this is where God lives. 'Night, Mommy. 'Night, Hawk."

Scott rolled to his side, drew his knees to his chest, and was instantly asleep. Dangerously close to tears, Miranda pulled the sleeping bag over his shoulders and tucked it beneath his chin. When she turned around and faced Hawk, her eyes were glittering with determination. "If you hurt him, I'll kill you."

"So you've said. And as I've said, it's not my intention to hurt him."

"Then what's all this for?" she cried, spreading her arms wide at the sides of her body. "Where's your bargaining power?"

"I won't hurt him," he said softly, "but he might never go home again. If your ex-husband doesn't come through for us, we just might keep Scott with us forever."

Issuing a growl of hatred, Miranda threw herself against him, claws bared. She scratched the side of his face and watched as slender threads of blood formed on his hard cheek. Her triumph was short-lived.

Hawk caught her arm and forced it behind her, cramming her hand high, until it lay between her shoulder blades. The pain was immense, but she didn't utter a single sound. She gritted her teeth against it. The tussle had alerted the others. They emerged from the darkness, ready to do their leader's bidding.

"It's all right," Hawk said, releasing her suddenly. "It's just that Mrs. Price doesn't like me."

"Are you sure?" Ernie asked around a laugh. He added something in his native language that caused all the men to laugh uproariously. Hawk glanced down at her. He snatched a blanket from the ground and ungraciously tossed it to her.

"Get into the truck and cover up with this."

Her pride was smarting as much as her arm . . . and her saddle-sore thighs and buttocks. She folded the blanket around her and clumsily climbed onto the tailgate. As she was doing so, Ernie made another comment that caused an outburst of masculine laughter, louder than the one before.

Having no doubt that whatever he had said was crude and in reference to her, she lay down beside Scott and squeezed her eyes shut. She listened as the men shuffled back to their sleeping bags around the campfire. She supposed she should be grateful that Scott and she had the pickup between them and any wildlife that might come prowling during the night, but the corrugated metal didn't make a very comfortable bed. She wiggled inside the blanket, trying in vain to find a softer spot.

"We only have enough sleeping bags for the men."

Her eyes popped open. She was alarmed to see Hawk standing beside the truck, watching her. He had blotted the blood from his face, but her scratches were still obvious. "Not enough for squaws, I guess."

"Not enough for an extra hostage we didn't count on having along."

"What did he say?"

"Who? Oh, Ernie?" His eyes moved down to her chest. "In so many words, he said you either liked me a lot or you were cold."

The shorts and top she had dressed in that morning were suited to a sunny summer afternoon spent in the foothills, but not for the late-season evening air at this elevation. Her skin was covered with gooseflesh. That wasn't what he was referring to. It was the distinct impressions her nipples were making against her blouse. A tide of heat washed through her, warming her momentarily, but doing nothing to relax her nipples, which still held Hawk's attention.

"I believed the latter to be true." He extended his hand and brushed his knuckles back and forth across one of the sensitive tips. "However, if my guess was wrong, I'd be happy to give you something else." His voice was as rough as the bark of the pine tree he'd sandwiched her against earlier, but as soft as the wind soughing through the needles of the upper branches.

Miranda shrank from his erotic touch. "What else did he say?" she asked through lips that had gone stiff and wooden.

Hawk withdrew his hand, but not his captivating blue gaze. "He said that I would sleep a lot warmer if I stayed with the blanket. On the other hand," he added, touching his scratched cheek, "he said I might not get any sleep at all."

She shot him a venomous look and pulled the blanket up to her earlobes, closing her eyes so she wouldn't have to look at his sardonic expression. She let a long while pass before she opened her eyes again. When she did, he was gone, though she hadn't heard a sound or felt any movement in the air. She wondered how long he had stood there staring at her before he moved away.

She listened, but all she could hear was the crackling and popping of burning firewood and Scott's soft, regular snores. Drawing comfort and faith from that sweet, familiar sound, she miraculously fell asleep.

Three

One moment she was asleep and alone. The next, she was awake and he was with her. Like liquid mercury, he soundlessly and heavily spread over her body to completely cover her. One of his hands closed over her mouth, the other held the tip of a knife at her throat. Into her ear he whispered roughly, "If you even breathe loud, I'll kill you."

She believed him.

Through the darkness, his eyes gave off an icy cold, unfeeling light. She made a slight bobbing motion of her head, indicating that she understood him. But he didn't relax his hand over her mouth. If anything, she felt his muscles grow more taut.

The reason became obvious seconds later when she heard the sound of a vehicle approaching the clearing from the uneven dirt road. A pair of headlights arced across the encircling trees. Dust swirled when the driver braked. Doors were pushed open.

"Stand up and put your hands in the air." The military sharpness of the command startled Miranda. Her eyes sprang wide as she gazed up at Hawk. He was mouthing swearwords. He feared the same thing she did, that the voices would awaken Scott.

She fervently prayed that he would sleep through this. If he woke up and started crying, there was no telling what might happen. He could be struck by a stray bullet during a shoot-out between his kidnappers and his rescuers. Or Hawk might realize that he had failed in his mission and, since he had nothing to lose, take everybody else down with him.

She looked at the man lying on top of her. Could he murder a child in cold blood? Focusing on the stern, hard, uncompromising line of his mouth, she came to the bone-chilling decision that he could.

Please, Scott, please don't wake up.

"Who are you and what are you doing here?"

Hawk's men had apparently been hand-picked for their acting abilities. They pretended to have just been awakened from drunken stupors, though Miranda knew that if Hawk had been alerted to the approach of a vehicle, the others also must have been. They appeared to be bemused and befuddled by the officers' terse interrogation and stammered nonsensical answers to each question. Eventually the lawmen lost patience with them.

"For heaven's sake, they're just a bunch of drunk Indians," one said to the other. "We're wasting our time here."

Miranda felt every muscle in Hawk's body quiver with fury. Close to her eyes, a vein in his temple ticked with rage.

"Did you see anybody on horseback today? Six or seven riders?" one of the officers asked the group. "They would have come from that direction."

There was a brief conversation between the Indians in their own language before some of them indicated to the officers that they hadn't seen any horseback riders.

One of the officers let out a deep breath. "Well, much obliged. Keep your eyes open, will ya? And report anything that looks fishy."

"Who are you looking for?"

Miranda recognized Ernie's voice, though he was deliberately sounding naive and humble.

"A lady and a kid. They were kidnapped off the Silverado excursion train today by a gang of horsemen."

"What did these horsemen look like?" Ernie asked. "What should we be watching for?"

"They were wearing bandannas over their faces, but it was a shifty and mean bunch from what folks on the train said. The leader stole some money from one of the passengers, ripped it right out of his hands. Hear tell the woman put up a helluva fight to protect her kid when they dragged him off the train. But the big one, the leader that is, snatched her up, too, and rode off with her. Can't say I blame him," he added on a lewd laugh. "They're passing her picture around for identification. She's a looker. Blonde, green-eyed."

Hawk glanced down at Miranda. She averted her eyes.

Good-byes were said. The car doors were slammed shut. The headlights swept the clearing again. Dust rose, then settled again with a ponderous silence. Eventually even the car's motor could no longer be heard.

"Hawk, they're gone."

Hawk removed his hand from Miranda's mouth, but he didn't lever himself up. He stared down at her lips. They were white and still. He stroked them with his thumb, as though to rub some color back into them.

"Hawk?"

"I hear you," he shouted impatiently.

For several seconds there was a tense silence around the smoldering remnants of the campfire. Gradually, sounds of resettlement could be heard. Then more silence. Still, Hawk remained where he was.

He eased the knife away from her throat. When she saw the razor sharpness of the blade, her eyes flashed with anger. "You could have killed me with that thing," she hissed.

"If you had given us away, I would have."

"What about Scott? If he had woken up and started crying, would you have killed him?"

"No. He's an innocent." He thrust his body upward, wedging his knee between hers and parting her thighs. "But everybody in the state knows you're not innocent. You heard the man; you're a looker. How many lovers did you seduce before your husband finally had all the unfaithfulness he could stomach and dumped you?"

"Get off me."

He looked at her through narrowed eyes. "I thought you would like it."

"Well, I don't. I don't like you. You're a thief and a kidnapper and—"

"Not a thief."

"You took money from that man on the train at gunpoint."

"He offered it to me, remember? I didn't steal it."

"But you'll spend it."

"Damn right I will," he said. "I'll consider it a gift from the haves to the have-nots."

"Oh, spare me. How do you see yourself? A twentieth-century Robin Hood? You're wrong. You're a criminal. Nothing more."

Wanting to shove him away, she placed her hands on his shoulders. That proved to be a mistake. His shoulders were bare and smooth. So was his chest. Shirtless, it was a sleek, supple expanse of bronzed skin, uninterrupted except for the disks of deeper color around his distended nipples.

Quelling an urge to run her palms over him, she tried to push him away. He lowered his head and nestled it in the hollow between her neck and shoulder. He sank his fingers into her hair. They enfolded her scalp and held her head still. He caught her earlobe between his strong, white teeth and flicked it with his tongue.

"Don't," she said breathlessly.

"Why not? Nervous? First time you've ever had it from an Indian, Mrs. Price?"

She was unable to think of an insult scathing enough for him. "If it weren't for Scott, I'd—"

"What? Give in? Take me right here? Does it bother you that your son is sleeping close by? Is that what's making you resist?"

"No! Stop this," she cried out softly.

"Oh, I get it. This is part of the making-it-with-a-savage fantasy. You resist and I overpower you. Is that how the game is played?"

"Don't, please. Please."

"Good. That's good. You can tell all your friends I forced myself on you. That makes for much more scintillating parlor conversation."

He stroked her lips with his tongue. Reflexively, her hands squeezed his shoulders. Her back arched, forcing her body up against his. "Good, you're warm," he said, groaning as he nuzzled the cleft of her thighs with his lower body. "I'll bet you're wet, too."

Then he kissed her, sending his tongue deeply, sensuously into her mouth while his hips rhythmically massaged her middle.

"Hawk?"

His head snapped up and he swore viciously. "What?"

"You said to rouse you at dawn." Ernie's voice came to them from out of the darkness, which was beginning to have blurred edges of gray. He sounded apologetic.

Hawk's eyes probed Miranda's as he eased himself up. Looming above her, he surveyed her mussed hair, kiss-rouged lips, splayed limbs. "Just as the news stories suggested, Mrs. Price, you are a slut. It's a good thing we kidnapped Scott. Ransoming you wouldn't bring us a plugged nickel."

He vaulted over the side of the pickup and walked away, hiking up the jeans he had hastily pulled on but left unfastened. Miranda's eyes smarted with tears of resentment and outrage. She blotted them out of her eyes. Using a corner of the scratchy wool blanket, she tried to scrub the taste of Hawk O'Toole's kisses off her lips.

But she wasn't very successful.

"Wake up, Randy. We're here."

Miranda's shoulder was given a hard shake. She raised her head from where it had been resting against the passenger-side window of the pickup truck. The awkward position had resulted in a crick in her neck. She rolled her head around her shoulders several times to work out the stiffness.

Blinking her eyes open, she looked across at the man sitting behind the steering wheel. Suddenly she realized they were the only two in the truck. Alarmed, she cried out, "Scott!" She reached for the door handle, but Hawk's hand whipped out and grabbed her wrist before she could cannonball out the door.

"Relax. He's with Ernie. There."

He pointed through the bug-splattered windshield. Scott was trotting behind Ernie like a trusting puppy. They were making their way along a path leading to a mobile home.

"Scott said he had to go to the bathroom, so I told him to go on ahead." Hawk unfolded a newspaper and slapped the front page with his fingertips. "You made headlines, Randy."

"Why are you calling me that?"

"That's how you're referred to in the papers. Why didn't you tell me that's what you're called?"

"You didn't ask."

"Was that your husband's pet name for you?"

"No, I grew up with it."

"I thought your reputation as an easy lay might have earned you the nickname."

She didn't waste her breath on a comeback. Instead she scanned the headlines. The stories of the kidnapping had been written according to eyewitness accounts. After clearing the barricade off the tracks with the assistance of several passengers, the engineer had returned the train to the station. He had radioed ahead of their arrival. The FBI, along with state and local law enforcement agencies, had been there to meet the train. Obviously, the media had been well represented too.

"Your ex was waiting for the train at the depot. He's all shook up."

The front page carried a picture of State Representative Morton Price. In the candid photograph, his handsome face was twisted into a grimace of anguish. He was quoted as saying, "I'll do anything, *anything,* to get my son Scott back. Randy, too, of course."

She laughed bitterly. "He's not breaking habit."

"Meaning?"

"He's milking the publicity for all it's worth. And as usual, I'm an afterthought."

"Do you expect me to sympathize?"

She gave him a level look. "I don't expect you to do anything but act like a bastard. So far, you haven't disappointed me, Mr. O'Toole."

"I don't intend to." He opened his door and stepped out. When Randy joined him on the other side of the truck, he made a sweeping gesture with his hand. "Welcome."

She gazed around her at the village. It was comprised mostly of mobile homes, although there were several permanent dwellings built of either adobe or wood. The one main street was deserted. There was a building that served as gas station, grocery store, and post office, but there was no one about. Another building looked like it might be a school, but its doors were locked. Beyond that, there wasn't much to see. Her eyes were drawn to the rocky road that snaked up the hillside until it disappeared over the crest.

"The mine?" Randy asked, nodding in that direction.

"Yes." He gazed down at her with a cynical expression. "The town isn't quite what you're accustomed to, is it?"

She chose not to pick up the gauntlet. "My estimation of your town will vastly improve if you'll direct me to a bathroom."

"I think Leta will make hers available to you."

"Leta?" Miranda fell into step beside him.

"Ernie's wife. And you can forget about trying to make a phone call. They don't have a telephone."

A telephone pole was the first thing Randy had looked for. She hadn't seen one. Almost as irksome as that was Hawk's ability to read her mind.

A goat, tethered to a stake, glared at

them as they crossed the dusty yard and went up the concrete steps. Hawk knocked once, then pushed open the door to the mobile home. The aroma of cooking food made Randy's stomach growl. Once her eyes had adjusted to the dimness, she saw her son sitting at the table. With a lamentable shortage of table manners, he was shoveling food into his mouth from the plate in front of him.

"Hey, Mommy, did you see Geronimo? That's the goat's name. This is Donny, my new friend. He's *seven.* This is Leta."

Randy acknowledged the introductions. Donny glanced away shyly. Leta, after staring at the scratches on Hawk's cheek, gazed at her with unabashed curiosity. Randy was shocked to see that Ernie's wife was not only much younger than he, but younger than Randy herself.

"Would you like some food?" the young woman asked her. "It's just hash, but—"

"Yes, please." Randy smiled at her pleasantly. Leta stopped nervously wringing her hands and returned the smile.

"I'm sure Mrs. Price is hungry," Hawk said, as he threw his long leg over the seat of a chair and straddled it, sitting in it back-

ward. "She must have been expecting buf-
falo jerky and fry bread for breakfast. When
we offered to buy her an Egg McMuffin, she
turned us down flat."

Ernie chuckled. Leta looked confused.
Randy ignored him. To Leta she said, "May
I use your bathroom, please?"

"Yes, of course. It's down the hall."

Hawk shot up. "I'll show her where it is."

Randy went through the kitchen and into
the narrow hallway leading to the back of
the home. Hawk reached around her and
opened the bathroom door. He peered
around it and gave the cubicle a cursory
inspection.

"What did you expect to find?"

"A window you might possibly squeeze
through."

She made an impatient sound and tried
to step around him. He remained where he
was. "Going in with me?" she asked
sweetly.

"I don't think that's necessary, but I'll be
on the other side of this door."

She propped her hands on her hips.
"Maybe you should search me."

The clear eyes traveled down her body
and back up again. "Maybe I should."

The heel of his hand gave her shoulder a slight push and her back landed against the wall. Before she could stave them off, his hands disappeared beneath the hem of her blouse. They moved over the lacy cups of her bra, kneading her breasts quickly and lightly. From there his hands moved to her back, running up and down her skin. At her front again, he unsnapped the waistband of her shorts and, flattening his hand, slid it down over her belly, then around to her hips where he palmed her derriere.

"Nothing there that shouldn't be," he said calmly, when he withdrew his hands.

Randy was too shocked to say anything. She only gaped at him breathlessly. Her face had gone pale, though blood was pumping through her system in hot, rapid jets.

"Don't ever dare me," he warned softly. "Not even by implication. I'll call your bluff every time." He gave her a gentle shove into the bathroom and closed the door.

Randy leaned against the door for support until she had regained her breath. She was trembling. At the basin, she turned on the taps and cupped several handfuls of water, scooping them up to her flushed face. After she had blotted it dry, she looked at her reflection in the mirror.

It was a sad sight. Her hair was a mess. It was littered with twigs and leaves, leftovers of the breakneck ride through the forest. Her clothes were dirty. Her makeup was more than twenty-four hours old.

"Ravishing," she said dryly. Then, remembering that she had almost been ravished, she frowned.

Taking up a bar of soap, she vigorously washed off her stale makeup. Using a finger, she brushed her teeth. Carefully, she picked the forest debris from her hair and worked through the stubborn tangles with her fingers. After using the toilet and brushing off her clothes as best she could, she left the bathroom.

Hawk wasn't waiting outside the door for her after all. He was sitting at the kitchen table, drinking a beer and talking softly with Ernie. He had subjected her to the "search" merely to insult her, not because he really feared that she would escape. When they noticed her standing in the doorway, the conversation came to an abrupt halt.

"Where's Scott?"

"Outside."

She checked the window. Scott was warily petting Geronimo while Donny encouraged him not to be afraid. Satisfied that he was in no immediate danger, she turned back toward the table and sat down in the chair Leta pointed out to her. It was midafternoon, an unusual time for a meal. She had been offered breakfast as soon as they had left the campsite early that morning, but she had declined. They hadn't stopped for lunch, so she ate all the food Leta put on her plate. The cup of coffee that followed it was strong, hot, and restorative.

She sipped it, then looked across the table at Hawk and asked bluntly, "What do you intend to do with us?"

"Hold you hostage until your husband—ex-husband—gets a guarantee from the governor that the mine will be reopened."

"That could take months of negotiation," she cried, aghast.

Hawk shrugged. "Maybe."

"Scott is supposed to start school in a few weeks."

"School just might have to start without him. Don't you have confidence in your husband's powers of persuasion?"

"Why don't you simply ask for money like an ordinary kidnapper?"

His expression hardened. Ernie cleared his throat and stared down at his hands. Leta fidgeted in her chair.

"If we wanted a handout, Mrs. Price," Hawk said coldly, "we could all live on welfare."

She could have kicked herself for making the thoughtless outburst. It had damaged Hawk's pride. His blue eyes might contradict his Indian heritage, but his fierce pride certainly didn't.

She took a calming breath. "I don't see how you plan to pull this off, Mr. O'Toole. Negotiating with any government involves miles of red tape. Morton probably won't be able to get an appointment with the governor for weeks."

Hawk thumped the newspaper that was now folded and lying on the table. "This will help, just as we planned. Your husband is running for reelection. He's already news. The kidnapping of his child puts him in the forefront of everybody's mind. Public pressure alone will force Governor Adams to meet our demands."

"You've apparently thought it out carefully. How did you know Scott and I would be on the Silverado train?"

She could tell instantly that her innocent question struck a nerve. Ernie and Leta looked uneasily at Hawk, who recovered quickly and answered, "A kidnapper makes it his business to know these things."

His glib reply told her nothing, but Randy realized that for the moment it was all she was going to get. "How do you plan to contact Morton?"

"We're starting with this letter." Hawk took a folded piece of ordinary typing paper from his shirt pocket. "It will be hand-delivered to his office mailbox tomorrow."

She read the letter. It was a ransom note straight out of a private-eye television series, having the message spelled out with letters cut from a magazine. It informed Morton that Scott was being held for ransom and that he would be contacted soon with the terms of exchange.

"Contacted? By phone?" Randy asked.

"His office telephone."

"The line will be tapped. They'll easily trace the call."

"Calls. Each one a single sentence long.

Too brief to be traced. They'll be originating from several western states."

She arched her brow. "Again, my compliments."

"The other Indian nations sympathize with our dilemma. When I asked for assistance, they readily provided it."

"Have you given any thought to what'll happen if you're caught?"

"None. I won't be."

"You've had brushes with the law before, haven't you? Once I had time to think about it, I remembered where I'd heard your name. I've read about you. You've been stirring up trouble for years."

Hawk came out of his chair slowly and leaned across the table so far that his face was only inches from hers. "And I'll go on stirring up trouble as long as my people are suffering."

"*Your* people? What are you, a chief or something?"

"Yes."

The word sizzled like a drop of water on a hot skillet. It silenced Randy instantly. She stared into his sharp, lean features and realized that she wasn't dealing with a run-of the-mill hoodlum. Hawk O'Toole was tantamount to a head of state, a holy ruler, an anointed one.

"Then as a chief you've made a grave oversight," she said. "As soon as you mention the Lone Puma Mine, this entire site will be swarming with FBI and state troopers."

"No doubt."

She spread her arms wide and laughed lightly. "So what do you plan to do when they arrive, hide under your beds?"

"We won't be here."

Having said that, he left the table and strode toward the door. He yanked it open with such force, it almost came off its hinges. "We leave in ten minutes."

As soon as the door banged shut behind him, Randy laid her hands on the table and appealed to Ernie and Leta. "You've got to help me. Mr. O'Toole's heart might be in the right place, what he's trying to do is noble and fine, but he's committed a serious crime. A federal crime. He'll go to prison and so will you all." She wet her lips. "But I'll see that you're dealt with fairly if you'll help me get away. Barring that, help me get to a telephone."

Ernie stood up and addressed his young wife. "Leta, is everything ready?"

"Yes."

"Put all the bags you've packed near the door. I'll load them into the truck."

Randy's shoulders slumped with defeat. Not only had they refused to help her escape from Hawk O'Toole, they wouldn't even discuss it.

Four

"Where are we going?"

"Wouldn't you love to know?"

Hawk's sarcasm grated on her temper like coarse steel wool. "Look, I couldn't find my way back to civilization if I had a compass in one hand and a map in the other. The only thing remarkable about this terrain is its monotony. Right now I don't even know which direction we're driving in."

"That's the only reason I didn't blindfold you."

Sighing her exasperation, Randy turned toward the open window of the pickup. A cool wind blew through her hair. A slender and unambitious moon cast pale light on her face. The dark outline of distant mountains marked the horizon, but she could barely distinguish them.

She had soon reasoned why the village near the Lone Puma Mine had been deserted. Everyone else had already moved to the "hiding place." Only those involved in the actual kidnapping and their families had remained at the village. Shortly after Hawk had stormed out of Ernie's mobile home, the caravan departed for a destination still unknown to Randy. Hawk's pickup was bringing up the rear, as it had all afternoon, but he never let too much distance get between them and the van they were following.

"How did you get to be a chief?"

"I'm not the only one. There is a tribal council made up of seven chiefs."

"Did you inherit the position from your father?"

As though he had clenched his teeth, the muscles in his jaw knotted. "My father died in a state hospital for incurable alcoholics. He was only a little older than I am now when he died."

Randy waited out a brief silence, then asked, "His name was really O'Toole?"

"Yes. Avery O'Toole was his great-great-grandfather. He settled in the territory after the Civil War and married an Indian woman."

"So you inherited the position of chief from your mother's family."

"My maternal grandfather was a chief."

"Your mother must be very proud of you."

"She died after giving birth to my stillborn brother." He seemed to enjoy Randy's stunned reaction. "You see, the doctor only visited the reservation once every two weeks. Her labor caught him on an off day. She hemorrhaged and bled to death."

Randy stared at him, compassion stealing over her. No wonder he was callous, having suffered such a tragic childhood. One look at his granite profile, however, and she knew he wouldn't welcome any pity, not even a kind word.

She glanced down at Scott. He was fast asleep, stretched out on the seat between them, his head lying in Randy's lap, his knees tucked against his chest. She wound a strand of his blond hair around her finger.

"No other brothers or sisters?" she asked softly.

"No."

"Has there ever been a Mrs. O'Toole?"

He cut his eyes toward her. "No."

"Why not?"

"If you want to know if I'm getting laid on a regular basis, the answer is that I do all

right. But your sex life is much more interesting than mine, so if that's what you want
to talk about, let's talk about yours."

"That isn't what I want to talk about."

"Then why all the personal questions?"

"I'm trying to understand why a man who
is as smart as you obviously are, would do
something so stupid as to kidnap a woman
and child off a train full of vacationing sight-
seers. You're trying to help your people,
fine. Your motives are admirable. I can appreciate them. I hope you succeed. But
through legal channels."

"That doesn't work."

"And crime does? What good can you do
anybody when they lock you up in a federal
prison for the rest of your life?"

"They won't."

"They might," she retorted bitterly. "They
should if you don't let us go."

"Forget it."

"Listen, Mr. O'Toole, hasn't this charade
gone on long enough? The men who
helped you, Ernie for instance, aren't criminals. They've treated Scott more like a fa-
vorite nephew than a hostage. Even you, in
your own way, have been kind to him."

She continued to make her sales pitch.

"If you let Scott and me out at the nearest town, I'll claim I never knew who our kidnappers were. I'll say that you wore masks the entire time and that for reasons unknown to me you changed your mind and decided to let us go."

"How benevolent of you."

"Please think about it."

His fingers wrapped more tightly around the steering wheel. "The answer is no."

"I swear I won't say anything!"

"What about Scott?"

Randy opened her mouth to speak, but no rebuttal came out.

"Right," Hawk said, correctly reading her mind again. "Even if I trusted you, which I don't, the first time Scott said anything about Hawk, the feds would be crawling all over me."

"They wouldn't be if you didn't already have a criminal record," she fired back.

"My record is clean. I've never been indicted."

"Close."

"Close doesn't count. If close counted, I wouldn't still be hard and you would know what sex with an Indian is like." She drew in a sharp gasp. Taking advantage of her speechlessness, he added, "I don't know which I wanted most last night—to see you humbled, or to see you hot."

"You're repulsive."

His laugh was harsh and dry. "Don't play lily-white with me. Your dirty laundry was aired when your husband divorced you for adultery."

"The writ of divorce reads 'incompatibility.' "

"Maybe officially, but your extramarital affairs were alluded to more than once."

"Do you believe everything you read, Mr. O'Toole?"

"I believe almost nothing I read."

"What makes accounts of my well-publicized divorce the exception?"

His eyes moved over her, taking in her windblown hair and pristine face, the clothes that were rumpled enough to have been slept in . . . and had been. "I know how easily you're persuaded. Remember last night?"

"I wasn't persuaded."

"Yes, you were. You just weren't willing to admit it."

Cheeks burning, Randy turned her head away to gaze out the window again. She didn't want him to see her embarrassment and know that he'd been right. It disgusted her to recall that, for a mere instant, she had enjoyed his kiss.

She had excused her wayward reaction because it had been so long since she'd felt a man's mouth against hers. Though her mind had denied him, her body hadn't. It had gravitated toward his masculine allure. It had reveled in the scent of his skin and the feel of his hair. The pressure of his hardness against her had sparked a glowing fire in her lower body that, even now, rekindled at the reminder.

She had hoped that her responses were so weak as to go unnoticed. Apparently not. He knew. He gloated over her momentary surrender not only because it fed his insufferable ego, but confirmed the allegations regarding her and her collapsed marriage. Much as she wanted to scream denials, she wouldn't. She hadn't before. She wouldn't now.

She closed her eyes against unpleasant recollections and let her head fall back against the seat. In spite of her mental turmoil, she must have dozed. The next thing she knew, the truck was at a standstill and her door was being opened.

"Get out," Hawk said.

Three things she noticed at once. The temperature was discernibly cooler, the air was thinner, and Scott was lying asleep against Hawk's chest, his arms folded around the man's neck. One of Hawk's hands was supporting Scott's bottom. He was holding the door open for her with the other.

She stepped out of the truck and onto the ground. Rushing water was flowing somewhere nearby. The roaring sound was unmistakable. The hillsides surrounding her were dotted with square patches of light, which, she realized after a moment, were windows belonging to numerous structures. In the stingy moonlight she could make out only a few vague outlines.

"Everyone situated?" Hawk asked Ernie, who silently materialized out of the darkness.

"Yes. Leta's taken Donny to bed. She said to tell you good night. The cabin reserved for Mrs. Price is up there." He pointed out an uneven path that zigzagged up a gradual incline.

Hawk nodded brusquely. "I'll see you first thing in the morning. We'll meet in my cabin."

Ernie turned and headed in the opposite direction. Hawk took the path Ernie had indicated. It came to a dead end in front of a small cabin that, as well as Randy could tell, was constructed of rough logs. Hawk went up the steps to a small porch and gave the door a nudge with the toe of his boot.

"Light the lantern."

"Lantern?" she asked timorously.

Cursing her citified ineptitude, he passed Scott to her. He struck a match and held it to the wick of a kerosene lantern, then adjusted the flame and replaced the glass lamp. It lit up the single-room dwelling, which offered no amenities beyond two narrow cots, two stools, and a square table.

"Don't look so horrified. This is the luxury suite."

Disdainfully, Randy gave Hawk her back and lowered Scott to one of the cots. He murmured sleepily when she removed his shoes and covered him with a hand-woven wool blanket. She bent down and kissed his cheek.

When she turned around and faced Hawk, he gave her a slow once-over. She knew that her fatigue must be evident. She wanted to appear unvanquished in front of him. Unfortunately, defeat was weighing down her proud posture and making her expression involuntarily bleak.

"Guards will be posted outside the cabin all night."

"Where would I run to?" she shouted in frustration.

"Exactly."

She drew herself up and looked at him haughtily. "Will you please give me some privacy, Mr. O'Toole?"

"You're shivering."

"I'm cold."

"Should I send in a young, virile brave to warm your bed?"

Her head dropped forward until her chin was almost resting on her chest. She was too tired and too dispirited to fight with him, even verbally. "Just leave me alone. I'm here. My son and I are at your mercy. What more do you want from me?" She raised her head and looked at him with open appeal.

A muscle in his cheek twitched. "A foolhardy question for a woman to ask a desperate man. I've got little else to lose. It won't really matter whether I treat you kindly or not, will it? I could be hanged in either case."

He seemed to be exercising tremendous control to keep from closing the distance between them. "I despise what you are," he said in a raspy voice. "Fair. Blond. Undiluted Anglo, with all the superiority that goes with it. But every time I look at you, I want you. I'm not sure which of us that discredits most."

With that, he stalked out, leaving her shuddering where she stood.

The sun was just cresting the rim of the nearest mountain. Hawk, standing at the window in his cabin, watched its progressive climb. He was already at the bottom of his third cup of coffee. He drained the tin mug and set it on the crude table beneath the window.

He hadn't slept well.

Years ago he had trained himself not to require much sleep, four or five hours a night at most. He was usually able to lie down and fall asleep instantly in order to maximize those four or five hours. But last night he had lain awake staring into the empty darkness, wishing that he felt better about the situation.

So far, so good. He had nothing to complain about. The abduction had been executed as planned, without a hitch . . . with the exception of including Mrs. Price. He couldn't put a finger on why he didn't feel exultant, why, in fact, he didn't feel good about it at all.

He didn't hear the other man's approach until he was almost on him. Reflexively, Hawk spun around and assumed a fighting crouch.

Ernie took a few steps backward and held up his hands in surrender. "What's wrong with you? You should have heard me coming."

Feeling like a fool, Hawk shrugged off his skittishness and offered Ernie a cup of coffee, which the older man accepted. "It was almost too easy, wasn't it? I keep asking myself what can go wrong," Ernie remarked, while waiting for the scalding coffee to cool.

"Nothing. Nothing can go wrong." Hawk injected more surety into his voice than he felt. "The letter will be delivered this morning. An hour later Price will get the telephone call from us, followed in quick succession by the others until our terms have been specified."

"I wonder when he'll contact Governor Adams."

"Immediately is my guess. The newspapers will keep us informed."

Ernie chuckled. "They become an asset to us criminals on the lam."

The comment reminded Hawk of what the woman had said the evening before. He picked up a shirt and pulled it on. "Do you feel like a criminal?"

He hadn't meant for Ernie to take his question seriously, but he had. "Not now." He raised his deep-set eyes to his younger friend. "I will if anything happens to the boy. Or to the woman."

The strategic pause coaxed a reaction from Hawk. He suspended stuffing the tail of his shirt into his waistband and gave Ernie a cold, unwavering stare. "What could happen to her?"

"Maybe you should tell me."

Hawk finished tucking in the shirt and buttoned the fly of his soft, faded Levi's. "If she follows my orders, she'll come away unscathed."

Ernie watched Hawk sit down on the edge of the bed to pull on socks and boots. "Leta says Dawn January has her eye on you."

"Dawn January? She's just a kid."

"Eighteen."

"As I said, just a kid."

"Leta was sixteen when I married her."

"So what does that prove? That you're hornier than I am? Congratulations." Ernie didn't crack a smile over Hawk's attempted humor. His taciturn face remained unchanged. Hawk stood up and began rolling his shirtsleeves up his sinewy forearms. "Aaron Turnbow is in love with Dawn. She's just feeling restless and flighty since he returned to college. I figure they'll get engaged when he comes home for the Christmas holiday."

"That gives you four months to enjoy her."

Hawk's body jerked around as though it had been machine-gunned. His eyes were as hard and still as frozen lakes. "I wouldn't do that to Aaron."

"You could."

"But I wouldn't." For several moments the atmosphere was thick with tension between the two friends. Hawk's lips finally relaxed into a near smile. He slipped a knife into the scabbard attached to his belt. "Isn't Leta enough to keep your libido occupied?"

"More than," Ernie said with a lusty chuckle.

"Then why do you find it necessary to meddle with mine?"

"Because I've seen the way you look at her."

"Who?"

The answer was so glaringly obvious that Ernie didn't even deign to speak the name. Instead, he said, "You need a woman in your bed. Soon. You're itchy. It's making you careless."

"Careless?"

"I could have killed you a few minutes ago. You can't afford to be preoccupied. Especially now."

"When I need a woman, I'll have one," Hawk said testily.

"But not her, Hawk. A woman like her, an Anglo, she would never understand you in a million centuries."

"I don't need you to tell me that."

"Nor do you need me to remind you of the consequences of taking an Anglo woman."

"No. But I see that you're reminding me anyway."

Ernie relented in deference to Hawk's foreboding expression. "Our people depend on you to exercise sound judgment," he said quietly.

Hawk drew himself up to his full height, which put him almost a head taller than Ernie. His proud, square chin jutted out. His voice was as chilling as his eyes. "I would never do anything to jeopardize the welfare of my people. And I have no intention of deserting them to live my life among the Anglos."

They stared each other down. Ernie was the first to look away. "I promised Donny we'd go fishing this morning."

Hawk watched him leave. The furrow between his brows was deeply engraved. That furrow was still there an hour later when he stood beside the cot on which Miranda Price was sleeping, her hands childishly stacked beneath her cheek. Her hair was spread over the pillow in a sexy tangle. Her lips, slightly parted, looked dewy and soft. The sight made his manhood strain uncomfortably against his fly. He cursed himself and his undisciplined body. He cursed her more.

"You should be up."

Having been awakened so abruptly, Randy bolted upright, clutching the blanket to her chest for whatever meager protection it offered. She blinked Hawk into focus. He remained a tall, black silhouette outlined against the sunlight streaming through the window.

"What are you doing here?" She checked the other cot. The rumpled covers had been thrown back, but the bed was empty. "Where's Scott?"

"Fishing with Ernie and Donny."

She flung back the blanket and stood up. "He doesn't know anything about fishing. He wouldn't be able to swim in the swift water I heard last night." She marched toward the door. Hawk caught her arm. "Ernie's watching him."

"I'd rather watch him myself."

"You'd rather turn him into a mama's boy."

She wrenched her arm free. "He still needs mothering."

"He needs to be with men."

"How dare you advise me on how to rear my son."

"Your son was terrified of getting on a horse."

"He was being carried off by a gun-toting man wearing a mask! What boy his age, or any age, wouldn't be terrified?"

"Donny told me that Scott was scared to death of the goat."

"That's not surprising. He hasn't been around many animals."

"And whose fault is that?"

"I've taken him to the zoo. Not much chance to interact with the lions and tigers."

"Pets?"

"We live in an apartment complex. Pets aren't permitted."

"Something else you should have thought about before taking Scott away from his father."

"His father didn't—" She broke off abruptly.

Hawk bore down on her. "What? His father didn't what?"

"None of your damn business." She rubbed her chilled arms, but, lest he mistake that for weakness, she addressed him with condescension. "I'm very glad to say that Scott is a sensitive child."

"He's a *sissy.* You've made him one."

"What would you have him be? A savage like you?"

Hawk grabbed her upper arms and yanked her against him. She landed hard enough to have the breath knocked out of her and to snap her head back. His breath was hot as it struck her face on each emphasized word. "You haven't seen me savage yet, Mrs. Price. You had better hope you never do." He continued to drill into her astonished eyes before releasing her abruptly. "They've got breakfast waiting for you. Come with me."

"I don't want any breakfast. What I would like is a bath and a change of clothes. Scott needs something warmer, too. We didn't know when we dressed two days ago that we would be kidnapped and carried off into the mountains."

"I can arrange for a change of clothes. In fact, Scott's already wearing his. The bathtub is this way." He turned and opened the door of the cabin. Curious, Randy followed him down the path.

The scenery was spectacular. What

darkness had obscured when she arrived the night before took her breath now. The sky was a vivid blue. The evergreen trees were tall and straight and symmetrical. The ground was rocky, but even the sun-bleached stones added a proper texture to the rugged terrain.

"Where are we?"

"Do I look stupid, Mrs. Price?"

Annoyed, she said, "I just meant to ask if this is part of the reservation."

"Yes. A vacation hideaway of sorts."

"I can see why. It's beautiful country."

"Thanks."

Randy had been right about the stream. As untamed as the rest of the landscape, it tumbled down the mountainside. The spar-kling spray that hung in the air like a mist caught the sunlight to create myriad rain-bows. The streambed was lined with stones that were as polished as mirrors. The cur-rent was so swift, Randy doubted she could keep her footing in it.

She followed Hawk's narrow-hipped, swaggering gait until he stopped a few feet from the stream and gestured with his hand. "Here you are."

She gaped at the crystal, swirling water,

then up into the amused face. "You can't be serious. *This* is the bathtub? That water will be frigid."

"Your son didn't seem to mind. In fact, I think he enjoyed it."

"You put . . . you put Scott into that freezing water?"

"Tossed him in naked as a jaybird. As soon as his teeth stopped chattering, he was fine. We almost couldn't coax him out."

"That's not funny, Mr. O'Toole. Scott isn't accustomed to things like this. He could get sick."

"I take it you're declining to bathe?"

"You're damn right I am." She spun on her heels and started back toward the cabin. "I'll wash with the drinking water."

"Suit yourself."

He let her pick her own way back up the path. When she reached the cabin, she slammed the door behind her. She had no way of heating the pail of drinking water that had been left for her and Scott. The cabin had a fireplace, but there was no wood stacked in it. However, the drinking water was warmer than the stream would have been. She washed as best she could with it and was about half done when someone knocked on the door. Wrapping herself in a blanket, she called out, "Come in."

Leta stepped inside. Her smile was sincere, but timid. "Hawk said for me to bring you these clothes."

It was impossible not to smile back at Leta. Her face was broad, her nose short, her lips wide. She wasn't pretty, but her luminous dark eyes and sweet demeanor made up for her lack of beauty. "Thank you, Leta."

She withdrew something from the pocket of her long, shapeless skirt. "I thought you could use this, too." She shyly handed Randy a bar of soap.

"Thank you again. I appreciate it." She sniffed at the bar. The fragrance was strong and masculine, unlike the perfumed soap she usually used, but she was grateful for it regardless.

"Here's a hairbrush, too," Leta added hastily, as she handed it to Randy.

Randy turned the items over in her hands. The ordinary grooming utensils seemed precious now. "You've been kind to me, Leta. Thank you."

Basking in Randy's compliment, she

turned to go. Only then did Randy take notice of the clothes Leta had laid on the table. The flannel shirt was gray and brown plaid. The long skirt was the drabbest color she'd ever seen. Even military camouflage was more attractive.

"Did Mr. O'Toole choose the clothes himself?"

Leta bobbed her head and ducked out the door, as though she feared Randy might hurl the ugly clothes at her.

Randy finished her sponge bath. She found underclothes folded between the shirt and skirt. The underpants would do, but the bra was several sizes too large. She had already washed out her own. It was still wet, so she had to go without. Not that it mattered. The shirt was as shapeless as the skirt. They hung on her slender figure like a shroud on a flagpole. It was another of Hawk's sneaky methods to try to diminish her will.

She had no mirror, but she did what she could to improve her appearance. She tied the long tail of the shirt into a knot at her waist, rolled the sleeves back to her elbows, and flipped up the collar. There wasn't much she could do about the skirt.

She put the hairbrush to good use, however. Once she had worked out all the snags, she used a shoelace out of her sneakers to make a ponytail.

She didn't know what was expected of her, but she wasn't about to sit in the cabin all day. The weather was lovely; it was a gorgeous day. As long as she was being held against her will in the mountains, she might just as well get as much enjoyment as she could out of them. Besides, she was eager to see Scott. She didn't like the idea of his being allowed to roam freely in this wilderness. He was unaware of the dangers.

She stepped out onto the porch and took in the scene spread out around her. There had been few people about when she had left the cabin with Hawk earlier. Now there were many. She would guess a hundred or more. She was also surprised to note the number of dwellings situated on the hillsides. The cabins seemed to be natural extensions of the rock, blending into their backdrops so well as to be almost undetectable.

Hearing Scott's voice over the sound of the rushing water, she set out in that direction. She came up short when she saw him at the water's edge in the company of Ernie and Donny. Standing on his knees and using a flat boulder as his worktable, Scott was using the knife Hawk had given him to disembowel a fish.

"*Scott!*"

He glanced up at her through the bangs that were hanging in his eyes and flashed her his gap-toothed smile. "Mommy! Come see. I caught some fish! Three of them. All by myself. I took 'em off the hook and everything."

He was so excited about his catch that she couldn't scold. She carefully made her way over the stony ground toward him. "That's wonderful, but—"

"Ernie showed me how to bait the hook, and pull 'em outta the water, and work the hook outta their mouths. Donny already knew all that, but he only caught two and I caught *three.*"

"Are you warm enough? Did you get in that water? Those rocks are awfully slick. You must be careful, Scott."

He wasn't listening. "First you cut their heads off. Then you split their bellies open. This is their guts. See all this squishy stuff, Mommy? You have to use a knife to get all the guts out so you can cook 'em and eat 'em."

Again, he attacked the fish with a relish that made Randy queasy. His tongue came out to fill the left corner of his lips, a trait that indicated the level of his concentration. "But you gotta be real careful with the knife and not cut your finger off or else it'll get cooked for supper, too. That's what Hawk told me."

"The boy learns well."

Randy whirled around. Hawk had moved up behind her. Though the top of her head barely reached his collarbone, she lit into him, poking his chest with her finger to emphasize each point. "I want you to do whatever is necessary to get us away from here. Call Morton. Get him to agree to your demands. Call Governor Adams himself. Go on the warpath. I don't care how you do it, just get us back home. Is that understood?"

"Don't you like it here, Mommy?"

She faced Scott again. His dirt-streaked face was filled with concern as he gazed up at her. The light in his eyes had dimmed. He was no longer smiling and animated. "I do. It's neat."

"It is not neat, Scott. It's . . . it's . . ." She

glanced down at the gore-strewn rock. "It's disgusting. You march up to the cabin right this minute and scrub your face and hands with soap."

Scott's lower lip began to tremble. He lowered his head with embarrassment. His shoulders drooped. Randy rarely scolded him so severely, and never in the presence of other people. But the sight of him having such a wonderful time with his kidnappers, in his innocence not realizing the potential threat they posed, had snapped her control.

Hawk stepped between Scott and her and laid a hand on the boy's shoulder. "You did very well on the fish, Scott."

Scott raised his head and looked up at Hawk dejectedly. "I did?"

"You did such a good job that I have another one for you now. Go with Ernie and Donny. As you know, we brought all our livestock with us. I want you to help groom the horses."

Randy made a sound of protest. Hawk spun around and stymied any others with one fierce stare. "Ernie?"

"Come, Donny, Scott," Ernie said.

Scott hesitated. "Mommy, can I go?"

Hawk's lips barely moved. In a voice only

loud enough for her to hear, he said, "I'll separate you from him. You won't know where he is or what he's doing."

She swallowed hard. Her hands balled into fists and she squeezed her eyes shut. She was backed into a corner, just as she had been the first time she heard an ugly and unfounded rumor about herself. She knew when she was defeated and this was one of those times. "Go with Ernie and Donny, darling," she said hoarsely. "Just be extremely careful."

"I will," Scott promised excitedly. "Come on, Donny. I'm not scared of horses anymore." She could hear his happy chatter as the trio made its way down the hill. Then, looking Hawk straight in the eyes, she said, "You hateful sonofabitch."

With one swift and fluid motion, he withdrew the knife from his scabbard and brought it to within an inch of her nose. "Clean the fish."

Five

Incredulous, Randy laughed. "Clean them yourself. Or better yet, go straight to hell." She slapped the knife away from her face. "For your information, Cochise, I'm no squaw."

"Clean the fish or you don't eat."

"Then I won't eat."

"And neither will Scott."

Calling his bluff, she said, "You wouldn't deny a child food, Mr. O'Toole."

Hawk stared at her for a full minute. Randy was beginning to feel smug, thinking she had scored a major victory. Then he said in a low, level voice, "Clean the fish or I'll make good my threat to separate you from your son."

He was no fool and that made him an awesome enemy. If he had plunged the knife between her ribs, he couldn't have found a straighter path to her heart. Knowing where she was most vulnerable, he had appealed to her greatest fear as a mother. Not knowing Scott's whereabouts, especially in this wild country, would be hell on earth.

Shooting him a murderous look, Randy took the knife from him. She studied it for a moment, running her fingers over the smooth ivory handle and the flat edge of the gleaming stainless steel blade.

"Don't even think about stabbing me with it," Hawk told her softly. "They would kill you before I even hit the ground."

When she looked up at him, he hitched his head in the direction of the compound. Several people had noticed them talking together. They appeared to be routinely going about their business, but their eyes were watchful and wary. What Hawk said was true. She wouldn't stand a chance if she resorted to violence. She hadn't considered actually killing him, but she *had* thought about inflicting some damage.

Defeated again, she sank down beside the boulder where Scott's fish lay.

"I don't know how to do this."

"Learn."

She stared at the carcasses with dismay. The smell alone made her want to retch.

Loath to touch the fish with her bare hands, she nudged one with the tip of the knife. "What do I do?" she asked helplessly.

"You heard Scott. First you cut off its head."

She finally worked up enough nerve to take the fish that was still intact by the tail. She laid the blade of the knife against its throat. Her first tentative sawing motion caused a crunching sound. With a soft cry, she dropped the fish and shuddered violently.

Muttering swearwords, Hawk reached down, grabbed a handful of her shirt, and hauled her to her feet. He retrieved his knife and sheathed it in the scabbard. He called out to one of the Indians. The teenage boy came jogging over. Hawk spoke to him rapidly in their native tongue. The boy looked at Randy and laughed. Hawk slapped him affectionately on the back.

"Aren't you going to make me do it?" she asked, as he led her away.

"No."

"There's no need to now, is there? You accomplished what you wanted to. You only wanted to humiliate me. Like putting me in these wretched clothes?"

"I didn't want you to clean the fish because I didn't want to waste them. You would only make a mess of it." He gave her a sidelong glance that mocked both her ignorance and her futile attempts to make the horrible wardrobe attractive. "Haven't you ever cooked fish?"

It was irritating to be put on the defensive. "One that I bought in the supermarket. I've never had an occasion to clean one."

"You've never gone fishing?"

She shook her head no. A reflective expression clouded her face. "My father wasn't much of an outdoorsman."

"*Wasn't?* He's dead?"

"Yes."

"What happened?"

"Why should you care?"

"I don't. But you seem to."

She remained stubbornly silent for several moments, then said, "He worked himself to death. He had a heart attack one day at his office and died at his desk."

"What about your mother?"

"She remarried and lives on the east coast with her husband." Shaking her head ruefully, she said, "She married the same kind of man as Dad. I couldn't believe it."

"What kind of man is that?"

"Demanding. Selfish. A workaholic. No plateau was ever good enough. I couldn't count the number of family vacations that were canceled because something came up and Dad couldn't—or wouldn't—leave town."

"Poor you. No vacations. You had to languish beside your backyard swimming pool instead of the beach."

Randy stopped in her tracks and glared up at him. "How dare you disparage me and my life? What do you know about it?"

He moved his face down close to hers. "Not a damn thing. There weren't any backyard swimming pools where I grew up."

She could have taken issue with him. She could have told him that she would have traded the swimming pool for some attention from her father. He had always been too busy for her and her mother. Whenever they complained about his excessive devotion to work, he defended himself by saying that he was working for them. Randy would then be made to feel ungrateful and guilty.

But with maturity came a deeper understanding. Her father had provided her with material things, but she had been short-changed nonetheless. He hadn't worked to provide her and her mother with luxuries. He hadn't worked for them at all. He had worked to satisfy a compulsive need within himself.

But she would be damned before she discussed her personal life with Hawk O'Toole. Let him think what he wanted to about her. She didn't care.

It seemed, however, that she was the only one who didn't value his good opinion. As they made their way through the compound, Hawk was stopped to admire a new baby, settle a dispute over a saddle, and assist in hoisting a generator off a flatbed truck.

They came upon a young man who was slouched against a tree sipping from a bottle of whiskey. He nearly jumped out of his skin when he saw Hawk. He hastily recapped the bottle and tossed it to the ground.

"Johnny," Hawk greeted him laconically.

"Hello, Hawk."

"This is Mrs. Price."

"I know who she is."

"You also know why we're here, how important this is to us."

"Yes."

"Just because the mine has been closed doesn't mean we don't have work to do. Let's utilize this time to do some long overdue maintenance work on all the trucks. I'm counting on you to give them thorough tune-ups. Understand?"

Johnny's dark eyes flashed and he swallowed hard. "Yes."

Hawk glanced down at the whiskey bottle. He didn't have to say anything about it. His eyes spoke volumes. "You're the best mechanic I've got. I depend on you. Don't disappoint me."

The young man bobbed his head. "I'll start on it right away."

Hawk gave him a brusque nod and walked away. "How do you know he won't pick up that bottle again?" Randy asked him when they were out of earshot.

"I don't. I hope he won't. Once he picks it up, he has a hard time putting it down."

"Isn't he rather young to have such a drinking problem?"

"He made a serious mistake and he's paying for it."

"What kind of mistake?"

"He married an Anglo." He gave her a hard look. "She hated living on the reservation. Johnny wouldn't leave it because he knew he could never come back. So his wife packed up one day and disappeared. He's been drinking ever since. His ego has taken a brutal beating because he fell for her in the first place, then when he got her, he couldn't keep her."

Randy ignored his sneer and addressed the topic. "You're trying to restore his self-confidence by giving him additional responsibilities."

"Something like that," Hawk replied with a negligent shrug. "Besides, he *is* an excellent mechanic and the trucks *do* need an overhaul."

"You're the tribal psychologist as well as baby-blesser and problem-solver. What other hats do you wear, Mr. O'Toole?"

He stepped up onto the porch of a cabin and swung open the door. "I'm the chief outlaw."

Up till then, Randy hadn't noticed where their walk was taking them. Now, she hesitated on the top step. "What do you mean?"

"Inside."

Hesitantly, she preceded him into the cabin. The dimness was an extreme contrast to the bright sunlight outside, so it took her eyes several seconds to adjust. Several men, whom she recognized as her kidnappers, were loitering around a rickety wooden desk on which sat the first telephone she'd seen since her abduction. Her heart gave a glad lurch, but the somber expressions of the men quelled it immediately.

"Where's Ernie?" one of them asked Hawk.

"He's watching the boy. He said for us to go ahead without him."

"If everything has gone according to schedule, it's time we put our call through."

Apparently Hawk agreed. He sat down in the only chair in the single room and pulled the telephone toward him. He looked at Randy and ordered curtly, "Come here."

"What for?"

His eyes, beneath the black, arching eyebrows, glittered dangerously. "Come here." She shuffled forward, until she was standing at the edge of the desk across from him. He said, "The conversation must be brief.

Thirty seconds, forty-five max. When I pass the receiver to you, identify yourself to Price. Tell him that you're safe, that you haven't been mistreated, but that we mean business. Say nothing else. If you do, you'll regret it."

He slipped the knife from the scabbard again and laid it within his reach on the table. "Our honor and our livelihoods are at stake. We're willing to die to protect both and to regain what is rightfully ours for future generations. Do you understand me?"

"Perfectly. But if you think I'm saying a single word into that telephone, you've got another think coming."

Her adamant statement elicited a reaction from the other men. They seemed aghast that she would address Hawk in such a disrespectful fashion. Hawk merely continued to stare at her with eyes that were as steady and blue as a gas flame.

After several moments, he turned his mouth down at the corners and, with a shrug, said, "Fine." Addressing the man nearest the door, he added, "Bring the boy. We'll let him do the talking."

"No!"

Randy's exclamation halted the man before he could take a single step toward the door. She swapped stubborn stares with Hawk. His stony expression was filled with resolve. He wouldn't relent. That she knew. She wouldn't let Scott be subjected to making the telephone call to his father. That Hawk knew. So it came down to a contest of wills.

Morton was no doubt frantic by now. His anxiety would be transmitted to Scott. There was also the fearsome knife lying on the desk to take into consideration. Subtle as that threat was, Scott was astute enough to pick up on it. What to him amounted to a camping holiday would become the nightmare it was for her. Just as Hawk had counted on, she would prevent that from happening at all costs.

"You win this time," she reluctantly whispered to Hawk. "I'll speak to Morton."

Hawk said nothing. He had been assured of a win before the contest had even begun. Picking up the receiver, he dialed the number he'd memorized beforehand. The line was busy.

Everyone in the room, including Randy, released a pent up sigh. She ran her sweaty palms over her skirt.

"What does that mean? Did somebody jump the gun, call before they were supposed to?"

"They're all too smart for that," Hawk said. "Remember, we knew when we were going to call, but the authorities didn't. Anybody could be talking to Price."

He dialed again. The call went through. The phone rang three times before it was answered. That would give the FBI time to set up the tracing mechanism, Randy thought. Little good that would do them or her.

The second Morton said a shaky hello, Hawk identified himself as the kidnapper. "I have Mrs. Price and your son Scott." He handed the receiver up to her. Her hands were so slippery with perspiration, she juggled it and almost dropped it before she got it to her ear. Hawk's eyes held her gaze like magnets.

"Morton?"

"Dear Lord, Randy, is that you? I've been so worried. How's Scott?"

"Scott's fine."

"If they've hurt—"

"They haven't." Hawk made a slicing motion across his throat with his index finger.

"We've been well treated." Hawk came out of his chair and reached for the receiver. "But do as they say. They mean business."

Hawk yanked the receiver away from her. Everyone in the room heard Morton's muffled voice frantically demanding information before Hawk hung up.

"Within seconds he'll get another call, the first in a series stating our demands," Hawk told the room at large. To Randy he said, "You did very well, Mrs. Price." She watched in silent misery as he held up the telephone wire and cut it in two with his knife. "We won't be needing this anymore."

Now that the connection had been irretrievably severed, Randy thought of a dozen things she might have done or said to give away their location. Any message of that sort would probably have cost her her life, but she could have tried. She rebuked herself as a coward and only excused her cowardice on the grounds that if something happened to her, Scott would be imperiled. She couldn't gamble her own life out of fear for his.

Hawk ordered one of the men to escort her to her cabin and lock her in.

Her despair gave way to anger. "For the entire day?" she shouted.

"For as long as I see fit."

"What will I do in there all day?"

"Fret, I would imagine."

She bristled. "I want Scott with me."

"Scott is otherwise occupied. Since he doesn't pose the threat of escaping that you do, I see no need to keep him cooped up indoors." He hitched his head toward the door. The man he'd directed to go with her grasped her elbow, though not unkindly. Randy angrily worked it free.

"I'll go peaceably." She said it with a sweet smile, but her eyes threw daggers at Hawk. "When they catch you, I hope they lock you up forever."

"They'll do neither."

As she was walking back to her cabin, it bothered Randy that he seemed so sure.

". . . and this was a really big horse, Mommy, not a pony. I got to ride it all by myself. At first Ernie held it on a rope, but then he slapped the horse on the rump— that's what it's called, the rump—and we took off." One of his hands slid off the other in a shooting gesture. "But I had to stay inside the corral. Hawk said maybe tomorrow I could ride out of the corral, but he'd have to wait and see."

"We might not be here tomorrow, Scott. Your dad might come and take us home. Wouldn't you like that?"

His small face scrunched into a perplexed frown as he contemplated that. "Yeah, I guess so, but I don't think I'm ready to go yet. It's fun here."

"You aren't afraid?"

"Of what?"

Of what? she asked herself. Of the evening shadows that seemed longer and darker than they were in the city? Of the purple dusk that came hours earlier when the sun sank below the peaks of the mountains? Of the strange sights and sounds and smells?

"Of Hawk," she said finally.

Scott looked at her, obviously puzzled. "Of Hawk? Why would I be scared of Hawk?"

"He did something bad, Scott. He committed a serious crime when he took us off that train against our will. You know what kidnapping means."

"But Hawk is nice."

"Remember all the talks we've had about never getting into a car with a stranger no matter how nice he or she might seem?"

"Like the yucky people who touch boys and girls in the bad way?" He shook his head positively. "Hawk hasn't touched me in the bad way. Has he touched you in the bad way, Mommy?"

She had to clear her throat before she could speak. "No, but there are other bad things people can do."

"Is Hawk gonna do something bad to us?" His flaxen brows pulled together worriedly.

Too late, she saw that her warnings were doing more harm than good. She didn't want to alarm Scott, but she also didn't want him to make Hawk into his idol. She forced a smile, and, after wetting her fingers with her tongue, smoothed down his stubborn cowlick. "He isn't going to do anything bad. Just remember that he did something that is against the law."

"Okay." He agreed too readily. Her admonition had been the proverbial water on a duck's back and had rolled right off. "Today Hawk taught me how to spear a fish from the bank of a pond where the water is still. He showed me how to sharpen a stick with the knife he gave me. He said it's good to have a weapon, but that it comes with res . . . responpablisity."

"Responsibility."

"Yeah, that. He said you should only use a weapon to get food, or to defend yourself, or . . ." He struggled to remember. "Oh, yeah, or to protect somebody you love."

Randy found it hard to believe that Hawk had ever loved anyone. His parents perhaps? His maternal grandfather who had been a chief before him? The people of his tribe? Certainly them. But a one-to-one love relationship? She couldn't fathom a man as hard-hearted as he loving a woman.

Disturbed over the thought, she said absently, "Always be careful with the knife."

"I will. Hawk gave me lots of safety lessons."

"You and Hawk had quite a lot to talk about. Anything else?"

"Uh-huh. Today when we were teeteeing in the woods, I asked him if mine would ever be as big as his and he said one day it prob'ly would be. His is *huge*, Mommy. Even bigger than Dad's. Hi, Hawk."

Randy, dumbfounded over the subject of Scott's meandering chatter, whirled around to see the topic of their conversation filling up the narrow doorway. Scott ran toward him. "I was just telling Mommy about—"

"The knife lessons," she interjected quickly. Standing, she faced him, hoping that he hadn't overheard Scott. "I think Scott is too young to be playing with knives."

"He is too young to be 'playing' with them. But every boy, even city-bred Anglos, should learn hunting skills. I'm here to take you to dinner. Ready, Scott?" Keeping his eyes on Randy, he extended his hand to the boy, who eagerly clasped it. They passed through the door together, leaving Randy to bring up the rear.

Scott kept Hawk engaged in conversation until they reached the center of the compound, where there was a buffet line of sorts. The main dish was chili being served out of enormous cauldrons, which had been simmering over the cookfire all day. Each family had contributed a side dish.

People had collected in small clusters around the bonfire. After having their plates filled, Hawk led Randy and Scott to a blanket. He crossed his ankles and lowered himself in one graceful motion. Scott tried to imitate him, almost upsetting his bowl of chili in the process. Hawk held his plate until he was situated as close to the man as he could get without actually sitting in his lap. Randy took a corner of the blanket—as far from Hawk as she could get.

The food was surprisingly good. Either that or she was inordinately hungry. In any case it was warm and filling and helped to ward off the chill in the evening air.

"Everyone's staring at me," Randy remarked to Hawk once they had finished eating. Most everyone was still sitting around the fire. Women were chatting and laughing together. Several men were strumming guitars and picking out tunes.

"It's your hair." The husky timbre of his voice drew her eyes up to Hawk's. "The firelight makes it . . ."

He never completed the sentence. That was disconcerting. So was the exclusively attentive way he was gazing at her. Randy had a sensation of suspension, of falling and being unable to catch herself. She desperately wanted to hear the adjective he had failed to speak, but the intimacy of the moment frightened her.

"I'm cold," she told him. "I want to go back to the cabin now."

He shook his head no.

"Please."

"If you go back, I'll have to send a guard with you." He made a gesture to encompass the circle of people. "They need the relaxation."

"I don't care what they need," she snapped. "I want to go inside."

Holding her hostile stare, Hawk raised his hand. Within seconds a young woman appeared at his side, smiling and eager to do his bidding. He spoke to her tersely. She faded into the darkness, reappearing in under a minute with a blanket folded over her arm. She extended it to Hawk, but he spoke another curt command. The young woman turned toward Randy. No longer smiling, her expression was rebellious and malevolent. She practically threw the blanket at Randy before stalking off.

Randy unfolded the blanket and wrapped it around herself. "What's the matter with her?"

"Nothing." He was frowning sternly as he

watched the young woman follow the perimeter of the circle and sit down almost directly across the fire from them. Even from that distance, her antagonism was obvious.

"She's been giving me 'drop dead' looks all night. What have I done to her?"

"She's just high-strung."

Randy didn't buy it. She knew jealousy when she saw it, and the young Indian woman was reeking with it. "Is there any significance attached to my sharing your blanket?"

"Families usually eat together."

"Is that an ancient tribal custom?"

"It is a recent custom that I instigated."

"Any special reason?"

"It's important for the children to recognize the family unit. Father, mother, children. It establishes unity and order."

"So why are Scott and I eating with you?"

"For the time being, you're my responsibility."

"In a roundabout way, your family."

"I suppose you could look at it that way."

"Apparently *she* does. And you needn't ask who. I'm talking about the high-strung girl with the sour expression for me and the cow eyes for you. What's her name?"

"Dawn January."

Through the flickering flames of the bonfire, Randy watched the girl. Dawn had classic Native American features—high cheekbones and long eyes that smoldered as hot as the fire each time they lighted on Hawk. They were brimming with lust and passion. Her sensuous mouth and ripely curved figure would have turned any man's head and appealed to his prurient instincts.

"She's jealous of me, isn't she?" Randy said intuitively. "She wants to be sitting beside you, sharing your blanket. Why don't you offer her father a complimentary number of fine horses? I'm sure she could be yours for the asking."

One corner of his lips tilted upward. It was as close to a smile as she'd seen on his austere face. "I saw that same John Wayne movie when I was a kid."

She made an impatient gesture. "You know what I mean."

"Yes, I know what you mean." His smile faded into his usual intense expression. "If I wanted Dawn, even for one night, I wouldn't have to pay anything."

"Ah," she drawled in a way that indicated she was impressed. "That kind of sexual favor comes with being a chief?"

"No. That kind of sexual favor comes with being Hawk O'Toole."

Properly put down, Randy safely lapsed into silence. She had little doubt that most women would find Hawk desirable. He was an intriguing man. His coldness challenged a woman's instinct to nurture. He was handsome, if one were attracted to the solitary, broody type. His lean, supple body was certainly appealing. Scott's innocent description of his manhood came back to haunt her now and she found herself taking surreptitious glances at his lap. Her cheeks grew warm.

"Something wrong?" he asked, as he stretched out his legs and propped himself up on one elbow.

"No, I just—" Her eyes were instantly drawn to the sizable bulge between his thighs. She hastily averted her head and groped for something to say. "You often refer to children and the future of the tribe. But you aren't fathering any children of your own."

"How do you know?"

Six

"Oh!" she exclaimed softly. "I just assumed . . . I mean you said there was no Mrs. O'Toole."

Amused at her stammering, he snorted a laugh. "There are no illegitimate children either."

She glared at him, furious because he had deliberately baited her. "Then why did you let me make a fool of myself?"

"Because you do it so well."

Randy's temper had been piqued and she was looking for a fight. "If you're so family oriented, why don't you have any children of your own? Wouldn't a few little O'Tooles strengthen the tribe?"

"Possibly."

"Well then?"

"I have enough to do. Why should I take on the additional responsibility?"

"A proper wife would take care of your children for you."

"Do you have any candidates in mind?"

"What about her?"

"Who? Dawn?" he asked, when Randy pointed out the girl still sitting on a blanket directly across the wide circle. "She's still a virgin."

"I'll bet," Randy said with a snicker. "Are you taking her word for that, or did you find it out for yourself?"

He didn't like her flippancy. Scowling darkly, he said, "I'm too old for her."

"I don't think Dawn realizes that."

"She could easily be my daughter. Anyway, she belongs to someone else."

" 'Belongs'?"

"One of the young men, Aaron Turnbow, has been in love with her since they were children."

"And that matters to you?"

The leaping flames of the campfire were nothing compared to those in his angry eyes. "Yes. That matters very much to me."

Randy looked away, privately admitting that she deserved the contemptuous look he gave her. She had no grounds on which to insult either him or the girl Dawn. Her only excuse was that she was feeling or-nery. And suspicious.

Having lived with her father first and then with Morton Price, she had pegged all men as selfish individuals who took what they wanted when they wanted it. Either Hawk O'Toole was a liar trying to impress her with his nobility, or he was a rarity she had never come across before.

She ruled out the possibility that he was homosexual. But what man would decline the open invitation of the voluptuous Dawn? There just wasn't that much altru-ism in the world. Randy found it easier to believe that Hawk was lying to her, though why he would remained a puzzle.

The conversation between them lapsed. Both seemed content to let it die. Snuggled within the warmth of the blanket, Randy breathed deeply of the crisp mountain air. It seemed to cleanse her from the inside out.

The ballads being sung softly to the ac-companiment of the guitars lulled the listen-ers. The repetitive rhythms of the songs were entrancing and seductive. Conversa-tions became quieter; some diminished to silence.

The children, Scott among them, who had been playing hide-and-seek in the nearby copse of trees, finally wound down. Scott returned to the blanket and wiggled himself between Hawk and Randy. Wrapping him inside the blanket with her, Randy drew his head to her breasts and sandwiched his cold hands between hers. She kissed the crown of his head, softly nuzzling the thatch of unruly hair.

"Sleepy?"

"No."

She smiled at his telltale yawn.

Couples began gathering their children and stealing away into the darkness beyond the circle of firelight. Randy saw Ernie lean over and whisper something into Leta's ear that caused her to coyly lower her lashes. Ernie shooed Donny toward their cabin. Arm in arm, they followed him.

Hawk had been watching them, too. "Horny old coot."

"Is that why he married a woman so much younger than himself?"

A corner of his lips quirked with a smile. "I'm sure lust had something to do with it, but not entirely. Ernie's first wife died soon after Donny was born. He had three other children by her. They're all grown now. Leta was an orphan who needed protection. Ernie was lonesome and needed a wife." He shrugged eloquently. "It worked out well."

Ernie had his head lowered close to Leta's, his arm protectively around her shoulders. Indians were usually depicted as being unemotional and stoic. Randy was surprised at Ernie's open display of affection for his young wife. She commented on it to Hawk.

"One's masculinity isn't measured by how shabbily he treats his woman, but by how well."

"Do you believe that?" Randy was amazed that he would profess such an untraditional doctrine.

"I don't have a woman, so it really doesn't matter what I believe, does it? It's just better for the community if the women aren't made to feel like second-class citizens."

"But weren't the Indian societies terribly chauvinistic?"

"Weren't they all?" With a tilt of her head, she conceded him the point. "Shouldn't societies be improved upon?"

"Definitely," she said. "It just surprises me that you don't hold more with tradition."

He made a noncommittal gesture. "Some traditions should be upheld. But what good is society if half its members feel worthless except to cook and clean and bear children?"

He was a man of contradictions. His mind was complex and his thoughts seemed to take more twists and turns than a mountain road. Randy was too tired to navigate them tonight. Her eyes gravitated toward Ernie and Leta again. She watched until the darkness swallowed them up completely. "They seem to love each other very much."

"She keeps him physically satisfied, and vice-versa, I believe."

"I was referring to a kind of love that transcends the physical level."

"There is no such thing."

Randy gave Hawk a careful look. He had just confirmed her speculations about his personal relationships, especially with women. "You don't believe in love?"

"Do you?"

She recalled Morton's treachery and the emotional hell he had put her through during their divorce proceedings. She answered Hawk honestly. "Idealistically, yes, I believe in it. Realistically, no." She touched Scott's cool, smooth cheek. He was fast asleep against her breasts, breathing damply through his mouth. "I believe in the love between a parent and a child."

Hawk made a scoffing sound. "A child loves his mother because she feeds him. From her breasts first, then from her hand. When he doesn't need her to feed him anymore, he stops loving her."

"Scott loves me," Randy claimed heatedly.

"He still depends on you to provide for him."

"And when the day comes that he no longer needs me, he'll stop loving me?"

"His needs will change. A man child needs milk. A grown man needs sex." He nodded down at the sleeping child. "He'll find a woman who'll give him that, and he'll soothe his conscience for taking it by telling her that he loves her."

Randy stared at him with astonishment. "According to this warped philosophy of yours, what does a woman require after she outgrows her need for mother's milk?"

"Protection. Affection. Kindness. A husband satisfies a woman's nesting instinct. That passes for love. She swaps him the nightly use of her body in exchange for security and children. If the two are lucky, they each consider it an even swap."

"What a callous man you are, Hawk O'Toole," she said, shaking her head in dismay.

"Very." He stood up suddenly. "Let's go."

He caught her by the upper arms and lifted her—blanket, Scott, and all—to her feet. The movement was so sudden, she was knocked off balance. He waited until she regained her equilibrium before releasing her.

Randy was glad that Scott's body acted as a barrier between Hawk and her. The evening had been vividly sensual. The spicy food, the chanting music, the brisk air, the warm blanket, all had enlivened her senses. Their conversation, especially its sexual references, had left her feeling agitated and restless, itchy from the inside out.

She was disturbingly aware of the tall

man beside her as they walked through the darkness toward the cabin. Occasionally their hips would bump together. His elbow glanced the side of her breast.

They had almost reached the cabin when a shadow separated itself from the others and stood directly in their path. Hawk's hand stealthily moved to the scabbard at his waist and withdrew his knife.

The shadow moved forward and caught a beam of light from across the compound. Randy's breath eked out in slow relief when she recognized Dawn January. Hawk didn't seem that pleased to see her, however. He addressed her in a harsh tone. She responded argumentatively. He said something more and emphasized it by making an impatient gesture. The girl shot Randy a look that oozed hatred, then whipped around and stalked off into the darkness.

Randy climbed the steps to the porch and entered the cabin. She felt her way across the rough plank floor toward Scott's bed, laid him down, and covered him with a blanket. He'd never slept in his clothes before. Now he was doing it for the third night in a row.

When he was safely tucked in, she returned to the open doorway. Hawk was standing as still as stone, staring into the night. "Did she leave?" Randy asked him.

"Yes."

"What was she doing here?"

"Waiting."

"For what?"

"To see that you got inside."

"I doubt she's concerned for my safety and well-being," Randy said sarcastically. "She probably thinks you're going to sleep with me."

"She may be right."

Her eyes snapped up to his, uncertain whether he was joking or not. He wasn't. When he turned his head and looked down at her, his sharp features were taut with intensity. He executed a graceful pivot that successfully anchored her against the doorjamb.

"You would have to kill me first," she told him breathlessly.

"No, I wouldn't." He brushed a light, arousing kiss across her lips. "You would trade me the use of your body for your child's safety in a second, Mrs. Price."

"You wouldn't hurt Scott."

"But you're not sure."

She swallowed hard and tried to avert her head. "You'd have to take me by force."

He angled his body forward, suggestively pressing it against hers. "I don't think so. I watched you tonight. There are aspects of our culture that you find extremely stimulating. Right now, your blood is running as hot as mine."

"No."

Her whimpered protest was smothered by his kiss. His parted lips rubbed against hers until they separated. His agile tongue claimed her mouth with quick, rapid thrusts, then made love to it with slow, delicious strokes.

Breathing rapidly, he lifted his lips off hers and opened them against her throat, drawing the fragile, fair skin against his teeth. "You like sitting on the ground with nothing over your head except the night sky. You like wrapping a blanket around you for warmth."

He kissed his way down her neck and nudged aside the placket of her shirt with his nose. He planted a fervent kiss on the soft, smooth slope of her breast. "You like our music, with its ancient, pagan, provocative beat. You feel its rhythm. Here." His hand came up to cover her breast. He fondled it aggressively, then more gently, lightly grinding her hardening nipple beneath his palm.

Her mind was chanting no, no, no. But when his mouth returned to claim hers, she responded hungrily. Her tongue searched for his. Her hands came up to grasp handfuls of his thick, dark hair. He slid one hand to the small of her back and, applying pressure there, lifted the notch of her thighs against the fly of his jeans.

He groaned. "Why do I want you?"

Randy doubted he was aware that he'd spoken the question aloud. It was one she could ask herself. Why was her body responding to him, when by rights she should feel nothing but revulsion? At what point had desire replaced fear? Why did she want to get closer instead of push him away?

When he rasped out the words, "I want to bury myself inside you," she trembled with arousal, not repugnance. "Damn you," he cursed. "You're my enemy. I hate you. But I want you." He spoke a gutter word, growled an erotic mating sound, and used the hand at the small of her back to secure her against him.

Then in the next heartbeat he shoved her away. He wiped off his mouth with the back of his hand. "How many have been there before me?" he snarled. "How many men have sacrificed their pride and their integrity for a few minutes of sweet forgetfulness between your thighs?"

He backed away from her as though she were something foul. "I won't be so weak, Mrs. Price."

Turning, he launched himself off the porch and down the steps. Randy stumbled into the cabin. She slammed the door shut and leaned back against it. Covering her face with her hands, she hiccuped dry sobs. Her breasts heaved with remnants of passion. At the same time, she was swamped with self-disgust. She quivered with rage against him and his false accusations.

How dare he rebuke her when he didn't know the truth? How dare he kiss her like that?

How dare she respond?

Eventually Randy lowered her hands and stared into the darkness of the cabin, which was relieved only by the meager moonlight coming through the small window.

Of one thing she was absolutely certain. She couldn't wait for Morton to respond to the Indians' demands. It was past time for her to seize the initiative. For Scott's own good, for her own, she had to get them away from Hawk O'Toole.

She had a plan for escaping, but it was so chancy that it barely qualified as a bona fide plan. From every angle, it was riddled with happenstance. So much of it relied on luck. Still, it was all she had. Impatient to act now that her mind was made up, she was going to ignore the risks involved and go with the plan.

It had occurred to her after several hours of floor pacing. She was grateful to whatever muse governed the memory. From out of nowhere, she suddenly remembered seeing the young man Hawk had called Johnny leaving a shed that, she had later discerned, was a garage.

At some point during the evening, she had spotted him slinking out of the building, clutching a whiskey bottle to his chest. As far as she knew, Hawk hadn't noticed him.

Instead of joining the others for the evening meal, Johnny had disappeared into the darkness with his bottle.

The young man's dependency on alcohol was tragic. It made her ill to think that she would be exploiting it, but it was the only feasible possibility she had arrived at. It was reasonable to assume that Johnny had been derelict in his duties and had left the keys in at least one of the trucks he'd been working on that day.

If she could make it to the shed undetected, and *if* she discovered a truck with the keys left in the ignition, and *if* it hadn't been disemboweled, and *if* she could get it started, she *might* be able to drive away before anyone discovered she was gone.

There were other considerations. For instance, she didn't know where she was, though she guessed the northwestern part of the state where the terrain was more mountainous. She didn't know how much gas would be in the truck. She had no money because her handbag had been left on the Silverado train. All those considerations could be dealt with as the need arose. First, she had to escape from the compound.

She chose the pre-dawn hour to put her plan into action. Hadn't she read somewhere that the last hour or so before dawn is when normal people are in their deepest sleep? Hawk O'Toole wasn't normal, but she tried not to let that bothersome glitch sway her determination. Besides, she wanted the cover of darkness, but she had to have enough light to see what she was doing and where she was going. She didn't want to use artificial light; she would depend on what was naturally available, which was the gray light just before sunrise.

One of the first obstacles she encountered was waking up Scott. He groaned and burrowed deeper beneath the covers when she tried to shake him awake. She didn't want to alarm him, but every minute that ticked by was precious.

"Scott, please, darling, wake up." She was gently persistent and eventually he sat up, though he was whining and crying. "Shh, shh," she cautioned, patting his back. "I know it's early, but you've got to wake up for Mommy right now. It's very important."

He mumbled another protest and dug his fists into his eyes, which Randy knew must feel gritty. Forcibly maintaining her composure, she knew better than to chastise him. That would probably result in a crying jag. So she appealed to his spirit of adventure.

"We're going to play a game with Hawk," she whispered.

His whining ceased. He straightened from his slumping posture and blinked her into focus. "A game?"

God, forgive me for lying, she prayed. She had never lied to her son, no matter how much the truth had hurt. She could only hope that he would be so glad to return home that he would forgive her.

"Yes, but it's a quiet game. You can't make a single sound. You know that Indians can hear everything."

"Like when they're in the woods, they can hear animals in their caves and bugs crawling under the ground and stuff like that?"

"That's right. So you must be quieter than you've ever been or Hawk will find us and the game will be over."

"Are we playing hide-and-seek? Is Hawk gonna come looking for us?"

"He'll definitely come looking for us." And that was no lie.

She wrapped him in a jacket that had been borrowed from Donny and tied his sneakers. Through the window she tried to locate their guard. She finally made out a hulking shape, wrapped in a blanket, propped against a nearby tree. He had obviously fallen asleep during his watch. So far God was answering her prayers.

"Now, listen, Scott," she told him, crouching down to his level. "We've got to get past the guard first. I'm going to carry you. But you can't say a thing until we're past him. You can't even whisper, okay?" He merely stared back at her, wide-eyed. "Scott, do you understand?"

"You said I couldn't even whisper."

She smiled and hugged him hard. "Good boy."

Gathering him in her arms, she slowly opened the front door. Its hinges creaked noisily. She froze and waited several moments, but there was no sign that she'd given herself away. She stepped out onto the porch. The bulk beneath the tree hadn't moved.

She felt her way down the steps. On the

path, she was careful not to lose her balance or to upset a rock. She didn't feel safe until they were a hundred yards from the cabin. Then she broke into a half run, keeping within the shadows as much as possible. A dog barked sharply twice, but she kept on going until she reached the shed.

The darkness inside was stygian. She released her hold on Scott and lowered him to the dirt floor. "Stay here by the door. I'm going to find a truck for us to use."

"I don't like it in here. It smells bad. It's dark and I'm sleepy, Mommy. I'm cold, too."

"I know, I know." She stroked his cheek soothingly. "You're such a brave boy. I don't know what I'd do without you to guard the door for me."

"Is that my job? Am I the lookout?"

"That's your job."

He thought it over and said grudgingly, "Okay, but I'd rather play something else. Let's hurry and finish this game."

"It will be finished soon. I promise."

Leaving Scott just inside the doorway and commissioning him not to "leave his post," she went in search of a truck with the keys left in the ignition. She got lucky on the second one she checked. From what she could make of it in the darkness, it was a truck used for hauling. It had high plywood sides attached to the trailer.

She considered scouting around, perhaps finding another that was smaller, more maneuverable, but decided that since time was of the essence and the sky outside was getting lighter by the minute, she'd better use this one.

She went back for Scott and urged him up into the cab of the truck. He went reluctantly. "Do you think Hawk can find us in this truck?"

"That's his part of the game. Our part is to get out of the compound without him seeing us."

Before that, however, she had to turn on the motor and risk waking everyone in the village with the racket. She only hoped that Johnny had worked on this truck before starting his drinking binge. Sending up a prayer and wiping her perspiring palms on her skirt, she reached for the key and gave it a twist.

The noise seemed louder than a rocket launch. The engine whirred in protest. Pressing on the clutch and pumping the accelerator, Randy urged it, "Come on. Please. Come on."

It sparked to life so suddenly that for a moment she stared at the steering wheel in shock. She glanced over at Scott and said, "It started."

"Didn't you want it to, Mommy?"

"Yes, it's just that—Never mind. Let's see if we can leave without waking up anybody."

"Can I invite Donny to play, too?"

"No."

"Please."

"Not this time, Scott."

Her harsh tone brought on a pout. She regretted being snippy with him, but she couldn't afford an argument now. She worked the stubborn floor stick into first gear, gave the truck some gas, and gradually let out the clutch. The truck lumbered forward.

Randy almost expected to be met with a wall of Indians armed to the teeth when she passed through the opening of the shed, but there was no movement anywhere in the compound. She gnawed on her lower lip with the effort it required to turn the truck, but she managed to do it. She guided it along, remaining in first gear, toward the entrance of the compound.

She resisted the impulse to thumb her nose at Hawk's cabin when the truck rolled past it. Driving the behemoth required all her physical strength, while her eyes continued to sweep the area beyond the windshield. Chilly as the morning air was, she felt sweat trickling down her sides. Reflexively, her fingers opened and closed around the steering wheel. All her muscles were contracted with nervousness.

There! She could see it. A gate with a cattle guard to keep the livestock from wandering out of the compound. The gate was open. She dared to shift up to second and accelerate. As soon as the truck rumbled over the cattle guard, she shifted into third. The engine protested, but she gave it more gas and it lurched forward.

"How far are we going to go, Mommy, before Hawk starts looking for us?"

"I'm not sure, darling."

She wiped her perspiring forehead with her sleeve. The road was so rough, it was hazardous. The truck jolted over each chuckhole. But Randy felt a relief in her chest, as though a boulder had been lifted off it. "Scott, Scott, we did it!" she cried happily.

"We won the game?"

"I think so, yes. It certainly looks that way."

"Good. Can we go back now?"

Laughing, she reached across the interior of the truck and ruffled his hair. "Not right away."

"But I'm hungry for breakfast."

"You'll have to wait a while longer. The game isn't quite over yet."

She drove for several miles. The road seemed to go on forever. Eventually it had to lead somewhere, she assured herself. According to the rising sun, she was heading east. That was good, wasn't it? She didn't know. For right now her goal was to reach a main highway. Then she would be as good as home.

The sun burst over the peak of the mountain like an explosion in the night, momentarily blinding her. She lifted her left hand to shield her eyes against it. But when her vision was restored, she was certain her watering eyes were playing tricks on her.

"It's Hawk!" Scott cried, jumping up to stand on his knees. He braced himself against the dashboard and hopped up and down. "He found us. He's smart, Mommy. He's a tracker. I knew he could find us. Hey, Hawk, here we are!"

Randy jerked the steering wheel around. The truck swerved, barely missing the man who sat astride his horse in the middle of the road. Neither the man nor the horse seemed concerned that they'd almost been run down. Neither moved a muscle.

A cloud of dust rose around the truck when Randy brought it to a wheezing halt. Before she could stop him, Scott bolted from his door and ran toward Hawk, who had dismounted. Randy stacked her hands on the steering wheel and defeatedly rested her head on them. She felt her failure from the marrow of her bones to every extremity.

"Get out."

She raised her head. Hawk had hissed the words through the open window. Even as he said them, he yanked open the door, encircled her elbow in a bone-crunching grip, and hauled her down to the ground. Several horsemen had joined them, including the ever-faithful Ernie. Scott was dancing from one foot to the other, crowing his delight over having come so far before being found.

"Mommy said I had to be quieter than I've ever been because Indians can hear everything. And I was the lookout when she got the truck. And then we drove away without waking up anybody. But I knew you'd find us." He spun around and charged back toward Hawk, tackling him around the knees. "Did you like the game, Hawk?"

His frigid eyes moved from Randy's pale face down to her son. "Yes. The game was fun. But I have something even more fun for you to do. How would you like to ride back to the camp on that?" He motioned toward a pony that Ernie had tethered to his saddle horn.

Scott's eyes rounded and his mouth dropped open. "You mean it?" he whispered reverently.

Hawk nodded. "Ernie will hold the reins, but you can sit on the saddle all by yourself."

Before Randy could voice her opinion of the arrangement, Hawk swung Scott up onto the small saddle. He gripped the pommel with white knuckles. His smile was uncertain, but his eyes were bright.

Hawk gave Ernie a terse nod. He and the other horsemen wheeled their mounts around and headed back in the direction of the compound. Keeping off the road, they crested a hill and disappeared.

Hawk's boot heel dug a crater in the earth when he turned on it and faced Randy again. "You made one bitch of a tactical error, Mrs. Price."

She wouldn't be cowed. Her chin went up a notch. "By trying to escape my son's kidnappers?"

"By getting on my bad side."

"Which wasn't too difficult, since you don't have a good side."

"I'm warning you. Tread lightly with me."

"I'm not afraid of you, Hawk O'Toole."

His eyes slowly scored down her body. He said nothing until they met hers again. Then he whispered, "Well, you should be."

Once again, he turned with an economy of motion and swung his right leg over his mount's back. Randy hadn't realized until then that he was riding barebacked. His thighs gripped the horse's sides. She stepped up into the truck.

"What do you think you're doing?" Hawk asked her.

"I thought I'd drive the truck back."

"That's for Johnny to do."

She alighted and faced him, hands on hips. "Then I suppose I'm to ride double with you again?"

He leaned low over the horse's neck. "No. You walk."

Seven

"Walk?"

"That's right. Get going." He flexed his knees and the horse started moving forward.

"It's miles back to the compound."

With an arrow-straight arm and index finger, she pointed in that direction. Hawk squinted his eyes as though calculating the distance. "About two and a half from here, I think."

Randy retracted her arm and folded it with the other across her middle. "I won't do it. Short of using physical force, you can't make me take a single step. I'll wait for Johnny to come after the truck, then ride back with him."

"I've told you more than once not to underestimate me." His silky voice carried sinister undertones. "You've already taken advantage of Johnny's misfortune once. Yes, I saw you watching him as he left the shed last night. I figured you'd try something outrageous like this. But would you exploit a misguided kid like Johnny again? What do you have in mind, enticing him with the promise of all the whiskey he can drink before he passes out? No, wait, it would be more your style to grant him sexual favors in exchange for your freedom."

"You're despicable. How dare you talk to me like that?"

"And how dare you take me and my people for brainless fools? Did you actually think you could sneak past me?"

"*You?* That was you asleep under the tree?"

"That was me, but I wasn't asleep. It was all I could do to keep from laughing."

"I didn't know you could."

The barb hit home. His jaw tensed. "I had a good laugh after you drove off. If you hadn't provided me with such an entertaining morning, I'd leave you out here for buzzard bait. Maybe I should anyway. You deserve no better. What kind of mother would deceive her child into thinking that he was playing a game?"

"A mother desperate to get her son away

from a criminal, a fanatic, a madman," she shouted up at him.

Unmoved, he hitched his chin toward the camp. "Let's go."

He nudged the horse forward again. Randy stood her ground, her expression stormy. She would have stood there until the elements petrified her if she hadn't thought of Scott. She became frantic every time he was out of her sight. As long as she was with him, she exercised some control over his fate. But when they were separated, she could think of little else but how precarious their situation was.

She sent up a puff of dust when she spun around and started marching in the direction of the compound. She wasn't as careful on the uneven ground as she had been before sunrise. Rocks rolled away beneath her tennis shoes, threatening a sprained ankle. She would have slowed her pace, but she was aware of each strike of the horse's hooves behind her. Hawk's eyes seemed to be boring a hole in the base of her spine. She could feel them there. Like his namesake, he had her in his sights. While she was under such close observation, she wanted to appear undaunted. Pride propelled her forward.

She ignored the blisters she was rubbing on her feet, and the sweat that was collecting around her waist, and the heavy, itchy feel of her hair against her neck. Her breathing became more labored with each step she took. She was accustomed to exercising, but not in this altitude. The thin air began to take its toll.

Her mouth turned as dry as the dust that swirled around her ankles. She was also very hungry. Maintaining the rapid pace soon sapped her reserve of energy. She grew light-headed. She couldn't keep the horizon level. It began to tilt.

She almost stepped on the scaly reptile before she saw it. It uncoiled a snakelike tongue. Randy leaped backward and screamed piercingly. The giant lizard, his bravado spent, scuttled for cover behind a boulder. Hawk's horse snorted. It pranced skittishly, almost trampling Randy. She uttered another sharp cry of fright. The horse reared. She dropped to the ground and barely managed to roll clear before his hooves came crashing down.

"Be still, dammit," Hawk commanded.

"And stop screaming." Using his knees, hands, and soothing voice, he managed to get the animal under control. He then maneuvered the horse closer to Randy, who was cowering, her teeth chattering with fright.

Hawk bent down and grabbed a handful of her loose shirt. He used it to pull her up. "Throw your leg over." She was too frightened not to obey him. Her right leg went over the horse's back at the same time she clutched the thick mane with both hands. Her skirt had become bunched up beneath her, leaving a good portion of her thighs exposed to the sun. She tried to tug the hem down at least as far as her knees.

"Leave it."

"But—"

"I said leave it!"

Her breasts rose and fell on a sob. "You won't be satisfied until you humiliate me completely, will you?"

"No. And I'm an expert in humiliation."

"Hawk, please."

"Enough." When she subsided, he placed his lips against her ear and whispered menacingly, "Enjoy the ride. These'll be the last peaceful moments you have for a long time." Then, possessively laying a hand on her bare thigh, he squeezed the horse between his knees and they moved forward again.

"Does it offend you to have my dark Indian hand resting on your white Anglo thigh?"

"No more than it offends me to have any creep pawing me."

A facsimile of a laugh broke through his stern lips. "Who do you think you're kidding? Certainly not me. Plenty of creeps have pawed you."

Randy's lips remained stubbornly sealed. She wasn't going to trade insults with him. It was a waste of time and energy. Let him believe what he would. Others had. Many had. She had survived their scorn. She hadn't gone unscathed, but she had survived. She could survive Mr. O'Toole's insults as well.

The horse plodded along. Randy began to think they'd never reach the compound, but her nose picked up the smell of wood smoke and cooking food. Her stomach growled indelicately.

Keeping one hand on her thigh, Hawk slipped the other into the waistband of her skirt and splayed it over her stomach. "Hungry?"

"No."

"You're not only a whore, you're a liar."

"I'm not a whore!"

"You were willing to play whore for me last night."

"I've never willingly played whore."

"No?"

His hand moved down. His fingers grazed the lace panel on the front of her underpants, which she had traded for the borrowed ones as soon as hers had dried. Her reaction to his touch was violently sensual. She felt it deep within her. She gasped audibly. Her thighs, already warm and sensitive from straddling the horse bare-legged, tightened reflexively. Her fingers curled deeper into the horse's luxuriant mane.

Hawk continued to feather his fingers over the lace. An involuntary groan rose out of Randy's throat. "Don't. Please."

He withdrew his hand. If Randy had turned her head and looked into his face, she would have noticed a discernible difference in it. His skin seemed to be stretched across his cheekbones to its absolute limit. His lips were thinly compressed. His eyes looked feverishly bright.

"I'll stop only because I don't want anyone to see me fondling you and mistake my disdain for desire."

The people of his tribe read their leader's mood well and gave the horse and its riders a wide berth. Randy's eyes darted everywhere, but she didn't catch sight of either Scott or Ernie. Hawk guided the horse to his cabin and agilely slid off its smooth back.

"I thought you'd take me back to my cabin," Randy remarked.

"You thought wrong." Reaching up, he again grabbed the front of her shirt and dragged her off the horse. She stumbled along behind him up the stony path. "Is this manhandling necessary?"

"Apparently so."

"I assure you that it's not."

"It wouldn't be if you hadn't tried to run away. If you were going to make the effort, you should have made damn certain you would succeed."

His critically derisive tone pricked her ego. He gave her a shove that sent her reeling through the cabin's door. She broke her fall against the table in the center of the room and spun around to face him, ready to do combat. Her bravery was instantly quelled when she saw him approaching her with his knife drawn.

"Oh, God," she cried. "If you kill me, don't let Scott see my body. Promise me that much, Hawk. Hawk!" She raised pleading hands. "And don't harm my son. He's only a child." Tears spurted from her eyes. "Please don't hurt my baby."

She threw herself against his chest and began beating it with her fists. His knife clattered to the table behind her. Hawk grappled for her hands and finally managed to secure her wrists. He carried them to her back, holding them behind her waist and rendering her unable to move, much less fight.

"What do you take me for?" he asked, angrily biting out each word. "I wouldn't hurt the boy. I never intended to hurt either of you. That wasn't part of the deal. He knew—"

Randy's vanquished head snapped up. Her eyes latched on to his just as her ears had latched on to his words. "*He?*"

Hawk's angry features smoothed out with

drastic speed. He reined in every emotion, until his face was an impenetrable mask and his eyes reflected no life.

"*He?*" Randy repeated on a shout. "Who?"

"Never mind."

"Morton?" she gasped softly. "Is my *husband* in on this? Oh, God! Did Morton stage his own son's kidnapping?"

Hawk abruptly let go of her wrists. He picked up his knife again and used it to cut a leather thong in halves. Randy followed each of his jerky movements, eager for some sign that her guess was correct.

The idea would have been preposterous had she not known Morton so well. She knew what made him tick. Since the kidnapping, his name had been appearing in headlines all over the state and beyond. He would like that. He would bask in the free publicity. He would milk it for all it was worth, giving thought to nothing else, not even his own son's welfare.

"Answer me, damn you. Tell me the truth." She gripped Hawk's sleeve. "Am I right? Did Morton put you up to this?"

Again Hawk placed her hands at her waist behind her back and began winding one strip of the leather cord around them. She didn't even struggle. She didn't think to. The probability that Morton was behind this nefarious scheme had erased all other thoughts from her mind. All she could think about was his convincing performance over the telephone. He had poured his heart and soul into his quavering voice, begging to know if Scott was safe. His anxiety had been phony, all for show.

She gazed into Hawk's face, but it revealed nothing. When he had secured her wrists together, he took the second half of the cord and led her to the bed. It had a wooden frame and was stronger and larger than either of the cots she and Scott had been sleeping on. He wound the end of the thong around the railing at the foot of the bed and tied a series of knots that would be impossible for her to untie.

Stepping back, he gave the thong a vicious tug. It didn't give a fraction of an inch. He nodded his head with satisfaction, then headed for the door.

"Wait a minute! Don't you dare leave until you answer me." Hawk came around slowly and pierced Randy with his blue eyes. "Did Morton Price plot this with you?"

"Yes."

Her chest seemed to cave in. She couldn't breathe. Now that she knew it for fact, she wanted to deny it. "Why?" she whispered in disbelief. *"Why?"*

"You'll be brought water periodically," was his nonanswer. "Since you chose to skip breakfast, you can wait for the evening meal to eat."

Only then did Randy fully realize she was tied up and completely helpless. Did knowing about Morton's involvement somehow increase the danger she was in? "You can't leave me here like this. Untie me."

"Not a chance, Mrs. Price. We tried it the other way, you took advantage of my good will."

"Good will! You're holding me hostage," she shouted. "If the tables were turned, wouldn't you have tried to escape?"

"Yes, but I would have succeeded."

Stung, she tried another tack. "I don't want Scott to see me tied to a bed, Mr. O'Toole. It would frighten him."

"That's why he won't be seeing you."

The blood drained from her face. "What do you mean?" she asked, her voice husky with dread.

"He'll be staying with Ernie, Leta, and Donny from now on."

Vehemently, she shook her head. Tears filled her eyes. "No. Please. Don't do that to me." The muscles in his face didn't relax one iota. "If you won't think of me, think of Scott. He'll miss me. He'll want to see me. He'll ask for me."

"When he does, he'll be brought here. You'll be untied during his visits. While he's with you, you won't do or say a damn thing other than what I tell you to do or say."

"Don't be so sure."

"Oh, I'm sure," he replied evenly.

"You've separated me from Scott. What more can you do to punish me?"

"As you've figured out, Price instigated this. Neither of us planned on your being a part of it. Your own foolhardiness is to blame for your involvement."

"So?"

"Scott's safety is guaranteed because he's valuable to Representative Price." His eyes moved over her contemptuously. "But his faithless wife sure as hell isn't."

"He'll never live up to his part of the bargain." She picked idly at the food on the tin plate. Irritated because he didn't acknowledge her remark, she tossed down her fork. The loud rattle caused him to look up at her. "Did you hear what I said?"

"You said that Price won't live up to his part of the bargain."

"Well, doesn't it bother you to know that?"

Hawk laid aside his fork and pushed his plate away. He curled the fingers of both hands around his mug of coffee and propped his elbows on the table as he sipped from it. "I know no such thing. That's what you've told me. I don't necessarily believe it."

"You don't *want* to believe it."

His eyes narrowed. "That's right. Because if Price doesn't uphold his end of the bargain, I've got no reason to keep you around. I'd be forced to . . . eliminate the problem."

"And Scott?" she asked raggedly.

"He would soon forget you. He's adapted to us very well. Children are resilient. Within a year, he'd be more Indian than Anglo." Her shattered features seemed to have no effect on him. He gave a casual wave of his hand. "Of course, he'd be another mouth to feed, another child to clothe and educate, another liability to the tribe. I'd much rather Price made good on his promises."

His matter-of-fact tone of voice instilled fear in her far more than ranting and raving would have. She had to clear the tension and emotion from her throat before she was able to speak. "What did Morton promise you, Chief O'Toole?"

"To bend the ear of the governor. He's going to plead our case with him to reopen the Lone Puma Mine."

"That much I know. In exchange for what?"

"The publicity generated by this fake kidnapping."

"It isn't fake to me," she snapped, thrusting her fists across the table and turning up her wrists so he could see the red welts left there by the leather thong. He took one of her hands and drew it forward for a closer inspection. He lightly stroked the scraped skin with his thumb. Randy snatched both hands out of his reach and shot to her feet.

"Sit down." For all its softness, his words carried a steely threat.

"I'm finished."

"I'm not. Sit down."

"Afraid I'll run away again?" she taunted.

He set his coffee cup aside and turned his gaze on her with the full blast of the intimidating power of those pale eyes of his. "No. I'm afraid you'll stupidly force me to do something I'd rather not have to do."

" 'Eliminate your problem'?"

She had come out of her chair quickly, but he was out of his before she could blink. His hand whipped out and curved around the back of her neck. "Sit down." He applied pressure to her shoulder and her knees buckled. Once she was back in her chair, he returned to his and stared at her across the table.

"Your husband saw a way for both of us to benefit."

"My *ex*-husband."

Hawk shrugged complacently. "I went to him several months ago because I had read in the newspapers that he advocates the Indian cause."

"Because it's expedient and fashionable, not because he's sincerely sympathetic to you. All his convictions revolve around himself. You were misled."

"I laid our case before him. The mine belonged to the tribe." His face darkened and, for a moment, his eyes seemed to be looking into another time and place. Then they cleared and focused on Randy. "It was bad enough when a group of investors bought it out from under us. You can imagine our outrage when we learned it was being closed, with no prospect for reopening."

"Why have they closed it? Is it losing money?"

"Losing?" he spat. "Hell, no. It's making money. That's the problem."

She shook her head with misapprehension. "I don't understand."

"The new owners planned all along to use it as a tax write-off, nothing more. They don't give a damn that we depend on it for our livelihoods. Selfish bastards," he said beneath his breath. "In years past they've juggled the books to appease the IRS, but they were being investigated on several counts. Initially, they curbed our production quota. Then they decided that in the long run the most profitable thing to do was shut down operation completely."

He left the table and went to the iron stove in the corner. Opening the door, he threw in a few sticks of firewood. There had been a marked drop in the temperature from the night before. But Randy had never experienced anything as cold as Hawk's eyes when he talked about the injustices heaped on the people of his reservation.

"What about the Bureau of Indian Affairs?"

"The BIA looked into it, but the owners have a signed contract and a deed. Legally, if not morally, they own the mine and can do whatever they want to with it."

"So you appealed to the state legislature?"

He nodded. "When I sought out Price, he listened and commiserated. Since I'd had so many other doors slammed in my face, his sympathy in itself was something. He promised to look into it and do what he could." Hawk's tone turned bitter. "His efforts weren't enough, but he promised to look into it further and get back to me." He returned to the table and dropped into the chair. "I was beginning to think he'd forgotten his promise, but a few weeks ago he approached me with this idea."

"Scheme."

"He convinced me that it would work."

"He manipulated you."

"We would both get what we wanted."

"He would. You'd be left with a criminal record."

"The case will never come to trial. He guaranteed that."

"He doesn't wield that kind of power."

"He said he would convince Governor Adams to intervene on our behalf."

"You'll face federal charges. If it comes down to that, I swear to you that Morton won't stick his neck out for you. He will disavow all knowledge of your agreement. It would be your word against his. Who is going to believe an Indian activist with a shady if not criminal record against a state representative? Admit it, your tale would sound outlandish. It would stretch even the most expansive imagination."

"Which side would you take, Mrs. Price?"

"*My* side. Given a choice between the two of you, I don't know who is worse, the manipulator or the guy he buffaloed."

His chair went over backward and crashed to the floor when he bolted out of it. "I was not buffaloed. Price will come through. He knows we've got Scott, but he doesn't know where. He loves his son. If he wants him back, he'll do as he promised."

Randy stood, too, so she wouldn't be looking up at him. "Your first mistake is believing that Morton loves Scott. That's a laugh." She swept back her hair with an impatient swipe of her hand. "If he loved him, would he volunteer him for something like this? Use him as a pawn? Endanger his life? Would you put a son of yours through something like this?"

Hawk's lips narrowed. Randy pressed her point. "Morton Price loves no one but himself. Bank on that, Mr. O'Toole. If he approached you, if this entire fiasco was his idea, then rest assured that he'll make the most of it and then some. He'll get what he wants out of it and leave you holding the bag. You'll be held accountable, not Morton.

"He's running scared about the upcoming election," she continued. "He's afraid he'll be defeated, and justifiably so. This stunt is a desperate measure to win the voters' attention and sympathy. Who could resist a suffering father, anguishing over the unknown fate of his only son, who happens to be, because of the state's unfair custody laws, living with his adulterous mother? He'll remind the public of me and my faithlessness. He's sure to blame my negligence, at least subtly, for letting Scott be kidnapped in the first place." She paused to draw a deep breath. "Did you put a time limit on it?"

"Two weeks. We don't want our children to start school late either."

"Two weeks of having his name in the headlines," she said on a scornful laugh. "Right up Morton's alley. He'll be the lead story on the newscasts every night." She rubbed her forehead, which had begun to pound with a headache. Then she looked at Hawk again. Flattening her palms on the tabletop, she leaned toward him. "Don't you see? He preyed on you worse than the men who closed the Lone Puma. He's using you and your people for his own gains."

Nervously, she wet her lips and pleaded with him. "Let us go, Hawk. You'll have much more leverage and credibility if you take us back and tell the authorities your story. I'll defend you. I'll testify that you were duped, that Morton put you up to it. When you've been cleared of all charges, we'll see what can be done about reopening the mine. What do you say?"

"You've got a deal. *If,*" he added, "you

put out for me tonight. Get naked and lie down on your back."

Stunned, she gazed at him in disbelief. "*What?*"

Hawk smiled, though it was more of a sneer. "You should see your face, Mrs. Price. You look like you just swallowed one of those fish you were butchering the other day. Relax. I just wanted to see how far you were willing to go to convince me of your noble intentions."

"Oh, you're a horrible man," she said, shuddering with revulsion. "And a fool. That'll soon become apparent. The news-paper accounts will let us know just how earnestly Morton is pleading your case. You'll see how naive you've been."

Randy made the mistake of laughing in his face. That ignited his temper. In two long strides, he rounded the table and pulled her up against him.

"Don't press your luck, lady. Your hus-band damn sure doesn't want you back. As far as he's concerned, you're mine to keep and do with as I please." His breath was hot and heavy on her upturned face. He held her head captive between his hands, which were strong enough to crack her skull. "You'd better hope and pray that Price comes across."

"Your threats are so much hot air, Hawk O'Toole. I don't believe you would kill me."

"No," he replied smoothly, "but I would send you back and keep the boy. I would disappear with him. When I got finished with him you wouldn't recognize him. He wouldn't be a sissy city kid any longer, not a clinging mama's boy. He would be meaner than a snake, a fighter, a trouble-maker, a pariah of society just like me. And just like I do, he would hate you for all that you are."

"Why do you hate me? Because I'm not Indian? Who's the prejudiced one here?"

"I don't hate you because you're white. I hate you because you, like most whites, have turned a blind eye to us. You conveniently keep us out of your consciences. It's time we got your attention. Taking a blond Anglo boy away from his blond Anglo mother and making him one of us ought to do it."

She was quaking on the inside, but she kept her chin high and her eyes defiant. "You couldn't disappear. They'd find you."

"Probably. Eventually. But I'd have time,

years maybe. That would be long enough for me to convert Scott into a hellion."

Threats on her life didn't faze her. This did. Her courage exhausted, she gripped the front of his shirt. "Please. You can't take Scott away from me. He's . . . he's my son. He's all I've got."

He slid his hands down her shoulders and arms to her hips. He cupped them and pulled her against him insultingly. "You should have thought of that when you were bedding down with all your husband's friends."

Randy gave his chest a furious shove and pushed herself away from him. "I didn't!"

"That's the story going 'round."

"That's all it is, a story."

"You're claiming that all the rumors about your infidelity are untrue?"

"*Yes!*"

The word reverberated in the explosive atmosphere. Then, "Mommy?"

Eight

At the sound of Scott's hesitant voice, Randy whirled around to find him standing in the doorway. Like a shadow, Ernie was behind him. The Indian was looking at Hawk curiously. But Scott was watching his mother, his young face filled with apprehension.

"Darling, hi." Even as she forced a bright smile, she was hoping that Scott hadn't overheard the last few words of her shouting match with Hawk. If he had, she hoped he hadn't understood them.

She dropped to her knees and extended her arms. Scott ran toward her and embraced her tightly. She hugged him back, cherishing his sturdy body, his cold cheeks, the smell of outdoors that clung to his clothes and hair.

Long before she was ready to release him, he ended the hug. "Mommy, guess what," he said, his eyes sparkling. "Ernie took Donny and me hunting today."

"Hunting?" she asked, raking the hair out of his eyes. "With guns?"

"No," he replied, looking slightly crestfallen, "Hawk said we couldn't use guns yet, but we set snares and caught rabbits in them."

"Did you?" She examined his face with loving attention to detail. Beyond a slightly sunburned nose, he seemed his normal, endearing self.

"Yeah, but we let 'em go. They were little and Ernie said we shouldn't waste 'em."

"I suppose Ernie knows about these things."

"He knows *everything*," Scott exclaimed, beaming a smile up to his new friend. "Almost as much as Hawk. Did you know Hawk is like a prince or a president in the tribe?" He lowered his voice and said confidentially, "He's real important."

Randy didn't want to get into a discussion of Hawk's merits. "What else did you do today? Did you eat a good lunch?"

"Uh-huh, bologna sandwiches," he answered absently, wriggling away when she tried to tuck in his shirttail. "Leta baked cookies. They were real good. Kinda better than yours," he admitted regretfully.

Tears formed in Randy's eyes. "I forgive you for that."

"What'd you do all day? Ernie said Hawk needed you to stay here in his cabin."

"Yes, well, I . . . I was busy all day, too."

"Did you play any more games with him?"

"Games?"

"You know, like we played this morning."

She shot Hawk a dark glance. "No. We didn't play any games."

He leaned forward and whispered to her. "I need to tell you a secret, Mommy."

Randy was instantly alarmed, certain that he was going to reveal that he'd been mistreated in some unspeakable way. "Of course, darling. I don't think Hawk will mind if we move over here for a private conversation." Looking at Hawk, she dared him to object as she drew Scott aside. She crouched in the corner of the one-room cabin and turned Scott to face her so that his back was to the room.

"What is it, Scott? Tell Mommy."

"I don't think Hawk liked our game."

His secret hardly warranted the seriousness of his expression. For a moment she was taken aback. Then, trying to keep her impatience from showing, she asked, "Why do you think that?"

"Because his face looked like this all day." He drew his brows together to fashion a scowl which, under ordinary circumstances, would have been laughable. "And I heard Ernie tell Leta that Hawk was in one of his black moods because of what we did." Scott laid a conciliatory hand on Randy's shoulder, as though their roles had been reversed and he was the wiser. "I know you were having a good time, but I don't think we should play that game with him again, Mommy."

"No. We won't." She didn't have to feign dejection. It distressed her to see how important Hawk's moods were to Scott. He wanted the man's approval. It was obviously important to him.

She drew Scott close to her again, tucking his head beneath her chin and wrapping her arms around him. "I love you, Scott."

"I love you, too, Mommy." However, now that he'd said his piece, his mind was already on something else. He squirmed out of the circle of her arms. "I gotta go now 'cause Donny's waiting for me. We're gonna pop popcorn. He invited me to sleep over at his house. Ernie said you wouldn't care 'cause you'd be staying here with Hawk."

"That's right. But don't worry about that."

"I'm not worried. I think it's neat that you've got a friend to sleep over with too. Are you gonna sleep in the same bed like the mommies and daddies do on TV?"

"Scott! You know better than that." Her stricken eyes moved to Hawk, who was watching her like a predatory bird from across the room. He couldn't have helped but hear Scott's piping voice, though his expression remained unchanged.

" 'Cause you're not really a mommy and a daddy?"

"That's right."

"Well," he said, tilting his head to one side as he pondered the issue, "it'd probably still be okay if you did. G'night, Mommy." He smacked a careless and obligatory kiss on Randy's cheek and dashed out the door, calling over his shoulder, "G'night, Hawk."

Ernie gave Hawk a steady look. Randy couldn't quite define his oblique expression, but it bordered on being reproachful. He closed the door behind himself, leaving them alone. After a moment of ponderous silence, Hawk said, "Well what's it going to be? The floor? Or my bed?"

"The floor."

His shrug indicated his supreme indifference to her choice. "Come here."

When she stubbornly remained where she was, he frowned, picked up the hateful leather thong, and brought it to her. She winced when he pulled her wrists together behind her back.

"I won't try to escape again. I give you my word."

"Why should I take your word for anything?"

"I wouldn't leave without Scott."

"But you would gain no small satisfaction by slitting my throat while I slept."

He dug into the pocket of her skirt and produced the knife. She had thought she had successfully taken it from Scott while they were hugging. That hadn't been her reason for hugging him so long and so tightly, but when she'd felt the polished ivory handle against her hand, it had seemed like a gift straight from God. She had seized the opportunity to snatch it.

Now Hawk robbed her of it, just as he

had robbed her of her pride. "These escape attempts are getting tiresome, Mrs. Price. Why don't you give them up?"

"Why don't you go to hell?"

She brushed past him with as much dignity as one could have with one's hands tied behind her. At the foot of the bed she sat down, where she had spent the entire day except during the evening meal and Scott's visit. Without a word, Hawk knelt in front of her and secured her wrists to the leg of the bed. From a cupboard in the corner of the room, he took down a blanket and a pillow.

He dropped the pillow onto the floor. "Lie down."

Randy wanted to rebel, but she was too weary of fighting him to make the effort. She would conserve her energy and her wits, both of which might do her more good later on. She lay down on her side and rested her head on the pillow. Hawk shook out the blanket and let it drift down over her.

"I'll be back," was all he said before he slipped out the cabin door. He took the lantern with him, leaving her in total darkness. More than an hour passed. Randy wondered where he had gone and what he was doing. Patrolling the camp? Conferring with the other chiefs? Making love to Dawn?

That possibility stayed in her mind. She envisioned them together, two bodies, one taut and sinewy, one soft and voluptuous, moving together in perfect synchronization. She saw Hawk's face, intense and virile, as his hips pumped against the woman's with supple grace.

She imagined his mouth at her breast, his lips opening and closing around it, his tongue gently teasing against a jutting nipple, his sucking motions fervent and strong when he drew it inside his mouth.

Randy groaned aloud at the longing that rippled through her. She hated her body's susceptibility, but she couldn't deny it. Her fantasy had created a shameless heat within her that demanded to be extinguished. Hawk was the man to do it. He would give his lover as much pleasure as he took. She could tell that by his touch. That morning, his deft caresses had made her ache. They had generated a carnal fever in her breasts and between her thighs.

A picture of his hand riding lightly on her thigh flashed through her mind. She bit her lower lip in an effort to stifle a low moan of desire to feel that hand inside her clothing, against her skin, inquisitive and investigative.

She was so lost in the fantasy that when Hawk shut the door behind himself, Randy started. She pretended to be asleep when he soundlessly approached her and held the lantern directly above her face. She could only hope that the color in her cheeks wasn't apparent and that her breathing had evened out enough to convince him that she was sleeping.

Apparently he was, because he said nothing. He set the lantern on the table and turned it out. She heard the clump of his boots as they hit the floor and the whisper of clothing as it was removed. The bedsprings creaked beneath his weight. She listened for soft snores or steady breathing, which would be her indication that he was asleep, but he outwaited her. While still listening, she fell asleep.

At some point during the night, she stirred and woke up to discover him bending over her. She flinched and stared up at him with alarm. Silvery moonlight coming through the window lined his face and body and lit up his incredibly blue eyes.

"Your teeth are chattering," he murmured in a low voice. He spread something
over her. The edge of it touched her cheek.
A sheepskin. She had seen many of them
around the compound. She burrowed
deeply into the instant warmth it provided.
Hawk silently returned to his bed.

For a long while afterward, Randy lay
there, staring at the window. She had seen
the bunching and relaxing of his biceps as
he spread the blanket over her. The skin
on his chest was as smooth and tight as a
drum. His nipples had stood out against it,
small and hard. His waist was lean, his
stomach flat. Patches of dark body hair had
beckoned her eyes downward.

Her breath caught with every recollection
of it.

Hawk O'Toole had been wildly, primi-
tively, beautifully naked.

Leta and she were acting as waitresses for
the men. They moved from cookstove to table and back again, carrying the heavy
enamel coffeepot and refilling cups as they
were emptied. The tribal council had met
this morning in Hawk's cabin to discuss

their strategy. It was the modern equivalent of a powwow.

Perhaps she should have resented them for talking about her as though she weren't there, but she didn't. For one thing, she would rather be informed than ignorant of what course of action they planned to take. For another, she was free to move about the cabin, which enabled her to watch Scott through the window. He was playing outside with Donny.

She could have been invisible for all the attention Hawk paid her. After last night, his disregard was a relief. When she had awakened earlier that morning, the cabin had been empty, but the thongs had been untied and her arms were free. When Hawk came in, Ernie and Leta were with him. It seemed to Randy that he had studiously avoided looking directly at her, just as earnestly as she had avoided looking at him.

During his discussion with the council, he spoke her name frequently, but he had looked at her only once, that being when she sneezed, surprising everyone in the room into momentary silence. As she self-consciously excused herself, her eyes met

Hawk's briefly, and she would be hard-pressed to say who had looked away first.

The purpose of the meeting was to await the arrival of the morning newspaper. Someone had been sent into the nearest town, which was still a considerable distance away, to buy a morning edition and bring it back. Finally the errand runner arrived. He shut off his pickup and ran up the path toward the cabin where one of the other men was holding open the door.

He had three copies of the newspaper tucked under his arm and distributed them around the table. His expression was grim. Hawk assessed the messenger's mood before lowering his gaze to the front page, which he read silently.

Randy could see a picture of herself and Scott beneath the headline. There was another picture of Morton, looking haggard. He was playing his role well. Only a truly devious man could carry off a hoax of this magnitude. Only a truly egomaniacal one would have the guts even to try. She was eager to read the accounts. Morton's quotes would make for interesting reading. She also wanted to know what measures were being taken to ransom Scott and her.

The men around the table began to shift uncomfortably in their chairs. Ernie raised his head once and stared hard at Hawk before returning to the newspaper. One of the men cursed and angrily left the table to stand at the window. It made Randy distinctly nervous that he fixed his stare on Scott.

She looked inquiringly toward Hawk. There was little comfort to be drawn from his expression, which turned darker with every passing second. He was grinding his jaw. His hands had formed fists where they rested on either side of the newspaper. His brows had formed a steep V over the bridge of his nose.

"Dammit!"

Randy actually jumped when he banged the table with his fists and swore violently.

"Maybe there's more in another section of the paper," Ernie ventured bleakly.

"I already checked," the man who had brought in the papers said. "There's nothing more. Only what you read there."

"The bastard barely mentioned us."

"When he did, he referred to the kidnapping as 'a savage, criminal act.' "

"I thought he was supposed to be sympathetic, to take our side, and plead our case with the governor."

One by one, each man voiced a comment. Only Hawk remained silent, ominously so. At last he raised his head and speared Randy with his eyes. Her insides shriveled in fear.

"Clear the room."

Hawk's sibilant words were barely audible.

Everyone glanced around warily, unsure what to do. The man at the window responded first. He stalked out. The others followed, muttering among themselves. Leta paused on the threshold, uncomfortably waiting for Ernie, who was standing at Hawk's elbow.

"Before you react," he cautioned the younger man, "consider every possible consequence."

"Damn the consequences," Hawk hissed. "I know what I'm doing."

Ernie didn't appear to share that opinion, but he and Leta filed out behind the others. Without having to ask, Randy knew that Hawk hadn't meant to include her in his terse order to clear the room. She remained rooted to the spot on which she stood.

The cabin fell silent. In the background there were familiar sounds—children playing, someone hammering, dogs barking. Horses nickered and snuffled. A contrary engine was gunned to life. But the ordinary noises seemed far away and detached from the thick silence inside the cabin. Except for the fire crackling in the stove and Randy's shallow, rapid breathing, there was no sound.

Finally, when she didn't think she could stand the mounting tension inside her chest a moment longer, Hawk moved. He stood up slowly, scraping his chair away from the table. He came around the end of it and advanced toward her, never relieving her of his stony stare.

When there remained only a few feet between them, he came to a stop. In an expressionless voice, he said, "Take off your shirt."

Nine

She said nothing, did nothing. Only the swift contraction of her pupils and a reflexive shudder indicated that she had heard him.

"Take off your shirt," he repeated.

"No." Her voice was little more than a hoarse croak. Then, shaking her head, she said more adamantly, "No. *No*."

"If you won't . . ."

The razor-sharp blade of his knife made a sinister sound against the leather scabbard when he slid it out. Randy fell back a step. Holding the knife in his right hand, Hawk reached for her with his left. She ducked. He came up with a handful of her hair. He wound it around his fist and pulled up. The pain prevented her from feeling him slice through the flannel shirt from collar to hem, but she sensed the movement of air against her skin. Glancing down, she saw the shirt lying wide open. Shock stifled the scream that filled her throat.

He let go of her hair, but she was too astonished to think of running. He caught one of her hands and, wielding the knife again, made a cut in the pad of her thumb before casually replacing the knife in the scabbard.

Randy gaped at the blood oozing from the wound on her thumb. Speechless and too stunned to move, she didn't even resist when Hawk peeled the shirt off her shoulders. He pushed her listless arms through the sleeves and removed it.

"Your stubbornness will serve our purpose. Having the shirt cut off you will look even better." He squeezed her thumb until the blood flowed freely over her hand and down her wrist. He pressed the shirt against the bleeding cut, mopping up the blood and smearing it on the flannel. "Your blood," he said. "They'll test it." Strands of her hair were wound around his fingers. He carefully removed them and snagged them in the fibers of the cloth. "Your hair." His lip was curled cynically. "They'll know for certain that you're the victim of a savage, criminal act."

"Well, aren't I?"

He looked down at her bared breasts.

Randy closed her eyes, swaying slightly with mortification, knowing that he was watching her nipples draw tight.

"Maybe you are." Stepping closer, he took her bleeding hand and drew it to his lower body. He cupped it around his full sex. "I'm heavy with lust for you, Mrs. Price. Should we smear the shirt with a specimen of another kind? One they don't need a microscope to identify."

He pressed her hand hard against him. She cried out sharply and jerked it away. She had cried out in pain, not in protest of his crude suggestion or of the caress he was forcing on her.

"What's the matter?" His voice had changed. It wasn't sugary with menace any longer. The concern behind it was genuine. No longer glittering and sinister, his eyes moved over her searchingly.

"Nothing," she said breathlessly. "Nothing's the matter."

He gripped her arm. "Don't lie to me. What?" He shook her slightly and, when she winced, he immediately relaxed his grip. "Your arm?"

Randy hadn't wanted to demonstrate any weakness, but since he was insisting, she nodded her head. "They're sore from sleeping on the floor in that position. I got cold before you . . . covered me," she finished softly, glancing away. "My muscles got cramped."

He backed away from her. When Randy looked up several moments later, he was still staring down at her. Turning away abruptly, he went to a cabinet and took out a fresh shirt. It was flannel, too, but much larger than the one she'd been wearing. Randy wondered if it was his.

He draped the shirt around her shoulders and guided her arms into the sleeves. The cuffs hung well below her fingertips. While she stood before him like a docile child, he rolled them back to her wrists. That's when he noticed that the cut on her thumb was still bleeding.

Randy's heart almost lurched out of her chest when he lifted her thumb to his lips and sucked on it hard. Their eyes met and locked as he ran his tongue lightly over the shallow cut he'd made. She drew in a staggering little breath that drew his eyes down once more to her breasts. They were covered now by the shirt, but accessible, as the shirt remained unbuttoned. The crests made distinct impressions against the soft cloth. It was sexier, somehow, than her nakedness had been.

His fingertips settled against her exposed throat, where he discovered the slight discoloration his strong kiss two nights before had left. He rubbed the mark tenderly. Randy saw regret, and an unmistakable trace of pride, in his eyes.

His fingers trailed down and edged aside the flannel to reveal one of her breasts. It looked pale and pink and fragile against the masculine material of the shirt and his bronze hand. He stroked the inside curve of it with his knuckle. His thumb fanned the delicate nipple until the texture changed and it no longer looked innocent, but erotic. His eyes swept up to hers. Hers were filled with wonder over this soft, caring side of Hawk O'Toole. His were hot with desire.

Then, as if angry with her, or with himself, he yanked his hand back and turned away. For a long moment he stood in the center of the room, his whole body taut and rigid. When he spoke, his voice was gruff. "It appears that your husband doesn't care if you are returned or not."

"I told you he wouldn't." She was having

difficulty speaking. Her knees seemed to have liquefied. The lower part of her body was throbbing and moist with want. The heat of shame burned in her cheeks. Quietly she added, "And he's not my husband."

"He's still concerned for Scott."

"Because that's what the public expects him to be."

"He says little about us, about our cause, to the press." He spun around and shook the blood-stained shirt at her. "That's what this is for. To remind him of the terms of our agreement."

"I doubt it'll do any good. He might not even publicly acknowledge that he's received it."

"I'm not sending it to him. I'm mailing it directly to Governor Adams, along with a letter detailing what we want and why the Lone Puma Mine is so important to the economy of the reservation."

"On that score, Hawk, I hope you get what you want. I sincerely do. But you must take Scott and me back. Sending bloody clothes through the mail, issuing silent threats of violence, that's dangerous and stupid. It'll hurt you far more than it will help."

"I didn't ask for your advice. I don't need it." His eyes moved down to the open shirt where the twin crescents of her breasts came together to form a soft valley. "I can think of only one field you might be an expert in," he said sardonically, "and I already know how to do it."

Leaving her aghast with rage, he stamped out and slammed the door.

"He hasn't had an easy life. That's why he seems so hard sometimes," Leta told Randy solemnly. "Underneath, I think Hawk is softhearted. He just doesn't want anyone to know it because that would make him look weak. He takes his job as a tribal leader very seriously."

Randy could only agree. They were at the table in Hawk's cabin, chopping up vegetables to go into a stew. Randy hadn't seen Hawk since he had slammed the door behind himself several hours earlier, taking the blood-stained shirt with him. She had been somewhat surprised that he had neglected to tie her up before he left, but that was explained a few minutes later when

Leta arrived. She had brought some mending and a basket of vegetables with her—along with a Band-Aid for the cut on Randy's thumb.

"You're my watchdog, I guess," Randy had remarked. When Leta's guileless smile collapsed, Randy regretted the unkind words. It wasn't the girl's fault that she was the captive of a man without a human heart. Leta was only obeying the directives of a man, a chief, which she had probably been conditioned to do since she could understand the language. "I'm sorry I was so cross with you, Leta. There's coffee left. Would you like some?"

It seemed ludicrous to play house when the lord of the manor had cut a shirt away from her body, assaulted her with a knife, and insulted her in the most demeaning way. Leta, however, had seemed unaware of the inconsistencies of the situation and gladly accepted the cup of coffee. She had started on her mending and when that was finished, began chopping the vegetables, chatting all the while.

Randy had been glad that the conversation had gradually and naturally turned to Hawk O'Toole. She had wanted to learn all she could about him without having to ask direct questions. As it turned out, there was no need to. Leta happily supplied her with uncensored information.

"I haven't seen much of his softhearted-ness," Randy said now, dunking one peeled potato into the basin of cold water and reaching for another.

"Oh, it's there. He still mourns his mother and the brother who died at birth. He misses his grandfather."

"From what I understand, he must have been the only positive and stable influence in Hawk's life."

Leta digested that, then agreed with a nod. "Hawk and his father fought like cats and dogs. Hawk didn't shed a single tear when he died. I'm too young to remember, but Ernie told me." She counted the carrots she had peeled and chopped and decided to add one more to the basin. "Ernie's old-est son and Hawk are the same age. They played football together in college."

"College?"

"Hmm. They both got degrees in engi-neering. Dennis does something with dams and bridges. Hawk returned to the reservation when his grandfather died. He gave up a career in the city."

Randy forgot about the half-peeled potato in her hand. "If he left a promising career in the city, he must have felt a strong compulsion to come back."

"I think it was because of his father and the mine."

"His father and the mine?"

"I don't know everything about it, but Hawk's father was the mine manager. He wasn't"—she lowered her voice—"he wasn't very reliable. Ernie says he was drunk most of the time. Anyway, he let these men talk him into selling them the mine."

Randy tried not to appear eager to hear more, but she wet her lips expectantly. "*He* sold the mine to the group of investors?"

"Yes. I've heard Ernie say the tribe was swindled. Most everybody blamed Hawk's father. He finally got crazy with liquor and had to be taken away."

"So Hawk assumed his responsibilities, along with the blame," Randy quietly finished the story for herself.

That explained a lot about Hawk O'Toole. He not only wanted to keep the mine operational for the tribe's livelihood, he wanted to get it back in order to redeem himself. With his college degree and leadership qualities, he could work mines anywhere in the world, but he stayed on the reservation, not only because he was an appointed chief, but because he was shackled to it by guilt.

"Ernie worries about Hawk," Leta went on, unaware of Randy's private musings. "He thinks Hawk should get married and have children. Then maybe he wouldn't get in his black moods so often. Ernie says Hawk is lonely. That's what makes him act mean sometimes. He could choose any unmarried woman in the tribe he wanted for his wife, but he hasn't."

"Does he ever choose one to . . . you know, to . . ."

Leta's eyes lowered demurely. "When he wants a woman that way, he goes to the city for a few days."

Randy swallowed with difficulty. "How often does he go into the city?"

"It varies," Leta said with a shrug. "Several times a month."

"I see."

"Sometimes he stays for days. But those

are the times when he comes back the grumpiest. It's like the longer he's with a bought woman, the less he likes it." She wiped her hands on a cup towel and gathered the peelings into the newspaper that had been spread out on the table for that purpose.

"Prostitutes won't get him children either."

"He's told Ernie that he'll never have any."

"Oh? Why?"

"Ernie thinks he's afraid to because of his mother. He watched her die." Most of Randy's antagonism collapsed upon itself. It was difficult to carry grudges against someone who had suffered such untold sorrow.

"If Hawk doesn't start having children soon," Leta said on a lighter note, "he'll have to work doubly hard to catch up to Ernie." She gave Randy a shy, secretive smile.

"You're pregnant?" Leta's eyes danced as she bobbed her head up and down. "Have you told Ernie?"

"Just last night."

"Congratulations to you both."

Leta giggled. "Ernie's got grandchildren already, but he's as proud as a peacock about the baby." Glancing down at her stomach, she affectionately smoothed her hand over it.

Her soft, loving expression made her plain face beautiful. Randy was glad for her, but she also felt a pang of jealousy. Leta's love for Ernie was so uncomplicated, their lives simple. Of course, he had committed a felony and might very well go to prison for it, but for nothing in the world would she have mentioned that to Leta and clouded the young woman's happiness.

A few minutes later, Donny and Scott came charging in. They stuffed down a lunch of sandwiches, which Leta and Randy made for them. Randy sat close to Scott, touching him at every opportunity without making it obvious and embarrassing for him.

"Gee, Mommy, sleeping over at Donny's house was fun! Ernie told us ghost stories, *Indian* ghost stories." He gulped his milk and wiped his mouth on the back of his hand. "Did you have a good time sleeping over at Hawk's house?"

Her smile faltered. "It was okay."

"Hawk said he would take us horseback riding after lunch. And he said for you to make him a sandwich. I'm s'posed to bring it to him."

She wanted to send back a message that Mr. O'Toole could damn well return to the cabin and make his own sandwich, but she didn't want to involve Scott in their quarrel, as, no doubt, Hawk had counted on. After handing Scott two wrapped sandwiches, she hugged him close. "Be careful. Remember you're a new rider. Don't take any unnecessary risks."

"I won't. Besides, Hawk'll be there. Wait, Donny! I'm coming."

He raced out the door, across the porch, and down the steps without giving her a backward glance. When she turned around, Leta was looking at her sympathetically.

"Hawk won't let anything bad happen to Scott. I know he won't."

Randy smiled feebly. "He won't as long as I cooperate. Which I intend to do." She took a deep breath. "So there's no reason for you to stay here with me. I know you must have other chores to attend to. Please go on with your business. I'm not going anywhere."

"You tried to run away."

"I won't try that again."

"You should have known Hawk would find you."

"I guess I did. But I had to try."

Leta, unable to understand Randy's determination, shook her head. "I'd rather have a man's protection than be alone."

The candid observation disturbed Randy. Why did being under Hawk's protection suddenly sound so appealing? She wanted to be by herself to think about that. Too, the rough night she had spent was now being felt. Her eyes were sandy from lack of sleep. She couldn't contain her yawns and had given up trying to politely hide them. She urged Leta to leave her alone. Eventually the younger woman capitulated.

As soon as the door closed behind Leta, Randy staggered to the bed. She lay down, pulled the blanket over herself, and buried her head in the pillow. If Hawk didn't like her taking a nap in his bed, that was just too damn bad. It was his fault she hadn't gotten much sleep. First he had forced her to lie on the hard floor. Then he had almost let her freeze to death before covering her up. Then he had appeared in front of her naked.

On that delicious memory she sank into a deep sleep.

He was in the cabin with her when she woke up. She eased herself into a sitting position, shivering with a slight chill, and glanced around the room. Hawk was sitting near the stove, unmoving, slouched in a straight-back chair. His booted feet were stretched far out in front of him, his hands loosely clasped over his belt buckle. His eyes were unblinkingly on her. She got the impression that they had been for some time.

"I'm sorry," Randy said nervously, throwing off the blanket and swinging her feet to the floor. "What time is it?"

"What difference does it make?"

"None, I guess. I didn't intend to sleep so long." Checking the degree of light in the window, she could tell that it was late afternoon. The sun had already slipped behind the mountains. Shadows beyond the cabin walls were growing long and dark.

"Aren't you curious?"

She rubbed her hands up and down her arms to ward off the chill. "About what?"

"About the shirt."

"Did you mail it?"

"Yes."

"I'm all for that, if it'll get us home sooner." She stood up and smoothed down the helplessly wrinkled shirt, which had been dreadfully ugly to begin with. "Did you take Scott horseback riding?"

"He did very well."

"Where is he?"

"I believe they're playing a card game in Ernie's cabin."

"I guess I'll see him at dinner."

"You missed dinner. We ate early this evening."

"You mean I won't be able to see Scott until tomorrow? Why didn't you wake me up?" she asked angrily.

He ignored both her anger and her question and asked one of his own. "Why do you keep rubbing your arms?"

"Because I'm cold. I don't feel well." To her mortification, tears began collecting in her eyes. "My head is stuffy. I ache all over, and it's your fault. I could use an aspirin.

The cut on my thumb catches on everything and keeps reopening."

"I sent you a Band-Aid."

"It came off while I was washing *your* dishes!" she shouted. "I want to see my son. I want to kiss him good night. You've kept him away from me most of the day."

He rolled off his spine and came to his feet. "You should have thought of that before you attempted to escape."

"How long will you go on punishing me?"

"Until I'm convinced you've learned your lesson."

Her head dropped forward in defeat. A tear rolled down her cheek. "Please, Hawk. Let me see Scott. Just for five minutes."

He placed his finger beneath her chin and jerked it up. He studied her face for several moments, then released her suddenly. He gathered the blanket off the bed and took another folded one from a shelf. "Come on," he said, heading for the door.

She followed him gladly, wiping the tears off her cheeks as she trotted after him down the path. She thought it odd that he headed straight for his pickup, but supposed that they were going to drive instead of walk to the other cabin. However, when he struck off in the opposite direction, she turned to him.

"What are you doing? Where are you taking me?"

"You'll find out soon enough. Just enjoy the ride. It's a beautiful night."

"I want to see Scott."

He said nothing, but continued to stare stonily through the windshield. Randy wasn't going to give him the satisfaction of seeing her cry again. She refused to beg. So she squared her body with the dashboard and continued to stare straight ahead, keeping her back rigid and her chin high. She could kick herself for crying and pleading. Not only had it humbled her, it hadn't done any good.

They didn't go far, but when Hawk brought the pickup to a stop, the surrounding landscape was considerably more primitive than the compound. Randy glanced at him with dismay when he cut the motor and pushed in the emergency brake pedal.

"Where are we? What are we doing here? Is this where you're going to bury my body?"

Saying nothing, Hawk got out on his side and came around for her. She stepped to the ground and waited until he took the blankets out of the pickup's bed.

"Up there," he said.

Warily, she preceded him up the incline. When they crested it she paused to catch her breath, not only because of the steep climb but because the scenery was breathtaking in the most literal sense. It seemed that the entire world was spread out beneath them and that nothing stood between them and the sunset.

Its hues were vivid, from the most flaming vermilion to the most iridescent violet. With each second of deepening darkness, stars were popping out like new flowers after a spring rain. Just above the horizon, the half-moon was large and as unblemished as fine china. A cool wind molded her clothes to her body.

"We have to squeeze through there," Hawk said close to her ear.

"Through where?" It seemed that he was pointing to a wall of solid stone.

"Here." Taking her hand, he drew her forward.

Upon closer inspection she noticed a crevice in the rock, barely wide enough to accommodate a slender person. Hawk

nudged her forward and she squeezed herself through. He followed. The passage
widened marginally at the other end. When
Randy stepped through, she was brought
up short.

Only a few feet in front of her was a small
pool of water. Steam rose out of it like a
boiling cauldron, covering the ground with
a swirling mist that curled around her ankles and calves. Underground springs
caused the water to bubble.

"Welcome," Hawk said, "to Mother Nature's version of a hot tub."

Ten

The prospect of submerging herself in the churning hot water was a delightful one. It had been several days since she had had a real bath. She hadn't wanted to bathe in the frigid waters of the stream, so, since her kidnapping, she'd had to make do with sponge baths out of a washbowl.

"Would you like to get in?" Hawk asked.

"Yes," she cried excitedly. Then, with more composure, she added, "If it's all right."

"That's why I brought you here. Maybe the hot water will clear your head and soak the chill out of your bones."

She took a step toward the pool before she realized that she was fully dressed. "What about my clothes?"

"Take them off."

"I don't want to."

"Then they'll get wet."

He began unbuttoning his shirt. When he

arched back his shoulders and pulled the shirttail from his waistband, Randy averted her eyes, knowing full well he was trying to intimidate her. She wasn't going to let him. Belligerently, she worked off her sneakers and peeled off her socks, carefully laying them on a dry, flat rock. She unfastened the skirt and let it fall around her feet, then stepped out of it. The oversized shirt reached the middle of her thighs, covering her adequately.

Hearing the rasp of Hawk's zipper over the gurgling of the water, she moved forward as swiftly as the stony ground would permit, and stepped into the pond. She yelped softly. The water felt scalding on her cold feet, but she forced herself to step into it. After a few seconds she became accustomed to it and eased herself down until the water bubbled around her waist, then her shoulders. Finally she was neck-deep in heavenly sensation.

A man-made hot tub would have to have a thousand jets installed to compare to this one, she thought. From every direction water gushed toward her, massaging the soreness out of her muscles, lubricating her stiff joints, and warming her chilled skin.

"How do you like it?"

She was afraid to turn her head and look at him, but she chanced it and was relieved to find that he, too, was submerged up to his chin in the water. Below the roiling surface, she knew he was naked. She tried not to think about it. "It's wonderful. How'd you find it?"

"My grandfather used to treat me to this after a day of hunting. Then when I got older, I'd bring girls here."

"I don't think I need to ask what for."

He actually grinned. "The water has a way of melting inhibitions. After a few minutes of it girls forgot how to say no."

"Were there a lot of them?"

"Girls?" he asked with a shrug. "Who was counting? They came and went."

"In adequate numbers?"

His laugh was low and self-derisive. "To a young man, is any number of women adequate?"

"And now that you're older?"

He watched her closely. "Is any number of women adequate?"

Knowing it would be prudent not to pursue the discussion, she plunged on anyway. "Leta told me about your trips into the city. Do hired women satisfy you?"

"Yes. And I satisfy them, too." Randy glanced away. "What about you?" he asked smoothly. "Are you ever satisfied? How many lovers does it take to put out your fire?"

She ground her teeth in an effort to hold in a scathing comeback. Instead she said, "You think I'm a slut. I think you're a criminal. Each of us thinks the other deserves to be punished. Fine. Can't we leave it at that and stop insulting each other? Especially now. Let's not argue and spoil this. Please. It feels too lovely. I don't want to ruin it by engaging in a silly argument."

He turned his head away. His profile formed a dark silhouette against the western horizon, which was quickly losing its battle with the night. Randy appreciated his profile for its masculine beauty.

How would she have felt about Hawk O'Toole if she had met him at another time and in another place, she wondered. If she hadn't married Morton Price so young to escape an unhappy household, she might have met a man like Hawk, strong but unselfish, working for causes instead of dollars, a leader without personal ambition. She might have fallen hopelessly in love with him.

Shaking her head to clear it of such ludicrous notions, she said, "Tell me about your grandfather."

"What about him?"

"Did you love him?"

His head came back around quickly, suspiciously. When he saw that she wasn't ridiculing him, he answered, "I respected him."

She encouraged him to talk, and soon he was relating stories about his childhood and youth. He even smiled at some of his fondest recollections. As he concluded a particularly amusing anecdote, however, his smile inverted itself into a frown.

"But the older I got, the more I realized that I had two strikes against me."

"What?"

"Being an Indian and having a drunk for a father. If folks weren't put off by one, they sure as hell were by the other."

She weighed the advisability of opening up a can of worms, but decided that she had nothing to lose and a lot to gain if she could understand him better. "Hawk," she began tentatively, "Leta told me about your father, about his losing the mine to the swindlers."

"Dammit." He sat up straight so that the waterline came to just below his waist. It sluiced down his smooth chest. Droplets got caught in the dark hair whorling around his navel. Randy wanted to stare at that intriguing spot, but his angry eyes drew her attention. "What else did Leta blab to you about?"

"It wasn't her fault," Randy said quickly. She didn't want the young woman to get into trouble for divulging tribal secrets. "I asked her about you."

"Why?"

She looked at him, puzzled. "Why?"

"Yes, why? Why were you so curious about me?"

"I thought that maybe if I knew more about your background, I would understand your motivations. And I do," she stressed. "Now I know why it's so important to you to regain ownership of the mine. You want to make up for your father's downfall." She laid a hand on his arm. "Hawk, no one blames you. It's not your fault that—"

He shook off her hand and stood up.

"The last thing I want from you is pity. If anything, Mrs. Price, you should be begging for mine."

He turned and was about to step out of the pool when Randy reached up and caught his hand. She used it to lever herself out of the water and at the same time to launch a verbal attack. "I don't pity you, you mule-headed jerk! I was only trying to get inside your head, to understand you."

He grabbed her by the shoulders, lifting her up so that only the tips of her toes touched the bottom of the pool. "You could never understand me because your skin isn't tinted. You haven't been laughed at by bigots or fawned over by phony bleeding hearts. You've never had to prove your worthiness as a human being every day of your life. Your successes weren't measured *in spite of* or your failures *because of*. You won acceptance by society the day you were born. I'm still struggling to earn it."

She threw off his grasping hands. "Doesn't that chip on your shoulder get awfully heavy? Don't you ever want to sling it off and be rid of it? No one is as prickly about your heritage as you are," she cried, poking his chest with her index finger. "No-body burdens you with your father's failings except *you*. You make things difficult for yourself because you feel you deserve the punishment for what he did. That's stupid. Crazy."

His features had evened out to convey indifference, but his eyes gave him away. They were turbulent, seething with rage. "You forget your place."

"My place!" she shrieked. "And just what might my *place* be?"

"Beneath a man," he growled, pulling her against him. He lowered his head and kissed her hard. She squirmed against him, trying to get away, but he was indisputably in control. His tongue continued to probe her lips until they separated, then it mas-terfully sank into the wet heat of her mouth. He used it to stroke and to tease, to wear down her resistance. It worked. Randy's struggles to be released became efforts to get closer.

She participated in the kiss, welcoming the wicked thrusts of his tongue. But she wasn't ready for the gentle suction he ap-plied, drawing her tongue inside his mouth. Once the electrifying shock had worn off, she explored it with rampant curiosity and carnal delight.

Her bare thighs pressed against his. The hard muscles of his chest rippled against her breasts each time he moved his arms to hold her tighter. She groaned audibly when she felt the steely evidence of his desire against her belly.

Hawk set her away from him. Their eyes locked and held for several moments while they regained their breath. The wind cooled their feverish bodies and the mountain air cleared their heads. The water bubbled around their legs. But nothing served to dissipate their passionate desire for each other.

His gaze dropped to her breasts and Randy heard him take a sharp, quick breath. Her nipples were tenting the wet fabric that clung to her body. Hawk reached for the top button of her shirt. Hypnotized by his eyes, she let him undo it. Then the second button. His knuckles bumped into her breasts and grazed her stomach as they moved down from one button to the next.

Finally all the buttons were undone and he pushed the clinging cloth aside. His eyes roamed over her for a long time, thirstily taking in the smooth, pale globes of her breasts and their dark, raised centers.

Making a low, hungry sound, he slipped his hands inside the shirt and beneath her arms so that her breasts fit into the notches between his thumbs and fingers. He tested their sensitivity by stroking the dusky tips. They responded. Quickly ducking his head, he took one into his hot, tugging mouth.

Reflexively, Randy's back arched. Her head fell back. Her hips slammed into his hardness. He raised his head and uttered a stream of blue words, sexual words, that shamefully thrilled her. Taking her hand, he dragged her with him out of the pool. Together they lay down on one of the blankets.

"Add another crime to my credit," he told her as he peeled off her underpants. He bent over her, kissed her belly, kissed her breasts, kissed her mouth again and again. The velvety tip of his sex was already pearled with moisture when he entered her. He stretched into her, reaching, stroking, unable to get high enough.

Randy gasped with the shock of his total possession. As he moved within her, the glorious sky seemed to open above her. She closed her eyes against the incandescent light, but it continued to shower her with sparks. Her body felt infused with a heat as intense as each burning star. She began to tremble. Only then did Hawk bury his face in her hair and surrender to an explosion of release.

Lying entwined between the blankets, she turned her face into his chest. She kissed it shyly and caressed the smooth, supple skin with her fingertips. "I'm just another of the girls whose inhibitions melted in the pool."

"No." He rolled toward her and slid his hand between her thighs, cupping her warmly. "None of the others had blond hair."

"Hawk." She spoke his name in an indrawn breath, which was the best she could do while his thumb was insolently moving across her mound. She struggled to keep her eyes open, to speak. "You called me Miranda."

His hand fell still. "What?"

"When you, uh . . . you called me Miranda." He withdrew his hand and eased away from her. His face was closed, as though a curtain had been dropped over it. "Hawk?"

"Come on, it's time to go back." He stood up and offered her his hand. She accepted it, surreptitiously grabbing her panties. She stepped into them, but Hawk didn't seem to notice her awkwardness. He was pulling on his own clothes with rapid, disjointed motions. Randy was loath to put the wet shirt back on, but she did so. When they were dressed, he took her hand again and led her back through the rock. They picked their way down the hill to his truck.

When they reached it, Randy pulled him around. "Why did you call me Miranda?"

"I didn't realize I had. Don't make a big deal of it."

"I wouldn't. But you are. It bothers you that you did. Why?"

For a moment he looked anywhere but at her. Finally he stared down into her face and said, "I wanted to be distinguished from the others."

"Others?"

"Your other lovers."

Little was said on the drive back to the compound. By the time he pulled to a stop in front of his cabin, Randy knew that he must regret what had happened at the pool. His face was closed, his lips thin with what she could only guess was disapproval of her wanton conduct. She hated seeing it, so she avoided looking at him.

He got out of the pickup first and came around to open the door for her. She alighted, but that was as far as she got because Hawk was blocking her path. She kept her eyes on the ground.

He tipped up her chin. "Obviously I didn't use a condom."

"Obviously I didn't even think about it."

After a ponderous pause, he said, "You've got nothing to worry about. I've never failed to use one before."

Everything inside her went very still. She could scarcely breathe. Inadvertently, he had told her that she was special, at least different. It wasn't much, but it was something. She would need all the justifications she could glean when she reviewed what had happened between them. "You've got nothing to worry about either, Hawk."

"You've taken care with your other lovers?"

She shook her head and blinked back

large, salty tears. Wetting her lips, she answered huskily, "There've been no other lovers. None. Only my husband. And now you. I swear it."

His eyes had never gleamed so brightly. As though to shut in the light, he narrowed them on her suspiciously. After a few moments he stepped back and encircled her elbow with his hand. "Come on."

"Where?" He was leading her away from the cabin rather than toward it.

"I thought you wanted to kiss Scott good night."

She stumbled along beside him, keeping her eyes on him rather than on the uneven path, trying to puzzle through this enigma of a man.

The mystery of Hawk O'Toole remained unsolved the next day.

After visiting with Scott for half an hour the night before, they had returned to Hawk's cabin alone. Selfishly, she was glad that Scott had remained with Ernie and Leta. He was happy to be there, and Randy was tingling with expectancy at being with Hawk alone all night.

But he didn't make love to her again, as

she had thought—even hoped—that he would. They slept together in the bed. He had undressed her slowly and leisurely, only growing impatient when he began to take off his own clothes. He then pulled her beneath the covers with him and gazed at her hair where it lay on the pillow beside his. His hands moved over her body with a sculptor's sensitivity to form and texture. But he didn't even kiss her.

Once, during the night, she awakened to feel his arms tightening around her and his legs moving restlessly against hers. Her name was breathed against the back of her neck as his lips softly kissed it. She felt him full and hard against her derriere. He took it no further, however, than to close his hand around her breast and draw her closer to him. Eventually he fell asleep, and, after the time it took to reduce the thumping speed of her heart, so did she.

When she woke up, he had already left the cabin. She got up and dressed, stoked the fire, made the bed, brewed coffee. She berated herself for behaving in such a ridiculously domestic way, but every time she accidently caught her reflection in a shiny surface, she was amazed by the lambency in her eyes and the perpetual smile on her lips.

Too, there was a constant, delicious ache in her lower abdomen. Her breasts felt heavy and flushed. Her nipples were sensitive to every stimulus. Hawk hadn't satisfied her hunger; he had created it.

At the sound of the door opening, she whirled around, breathless. Hawk paused on the threshold. Their gazes held for a noticeable length of time before he came through the door. The other chiefs filed in behind him. They seemed not to notice the charged atmosphere. None but Ernie, who eyed Hawk and her shrewdly.

"Get everyone coffee," Hawk ordered harshly. Randy's spine stiffened. "Please," he added in an undertone.

She complied, not necessarily because the command had been politely amended, but because they had brought with them a newspaper. She was curious to know what the governor's reaction to receiving her bloody shirt and the accompanying letter had been.

"At least we've got his attention," Hawk reported, when he had finished reading the newspaper account of this latest development in the case. "He promises to check into the closing of the mine. He's also side-stepping Price and conferring personally with the FBI. He wants to be acquainted with every aspect of Randy and Scott's kidnapping. On the other hand, he warns that if Randy has been physically assaulted in any way, he'll exercise his authority to see that we're punished to the full extent of the law."

He glanced up at Randy. Feeling color mount in her cheeks, she lowered her eyes. She wondered if he realized that he had referred to her by her first name.

"What do we do now?" asked one member of the council.

Hawk sipped from the mug of coffee Randy had handed him. "I'm not sure. Let me think about it. We'll have another meeting this evening just before dinner and discuss our plans then. In the meantime, continue to enjoy the time off." His gaze traveled around the circle of faces. "Hopefully, we'll all be going back to work soon."

After the men left, Leta came in with Donny and Scott. The boys wrestled on the floor while Hawk and Ernie discussed their options. Randy was curious to know what they were saying, but they kept their voices low. It seemed that Hawk was pitching an idea to Ernie, but Ernie kept rejecting it. Apparently she wasn't to be consulted, so she helped Leta cook breakfast. They ate together, sitting around the table in Hawk's cabin.

The conversation flowed easily. Looking in, one would never guess that Scott and she were hostages, Randy thought. Scott asked for Hawk's help in repairing a slingshot. Along with the repair, he received a lecture on its safe usage.

"We don't have to go home yet, do we, Mommy?" Scott's question came as a total surprise. She didn't have an immediate answer.

"I . . . I don't know. Why?"

"I hope we can stay a long time. I like it here."

That said, he dashed out the door behind Donny. The adults were left to cope with an awkward silence. Leta was the one to break it. She braced her hand on Ernie's shoulder and unsteadily rose to her feet. "I don't feel well." Ernie moved faster than Randy had ever seen him. He hustled her out.

"What the hell was that all about?" Hawk demanded, as soon as Randy closed the door behind them.

"Leta's pregnant."

Hawk stared at her for a moment, then at the door, as though he could see Ernie and his young wife through the wood. Muttering a foul curse, he plowed all ten fingers through his thick, straight hair and held it away from his face. He propped his elbows on the table and rested his head in his hands.

Quietly, Randy approached him. "Aren't you happy for them?"

"Very."

"You don't seem to be."

His head came up quickly. "If Ernie is convicted of this crime, he'll go to prison."

She dropped into a chair across the table from him. "Well, welcome to the world of the clear thinking, Mr. O'Toole. That's what I've been telling you for days. You'll all go to prison."

He was shaking his head no. "I made the deal with Price. I told the others that if it didn't go as we had planned, I would take full responsibility. I made them take a blood oath that if I was arrested, they would scatter and go underground."

Randy thought that he was being generous to a fault, but she couldn't help but admire his self-sacrifice. "Your gesture is noble, still, the best they could hope for is lives as fugitives."

"That's better than prison."

"That's arguable. What about Ernie? Didn't he take the oath?"

"Yes, but he's already told me that if I go to prison, he'll surrender himself."

"I take it that Leta doesn't know that."

"I doubt she does."

He stood up and began pacing the width of the cabin. Randy cleared the breakfast dishes off the table and washed them in a basin with water from the pump that she had heated on the stove. She was so absorbed with Hawk's dilemma, she barely noticed the lack of amenities.

When she was finished, she turned to find Hawk unlocking a small metal strongbox with a tiny gold key. "What's that?"

"The Lone Puma's files. I brought them with us."

She stared at the unorganized heap of

papers he dumped on the table. "That scrap pile is your filing system?"

"I'm an engineer. I know where the silver is and how to bring it out safely and economically. I also do . . . did the marketing. I'm not a bookkeeper."

"You could have hired one."

"I never got around to it." He lowered himself into a chair. "I thought there might be something here that I've overlooked, something I might use as leverage."

Again Randy sat down across the table from him. As he scanned and discarded the papers one by one, she drew them toward her and read them herself. She began to separate them into stacks, segregating tax records from payroll records, from bills of sale, from plats.

Swearing colorfully, Hawk tossed aside a copy of the contract that had transferred ownership of the Lone Puma Mine to the investors. Randy read it. It was standard as far as she could tell at first glance. The amount of money the Indians had received on the sale seemed impressive until one considered the length of time for the payout versus the potential of the mine that was being wasted.

Then, going over it more carefully, her mind snagged on one particular clause. Her heart lurched with excitement, but she carefully reread what she had just gone over to make certain she wasn't optimistically jumping to conclusions.

"Hawk, what is this?" she asked him, holding up one of the surveys of the property.

"It's a plat. Surveyors make them to determine—"

"I *know* that," she said with irritation. "I work in a surveyor's office."

That information took him completely by surprise. "You do? You work?"

"Of course I work. How do you think I support Scott and myself?"

"I figured that Price—"

"No," she said, giving her head an adamant shake, "I didn't ask for any money from him. Not even child support. I didn't want to be even that obligated. Anyway," she said, spreading the plat out on the table between them, "what is this? This area of land right here." She traced around the dotted lines on the plat that marked the area she was referring to.

Hawk's mouth curled bitterly. "It used to

be open ground, pastureland where our cattle grazed."

"Cattle?"

"The tribe owned several hundred head. We raised it for beef."

"No longer?"

"No pastureland, no cattle. We lost it with the sale of the mine."

To his surprise, Randy smiled. "You mean that the new owners seized control of that land in addition to the mine?"

"There's a barbed wire fence around it now. No-trespassing signs are posted every few yards. I take that to mean they've seized control of it."

"Then they did it illegally."

His brows drew together. "What do you mean?"

"Look, that pastureland . . . several square miles, right?" She got an affirmative nod. "That land is designated on the plat, but it's not even referred to in the deed."

"Are you sure?" He couldn't contain the excitement in his voice.

"Hawk, I study plats like this all day long, checking out every detail before property changes hands. I know what I'm talking about. Those investors weren't only swindlers, they were stupid swindlers. They bought in a hurry, obviously to acquire a tax shelter at the end of the year."

She reached for his hand and pressed it. "The tribe still owns that pastureland, Hawk. And if you presented this material to the governor, I'm sure he would authorize a full investigation of the sale. Morton would be superfluous as a go-between. This," she said, slapping the contract and plat spread out in front of her, "would do you much more good than his intercession could do in a million years."

He was staring at the legal documents. "I never went over that contract with a fine-tooth comb. Damn! I was too angry. Every time I thought about it, it made me sick to my stomach. I couldn't bring myself to even look at it."

"Don't blame yourself for past negligence. Just act on the information now. Hindsight is better than no sight at all." Randy watched him gather up all the papers and stuff them back into the strong-box, undoing all the careful categorizing Randy had done. "Your filing system still leaves a lot to be desired."

He merely gave her a lopsided grin. Re-locking the strongbox and tucking it beneath his arm, he came around the table. As he drew up beside Randy, he gripped a handful of her hair and pulled her head up and back. "Tell me about the lovers."

Her gaze didn't waver. "I told you last night. There were none. They didn't exist."

"Why didn't you deny the nasty allegations?"

"Why should I? They were untrue. I refused to honor them with denials. Morton had the lovers. He was unfaithful to me almost from the beginning of our marriage. After he won his congressional seat, he seemed to think that extra women were his due, a bonus he was entitled to take. He flaunted his affairs in my face, knowing that I wanted to keep the family intact for Scott's sake. When I finally had my fill of it and couldn't tolerate his infidelity another day, I demanded a divorce. He threatened to file for sole custody of Scott if I divorced him on the grounds of adultery. That wouldn't have been good for his image."

"He would never have gotten custody of the boy."

"Probably not. But I didn't want to put Scott through a well-publicized, messy trial like that, and Morton knew it. Besides, I wasn't absolutely confident that I would win. He had enough friends in high places lined up to testify under oath that I'd slept with them, seduced them."

"What friends?"

"Men who owed Morton political favors."

"When I accused you of being a faithless wife, why didn't you deny it? Why did you let me torment you?"

"When Morton began leaking gossip about my many affairs, my own mother only said tsk-tsk and reprimanded me for not being more discreet. I didn't deny it to her either. If she was willing to believe that kind of lie about me, I was willing to let her. Since she obviously had very little faith in me, I ceased to care what she thought about me."

"Then why did you tell *me*?"

The unspoken answer vibrated between them. Hawk's opinion of her mattered a great deal.

His fingers had maintained a tight grip on her hair. Her arching neck should have felt the strain, but it didn't. She felt only the heat of Hawk's eyes pouring over her face. He applied a slight, unintentional pressure to the back of her head, drawing her face closer to his lap. Instinctively, Randy raised her hand and laid it high on his thigh. He released an involuntary groan.

Between choppy breaths he said, "If you keep looking at me like that, you'll have to—"

The knock on the door broke them apart. Randy quickly withdrew her hand. Hawk released his grip on her hair and stepped back. "Come in."

His voice was as dark as his unwavering eyes, which held her stare. Ernie stepped through the door and assessed the situation at one glance. The air crackled with electric sexuality. "I can come back later," he said, retracing his steps through the open doorway.

"No," Hawk said. "I was coming to look for you. We've got a lot to talk about."

He didn't even lock the cabin door behind him when he left.

Eleven

The mood around the bonfire that night was almost festive. The tribal council had a plan that would restore the mine to them. The people didn't know exactly what the plan was, nor did they care. They merely trusted the council to come through for them. All the chiefs, but especially Hawk, were treated with more respect and deference than usual.

Johnny approached Hawk's blanket while he and Randy were eating. Since the day of her aborted escape attempt, every time she'd seen the young man, he'd been diligently at work, as though trying to redeem himself for his previous negligence. Now, he held out his hands parallel to the ground. They were no longer shaking. "I've been sober for three days," he said.

Hawk didn't crack a smile, but the young man wouldn't have expected him to. "You've done a fine job on the trucks and restored my confidence in you. When we return to the mine, the specialized equipment will need to be overhauled. I'll appoint you permanent overseer of the garage if you'll agree to attend a mechanics school in the city. The tribe would pay for your tuition. Are you interested?"

"Yes."

Hawk gave him an appraising stare. "I'll check into it as soon as possible." Johnny's dark eyes glowed, but he said no more before leaving them. He didn't wander off by himself as before, but mingled with the others. Randy saw him approach one of the young women and hesitantly strike up a conversation with her.

"I think his broken heart and wounded ego are on the mend."

Hawk absently agreed, but his attention had already been diverted to the couple approaching them, walking hand in hand. The handsome young man was standing proud and tall, but the woman was demurely keeping her eyes on the ground in front of her.

"Welcome back, Aaron," Hawk said to the man.

"I'm only here for two days. I've registered, but I don't actually start classes until Monday."

"You had enough money to pay for everything?"

The young man nodded. He glanced down at the girl and for the first time began to show signs of nervousness. He wet his lips before speaking to Hawk again. "I'd like your permission to marry Dawn January."

Hawk's eyes moved to Dawn. She looked at him briefly, then cast her gaze downward again. "What about school?"

"I graduate in May," Aaron reminded him. "We'd like to marry next June. Next fall, we'd like for Dawn to enroll in college and get her degree also."

"This is something you need to bring before the council."

"I wanted to this afternoon, but didn't because I knew the other matters under discussion were so pressing." He glanced at Randy. "I've privately consulted with all the other chiefs on the council. They've granted their permission."

"Is Dawn's family agreeable?"

"Yes."

"And she?"

The young man pulled her forward

slightly. She spoke in a soft bride's voice. "I want to marry Aaron Turnbow."

"Then you have my permission," Hawk said. "But not until you graduate, Aaron," he qualified hastily.

They thanked him with proper deference, then turned and rushed off. Before the darkness swallowed them up, Randy and Hawk saw Dawn cross her arms behind her fiance's neck and plaster her body against his.

"I doubt they'll wait until June to consummate it."

"I doubt they'll wait until morning. Not if Dawn has anything to say about it," Randy remarked snidely.

Hawk's head came around quickly. His stern face tried to hold back a smile at her catty comment. "I just hope he doesn't get her pregnant and force me to move the wedding date up by several months. We've invested heavily in Aaron's college education. So far he's lived up to our expectations. I was afraid he would meet an Anglo girl at college and—"

"What?" Randy asked, when he came to an abrupt and incomplete end to his sentence.

"Nothing."

"And what?" she persisted.

"And want to marry her."

"Would that have been so terrible?" Her heart was hurting. She didn't want to hear his answer, but knew that she must.

"We need strong, intelligent young men like Aaron. If he had married a white woman, in all probability he would have left the tribe."

"And never been welcomed back," she said quietly, adding what he had deliberately omitted.

"He could have lived on the reservation, but he couldn't have held a position on the council. It's very difficult, if not impossible, to straddle two cultures. Once you choose, it's a lifetime choice."

He turned his head away. Randy studied his profile, which was cast in relief against the mellow glow of the fire. He was a tough, but fair, leader. She admired his sense of justice. His chastisements were subtle, but effective. Because his praise was rare, it was valued greatly. He took to heart the problems of each member of his tribe. She was glad she had met this one man, in her entire lifetime, who wasn't always looking out for number one. Until she knew Hawk O'Toole, she hadn't thought that one existed.

But as she continued to watch him, something occurred to her. Hawk was alone. Even though he sat amidst people who obviously revered him, he was removed from them. There was a separateness about him that caused her heartache. Sadness lurked in the depths of his blue eyes. He kept it carefully screened, but in unguarded moments it became apparent to anyone looking for it. For his unhappy childhood and the guilt he bore, he suffered in silence and he suffered alone.

Before she could closely examine the emotions churning inside her, Scott appeared and sat down on the blanket beside her.

"Hi, Mommy." Uncharacteristically glum, he snuggled close and laid his head on her chest.

"Hello, darling. Where have you been? I haven't seen you for a while. What have you been up to?"

"Nothing."

She looked at Hawk inquiringly, but he shrugged, indicating that he didn't know what had brought on Scott's melancholia. "Is something wrong?"

"No," Scott grumbled.

"Are you sure?"

"Yeah, only . . ."

"Only?"

He sat up. "Only Donny's getting a new baby."

"I know. I think that's wonderful news. Don't you?"

"I guess, but he's telling everybody." He made a broad sweeping gesture with his hands, as though encompassing the world. "He said I wasn't getting one. Can we get one, too, Mommy? Please?"

For a moment the request rendered her speechless, then she laughed softly and gave him the universal parental put-off. "We'll see."

"That's what you said about the bunny rabbit, and I never got to get a bunny rabbit. I promise I'll help you take care of the baby. Please."

"Scott."

The boy's earnest pleadings ceased abruptly when Hawk spoke his name. "Sir?"

"Where's your knife?" Scott pulled it from

his belt. Hawk took it, studying it as it lay in his palm. "You haven't lost it again?" Obviously when he had returned the knife to Scott, he hadn't told him that his mother had taken it from him while they were hugging.

"No, sir."

"Hmm. I think you deserve a reward for taking such good care of this knife. A scabbard."

"It's already got a scabbard, Hawk."

"But not like this one." From his shirt pocket, Hawk removed a tooled leather scabbard. He slid the knife into it and handed both back to Scott, who accepted them with a reverence reserved for holy relics.

"Gee, Hawk. It's neat. Where'd you get it?"

"From my grandfather. He made it for me when I was about your age. I want you to keep it."

To remember me by. He didn't say that, but Randy heard the words in her head, spoken in Hawk's voice. The gift seemed like a going-away present. The thought caused her heart to flutter in panic, which made no sense at all. Hadn't she tried to get away only a few days ago? Now the thought of leaving and never seeing Hawk O'Toole again was a dismal one. What had brought on this reversal?

Before she had time to muddle through it, Leta and Ernie approached with Donny, who was so impressed with the scabbard, he stopped bragging about his awaited sibling.

"Do you want Scott to stay in our cabin again tonight?" Ernie asked, looking from Hawk to Randy and back again.

"You've got more room in your cabin than I do in mine," Hawk observed. "It would make better sense for that reason."

"He and his mother could stay in the cabin they occupied when they got here."

Ernie's alternative didn't meet with Hawk's approval. "The stove hasn't been lit in days. It will be too cold."

"Scott is no trouble at all," Leta said, unaware of the underlying tension. She shepherded the boys away. Ernie, looking like he had more to say but thinking better of it, followed his family.

"I don't think Ernie likes me," Randy said, after they were out of earshot.

In one smooth motion and without using

his hands, Hawk came to his feet and helped Randy to stand. Together they started walking through the compound toward his cabin. "Ernie doesn't like Anglo women in general."

"I gathered that."

"He thinks they're aggressive and too smart for their own good."

"We're not submissive enough."

"That sort of sums it up."

"What do you think?"

"I think Ernie is a lost cause as far as the feminist movement goes."

"I mean, what do you think about Anglo women?"

"Any one in particular?" By now they had reached the cabin. He firmly shut the door just as he asked the question.

Randy turned to face him. "What do you think about me?"

He advanced into the room until only inches were separating them. "I haven't finished forming my opinion of you yet."

"First impression?" she asked coquettishly.

"I wanted you in bed."

She sucked in her breath. "Oh."

The only light in the room was coming

from the fire burning in the stove. Graceful shadows danced across the rough log walls, across the floor, across the two people staring into each other's eyes.

For a long while, that's all they did. Then, moving with painstaking slowness, Hawk put his hands in her hair and combed his fingers through it. He lifted it off her neck and held it out at the sides of her head, watching the firelight filter through the blond strands. "You've got beautiful hair, especially in firelight."

Randy found it difficult to speak, but she said a gruff thank you.

Hawk cupped her face between his hands and ran his thumbs along her lower eyelashes. "You've got eyes the color of the first leaves of spring."

He slid his hands down to her neck and momentarily closed his fingers around it before letting them move down to her chest. She had been given a fresh shirt that morning. It was no more attractive than its predecessors. Hawk didn't seem to notice. He seemed more interested in the way she gave shape to the front of it. The manner in which he looked at her made her feel more beautiful than she had ever felt.

His hands glided over the soft mounds of her breasts. "Take it off," he said, lowering his hands to his sides.

She ducked her head only once and that was to locate the top button. After that, holding his gaze, she undid the buttons and peeled off the shirt. She dropped it to the floor. She saw Hawk swallow, saw his hand reaching for her, but her eyes had already closed by the time he touched her.

"Beautiful breasts." He cupped her gingerly. "Beautiful, sensitive nipples." He let out a long, raspy breath when her nipples hardened against his caressing fingertips. Lowering his head, he stroked one of them with the tip of his tongue. Randy's stomach quivered and she moaned softly. He continued the love play, encircling the rigid crests with his nimble tongue until they were distended so far they almost touched him.

Which was obviously what he wanted. He rapidly unbuttoned his shirt and shrugged it off, unable to get rid of it fast enough. Placing his strong, dark hands in the center of her back, he drew her against him. Her breasts left damp impressions on his chest. Groaning his pleasure at the sight, he lowered his head and kissed her.

It wasn't a hard, demanding kiss, but deep and questing, as though he wanted to touch her soul with his searching tongue.

They continued to nuzzle each other, rubbing noses and cheeks and chins and lips together. Randy soon realized why he wasn't embracing her. He was unbuttoning his jeans. When they were undone, he took a step away from her.

Their breathing was unsteady and swift as they looked at each other. Finally Randy's eyes lowered to his chest. It was incredibly smooth and sleek, marvelously formed of muscle and bone and skin. Her fingertip traced the line that squared off his pectoral muscle. When she reached the sternum, she followed the shallow indentation down, over his ridged stomach, beyond his narrow waist, to the ribbon of dark, glossy hair. She traced it into the dimple of his navel. There she dallied, wondering what was expected of her.

She didn't have to wait long to find out. Hawk took her hand and moved it into the open wedge of his jeans. But he left the decision up to her by removing his hand and leaving hers, open, against him.

Randy closed her eyes and inclined for-

242 SANDRA BROWN

ward. She turned her head to one side and laid her cheek against his chest. Only then did she slide her hand into the dense thatch of hair. When she touched him, he shuddered. When she cupped him and lifted him up and out, he cried, "Miranda," and wrapped his arms around her.

She tilted her head back to receive his tempestuous kiss. He reached beneath her skirt and rid her of underpants. He then gathered the fabric of her skirt in his hands and tilted her hips toward his. They touched; the contact was more than they could stand.

Hawk moved to the bed. He sat, half reclining, against the wall behind it and pulled her over his lap. With his hands supporting her hips, he drew her body toward his mouth and kissed her through her skirt. Lifting it, he kissed her belly, her smooth thighs, the patch of tawny hair between them. He sank lower, continually kissing, separating and investigating the silky furrows of her femininity with his tongue.

Almost instantly Randy reached a shuddering, heart-stopping climax. Before she had fully recovered, he lowered her hips and impaled her upon his rigid heat. Their lips met in a fierce and hungry kiss. His hands, applying subtle pressure to her hips, guided her motions.

Desperately wanting to please him, she shed any and all inhibitions and gave more than he asked for. Their bodies were shiny with perspiration and hot with fever when they surrendered to the passion that threatened to consume them.

Replete, barely having the energy to move, they separated long enough to remove the rest of their clothing. Hawk then drew her naked form against his and pulled a blanket over them.

"Ernie wouldn't approve," she whispered against his neck.

"The hell with Ernie." His chuckle vibrated in her ear.

Her smile of satiation faded upon reflection of what had just transpired. "Hawk, I don't want you to compromise your position in the tribe because of me."

He tipped her head up. "Nothing that has happened tonight will make a difference."

"You're sure?"

"Positive."

"But I thought that if—"

"Shh." He lightly ran his thumb over her lower lip. "Your mouth is bruised."

"From kissing you so hard."

"I'm sorry I hurt you."

"I'm not." She inched up and pressed her lips over his. They shared a long, sweet, melding kiss while his roving hands cherished her.

Randy remembered little else after that. Sprawled across his chest, with her hair covering his copper skin and his heart beating out a cadence in her ear, she slipped into sleep.

She was awakened by the absence of his body heat. Before opening her eyes, she tried to snuggle closer. Her hands reached for him, but came up empty. She opened her eyes and discovered herself alone in the bed. Startled, she swung her head around. She lay back down, relieved to have spotted him standing at the window. His shoulder was propped against the sill. He was staring through the windowpane, unmoving.

He was still naked, seemingly impervious to the chill in the room. Drawing the covers up over her shoulders, Randy took advantage of his lack of awareness to watch him. His shoulders were broad, his torso long and beautifully proportioned. His buttocks were taut and narrow, gracefully swelling out from the small of his back. He had long thighs and sinewy calves. Arms, hands, feet—she couldn't find a single flaw.

She admired his body as one of God's finest creations. As a woman, she desired it. It was capable of giving her incredible pleasure, of coaxing feelings and sensations from her that she hadn't known were there. He had brought to life erogenous parts of her body that had lain dormant since she was born. He exercised a powerful and wonderful magic over her body.

Brimming with emotion, Randy eased back the covers and padded over to him. She moved up behind him and pressed the front of her body against his back, then slipped her hands beneath his arms and crossed them over his chest.

"Good morning," she said, pecking a kiss on his shoulder blade.

"Good morning."

"What are you doing up so early?"

"Couldn't sleep."

"Why didn't you wake me?"

"There was no need to."

Maybe she should have left him to his private thoughts. He wasn't in a talkative, receptive mood. But she didn't want to return to the bed that seemed so empty without him. "What are you looking at?"

"The sky."

"What are you thinking about?"

His chest rose and fell with a deep sigh, though he didn't make a sound. "My life, my mother, father, the brother who was stillborn. My grandfather. The Irishman who took an Indian girl for his wife and left me with Anglo eyes."

She wanted to tell him what stunning eyes they were, but she was certain he already knew. She was also certain how he felt about their distinctiveness. "You resent your eyes because they're not Indian, don't you?"

He shrugged indifferently, but she strongly sensed that her guess was right. She kissed his spine and splayed her hands on his stomach. Slowly she let them coast down. They skimmed his lean hipbones, sifted through his body hair, glanced his sex, before moving to the tops of his thighs. She felt his body tense, but he didn't overtly respond.

"You're beautiful, Hawk O'Toole. All of you is beautiful."

Her hands began moving back up, only this time her touch was less analytical and more sexual. Suddenly, he caught her hands and held them still. "Go back to bed," he said in a harsh, curt voice. "It's cold."

Randy uttered a small cry of dismay and quickly withdrew her hands. Feeling brutally rejected, she spun away. Before she had taken two steps, however, his hand closed around her wrist and drew her up.

"You think I don't want you." It was a statement rather than a question. "I don't," he growled.

Randy had no time to react before he lifted her against his lap, braced her against the wall, and thrust himself into her. Palm to palm, their hands were flattened against the wall on either side of her head. Burying his face in her hair, he ground his hips against hers.

He moaned. "Oh, dear Lord. I don't want to want you, but I do. I don't want you because you make me weak."

At first overwhelmed, Randy encircled his waist with her legs and drew him closer. Reflexively, her hips began to move.

"No, don't move," he said raggedly. "Don't . . . don't do anything but hold me tight inside you. Make it last. Glove me. Just let me feel you surrounding me. Let me stay . . . Oh, no, no . . ." The staggering words gave way to the warm jetting tide. His groan of release was low and long and tinged with desperation.

Some minutes later, he set her on her feet. Randy searched his averted face for an explanation. She wasn't offended. She was perplexed. Her bewilderment was tinged with fear, but of what she couldn't say. Before she could press Hawk for meanings behind his behavior, she heard noises that were out of keeping with the breaking dawn.

Going to the window, she looked out. The rising sun was just spreading its glow over the mountainside. The figures alighting from the convoy of cars below looked like black insects as they scurried about over the rocky ground.

"Hawk!" she cried out in alarm. "It's the police. How'd they get here? How'd they find us?"

"I sent for them."

Twelve

"You sent for them! *Why?*"

He reached for his jeans and pulled them on. "To turn myself in." He broke the news to her without any expression of emotion either in his face or his voice. "You'd better get dressed. They'll expect you down there soon."

"Hawk!" she cried, grabbing his arm and forcing him to look at her. "What is going on? Why are you doing this? I thought you were going to send the deed to the governor."

He shook off her hand and began tossing her clothing at her piece by piece. "A copy was delivered to his office yesterday. After giving him a few hours to read over it, I called him."

"You talked to him directly?"

"It took some doing, but after I made a few veiled threats regarding your life, he agreed to speak to me."

"Well, what did he say?" she asked impatiently, when he turned his back to her and started pulling on the rest of his clothing.

"He said he would give the matter his full consideration, *if* I surrendered myself to the authorities and released you and Scott. I agreed, but only if he would guarantee that I would be the only one held accountable for your kidnapping. He gave me that guarantee."

"Hawk," she said miserably, clutching her clothes to her chest. "That's not fair."

"Not much in life is. Now, get dressed."

"But—"

"Put your clothes on, unless you want me to drag you naked down to the gate. I don't think your ex-husband would appreciate that." He hadn't behaved in this hard and uncompromising way since that first night at the temporary camp just after the actual kidnapping. His jaw was rigid with resolve, his eyes glittering with hatred.

"What role does Morton play in your surrender?"

"I don't know, but he's sure to be waiting there with open arms to welcome Scott and you back."

"You want me . . . *us* . . . to go back to him?"

His eyes were cold and unfeeling as he said, "I couldn't care less. You were a pleasant diversion while you were here. Nice to look at. Nice to feel. Nice to . . ." He hitched his chin in the direction of the rumpled bed. "If it's true that you never had lovers before or since your divorce, your talents were being wasted."

Randy's chest heaved with the need to cry out in emotional agony, but she contained it. Giving him her back, she clamped her teeth over her lower lip. Her coordination was so bad she could barely pull on her clothes. When she was finally dressed, she turned to him. He was holding the door open, his face stony.

At the end of the path leading to the cabin, Ernie was waiting with Scott. The little boy's eyes were still puffy with sleepiness. They were also troubled. As she and Hawk approached, he ran to her.

"Mommy, Ernie says I gotta go home now. I don't, do I? Can't I stay longer?"

She took his hand and gave him a watery smile. "I'm afraid you can't, Scott. It's past time for us to leave."

"But I don't want to go home yet. I want to stay and play with Donny. I want to see his baby brother when he gets borned."

"Scott."

The single word from Hawk stopped his flow of whining protests. "But, Hawk, I—"

One look into Hawk's unblinking eyes silenced him. Dejected, Scott lowered his head and stood subdued at Randy's side. Ernie stepped directly in Hawk's path.

"Let me go with you," he said.

"We've been over this a hundred times. Don't be foolish. You'll be needed here to take care of your sons. See that they grow up smart and strong. Make them men of conviction and purpose."

Ernie's lined face seemed to stretch longer. Sadly, he laid his hand on Hawk's shoulder. They shared a long, telling stare. At last Ernie dropped his arm and stepped aside.

With Randy and Scott leading the way, the procession started down the central street of the compound toward the gate. Randy was aware of eyes, solemn and bleak, watching them from behind window-panes. Beyond the gate, officially marked cars from the capitol city formed an intimidating semicircle. She recognized the man standing in its center as the governor of the state. And next to him, Morton. At the sight of him, she wanted to retch.

"That's Daddy," Scott remarked on a low, disinterested voice.

"Yes."

"How come he's here?"

"I guess he missed you and wanted to see you."

Scott said nothing. Nor did he increase his pace in anticipation of seeing his father. If anything, his footsteps became more laggardly.

"Mommy, what are all these policemen doing here? I'm scared."

"There's nothing for you to be afraid of, Scott. They want to give you a police escort home, that's all."

"What's that?"

"It's something they only do for very important people, like the president."

"Oh." The idea of a police escort didn't seem to excite him either.

Before they reached the gate, Hawk halted. Randy turned and looked at him, her eyes bleak and questioning.

"They're expecting you to come ahead of

me. I asked them to take you and Scott away before I'm arrested. For the boy's sake."

Hawk in handcuffs, being stuffed into the backseat of a police car. Inwardly, she shuddered to think of Scott witnessing that. "I'm glad you thought of it. That's best, of course."

Despite the harsh words he had said to her earlier, Randy's heart was tearing in two. She wanted to memorize his face. This might be the last time she would see it set against its natural setting, against the sky, which was the very color of his eyes, against the mountainside, which was as rugged and indomitable as his profile.

His body was as tall and lean as the evergreens in the background. The wind lifted his hair and she was reminded of the black, glossy wings of a magnificent bird of prey.

"Hawk, aren't you coming with us?" Scott asked him in a quavering voice. Even if he didn't understand the repercussions of what was happening, he sensed that something was amiss.

"No, Scott. I've got some business to do with these men, but not until after you leave."

"I'd rather just stay with you."

"You can't."

"Please," he asked, his voice cracking.

A muscle in Hawk's cheek twitched, but he maintained his proud posture. "Where are your knife and scabbard?"

Scott, his eyes shimmering with tears and his lower lip trembling, touched them where they were attached to his belt.

"Good. I'm depending on you to watch over your mother."

"I promise I will."

He clasped Scott's shoulder firmly, much as Ernie had bid him good-bye, then he withdrew his hand and stepped back quickly, as though severing an invisible cord. He gave Randy a piercing stare. "Go on. Before they become impatient."

There were a thousand things she needed and wanted to say, had she the time to say them and had Hawk wanted to hear them. Drawing from an inner resource of strength, she turned, bringing a reluctant Scott around with her.

Together they moved through the gate. Morton rushed forward and gripped her shoulders. "Randy, are you all right? Did he make good his threats and hurt you?"

"Get your hands off me," she spat.

Morton blinked at her in astonishment, but to save face with all the spectators, he complied. "Scott? Scott, are you all right, son?"

"I'm fine, Daddy. How come I have to go home now?"

"Wha—"

"Governor Adams?" Randy addressed him.

The statesman had been blessed with oratory skills and a keen political mind to make up for an unimpressive, paunchy physique and prematurely balding head. He stepped forward. "Yes, Mrs. Price? What can I do for you?" he said, taking her hand. "I realize that you've been through a terrible ordeal. Anything I can do to help you, you've only got to ask."

"Thank you. Will you please instruct those officers to put their guns away?"

Governor Adams momentarily lost his composure. He had expected a request for food, water, fresh clothing, medical attention, protection. Randy's request took him totally off guard.

"Mrs. Price, they have their weapons drawn for your protection. We couldn't rely on Mr. O'Toole's promise to deliver you unharmed."

"Why not?" she demanded. "Do we look harmed in any way?"

"Well, no, but—"

"Didn't Mr. O'Toole give you his word that he wouldn't harm us?" It was a lucky guess, and by the embarrassment on the governor's face, a correct one.

"Yes, he did."

"Then have the weapons put away or I'm not moving from this spot. The guns are frightening my son."

Morton propped his hands on his hips. "Randy, just what the hell do you think—"

"Do not address me in that condescending tone of voice, Morton."

"Yeah," Scott piped up. "Hawk'll get mad at you if you yell at Mommy."

"Now see here—"

Governor Adams held up his hand. "Please, Mr. Price. Apparently Mrs. Price has something to say."

"That's right. I do. The guns?"

Adams gave her a measuring stare. He glanced beyond her shoulder to the man standing above them on a ledge of rock outlined against the sky. With a wave of his hand, he summoned the senior FBI agent forward. They held a brief and furtive discussion. Randy had to argue her point with him just as she had done with the governor, but finally the order was given for all weapons to be put away. Only after she saw that they were did the knot of tension in her chest begin to loosen.

"Yesterday, did you receive a folder of Xeroxed material from Mr. O'Toole?"

"Indeed I did," Governor Adams replied. "Very interesting reading."

"And didn't you speak with him by telephone regarding this material and an ensuing investigation?"

"I did."

"Then there is no call for all this." She spread her hand wide to encompass the patrol cars.

"The man has agreed to surrender himself to the authorities."

"For what?"

"For what?" Morton exclaimed. "He committed a federal crime."

"He executed it. Who *planned* it?" she fired at him. Morton went whey-faced. While he was temporarily rendered dumb, Randy turned back to the governor, whose brows were drawn together in disapproval and suspicion. "Governor Adams, Morton is ultimately responsible for this entire incident. He duped Mr. O'Toole into thinking that conditions on the reservation could be improved upon and that the Lone Puma Mine would be restored to the tribe if he did Morton this little 'favor.' Needless to say, Morton had no one's interest at heart except his own. He instigated this kidnapping for the publicity it would give him before the election in November."

The governor's glower could have turned Morton to stone. It said that he would be dealt with properly later. In the meantime he wanted to proceed with matters at hand.

"The fact still remains, Mrs. Price, that Mr. O'Toole kidnapped you and your son off that train."

"If he's prosecuted, I'll swear that he didn't. I'll testify that we went with him willingly," she said staunchly.

"He stole money from one of the passengers."

"He took money that was practically pressed into his hand by a loudmouth who thought he was being cute. When witnesses are put on the stand, they'll have to testify to that. Everyone thought the 'holdup' was a hoax. No one was in any danger. Ever."

"No one but you and your son."

"Never," she said, shaking her head adamantly.

"I received a ripped shirt with your blood on it."

She held up her wounded thumb. "A kitchen accident," she lied. "The shirt didn't belong to me." That was sidestepping the truth. "Putting my blood on it and sending it to you was a desperation move on Mr. O'Toole's part to gain your attention. We were never in any real physical danger. Ask Scott."

Governor Adams looked down at Scott, who was following the conversation as well as his limited vocabulary would allow. The governor knelt down and said, "Scott, were you ever afraid of the Indians?"

He screwed up his face and thought back. "A little, when I first got on the horse with Ernie, but he kept telling me that he wouldn't let me go. Then I was kinda scared of Geronimo 'cause he kept trying to butt me with his head."

"Geronimo is a goat," Randy said for clarification.

"I still don't like him very much," Scott admitted.

"Did Mr. O'Toole ever hurt you? Or threaten to hurt you?"

Puzzled by the question, Scott shook his head. "No. Hawk's neat." He glanced over his shoulder and happily waved at the stalwart silhouette. "He's not waving back 'cause he doesn't like all those cars parked on the grass and making trails. He says that sometimes men do bad things to the land. That's why they mine the silver the way they do so it doesn't mess up anything on top of the ground."

The governor was obviously impressed by what he heard, but he asked Scott one last question. "Did Mr. O'Toole ever hurt your mother?"

Scott shaded his eyes against the sun and looked up at her. "No. But he had a knife—"

"A knife?"

"This one." Scott pulled the knife from its new scabbard. "He gave it to me and said that if he ever did hurt my mommy, I could stab him in the heart with it. He never did though, so I didn't have to stab him. I don't think I would anyway, 'cause Hawk said that knives are okay to skin animals and gut fish, but I shouldn't ever turn it on a person."

Morton rounded on Randy. "You let my kid play with knives? You want him to be as savage as your new lover?" he asked nastily, flinging his hand toward Hawk. He reached for the knife. "Give me that thing."

"*No!*" Scott screamed, and bent double to protect the knife.

Morton lunged for him and roughly grabbed his small arm.

Hawk leaped from the shelf of rock and came racing forward. Automatic weapons, which had been previously concealed, were snapped into place again and aimed at him.

"Don't fire!" Governor Adams yelled, holding up his hands.

After a tense moment, Governor Adams turned to Randy. "Mrs. Price, you've been most instrumental in clearing up this"—he paused and shot Morton a scathing look—"disgraceful misunderstanding. But I'm afraid I can't just dismiss the issue."

"Why not?"

"This episode has cost the taxpayers a tremendous amount of money."

"So will needlessly arresting Mr. O'Toole."

"The public will demand a satisfactory explanation."

"I'm certain you can rise to the occasion, Governor Adams. Think what an opportunity it will be for you to rally support for the Indians' cause, which I'm certain you feel strongly about."

He assessed her shrewdly. "Very well, I give you my word that I'll look into the Puma Mine swindle immediately. Now, may I offer you and your son a ride back to the capitol in my limousine?"

"Thank you, Governor, but we're not going back."

"You mean we can stay?" Scott cried. "Oh, boy, can I go tell Donny?" Without waiting for permission, he brushed past his father and charged through the gate.

Morton sputtered, but Adams silenced him with a brusque wave of his hand and turned his attention back to Randy. "In that case, will you deliver a message to Mr. O'Toole?"

"Gladly."

"Tell him that I'll arrange a meeting with representatives from the Inter-Tribal Council, the BIA, lawyers from my office, and the current owners of the mine. I'm sure an IRS agent would like to be in on that meeting, too. As soon as we designate a time and place, I'll be in touch with him. In the meantime I suggest that he return to the village near the Lone Puma."

She gripped his hand. "Thank you very much, Governor Adams. Thank you."

She didn't even give Morton a backward glance, though he called her a dirty name as she went past him. The epithet, his disdain, didn't matter to her in the least. She kept her eyes trained on the man standing just inside the gate. Her heart was beating wildly, but her footsteps were sure and unfaltering as she moved toward him.

When only inches separated them, she looked into his stern face and said, "You took me off that train by force, so you're stuck with me. I know you desire me. I suspect you even love me, though you don't want to admit it. More than anything, you *need* me, Hawk O'Toole. You need me to hold you in the night when you're alone. You need my reinforcement when you're in doubt. You need my love. And I need yours."

His face remained impassive. She wet her lips nervously. "Besides that, you're going to make me look like a damn fool if you send me back now."

She saw a flicker of amusement in his eyes. He moved, reaching out and gathering a handful of her hair in his fist. He wound it around until he controlled the movement of her head. Then he drew her mouth up to his for a scorching kiss.

Epilogue

"Isn't he beautiful?"

Randy smoothed the crown of her new-born son's head. It was covered with straight, dark hair.

"For a half-breed, he's okay."

She swatted Hawk's caressing finger away from the baby's cheek. "Don't you dare say that about my son."

"*Our* son," her husband corrected with an affectionate smile. He replaced his finger against the baby's cheek. It puffed in and out as he vigorously suckled his mother's breast. "He is beautiful, isn't he?"

Hawk's face was filled with wonder and awe. His visage was normally stern. That hadn't changed. But contrary to a year ago, his features softened more frequently now—when he laughed at Scott's antics, when he made love to Randy, when their eyes met in a public place and they could only communicate their love silently.

"He certainly is, but I already see strains of your temperament in him." She pulled the infant away from her breast. His balled fist boxed the air and his newborn features contorted with fierce displeasure. "Relax, you're only done on that side," Randy scolded gently, as she transferred him to her other breast. He latched on to the nipple and started sucking noisily.

Hawk smiled at the gusto his son demonstrated. "If he keeps eating like that, he's going to grow up to be a halfback."

"I thought Scott was going to be a halfback."

"There are two on every offensive team. We could have two more sons and round out the whole backfield. We'll sell them to the highest-bidding NFL team."

"Do I have anything to say about this?"

"You could say no every night when I reach for you." He leaned down and brushed a kiss across her lips. "But you never do."

She lowered her lashes. "How indelicate of you to point that out, Mr. O'Toole."

Just then a hospital nurse came in carrying a vase of roses. "More flowers," she said to Randy, setting them on the nightstand. "How are we doing here?" She peered over Hawk's shoulder.

"I believe he's finally full." Randy gazed down at her son lovingly. He had stopped sucking and was sleeping contentedly. "I'll take him back to the nursery."

"Just a minute." Hawk slipped his hands underneath his son and lifted him up. He pressed a soft kiss on the baby's forehead, nuzzled his cheek, and admired the sleeping face and strong limbs before passing the child to the nurse.

He escorted them to the door as though seeing them safely on their way back to the nursery. When he turned toward the bed, he was alarmed to find Randy's eyes cloudy with tears. "What's the matter?"

She sniffed. "Nothing. I was just thinking how much I love you." He sat down and kissed her softly. "That kiss is from Scott, who wants to know when you're bringing his baby brother home."

"Tell him only two more days. How is he?"

"Busy working on a drawing for you, which he promised should be finished by tomorrow."

She smiled. "I'll look forward to that. Who are the flowers from?"

He read the attached card. "Ernie and Leta. I'm sure they were Leta's idea. Ernie's chapped because my son weighed more at birth than his."

"How well I know." Wincing, she laid a hand on her unfamiliarly flat tummy.

"Are you in pain?" Hawk asked, his mouth tensing. Because his mother had died as a result of childbirth, he'd been anxious over Randy's health all through her pregnancy. The day he drove her into the city to the hospital, he'd been far more concerned about the delivery than Randy herself had been.

"No, I'm not in pain," she assured him. "I was only teasing."

She brushed a strand of hair off his forehead. For a while after they were married, she had been hesitant to openly express her affection for him except when they were in bed. Soon, however, she had discovered that Hawk enjoyed her spontaneous caresses, probably because he'd experienced so little affection in his lifetime.

"Ernie still doesn't like me," she said, glancing at the roses.

"You're my wife."

"Meaning?"

"If a woman doesn't reside in his kitchen and his bed, he's indifferent to her. You mistake his indifference for dislike. I know that he respects you in spite of himself."

"His attitude toward me improved—marginally—when he became convinced that I wasn't going to lure you away from the reservation."

He stroked her neck with the backs of his fingers. "He could see that first night I climbed into the pickup with you and held a knife at your throat just how powerful a lure you could have been."

Giving birth had left her emotionally tremulous. On the brink of tears again, she steered the conversation away from their personal life. "I'm proud of their new house for Leta. They needed the additional space for their growing family."

"They've prospered this year. We all have. Thanks to you for restoring the mine to us," he added quietly.

"I only set things in motion. It was your power of persuasion that made them happen."

He braced his arm on the pillow behind

her head and leaned over her. "Have I thanked you?"

"At least a million times."

"Thanks, one more time." He kissed her sweetly, chastely. "That kiss is from me."

"I thought I felt your special touch behind it."

"Have I mentioned how much I miss you, how empty my bed is without you, how much I love you?"

"Not today."

He kissed her again, keeping it innocent, until her tongue came in search of his. With a moan of longing, his mouth sank down upon hers. His hand moved to her gown and opened it. He covered her breast fondly and possessively. When he felt the sticky moisture, he raised his head and gazed down at her. "I love to watch my son nurse."

"I know. I love watching you watch him."

Hawk lightly stroked her dusky nipple and a bead of milk formed on the pad of his thumb. "He didn't drink it all. You've still got milk."

"Plenty," she replied huskily.

His inquiring eyes flew up to hers. They held for several misty seconds. Then Randy lovingly curved her hand around the back of his head and drew it down.

"May I come in?" he asked politely. If he
had had a hat, it would have been in hand.

"No."

"Please?"

"Why?"

"I want to talk to you."

"And hurl more ugly accusations? No,
thank you, Mr. MacKensie." Ria started to
close the door. He stuck out his hand and
caught it.

Ria looked at him closely. What she saw

made her feel better. If his appearance was any indication, he'd had a hellish day. His dark hair was mussed. His tie had been loosened and the collar button on his shirt undone. He was holding his suit coat over his shoulder by the crook of his finger. He looked haggard and worried and tired. For a man who had gone through a heated campaign with nary a wrinkle, his dishevelment was a dead giveaway that he'd suffered some recent mental anguish.

Too bad, Ria thought. She refused to be moved to pity, not after the things he'd said to her. "Just go away and leave me alone. Forget everything I said this morning."

"I can't."

"I never should have told you."

"Of course you should have."

Annoyed, she shifted her weight from one foot to the other, while still blocking his entrance. "Need I remind you, Mr. MacKensie, that you didn't take the news too well? You were insulting and abusive."

"That's one of the reasons I'm here, to apologize for my knee-jerk reaction. Grant me one point."

"What?" she asked cautiously.

"That my initial reaction was just a teensy bit justified."

His eyes were intensely blue. They were set off by his dark hair and tanned face. Wary of their persuasiveness, Ria lowered her gaze to his vest. But that, too, evoked memories. Was it really possible that she had once unbuttoned his vest in a lustful hurry to touch him? Had her fingers fumbled in their rush to gain access to him? She couldn't imagine reaching out to touch him now.

She cleared her throat uneasily. Reasoning that she owed him the courtesy of accepting his apology, she decided to be conciliatory. "I suppose that what I had to tell you did come as quite a shock."

"Then will you please let me come in, Ria?"

Maybe it was because he addressed her by name. She couldn't explain it to herself afterward. But for whatever reason, she stepped aside. He came in. She closed the door behind him and they were alone.

The room had changed. It was filled with golden afternoon sunlight rather than flickering firelight. The fireplace had been cleaned out and a potted philodendron with leaves as large and flat as place mats stood in front of the brass screen. A leafy ficus occupied the spot where the Christmas tree had been.

"You have a green thumb," he remarked.

She inclined her head in acknowledgment of the compliment and indicated a chair. She sat down in a bentwood rocker. Both of them avoided the sofa, looking past it as though it weren't there. The room might have changed with the season, but the atmosphere still teemed with vivid and disturbing memories of a snowy night.

"Would you like something to drink?"

"Not if that's all you've got." He nodded toward the glass sitting on the end table beside the rocker. "What is that?"

"Alka-Seltzer."

"Are you sick?"

"I get indigestion every afternoon."

"Oh."

"I can get you a soft drink," Ria offered. "Or something stronger."

"No, thanks."

A clock was ticking. It seemed very loud. The rocker squeaked slightly each time it moved to and fro. Whenever their eyes accidentally met, they guiltily looked away, like children who'd been caught playing doctor the day before.

Ria wished she hadn't changed out of her tailored suit and into the old jeans and T-shirt. She wished she had on a brassiere. She wished she had on shoes. She knew that she needed to take a firm stand with this man. Bare feet weren't a very reassuring platform. Her hair was a mess. After taking down her bun, she'd only shaken it out. It hung unbrushed and untamed around her shoulders.

She knew the strain of the last twenty-four hours was evident on her face. She hadn't been able to hold down much food lately. Her cheeks were gaunt. No amount of Erase would hide the violet crescents beneath her eyes. She hadn't slept at all the night before, worrying over her dilemma and planning what she was going to say to Councilman MacKensie the next morning.

In the end she had decided to take the straightforward, honest approach. And just look what honesty had gotten her. His temper. His suspicion. His contempt.

"How long have you lived here?"

She roused herself to answer his conversational question. "Going on three years. Ever since I started working at Bishop and Harvey."

"It's a nice house."

"Thank you."

"Cozy."

"Uh-huh."

"Did you decorate it yourself?"

"Yes."

"This is a good neighborhood."

"The city keeps the garbage picked up and the streets repaired," she said, smiling sickly.

"Ah, well, that's good to hear." His smile was just as puny as hers. "It felt almost like spring today."

"Yes. I saw some daffodils already in bloom."

Sitting on the edge of his chair, his knees widespread, Taylor stared at the hardwood floor between his feet. The fingers of one hand were nervously doing push-ups against the fingers of the other. He forced a cough. "When, uh, when did you know about, uh, the, uh, baby?"

From all she'd read, heard, and experienced firsthand about Taylor MacKensie, stuttering was totally out of character. His voice frequently rang out in the City Council chambers as he waxed eloquently and intelligently on the topics presented for the council's review. His campaign speeches had been incisive, amusing, and articulate. Reporters' questions, even the most probing or complex, never left him at a loss for words.

It was gratifying to know that he was as uneasy now as she had been that morning before entering his office. Diving off the cliffs at Acapulco couldn't compare to how she'd felt when she'd walked through that door and faced him for the first time since Christmas morning. Especially in light of what she had to tell him.

"When did I know?" Ria kept her eyes averted. "I missed a period."

He fidgeted on the edge of his seat. "I understand that happens sometimes."

"It does. But never to me. I'm always like clockwork."

This time it was she who coughed. It flustered her to talk about such personal things to this stranger. Well, not exactly "stranger." Yes, this stranger. What did she really know about him? That he was handsome. That he knew how to open a bottle of champagne correctly. That he was a good driver on snowy streets. That he could charm the pants off a woman. Literally.

She began again. "I started feeling sick . . . not really sick, just . . ." She foundered, looking for a word that precisely described that bloated feeling, that lassitude, that inability to draw enough breath, that feeling of being full to bursting even when she was hungry. There wasn't a word descriptive enough. "There were just symptoms," she said conclusively.

"Like what?"

"Upset stomach. Emotional instability. Itchy—"

He cocked his head inquisitively. "Itchy . . . ?"

"Breasts," she supplied huskily, having to force the word through her lips.

"Oh." He looked down at her chest and kept looking in that vicinity for a long, uncomfortable time. "I'm sorry."

She crossed her arms over her stomach, wishing she could place her hands over her breasts to shield her hardening nipples from his piercing eyes. "You know the symptoms," she said shortly.

Taylor looked completely baffled. "Yeah, I guess."

"Then I skipped another period last month. I finally went to the doctor yesterday, and he confirmed my own diagnosis. My due date is September twenty-sixth."

He expulsed a deep breath. The jury had just brought in a guilty verdict. "I guess that cinches it."

"There was never any doubt about the child's father, despite what you might think of my sex life, Mr. MacKensie."

"Make it Taylor, okay?" he demanded crossly.

Just as crossly she said, "Regardless of your 'experience' with me, as you so ungallantly referred to it, I don't sleep around."

"Forgive me for saying that. I shouldn't have."

Her angry outburst had exhausted her. Her shoulders slumped, and she rested her head on the caned back of her chair. "I suppose you had every right to think that." Her soft laugh was bitter and self-disparaging. "On Christmas Eve, I was an easy lay."

"Don't say that."

"Well, wasn't I?" She raised her head and looked at him directly.

"I never thought that. Then or now."

"You thought that this morning."

He ran a weary hand down his face and blew out another gust of carbon dioxide. "We're going in circles and getting nowhere." He held her gaze for a moment. "Look, I don't think you're an easy lay. Because if you are, then I am. And I'm more discriminating than your average tomcat.

"So let's just drop whatever recriminations we're harboring, self-imposed or otherwise, and try to figure out what we're going to do about the consequences, okay?" Ria only nodded. "What about this guy you told me you're seeing? The one with the elderly mother in Florida."

"Funny, Guy happens to be his name." She was surprised that he remembered the details. "Guy Patterson. He's an associate in the firm."

"Have you told him yet?"

"Yes. As soon as I'd told you. I felt I owed him that."

"And?"

Guy Patterson had taken the news of her pregnancy no better than Taylor had.

Worse, in fact. He'd been livid, calling her in explicit terms the names Taylor had only implied.

"He's permanently out of the picture," she said without elaboration.

Actually, having Guy out of her life was a relief. Older by fifteen years, he was somewhat stuffy. She was tired of his staid, conservative ideas. Their conversations were boring, because he directed them to topics only he was interested in. When you got right down to it, Guy was a persnickety old maid, and not much fun to be around. The only reason she had been dating him was that nobody better had come on the scene. She wouldn't have chosen this earth-shattering way to break it off with him, but she was glad it had been done so irrevocably.

"You could have passed the child off as his," Taylor said tentatively. "Why didn't you?"

"I never would have done that," Ria exclaimed, taking umbrage. "What kind of woman do you think I am?"

"All right, I'm sorry."

"Besides, I couldn't have deceived him

even if I'd wanted to. Guy had a vasectomy years ago."

He'd made no secret of it. When their relationship had developed into more than that of working associates, he'd told Ria that he might consider marriage, but children were out of the question. There was another reason why Guy couldn't possibly be the father of her baby, but she'd let Mr. MacKensie think what he would.

"Has this ever happened to you?" she asked suddenly.

"You mean fathering a child? No. How 'bout you? Have you ever been pregnant?"

"No." She wondered why she was pleased to know that this was new to him too. There was no explanation except that she would have hated knowing she was one of a group of unfortunates. Taylor's Tarnished.

He studied her carefully for a moment, but lowered his eyes before asking, "Did you come to me for financial assistance?"

"Financial assistance for what?"

"Any number of things."

"Like . . . ?"

"Abortion. Is that what you plan to do?"

Ria turned her head, giving him her profile. Tears were glistening in her eyes. They reflected the light of the setting sun coming through the window.

"No. Mr. Mac— No, Taylor. I believe in living with my mistakes, not burying them. And for your information, abortions come cheap these days."

"I was only asking because the timing is right. I know there's a deadline before that, uh, solution becomes unfeasible."

"Are you sure you're not suggesting that's what I should do? Before you answer, I should warn you that that's a rhetorical question. I won't be having an abortion." She turned her head and looked at him squarely, almost defiantly. "Why else do you think I'd come to you for money?"

"To help with supporting the child, before and after it's born."

"I earn a very good salary, in addition to the commission I make on each job. Thank you very much, but I don't need your money, Mr. MacKensie." Leaving her chair, she picked up the Alka-Seltzer-coated glass on the end table and made a beeline for the door across the room.

Taylor followed her. Her kitchen was alive with a jungle of plants. He had to swat aside a leaf as he went in. She was rinsing out the glass in a stainless-steel sink.

"Why do you bristle at everything I say?" She swung around to face him. "Because I find everything you say offensive."

"Well, pardon me, ma'am, but I'm not quite myself today." His tone of voice bordered on loud. "Forgive me for pointing out that we're a little old to be caught 'in trouble' like a couple of teenagers. This didn't happen in the back of Dad's Ford after the prom."

"That's why I don't see why we can't be adult about it and stop throwing blame on each other."

"We can. But the idea of a baby is going to take some getting used to. You've had weeks to reckon with it. It's new to me. Don't expect me to be my normal, glib self today. I've suffered a shock."

"So have I!" she yelled back. "It's not your body that is going through all these changes, it's mine. Think about the adjustments I've had to make."

"I can appreciate that," he said, striving for calm.

"You have a damn funny way of showing it."

"I said I was sorry."

"Then stop making unflattering innuendos about my milking you for money, etcetera. I'm willing to live up to my obligation. Why aren't you? We share this responsibility equally. We were both on that couch. We both enjoyed it. It was a simultaneous—"

Horrified at what she heard herself saying, Ria turned her back on him again. Her cheeks were on fire. She hadn't blushed before or since Christmas Eve. It seemed that she'd packed a lifetime of blushes away and saved them all for Taylor MacKensie.

Her heart was thudding. Her mouth was dry and her palms were wet. In her ears she heard a roar as loud as crashing waves. In fact, it felt as though they were ebbing and flowing through her burning earlobes.

It took a moment for her to collect herself. "All I meant is that I'm willing to assume responsibility for my actions that night," she said in a shaky voice. "It's not going to be easy for me to have a baby, but I am and that's that. You don't know me very well or you never could have thought I'd have an abortion." She shuddered.

"Why did you bother to tell me about the baby at all?"

She came around slowly, clearly mystified by his question. "You didn't want to know that you had fathered a child? I considered it my moral obligation to tell you."

"Your integrity is admirable."

"But you'd just as soon I hadn't involved you," she said with a humorless laugh. "Won't the ski bunny like it?"

"The ski bunny?"

"The woman who got ticked off when you didn't go on the ski trip with her."

"Lisa?"

Lisa. Ria had wondered later what Lisa would have thought of Taylor's Christmas Eve. Would she have been jealous? Or had she been making it with a ski instructor at the same time? Were they sophisticated enough to tell each other about their escapades? Had he regaled Lisa with a detailed account of their lovemaking, perhaps for the purpose of stimulating her?

The thought made Ria ill. She pressed one hand against her stomach and covered her mouth with the other.

Taylor jumped as if he'd been shot. "What's the matter?"

"Nothing."

"Something, dammit."

"Nothing!"

"You're green!"

She drew a deep breath through chalky lips. "I'm a little queasy, that's all."

"Sit down." He yanked a chair away from the table.

"I'm fine, really."

"Sit down." The order was issued in a terse, authoritarian voice that Ria was too weak and woozy to argue with. He pulled out a chair for himself and dropped down into it, plowing his hands through his hair and cursing. "Don't scare me like that again. Can I get you something?"

"No." She glanced up at him. He was glaring at her sternly. "All right. A cracker. That helps settle my stomach sometimes."

She told him where he could find a box of saltines in the pantry. He shook crumbs all over the table as he wrestled two crackers out of their cellophane package. The box fell to the floor when he bumped the edge of the table with his thigh as he sat back down. Nibbling the cracker, Ria began to laugh.

"What?" he grumbled.

"For a man who's so adept at uncorking champagne, you don't handle saltines very well."

He smiled with chagrin. "Well, I've had more practice with champagne than with pregnant ladies."

Ria sobered instantly. She dusted salt off her hands as she said softly, "I'm sure you have."

It surprised them both when he reached across the table and covered her hands with his. "Please don't take offense," he said. "I didn't mean anything by it."

She stared at his hand. It was a beautifully masculine hand. Blunt, well-trimmed fingernails. Her stomach experienced a sinking sensation when she remembered those very hands moving over her body, massaging the breasts that even now ached to be touched. Those fingertips had stroked the secret-most part of her body, lifting her toward ecstasy, taking and giving pleasure in equal quantity. At least she thought he'd taken pleasure in caressing her. She hoped so.

Discomfited by her thoughts, she brought her head up and looked straight into his blue eyes. "Did you tell Lisa about me?"

"Of course not." He abruptly withdrew his hand from hers.

"I don't think I could have stood that." She felt weepy, as she had in the last several weeks, and hoped to heaven she didn't burst into tears over the thought of him and Lisa having a good laugh at her expense.

"I'll confess to going out with a lot of women, but I'm not a complete jerk, Ria."

"I thought you might have used Christmas Eve to make Lisa jealous."

"Did you use it to make Guy jealous?"

"I don't play games like that."

"Neither do I."

She saw that he was telling her the truth. "I didn't tell anybody."

"You had to tell Guy when you told him about the baby."

"I wasn't specific about the date. I didn't name you. Are you still seeing her?"

"Lisa? Yes."

"What will she think of the situation?"

"It isn't any of her business."

Ria stared at him, aghast. "She may beg to differ."

"It isn't like that between us."

He'd felt free to take another woman to bed on Christmas Eve without having to grapple about it later with either his conscience or his steady lady friend. That typified more than anything what a casual, forgettable event their lovemaking had been for him. Ria's heart was aching around the edges, as though the border of her soul had been trespassed.

"Now that we've acknowledged our dual responsibility for this child," he said, "and eliminated abortion as an alternative, what do you suggest we do?"

Ria steadily held his gaze. "You're going to marry me, Mr. MacKensie."

CROSSTOWN SABBATH

Frederic Morton

CROSSTOWN SABBATH

A Street Journey Through History

GROVE PRESS, NEW YORK

Published by Grove Press, Inc.
920 Broadway
New York, N.Y. 10010

Some of the material in the first three pages of this book
appeared in different form in the *Village Voice*.
The author is grateful for permission to reprint.

Library of Congress Cataloging-in-Publication Data

Morton, Frederic.
Crosstown sabbath: a street journey through history.
I. Title.
PS3525.0825C7   1987   813'.54   86-33466
ISBN 0-394-56070-1

Designed by Helen Barrow
Manufactured in the United States of America
First Edition 1987

10 9 8 7 6 5 4 3 2 1

For Marcia

✤

✣ IN THIS BOOK New York is always New York; I am always I; my parents and my daughter are not always my parents and my daughter—sometimes they are the fictional instruments of my point. Being related to a writer is a hazard. I apologize.

—F.M.

FOR MANY YEARS NOW I haven't been able to stop the Factory. Regardless of what corner of the week, what hour of the day, the Factory hums away, unstanched, inviolable. It hums in great metal halls, in shopping centers, on brownstone stoops, under post-graduate pipe smoke, on highways and around the coffee table. Nothing remains exempt from it. Not the shade under the juniper tree, not a cockroach's crevice on West End Avenue. It whirs on, whirs in me and through me, through lunch, through strolls and dreams, smoothly, without respite. Now nobody can stop it. Yet once upon a time we did, my father and I, every Saturday afternoon.

The Factory is old, nearly six thousand years. For a while, though, my family worked an easier shift. For some generations we lived in a Jewish village called Duna Serdahel, in Slovakia. All around us the great mill ground out epochal events. In Duna Serdahel we practiced what we did not know

was provinciality. We kept an inn, fed geese, stacked hay, chanted in the prayer house, wept at the cemetery, danced on feast days, never exerted ourselves enough to produce a rabbi, poured sweet wine, slept on high beds, ate kosher from wooden plates, cheated and bragged never more than was necessary, and thanked the Emperor for keeping off the Cossacks. One day the whistle blew all that away.

One day, in the 1880's, the Factory's whistle cut through Duna Serdahel. We woke up to discover ourselves small, remote. Our very clocks began to stutter with impatience. *Tick— tock—tick—tock* became *ticktockticktock*. The whistle shrilled into the air an acceleration, a cumulating need for something bigger. The cozy turned muddy in Duna Serdahel. The familiar became restrictive. The whistle blew, it blew us into a third-class compartment of a train bound for Vienna. It drove us into a basement in the capital. Here we relearned the Factory. We learned to lathe brass and to work iron. We crafted and designed, and expanded beyond the basement. We saved and invested and built the walls and the roof of the Factory, *a* factory, our very own. We made watch chains by the thousands and hobnails by the hundred thousands. We bought the Emperor's bonds, we wore top hats and silk bonnets. The Emperor died, war broke the Empire, the bonds expired unredeemed, like soldiers. We were poorer, but not quite poor, and the factory whirred on.

The factory whirred on, into the Republic, on borrowed funds. We made cuff links and shoehorns. We wore fedoras and toques. My scooter had a chrome-framed speedometer. We had become bigger again. We would become bigger still if we

produced a latter-day rabbi, that is, a doctor. The factory whir-ring, we exerted ourselves. In vain. The swastika fell upon the city. Some of us were shoveled into freight trains; others scrambled onto a last plane out. And all the while the Factory pounded, until today I can stop it no longer. We came to New York, into the Factory's heartland. We started a mother-of-pearl workshop and a gold smithy. On new soil we joined, sweating, the Factory's newest accelerations. We married and multiplied and retired and died, always to the sound of the whistle, to its demand for something bigger.

We closed the workshop and started academic careers, to wear doctoral mortarboards after all. We clawed our way into tenure and overcame rejection slips from *Harper's* magazine. We milked the dream and were betrayed by it. We hired nursemaids, wore blue jeans or blazers, drowned in garbage, wrote a book that sold eight thousand copies a week, and stag-gered full of Thorazine to our daily shrink. We almost made it. We knew there was a way to lick it. We had it up to here. We stuck it out. We fought past divorce and bankruptcy and got by, by a hair's breadth, and went right on sweating. Why? Because the Factory did and does. I can no longer stop it Sat-urdays, as I once could, in Vienna, with my father.

My father and I stopped it every week at 2:00 p.m., yet every Saturday it seemed unstoppable. At noon my school let out for the weekerd. By 12:15 I'd reached our street, the one in which we lived together with our factory. I walked past the house my grandfather had built. Lion heads crowned the pedi-ments of its windows. From the lions came a roar—distant, tumultuous, royal: the wrath of pistons, the stompings of

presses, the screaming bite of drills. A manifold powerful pulse pounded somewhere in the beasts' great common belly— the factory hall beyond the backyard. It pounded at me. I swung my satchel. I swung it past the next building, each of whose six windows carried a *bas relief* of Aesculapius's healing serpent. The serpents' eyes clocked my passing. Right now they guarded Frau Migsch's rooms and her grocery. But Frau Migsch was not the reason why my grandfather had raised up this Aesculapian house. I was the reason. I was to be the doctor on our street. My M.D.'s sign was to authenticate our bigness. It was for me, for our arduous fulfillment here, that the whistle had blown our village to pieces. One day I must officiate here, in the ermine of a medical smock, sceptered with a stethoscope. The heraldry of my chores to come had been chiseled into stone before my birth. I'd left my mother's womb as the Factory's inchoate instrument. Now I must complete myself. I closed my eyes as I passed the windows. I swung the satchel, but nothing helped. Serpents and lions enforced the Factory's purpose. Could I really stop it with my father, if only for an afternoon?

In New York I can no longer close the Factory. The party to which I must bring my daughter this Saturday is Factory-business continuing in secret session. But in my Viennese childhood Saturdays, it was the other way around. Walking from our street to the synagogue, I came through a market whose business always struck me like a sudden party. The market men wore caps and boots; the women, aprons and babushkas. They'd come in from the country for the day and they looked like old-fashioned dolls, like stories told me of

Duna Serdahel, my great-grandparents' village. The market
dolls whooped out the price of a ladleful of honey. They
napped amidst flies in the wagons that would take them back to
the meadows. Once upon a time, perhaps, we had been able to
whoop or nap like them. And their children—their children
shot about on scooters that were crate boards nailed together
and mounted on rusty rollerskates. On these makeshift won-
ders the market children seemed to live as the Tartars once
lived on horseback. *My* scooter gleamed, being polished steel;
it carried on its handlebars the enameled trademark of a rampant stag. I was allowed to ride it thirty minutes a day on
weekdays. If I rode it longer, the stag might run amok, might
pull me down a Tartar path that would never lead to the windows with the healing serpents. I would not arrive there as a
doctor. I would not go on from there and ascend to University
Professor of Medicine. I would fail the Factory. It was not to be
failed, though my father and I could stop it on Saturday.

✛

Today, New York time, my daughter dwells in the Factory. I
have no way to free her. This Saturday I'm bringing her from a
sleepover date to a gambol that will move to the Factory's whistle. My daughter's friend Viv has invited special friends to her
place on Fifth Avenue. Few things are harder work than a se-
lect party, even a children's party that admits poorer children
like my daughter. A corner of Viv's room is a miniature replica
of Pharaoh's temple at Dendur; its marble flooring is perfect for

jacks. My daughter has been invited as jacks champion. In the Factory everyone pulls his own weight. Hard. Even for young apprentices hard pulling becomes automatic, like breathing. You don't notice your own sweat.

In New York neither my daughter nor I need serpents to spur us to our labors. We don't require lions. We sweat freely without any such. Yet here, too, my Saturday is full of animal images. Instead of being carved in stone they are printed, archly, on polyester and subject to city sales tax. I am at the Aux Chachkas boutique, shopping for some highly strategic fun. On a New York Saturday all fun is calibrated by the Factory, in terms of cost, timing, and purpose. The invitation to the Pharaoh party asked both child and escorting parent to "come anciently." But I cannot appear with, say, togas when picking up my daughter at the sleepover; the sleepover friend should not suspect that our next stop will be a party (that is, a chic Factory-session) to which she has not been elected. Hence I'm shopping for an "ancient" thingamajig, something concealably foldable we can don after leaving the friend. I'm shopping for T-shirts with a primordial gag.

I never expected to stumble on my childhood in the Aux Chachkas boutique. Its shelves are heaped with cheap hip. Here you can buy your sophistication for a song. Six bucks will camp up the Stone Age—as does the T-shirt I finally choose. On its Dacron breast prehistoric art has been emblazoned. It is the famous running deer originally drawn in the cave of Lascaux. The loveliness of its shape prevails even against the psychedelic purple with which it has been daubed. Of course it

has a cute caption: THE FIRST GRAFFITI. It will have to do for
me. In that I will "come anciently."

For my daughter I buy a myth-joke: a T-shirt-within-a-T-
shirt. It shows a centaur harnessed to a plow on which rides an
Amazon splendid with bikini and cigarette holder. Both centaur and Amazon wear T-shirts in turn, both inscribed. His
says MALE CHAUVINIST STALLION; hers, JEWISH PRINCESS
AT WORK. So clad, my daughter and I will enter the cute
sweatshop of the party. But those two witticisms I have pur-
chased are not just cost-effective. I look at them while the
clerk writes out the sales slip. They exhale, unexpectedly,
whiffs of a genuine old paradise. The Jewish Princess bestrides
the plow in almost exactly the position I once rode my scooter.
And the running deer of Lascaux could be a cousin to the
rampant stag, my scooter's trademark . . . my scooter streaking through my Vienna Saturday. From those two shirts come
the breath of an afternoon when my father and I could still lock
up the Factory.

I know what I'll do after I spring my daughter from the pharaonic labors of that party. We'll still be wearing our T-shirts—
I, the running-deer one; she, the centaur-princess. We won't
be able to stop the machines. But we'll be out of that party and
we'll run into Central Park and try to climb a tree together. On
the topmost branch we might be able to glimpse a valley
beyond the Factory. We might spy the village of Duna Serdahel as it was the minute before the whistle blew it to pieces.
Don Quixote—he with his armor as preposterous as our T-
shirts—didn't he see something like that, for a moment, dangling from the highest point of a windmill wing?

❖

The No. 18 bus is an oblong, panting, snooty scarecrow. It snubs some thirty of us at the bus stop. Whiskey advertisements cover it like a rash. It chokes out diesel coughs while squatting on four splayed-out wheels. The splintered glass snout is clenched tight against us. Not that the No. 18 is a beast. It is not alive. On the contrary. Being a bus, it is the perfect machine: marvelously addictive and hence poisonously indispensable. I need it to get to my daughter's sleepover on the East Side. But I also need something supremely unmodern to sustain me against it. Out of my Aux Chachkas bag I pull the T-shirt with the running deer. I try to ignore the caption and the coloring-in; try to drink in the grace of it, the flow of its shape. And I remember Roger Fry.

Roger Fry, art critic, curator at the Metropolitan Museum of Art in New York, saw such cave pictures as a kind of specific against latter-day ugliness. With his eyes I see the running deer as an anti–crosstown bus. Roger Fry thought these cave-wall images had a truth surpassing that of any painted animal in any museum. To him this deer was perceived with an immediacy impossible for our much sootier senses. The motion conveyed by Paleolithic painters, he said, "is seen by us to be true only because our slow and imperfect vision has been helped out by instantaneous photography."

Nostalgia literally means the pain caused by one's absence from home. As a rule this is a home we never had. If we had

ever had it, it would, even after we'd left it, abide in our soul; then its absence wouldn't be so total and so painful. Standing before the No. 18 bus, brooding over Roger Fry, I am a helpless, shameless, rabid, rapturous nostalgic. Backwards I long, back beyond my scooter years, even far beyond the two centuries during which my family rusticated in Slovakia. In the crosstown wilderness of Manhattan I long for the home I never had. I long for grass bent by hooves thirty thousand years ago, the green blades through which the deer ran.

This deer brings home anthropology's subversive moral. It's a moral pointing to the inner destruction which accompanies the outward streamlining of the Western enterprise. Though this moral has enjoyed moments of raffish vogue, most of us are not in a position to think it through. We can't afford to let it affect our daily business. For the last ten thousand years too many of us have made a living, in one way or another, by making life ultimately less endurable. In too many of our jobs we work at next year's model of occidental civilization. And next year the growth curve must rise together with the bacteria count and the stress factor.

The moral of the deer, then, renders absurd progress in general or any metropolitan bus stop in particular. The moral lies in the difference between us and the man who drew the cavewall deer. He enjoyed seamless intimacy with every breath and stir of life around him. He knew so intimately the rush of the deer's limbs, the tang of its meat upon the tongue. Above all, he knew the group-warmth, the excitement of being at one, moving at one with his fellow hunters in the sacred commu-

nality of the chase. Along with true joy, such intimacy is long extinct in us today. It lived in him.

Important: he was no artist. He drew with no "creative" cunning. His charred stick against the wall moved and limned spontaneously by way of a ceremonial of which the actual pounce of the hunt was just part. He had no idea of esthetics. Esthetics are a recent middle-class science responding to alienation—to the estrangement between the pleasing and the everyday. No, he performed the kind of everyday magic possible only before the advent of the Factory, when the world was whole.

✣

While the crowd still waits for the bus to open, I put the deer back into the Aux Chachkas bag. If the others heard my thoughts, they'd tell me to go sing my naïve ballads elsewhere. But it's their space-age naïveté which assumes that cave art was just nice, primitive caveman stuff. If the others were able to see the deer unnaïvely, they might surmise something quite different. They might recognize not only that the deer was drawn on a day fresh beyond our imagination, but that this freshness lasted longer than our own age has so far. To the majority of human generations, home has not been the likes of Broadway and 86th Street. They lived in the hunting village for many hundreds of thousands of years. The village lasted so long, perhaps, because it stayed so small. In it every one of us recognized the face of all the others. Here we were still to-

gether. The activity we now call Art was a spontaneous expression of the impulse we now call Religion. Art was still dissolved unselfconsciously into the rite that joined a man to men, and men to something higher. He who drew the deer invoked his unison with the prey as well as with comrade hunters all moving in your-face-my-face concord. Directly or indirectly all shared in the continuum: drawing the deer on the wall, mythologizing it, stalking it, spearing it, skinning it, roasting it, distributing its delight to peers and higher spirits. . . . The communality of the chase embraced all those things later separated by Factory clerks into a) food production, b) church religion, c) gallery art, d) encounter therapy.

"Man," said the anthropologist Lionel Tiger, "is a creature evolved for living in bands of fifty." The reason why the Japanese economy works with such smoothness and efficiency, says the sociologist Kurt Singer, "does not reside in the rationalized perfection of its mammoth organizations, but in the dense tissue of its small society relationships." "When a plant starts edging toward fifteen hundred people," said the president of Motorola, "somehow, like magic, things start to go wrong." Voter alienation has increased because (as Byron Shafer writes in the *Journal of Law and Politics*) "local political parties, racial and ethnic associations, neighborhood groups and others . . . no longer play an important role. . . . That role has shifted to professionals operating on the national level." They ordered these things better in the Pleistocene underbrush, those happy few, chasing deer.

✤

Inside the crosstown bus—still empty and immobile—the driver keeps the door clenched shut, and lights a cigarette. Outside, I hymn the Noble Savage. Of course the Noble Savage is, like Santa Claus, a fantasy of us Factory menials. And yet the term is not quite a misnomer. The Savage was noble all right, in the early, forgotten meaning of the word: *nobilis*, meaning well-known. Every Paleolithic hunter was well-known to everyone else in his horizon. All his fellow villagers were well-known to him. Compared with today's world, his was a coziness of familiar eyes. And that's just why he wasn't savage. During our million years as hunters, one settlement might skirmish with another. Yet, by and large, hostilities were not lethal but ritual, like the abduction of the exogamous bride. Organized slaughter remained as rare as internecine murder. Hunting then was much more peaceful than shopping today. Then, in the "jungle," we had a joint venture of companions, mutually familiar and mutually ceremonious. Today, in the A & P civilization, humanity has been diminished to a sullen anonymous checkout line where each envies the stranger ahead, suspects the stranger behind, boils at the slowness of the cashier, resents the prices, distrusts the packaging, smolders alone in a sea of misgivings. None of us knows the others. We are all ignoble. It's the way of the Factory.

We are all ignoble, and at the bus stop everyone is far away. There are three buses by now, three oblong eyesores smeared

with whiskey ads. We are waiting not only for the opening of at least one door by one driver. We are waiting for some nearness to happen. We are not near to one another, we bus-stop waifs, no matter how closely packed we stand. Not near enough for one of us to complain to our neighbor. We're all frozen into separate, stranded selves, each one shrouded alone in diesel fumes. How did it come to pass, this decline from the deer's warmth to us lockjaw zombies far away on the crosstown curb?

All I have for a resort is my introspection, and the impulse to slap my Aux Chachkas bag against the bus door.

Smack.

A snicker at this from somewhere among the statuary of the crowd; inside the bus, the driver yawns and lights another filter-tip Kent. My *smack!*, though not particularly productive, was at least symbolically right. The bag contains the secret that reduces cave to crosstown bus stop. After all, the bag holds also the other T-shirt, the one for my daughter, and this one displays the tool which did us in. I mean the device to which the man-faced horse is tethered and which the Amazon rides like a scooter. I mean the plow. The plow produced a wealth of yoked centaurs and frantic princesses. It fathered all the ingenious, tortured monsters of progress.

Never mind that the plow is the heart of farming and that among the asphalt dunes of Broadway, "farm" suggests a last enclave of freshness. Never mind: the first furrow in a clearing was the initial wrinkle of degeneration. The long, treacherous progress to the bus stop of zombies began with the plowing of a field.

For the hunters, the chasing of the deer was as exciting as

the eating of it together. Both acts composed the same communal arc, the same collective joy. But with the plow, the first
bisection of life was invented: monotonous effort here—mere
gorging way over there. The solitary plower drudged away on
behalf of the nearly invisible seed. He dug, planted, ground—
nothing but flat moil. Then he waited. Then he milled and
baked. And then he ate. True, he ate more, and more reliably,
than the hunters did at their less regular feasts. But he ate with
less ceremony and less community. He ate a lonelier, grayer
abundance that would one day become the sad cornucopia of
the supermarket, so plastic and so futile. It was in agriculture
that the instincts of the Factory were bred.

The hunters lived, lunged, consummated in the gregarious
instant. The plower sweated in lone postponement; he heaved
and strained for an abstraction, for the crop that is not yet. His
harvest might be copious in the end. It might feed him for
much longer, but it was also more arduous for body and soul. It
was not blessed with the spontaneous savor of the hunters'
feast.

✤

In the bus the driver turns the pages of the *Daily News* while
he keeps the door closed against us. And from the throng of us
excluded ones explodes a blast—Rolling Stones clangor from a
portable. An outcry at the heartlessness of the controller of the
door. A scream against indignity. The bus driver just blows an
oval smoke ring. To passers-by we are a familiar sight: yet

another catatonic congregation forsaken by its priest and wailing in vain through some wired mouth.

The hunting village would not have understood our bus stop. Hunters knew trouble and sickness. But they didn't know toil nor habitual desperation nor routine estrangement from their Higher Spirit; that is, from Him Who controls the door. The sacrifice which hunters offered to their Higher Spirit was almost comradely. They roasted part of the animal for themselves, and burned the rest for Him or poured out the blood for His consumption. It was a sharing.

But the plower took the first step toward the bus stop and its angry abasement. He no longer dared divide his feast with Him the way a junior partner would with a senior. Instead he surrendered food as tax demanded by a choleric overlord. "We can affirm," said the orientalist Robertson Smith, "that the idea of the sacrificial meal as an act of communion is older than sacrifice in the sense of tribute, and that the latter notion grew up with the development of agricultural life."

The coercion boiling in the word "tribute" is important. The plower had to push and push and push the plow blade through furrow after furrow after furrow. He would not bend his back to wearisome rote unless driven by an exacting king, by a rigorous godhead. The plower made his offering to a Deity Who was too peremptory to permit inferiors at His table. This God ate alone and He ate every shred. The plower, a fearful, resentful, sinful toiler, submitted his grain to appease a wrathful, jealous all-consuming God. And, of course, his God accepted nothing but a *holocaust*—that which is *wholly burned*—nothing but the sort of drastic homage that finishes entirely in

ashes. There was no holocaust, no real war, no large-scale systematic slaughter until the plower's anger and fear. Only the plower's storable grain could feed soldiers: those professionals of fear and punishment. Only a surplus of storable grain could maintain a class of non-working slayers. Two pre-eminent historians of religion have been struck by the same contrast: "the childlike spirit of the mythology of the paleolithic hunt," on the one hand; and, on the other, "the horrendous myths and rites of the planting cultures." And so the evil clustering at this Broadway corner has a long genealogy. Listen:

Abel was a herder and a hunter of animals. Cain tilled the ground. He plowed. Cain brought the fruits of the ground, the holocaust, as an offering to the Lord. Abel brought the firstlings of the flock and the fat thereof. And the Lord had respect unto Abel, but unto Cain and his offering he had no respect. And the Lord said unto Cain, the plower, Why art thou wroth, why is thy countenance fallen? If thou doest not well, sin lieth at the door. . . . And Cain rose up against Abel his brother and slew him. . . .

Still, in those days the Factory had not yet begun to cover the continents. Cain's earth was still better than ours, pitted as ours is with bus stops. In those days Cain was still the only man who was not his brother's keeper. It was his singular lack, his unique stigma before the world. Today the Cains are legion. The No. 18 bus has opened its doors at last, and we, the waiting crowd, have finally become aware of our brethren, by way of muted fratricide. With subtle virtuoso motions we are fighting our neighbors, we are shoving and elbowing deftly in the crush by the entrance, kneeing and jostling to be the

first ones in. Not keeping our brother is no sin today. It's our democratic bag, our red-blooded with-it way of life. What ambitious Factory hand wants to keep the competition? Being Cain constitutes our deepest ethic and gets us bus seats. We have become so civilized that we are more adept at contending against each other than talking to each other. Being Cain is where it's at, man, uptown or down.

But before Cain became just anybody, he turned into someone very special. Before he multiplied into millions of mean hustlers, he attained extraordinary distinction. He started as a "tiller of the ground." In English "till" derives from "tillian," Anglo-Saxon for "strive." Therefore the phrase in the King James Bible is not just translation but implication. As the one willing to kill for strife's sake, Cain became *the* arch-striver. His mark, Cain's mark on the forehead, stood out as an ensign recognized as royal in the end—the crown. Cain waxed to Pharaoh, King of the Tillers.

Pharaoh, being Cain, was set apart from humanity by divine decree. By divine decree Cain must not be touched. The mark on his brow announced that he was inviolate; beyond ordinary death. Cain's unique crime led to heroic accomplishment. "He builded a town," reports Genesis 4:17. "He tried to immortalize his name by means of monuments," says a midrash. "He introduced a change in the ways of simplicity wherein men had lived before and he was the author of weights and measures. And whereas men had lived innocently and generously while they knew nothing of such arts, he changed the world into cunning craftiness." His descendant Tubal-Cain "was the instructor of every artificer in brass and iron," says Genesis 4:22. No

great surprise this, since in Hebrew Cain means "smith."
Cain-Pharaoh founded the Factory I cannot close today.

Cain-Pharaoh was the first manufacturer. Manu-facturer.
With hand, he made. More precisely, he made with hands not
his own. Pharaoh started the Factory employing others' fingers,
fingers without number. We, inside the bus or out, are the
countless offspring of countless such fingers. How did Pharaoh
get so many? He recruited them from the hunting villages,
which had lasted for so long, and from the plowing villages,
which were newer and angrier. Their hands served him because their stomachs had grown dependent on his governance.
His deployment of canals, ditches, embankments tamed the
unruly earth into obediently productive soil. This system
worked best over an area that was royal in size, administered
through the centrality of a capital. It could be supervised best
by a chief engineer of divine provenance who wielded all the
regalia of supremacy including those of murder. With his great
killing, striving might Cain-Pharaoh welded the villages together into the agro-factory.

✛

The bus, having taken off, is towing a daredevil. Not just a
daredevil—I watch him from the rear window—but a candi-
date for Pharaoh. Superfly has hooked a baling hook into the
tailgate of the bus and lets his three-wheel delivery wagon be
pulled pell-mell over potholes and manholes, across town. I
know his name because on his wagon a golden legend has been
sprayed: SUPERFLY SIR JUAN WOW!

Does Sir Juan Wow! know about Cain's high career? I'd imagine it's not particularly his bag, this brooding about Genesis, Chapter Four. But probably his blood understands Cain's anger and audacity. If he's not read it in the Bible, he's seen it in the comic books or watched it in the movies. It activates the basic Judeo-Christian scenario: the nobody, the nothing, who in the end can do everything; the outlaw who alone can found a city and assume the crown; the Cain who becomes Pharaoh; the outsider, the peon who becomes Numero Uno; the disgrace who finds grace; the pariah who will rule and save.

I watch Sir Juan Wow! from the rear window of our bus, our rolling cage of zombies. I watch him soar on a delivery wagon turned rocket; watch him break the traffic laws, listen to those heavy tricycle wheels clash like cymbals across road cracks. I watch his majestic hand-waves, only half playful, with which he rewards imaginary ovations left and right. Yes, five thousand years ago someone like him might have gotten away with forging the first Empire along the Nile. Someone like Sir Juan Wow! might have taken the village hunters, those painting, ritualizing, feasting congregations, and split them apart and chipped them down into ten-fingered tools detached from one another. Someone like him would have set those live tools digging irrigation ditches. He'd have made them pull plows, pile up stones as his, Pharaoh's, dynastic wedges into the sky, smelt metals into weapons. Out of agriculture's deep breach, out of the breach between effort and reward, between drab toiling now for the sake of drab gorging later, someone like him might have made a huge dominion and "builded a city." He would have reduced the great rhythms of the sun to segments of the grain-manufacturing process, to thermal phases of the

agro-factory earth. From the surplus of food so produced he would have supported all the nonproductive members of his priesthood, of his bureaucracy, of his army.

And, sitting in the crosstown bus today, I think that would have been all right with me. True, I envy the cave people before Pharaoh's time; being so much more intimate with life, they were no less intimate with dying. They were so much closer to accepting—and to ritually absorbing—the last cough of a sick man as part of the circular force which produced the first cry of a baby. And yet it would be all right for some Sir Juan Wow! triumphant to destroy this sense of Eternal Return that's possible only through the enactment of intimate, communal, your-face-my-face mysteries. It would have been all right for him to destroy the Eternal Return, leaving us at the mercy of Factory Time—that is, of the one-way moment that wrinkles and wilts and putrefies forever. It would be all right for him to scorch the evergreen village common and to fashion out of the burnt loam those solitary temporary utensils who must drudge and decay far away. It would be all right *if*.

It would be all right for Sir Juan Wow! to do all that as long as he went a step further as well. After all, the truly pharaonic thing about Pharaoh was not merely that he organized the Factory, but that he made it holy. He told his workers with a charismatic *wow!* what the sweat was for. Nobody can manage such telling today. We sit in the crosstown bus, being thrown about on some bottomlessly profane flywheel; we are in thrall to a Factory we cannot close and no longer know. Under the true Pharaoh the Egyptians did possess such knowledge. They incised it on the sovereign's great stones: THE KING OF UPPER

AND OF LOWER EGYPT IS A GOD BY WHOSE DEALINGS ONE LIVES, THE FATHER AND MOTHER OF ALL MEN, ALONE BY HIMSELF WITHOUT EQUAL.

ALONE BY HIMSELF. Pharaoh alias Cain was the first individual. He was the singular, transmoral, sacred outsider. He lived outside society and he reached beyond nature in order to reconstitute it as his workshop. He transcended weather, its floods and droughts. Through his myriad hands he devised a controllable, manipulable rain—a landscape of irrigating ditches. And he placed himself on the far side of mortality so that he could fight it better. With his infinitely fingered machine he raised up a gigantic rampart against death. The pyramid was his palace in eternity. He started building it the moment he started reigning. He resided close by; he kept his court in the shadow of his tomb. This great structure was his fame, the media which broadcast his rule over the afterlife. It was his manifesto to the populace, his proclamation that in there he would breathe again forever; and perhaps through him so would his people "who lived by his dealings."

✣

Breeeem!!! The bus has stopped at Columbus and 86th. Sir Juan Wow! has reached into his delivery wagon, hauled out, let go. Glass splashes in the doorway of Los Hidalgos Social Club. The bus jolts forward. So does Sir Juan, being still hooked to our tailgate. Forward he sweeps with a grin triumphant.

I notice no particular stir on the street. Everything is normal. Sir Juan has only done the necessary. Los Hidalgos must be a rival principality of Juan's. Thus they invite being wasted. Sir Juan, prince of his territory, cannot allow the existence of other realms to go unpunished. That bottle was thrown by a pharaonic reflex. The first dynasty along the Nile fired the first such missile. Since then the volleys have not stopped. It doesn't matter whether the front lines run between towering empires or between littered turfs of ghetto blocks. Supremacy is a king's duty and must be discharged without compromise at home or abroad. It might accommodate a truce, even a long one, but never a true peace. By the time Plato said, "Every city is the natural enemy of every other city," this sentence was a weathered platitude. The first surviving image of a city—depicted on an Egyptian palette—shows the destruction of a city.

❖

The bus halts well before our next stop. Why? Because in the rearview mirror the driver has discovered Sir Juan Wow! hooked into the bus's tailgate. The driver curses. This here vehicle won't move a goddamn inch till that animal back there lets the hell go. The animal, Sir Juan Wow! wearing his sovereign grin, will not let go. Meanwhile the passengers have found a bond at last: a common anger at that little spick. How does he get away with it? Why should he sport untouched past the Factory which beats the rest of us down? I, too, have

started to dislike him. If he keeps sporting and we keep stand-ing, I'll get my daughter to the party too late.

In a way, something like that happened forty years earlier on my Vienna Saturdays. It always happened the hour before I closed the Factory with my father. The market kids looked like Sir Juan Wows!—happy rogues on forbidden scooters. I kept watching them, fascination curdling to envy. I kept watching them, though I knew I must go on. The Factory, to which they seemed immune, kept me to a stringent schedule. High time to hurry away to the Hubergasse around the corner, into the syn-agogue before it closed its door. If I didn't arrive in time I would not get my Religious Attendance card; and if I failed to present the card to my teacher Monday, I would be penalized with a demerit. I would endanger my progress toward doctor-hood. I would not become somebody big, I would offend against the mandate of the Factory.

At last Sir Juan Wow! unhooks himself from our tailgate, gives us the finger superbly, pedals off on his regal tricycle. Our bus moves again. Decades earlier, on my Vienna Satur-days, I'd also finally manage to move once more, to tear myself away from the market kids. I'd reach the synagogue, running, just before it closed its doors. I got my attendance card. Yet I never had a chance to feel relief. I'd sit down in my pew in time to receive a cursing worse than the one the driver now flings at Sir Juan's back.

All of Rabbi Fluss's sermons were variations on the same polemic: we Viennese Jews had been living in treason for at least one generation. When our forebears had left shtetl for city, they had walked away from the Eternal. They had aban-

doned our faith and our folk-self for the fleshpots of the boule-
vards. And we young ones, sitting there in our gentile sailor
suits, we refused to show any sign of undoing the desertion.

I sit in chinos in the crosstown bus jolting fast to make up
for lost time, and I live with censure. Much of it comes from
within me, some from the outside. Yet Rabbi Fluss's maledic-
tion, still echoing from the Vienna pulpit, cannot hurt me in
New York. Today I know better. My forebears who left the
shtetl were, by their very act of leaving, orthodox. Orthodox
Jews in an ultimate sense, the way Sir Juan Wow! is, ultimately, an orthodox American. True, my grandparents abandoned their folk at Duna Serdahel. Yet it is equally true that
this act of rupture was profoundly Jewish. It was not a negation
but an expression of the Hebrew creed.

The arrow forged by the Factory six thousand years ago
started pointing outward and away in Mesopotamia. My grandfather only obeyed a call heard by the first patriarch. I ride the
crosstown bus with the Lord of Hosts resonating in my ear.

"Get thee out of thy country," the Lord had said to Abraham. "Get thee out of thy kindred and from thy father's house,
unto a land that I will show thee . . . and I will bless thee and
make thy name great. . . . In thee shall all families of the
earth be blessed. . . ."

In Mesopotamia Abraham had listened to the Lord. But in
Vienna Rabbi Fluss misheard Him. It is very Jewish to go forth
among gentiles, to strive abroad, to covet the fleshpots of a
strange land. "Hebrew," the old Semitic "Ibhrim," means "the
ones from the other shore of the river." In accepting Yahweh's
covenant to cross over into foreign soil, the Hebrews collec-

tively took on Cain-Pharaoh's burden. For the first time a
whole tribe moved to an injunction which before had distinguished only one individual—the one man who roams beyond
the pale, who crosses over and strives his way to the very pinnacle of the new territory. Before, it was just Cain-Pharaoh
who had left the familiar, the natural, the touchable, the
peaceable, the comfortably bounded. Before, it was just he
alone who had left all that for an abstract and infinite greatness
("in thee all families of the earth shall be blessed . . .") ordained by an infinite and hence invisible God.

But now it was all the Hebrews, all those "from the other
side," who together became the outsider-nation. They were
conditioned for the role. The animators of their history were
outsiders: younger brothers and barren wives, ordinarily deprived figures at the outer margin of the clan. Yet each broke
through into centrality. Among younger brothers—dispossessed by the very date of their birth—it is Cain (not the
older Abel), Isaac (not Ishmael), Jacob (not Esau), Joseph (not
Reuben), David (not Eliab), Solomon (not Adonijah) who provided the dynamic legends. And it is the women with "shut"
wombs (Sarah, Rebecca, Rachel, among the matriarchs; the
mother of Samson; the mother of Samuel; even the mother of
John the Baptist in the New Testament) whose tardy progeny
redeemed them in the end. The younger brothers overcame the
laws of inheritance. The barren women transcended nature's
edict by conceiving in old age. All these stories educated the
Hebrews in puissant outsiderdom; equipped them to leave for
the outside, for the river's other side; primed them to master
the beyond. Israel was God's chosen outsider-nation just as

Pharaoh was God's chosen outsider-son, outside the commonality's limits and sanctions, outside the earthly seasons. And so the small nation of the Jews consecrated itself to the labor of greatness, just as Pharaoh, one finite man, claimed the boundless scope of infinity. Israel became a hallowed nomad, a singular and martial warrior, as Cain had been a taboo and dangerous wanderer; as Cain-Pharaoh, holy and solitary— ALONE BY HIMSELF—kept burnishing and improving and expanding the kingdom he had wrought.

My grandfather was an outsider who went and strove in a strange land. My father built on his labor. I renewed the effort on another continent, an effort aiming at greatness more vainglorious than the land's fat. Riding the crosstown bus over ground on which I was not born, I operate the Factory between my temples, a writing wheelworks built of a language to which I am not native. It must grind out fame, my bigness, my doctorhood writ large. On the newsstand at Central Park West I see the Sunday sections of the *New York Times* heap up, as they do on all Saturdays. Will some page print my name? Will it say *Sir Frederic Wow!* . . . ?

✢

We may not know it, most of us in the crosstown bus, but one reason why we are such jolted, pale-souled sufferers in transit is that we miss Pharaoh badly. He is no longer with us, everybody's mother-father through whose dealings we can live. Our orphanedness started with Israel. The Hebrews had to live and

strive by their own dealings, not just through their leaders. They had many fallible captains; never one all-sheltering Pharaoh. Even the greatest of their princes were flawed in character or accomplishment: from Moses who was not allowed into Canaan; through the sins of David, through Solomon's vanities; down to the last doomed post-Maccabean satrap under Caesar. In Israel it was not the anointed monarch but the chosen people who must struggle under the burden of perfection. The Hebrews, quintessential outsiders, must hew a homeland out of hostile earth, must construct their righteousness nail by resisting nail. Must, must, must, all alone.

On the crosstown bus, the fatigue on the passengers' faces is Judeo-Christian. We are all toiling in the same orphanage, parentless on earth and, because of that, doubly possessed by God. Our hard labor is *imitatio dei,* the imitation of God.

On this bus, as elsewhere in the West, we are all imitating the God of our civilization. Yahweh created the world under working conditions grittier and more rigorous than those of any other cosmogony. Other Near Eastern religions show the universe born of monsters' duels and titans' swashbucklings, of volcanic adventures and stellar quests, of the inter-incandescence between deities, of copulations that heaved mountains and valleys into being. Yahweh, however, did the job as the Workaholic Supernal. He buckled down to it in unremitting, solitary toil. He assembled the world in Factory terms. Each time He had completed a part of the product, He stepped back to see if it was good—He was His own quality-control department. For one hard work week He created away at a masterpiece of majestic drudgery.

His people, made in His image, must match His productivity—His output of the unflawed "good." There must be no sagging in their pursuit after absolute piety. But they had a problem: they were flesh. Flesh needs to be tempted into holiness. And Yahweh knew how to tempt with the proper incentive.

After all, He was the God of the gratification-postponers. He was the Lord of the nomads who kept wandering and fighting in hope of Zion. Later He became Lord of the plowers who must sweat before they may harvest. Later still He was the God of workers that stoop and push for wages to come at the end of the week. He is the God of the crosstown passengers today who stick it out and bite the bullet overtime because there's got to be someday, somewhere, that little pot of gold.

And way back then, near the Factory's start, Yahweh held out a paycheck of unprecedented size. He released the kind of hope among his people nobody had experienced before: hope for a glory richer than Pharaoh's empire, for a satisfaction the hunting village had never known or needed. "I will do such marvels," he said in Exodus 34:10, "as have not been done in all earth or in any nation."

A promise tendered before to Israel and to be repeated again yet more hypnotically, paternalistically, magisterially, in a series of covenants. These resembled a supreme industrialist's dealings with successive intemperate generations of employees dear to him. Nearly every new generation underwent new and necessary trials: necessary as penalty for violation of the commandments from on high. The scourge of Babylon? The Assyrian sword? Both acted as agents of the Lord's anger. Israel

kept falling short of the standards demanded of God's "peculiar treasure above all people." Israel had been chosen to dig and dredge and mine righteousness from the world's mud. "Be thou perfect," He had said to Abraham. Yet Abraham's people lapsed and became muddy themselves. They required disciplining. They suffered and recanted and made a new pact to be industriously observed. They gathered up new moral energy and were restored, for a while, to deserved expectations of Yahweh's "marvels." To help them He gave His faithful a periodic down payment on that tremendous field day in the future when they would no longer need to conquer or strive; when the earth would surrender its riches to them on the instant: "Every place where the soles of your feet shall tread shall be yours." As a foretaste of the age that would be no work and all celebration, the Jews were allowed to set aside their labors at regular intervals. God gave them the Sabbath.

His gift unyoked the Hebrews for one day from the compulsions ruling their week. Before the Hebrews, no other people had a Sabbath. No other people needed one. And today, in the crosstown bus, we sit, inheritors of the endless Hebrew chore of advancement and perfection, starved for a little ease, muddy and famished, fatigued. Our Sabbath is gone. The Factory can no longer be closed.

The Factory cannot be closed and the golem rises from his seat. He is on his feet, the harmonica in his mouth, the moment we jolt from the Central Park West stop into Central Park itself. I know my golem. He works the crosstown bus Saturdays, when the passengers are more affluent. They're off to do East Side shopping and there's more money in their purse for

him. He is a blind, bearded bus-musician. At least he's gotten up as such. He reminds me of the centaur on the T-shirt. There's a certain vulnerable animality to the blind, and, like the centaur, he has a Vandyke and wears a pendant. Only his pendant is a tin cup. With one hand he moves the harmonica between his lips; with the other he gropes wildly from strap to strap, feeling his way along the connecting bar. A dramatic sight. Certainly a good show. He lurches about to make the most of the long stopless ride through the park. His playing of "Sweet Molly Malone" is stopless too, and too fast, and yet somehow still lyrical and haunting. He staggers down the bus with his clacking cup and smoked glasses, playing extra loudly today as if to overcome the ill-will left by Sir Juan Wow! . . . *cryingcocklesandmusslesalivealiveohh* . . .

We clink our coins into the tin cup; but not really by way of compassion. We drop in dimes, but not as a thank you for the music. We do it as a bribe, a plea saying "Stop . . . enough!" Which is exactly why he will not stop; he cannot stop; this now is his chance to exact more clinks. . . . *SweetMollySweet-MollySweetMollySweetMollySweetMollyMalone* . . .

He is another pain added to an already burdened Saturday. And the thing that should be sweet in his mouth becomes a curse of the Sabbath that is lost.

⁜

The first golem in Prague had a sweet thing in his mouth, and he had a Sabbath. Rabbi Loew had built him as a marvelous manlike machine, able to take on all heavy labor, which other-

wise would have to be done by the city's Jews. But he could perform his chores only if the Rabbi slid under his tongue a slip of paper on which was written the mystic and ineffable name of God.

Thus the golem worked on behalf of the Jews. Every Sabbath the Rabbi removed the slip of paper from his mouth, so that he could stop working. A golem, too, must rest on the Lord's day. But one Friday evening, Rabbi Loew forgot. The golem kept working as the others went home. The golem kept working while the women lit the candles. The golem kept working as the men gathered to pray before the ark. The golem kept working harder and more furiously. His factory would not close. His huge body became inflamed with the loss of his Sabbath. He swelled into a size yet more giant. He raised his giant fists unto heaven. He turned into a titan running amok. He roared and reared before the synagogue and was about to smash it and the Torah into a thousand pieces—when Rabbi Loew rushed out at the very last minute. From that foaming huge mouth the Rabbi snatched the holy name of God. And then, at last, the golem could rest. His limbs crashed lifeless to the cobbles.

⁘

In the crosstown one golem staggers and blows into the mouth organ, and listens to the coin-clink, and staggers on. The other golems, us, jolt along with him, on the same bad springs, on the same sad rampage. Who'll take the slip out of our mouths? Who'll relieve us of obsession and replace it with holy rest?

Where is the Sabbath? The Factory speeds and jolts us on its mad moving belt, and jars our spines and works our limbs like pistons . . . we can no longer lock it up.

Yet once upon a time I could, in Vienna, with my father.

Not that it was ever simple. Locking up the Factory was each time something of a hairy thing. I was not sure we could do it until it was actually done. Gingerly I would begin my side of the endeavor when I returned from the synagogue's youth service on Saturday, after 1:00 p.m.

By the time I entered the Factory building with its lion-headed windows, all the workers had left. The great presses stood mute. But what I heard was never plain silence. In my ears trembled a lull before the brink. I felt all those machines were coiled back upon themselves, breathless. When would they let go and cough out their sledgehammer breath?

The imminence charged those Saturday seconds when I met my father. I didn't go to his regular office where, on weekdays, he dictated to his secretary or conferred with his foreman. No, on Saturdays I went to the more mysterious "Customers' Room," a sanctuary designed to receive out-of-town buyers— removed from the plant, from all grubby commotions, with green-leafed wallpaper enclosing an upholstered silence.

But I knew better. I knew that just here true quiet was uncertain, even unnatural. Here my father kept his confidential desk. On it converged invisible wires from every cogwheel of each machine. The desk's corrugated rolltop was open: I saw the various compartments in which lay compressed the future with its need to get our flywheels blurring again, our pistons boiling; the future with its demands for all the work yet to be

done to justify our chosenness in a strange land, to redeem our desertion of the shtetl against which the Rabbi had thundered.

At the desk my father bent over papers that programmed all our tasks ahead. I knew which documents belonged to which secret compartment. Often my father had shown me. There, the sketch book of designs for the shoe-buckle line to be manufactured next season; there, the price calculations whose lower margin aimed to win a bigger share of the market away from the competition; there, a cost estimate for more highly automated lathes that would put us ahead of the pack; there, the blueprint of the new floor which would be built on top of the existing plant next year, increasing its capacity. There, the bonds that would pay for my medical studies a decade from now and for my bachelor flat near the university. There, other bonds that would finance my future professional suite in a style worthy of a rising young physician, a university-professor-to-be, famed for his surgical feats and research labors. . . . The desk held, in concentrated form, the sweating schedule of the Factory for tens of thousands of hours of work to come.

Toward this very desk I walked. I laid on it my school satchel. That is, I deposited the record of my own latest contribution to our family effort. Inside the satchel were my test marks of the last six days. Now they had to be submitted to parental inspection. Had I done well enough in my preliminary toil to qualify for the more elevated kind later at the Medical Faculty? Was I grinding my way properly toward bigness? Had I obeyed the Factory's mandate this week?

Every Saturday my chest contracted as I put the satchel on my father's desk. Every Saturday my father put his hand on the

satchel's thong. "Shall we have a look now?" he would say.
Every Saturday I took a reckless, hopeless deep breath and
shook my head. "Or maybe tomorrow will do as well," my father said. (He returned to his office even on Sundays.) I nodded with my eyes shut tightly. "Well, in that case," my father
said. And then, every Saturday, he amazed me anew. He
closed the rolltop desk over those inexorable papers and even
over my satchel, the satchel which—though I no longer
touched it—stung my nerves.

Yes, my father actually rolled down the rolltop with a defini-
tive thunder, followed by the hissing creak of his key turning
the lock. Those motions, those sounds were the beginnings of
our approach toward the Sabbath.

But we still had before us a complicated journey. My father
still had stiff weekday eyebrows as we walked down the cor-
ridor. Our steps echoed into the Factory Hall itself. Its immo-
bility always struck me as a frozen ambush that could thaw and
pounce at any moment. The rows of lathes and presses with
their hard angular limbs; the spindles, the screw-handles and
pulleys; the webs of transmission belts and the huge wheels
soundlessly towering . . . they all composed a giant body
whose fierce tangle of organs now lay in a state of macabre
arrest. We walked through a quiescence not to be trusted. Our
footfalls sounded in a landscape of petrification, not of repose.
The Lord's day had not entered this sooty hall. Not at all. Not
yet.

But my father began to change that. He began to smuggle
the Sabbath into the Factory. First he went to the Electroplating Room with its acid tanks still foaming, its corrosive odor

and its endless shelves of raw tin buckles needing to be bronzed for Monday's order sheet posted on the door. My father went to this door, and locked it. He locked away the acid, the corrosion; above all, he locked away Monday's coming. He locked away time, with its striving and strife. And he let me join in the locking. I was permitted to do the second, conclusive, turning of the key. Then we went to the Dye Room whose ether solvent pinched my nostrils and flooded my eyes. Fat vats of dye stood here next to enormous barrelfuls of brass eyelets which must be colored and wrap-ready by early next week. All that we locked away. We turned the key on "next week." We shut in the "must." Then we went on to the Soldering Department: smell of molten lead, blackened gas torches, high heaps of brooches that had to be fused with as many tens of thousands of brooch clips for delivery in Sweden before the first of the month. My father explained the reason for the deadline. And he grinned. Grinning, we put the deadline in a dungeon by putting between it and us the heavy fireproof door—locked twice, first by my father, then by me.

All that locking-away, my father had once explained, was demanded by the insurance companies. Yet I knew the other, still better reason. I could read it in my father's eyebrows. They had loosened into an easy curve now. He was whistling. He had begun to turn off the various motor switches by the foreman's desk. He turned off the gas motor switch which was a heavy nightstick-like lever. He turned off the electric switches, which looked like clock hands on a dial. He turned off the diesel switches resembling gear shifts in a car. He was whistling more loudly. And I, without even asking him,

grabbed my scooter. I snatched it from where it leaned against the door leading to my father's "regular" office. The scooter was perpetually parked there to keep my passion for it under control. After my homework was done on weekdays, I could pick it up here, ride it for thirty minutes—no more—and return it. Now I rode it beyond time because time had been turned off by us with my father's key. I rode my scooter with supernatural voluptuousness because I rode it through the Factory itself. Magically I slalomed between the big machines. Those fierce iron creatures were dozing now and I, swiveling past them, I was their flighty dream. My father passed his hand over their cutting tools as over slumbering eyelids.

Finally, to clinch the stillness of the plant, we swung shut the great portal of the building itself. We locked each of its three locks—my father, the first; I, the second; my father, the third. And then it did all stop. Then we really felt it: the Factory, that mighty combustion engine which had built the twentieth century and kept building and pounding it into the twenty-first—had stopped. It had really stopped. It was no longer happening—not to us. Right now it had never happened. We were free from the claims of next Monday's process sheet. A yoke had taken wing and floated away from our necks. We had been liberated from the future. We owned this moment. Our Sabbath had begun.

And since we owned the moment, we owned our impulses. They were no longer wired to non-Sabbath strategies. We didn't just walk out into the street. We pranced. Or rather my father did, with me sitting behind his head. He carried me piggyback even though on weekdays he was too dignified for

that, and I a bit too old. But this was the Sabbath. He skipped, I floated around corners. He was my scooter, I was his baby, and the world was heedless play.

We skipped into the Cafe Hernalshof. Outside of Saturday afternoon the Hernalshof did not exist. Not for us, not for factory proprietors who must not only manufacture bigness but cultivate size. The Hernalshof was a café for the small, like some of our relatives.

My Uncle Joseph got up from the mended plush and lifted me down from my father's neck. The hands that stroked me had fingernails that were Saturday-magical with moons very white and nail-rims black from his cobbling, My Uncle Mischa hugged me, his kiss smelling of wine and glue, logically, for his job consisted of pasting labels on bottles. But the Sabbath shrugged away his job as well as the coarse discriminations of ordinary days. My mother came running. In the Hernalshof on Saturday she could buss me rabidly in public. Here there was no need to wear lipstick. Her lips weren't constrained into a non-touching pursing at my cheek. She could grab me and kiss me. And this was the day when she didn't have to produce a sensible midday meal. Here on Saturday afternoons she forgot fashion and laughed at waistlines. She ordered pancakes in heavy cream, the Hernalshof's most uncorseted dish. My father didn't ask for the London *Financial Times*. This was the *de rigueur* paper in coffeehouses licensed by the Factory. But now the Factory was vapor. It was part of the Cafe Hernalshof's Sabbath genius not to have the London *Financial Times*.

What the Hernalshof did have was cracked tarok cards. My father dealt them out, biting the enjoyable cheap cigar allowed

him only here. And me—I could state my wishes directly to the waiter without surveillance by my parents. I ordered coffee just because on other days I was limited to hot chocolate. I asked for chocolate tarts which on other days, but not on this one, caused pimples and provoked cavities. And I quite openly reached for the magazine called *Schöne Kunst*. Its pages featured ladies with earrings but nothing else, conversing, wondrously nippled, in artistic wicker chairs. In my life, only the Sabbath was capable of such apparitions.

I tasted, sipped, and looked. I was free with tongue and eye. Most of all I listened. Sound was the most important thing on my Hernalshof Saturday. I heard something not known at other times. I listened to my parents speak not High German but a language flecked with Hungarian and a little Yiddish.

"Get thee out of thy kindred and from thy father's house," the Lord had enjoined. "Get thee out of thy father's house . . . and I will make thy name great." But at the Hernalshof on Saturday the command was in abeyance. We got back to our own kindred. We came back into our father's house. We did not have to be great beyond the river. There was no need to be Sir Juan Wow! abroad. From strife in mighty exile we returned to the cozy village corner. At the Hernalshof we knew that the only peace possible is small-textured, sensuous, your-face-to-my-face. On worn coffeehouse upholstery we regenerated the shtetl.

Our Sabbath satisfied few of the Talmud's requirements. Yet it obeyed the law's primary intention: we celebrated, as we were meant to, reprieve and relief from being chosen to do God's work. Our Sabbath had, in fact, only one untraditional

aspect. Its length. Something always happened to it after two hours.

At the Cafe Hernalshof my mother was always stung, suddenly, by her wristwatch. *Four p.m.!* Time to go home, to bathe and dress! She mustn't stay one minute longer! If she did, she'd order more pancakes and would no longer fit her one skirt that was right for the Opera Restaurant tonight.

My father put out his cheap cigar. He must pick up a Swiss newspaper before the downtown kiosk closed. The rendezvous my parents had at the Opera Restaurant was with business acquaintances from Zurich. My father said he'd better get the Swiss lay of the land in advance. And I knew it was high time for me too. The moment would come when my father would again roll back the corrugated top of his confidential desk. Underneath he'd find my shame: the school satchel with the C-minus math test. I foresaw the stiffening of my father's eyebrows. I'd better apply myself tonight to the arithmetic exercise book I kept at home. I must display the new leaf I was turning. Perhaps it would appease my father tomorrow.

Tomorrow.

Tomorrow had come back into the world.

Suddenly the Cafe Hernalshof looked sleazy-lazy and sinfully small-time. Serpent-shaped ceiling cracks ran around its dusty chandeliers. One by one our small relatives kissed me goodby. "Goodby, goodby, Mister University Professor," said my uncle with the white moons and the black rims on his nails. He was teasing me a little resentfully. But he understood that we, my father's part of the family, were big. That we had to constantly enact and groom our bigness; that we had to defend

it by enlarging it; had to entrench and justify it; to nourish, vitalize, and rehearse it; to study, ornament, amplify, and exemplify it; to underpin, to re-earn, and to rework and refine this bigness of ours. We had won it in a foreign land, on the other side of the river, and we must pursue it further abroad, far from the tribal warmth of the Hernalshof. We must be off.

The afternoon had waned so fast. Something else was starting. Behind the lion-headed windows of our street, in the locked, deserted plant, shadows had begun to move with unmerciful precision. The Factory's ghost pulsed in our temples. As we hurried home, the future came down on us from a darkening blue heaven. Once more it fastened on our necks. The Sabbath was over.

✛

The Sabbath is over, a Sabbath begins. In New York a gaudy facsimile thereof waylays my crosstown journey, unfolding athwart the path of our bus. Two stoplights ahead, beyond thirty cars of stalled traffic, I see festive lights dazzling up. Neon-tinted shakos, high kicks of sequined boots, drums booming, French horns in full fettle, silver staffs floating atwirl. Campy epaulettes, gilt braidings, pennants and transparencies, celebrating the Puerto Ricans or the Polish . . . I can't quite distinguish which.

Our bus bumps closer into a better view. It develops that distinctions are immaterial. Nobody cares. Police barricades line Fifth Avenue to no purpose. The sidewalk is crowded, but

with legs that hurry, not with eyes that watch. There are no faces looking from the windows, just air-conditioners hissing. Doormen bend over ribboned packages to be carried into lobbies. Cops remain in tight conference with their walkie-talkies. Nobody pays much attention to the parade except drivers. That they do furiously. After all, they're being blocked. Horns curse in front and behind our bus.

The parade, on the other hand, needs no cheers for vindication. What will justify it in the end, what will authenticate it, is the truck riding along with a TV crew in action. The legend on the camera says *NBC*. Three letters that shed a future radiance, a transfiguring promise: tonight some ninety to one hundred fifty seconds of this celebration will saturate the network air between Mr. Clean and the squeezed Charmins. This bash will be a media heavy among media heavies. After that it will be certified as an event. Only after it has been broadcast will it have actually taken place.

No matter, therefore, if it isn't much happening here and now as a true jubilee with clapping throngs and a specific ethnic color. Here and now is local: provincial. Here and now is small potatoes. But, boy, tonight the parade's going to go national—top-Nielsen imperial—coast-to-coast prime time, and that's the only time that's big and therefore real. So what if right now, in local penny-ante time, the parade is just a bright nuisance and a noisy obstruction? Who gives a damn that in the crosstown bus the passengers shake their slob heads? "For Christ's sake," my neighbor says.

For Christ's sake. An outcry become curse which yet remains an outcry. Christ did arrive for the sake of a great march

gone wrong and requiring redemption. But he didn't arrive until the wrongness cried out to heaven. When those royal drums first started, way down at the Egyptian end of Fifth Avenue, the parade was still right.

"Come anciently," says my daughter's invitation to the party, winking with that arch nostalgia that's half-serious and suspects that way back there may have been a stretch of street when we weren't lost. In very ancient times the first flag ever carried in a procession was a representation of Pharaoh's placenta. Through his birth we were born. We marched behind it in true celebration.

"To celebrate" means "to find a place to frequent together"; that is, to establish a mode or site embodying our bond to others. "Pharaoh" means "him of the big house," and it was in and through his house and through his life that his subjects celebrated. That's why he was the one "by whose dealings we live, the mother and father of us all." He was the mode through whom we frequented together. He was the king of one country, of one language and one divine scheme. The parade he led didn't look for deliverance beyond the horizon. No need to justify it through some splendor later on. It was really and fully happening when it happened—still safe within the moment.

Unlike the crosstown traffic, history will not be stalled. That's the problem. Cain who became Pharaoh waxed yet greater into Caesar. No pageant was mightier than Rome or more productive. Gathering many tongues and nations, it marched from triumphal arch to triumphal arch. It was a mixed multitude, marching away from the countryside, which had become "provincial,"; marching away from their native selves; marching away from sundry pharaohs now become so feebly

local, marching toward the huge cities that were the true cosmopolitan Rome, marching toward their imperial working niches.

Tremendous drums in that cavalcade, less and less tune. Here rolled a pageant of legions, not of faces. Less and less could it speak or sing to other faces along the way. Rome's many millions could not frequent together. But they did mesh efficaciously, as cogs do in a wheelworks. That is, they connected with cold edges. Under Caesar, the Egyptians produced the wheat that fed the iron workers in Tuscany who produced the swords with which the legionaries defended Egypt. Egypt and Tuscany were departments in Caesar's factory; so were electroplating and dyeing in my father's.

In the bus, the golem with the mouth organ launches a sudden encore of "Molly Malone." Is he entertaining us while the bus is immobilized by the parade? His chords grate against the cawings of the car horns. Dublin's fair city fractures in dissonance with the Polish–Puerto Rican woodwinds. Rome must have blared like that under the later Emperors. That vast expeditious clangor broke down into cymballing gibberish.

Marchers through the *pax romana* began to suffer Hebrew pangs. With Pharaoh you worked and died under the protection of his dealings. During the early Roman republic every farm family was sheltered by the *lares et penates*, the household gods who were local and cozily numinous like the baalim of Canaan. But later, during the Roman empire, families drifted off their farms to swell the urban jetsam in the capital. And in that capital of conquerors Caesar recruited the gods of the conquered into the Roman pantheon—a motley of celestial field marshals that could threaten or dazzle but not shelter you.

What had once been the near, tribal earth turned into an imperial desert whose sands blew far across many nations. Latins, Gauls, Iberians or Greeks, rich or poor, orgiasts, pretorians, scullions . . . more and more denizens of the Empire found themselves far away, on the far shore.

They began to feel the famine of a diaspora. What had happened to the commons and the clan? Everything comprehensible and cherishable seemed to have drained away. Now they were citizens of a grandeur that was grand precisely to the degree that it was alien. Israel had been a nation of outsiders; Rome grew into an outsiders' empire. To be part of Caesar was to have crossed from the home side of the river into contentious infinity. In this endless, ceaseless arena of boots trooping, workers straining, gladiators slashing, there had to be a stop. There had to be a sabbath.

A special sabbath. An imperial sabbath. In size and intensity the balm and bounty of that sabbath-to-come must match the peonage engulfing the world now. This sabbath must be vast, for the Roman Factory had churned up so much of the known world. In fact, this sabbath must be beyond earth because all things earthly had been contaminated with travail and confusion. This sabbath must be a raising unto heaven. It must be a permanent sabbath, announced by a blessed convulsion, a sacred catastrophe that would be the sabbath's trumpet. A Factory so titanic must be blown away on all continents, with the blast apocalyptic.

The apocalypse is an "uncovering," a "revealing." From the window of my stalled bus I see a woman limping down the path to the park entrance at Fifth Avenue. Her gown, long and

somehow vestal, is torn at the ankles and ripped at the collar. She wears sneakers and a smudged nurse's hat tilted down on her black face. One of her arms ends in a catcher's mitt from which the stuffing spills. The mitted hand carries a bird cage without bird. On the perch where a canary ought to twitter is strapped a mute white doll with the face of an astonished clown. The woman talks at it fiercely as she walks. I think she is preaching it the apocalypse.

She is not a remarkable sight. At least no more so than many such in the city. Nobody pays much mind to her or the parade. One person, though, seems to laugh at her voice . . . a girl about twenty years old, ten feet above the ground.

I wouldn't have noticed this girl if the cage-carrier hadn't looked up for a minute. The girl sits on a low tree branch, laughing. Lightly she slaps her beautiful brown suede pants. On her shirt a strand of pearls heaves with her laughter. She keeps laughing after the cage-carrier has vanished. Steadily she keeps laughing at nothing, nothing and nobody whatsoever. Maybe she and the cage-carrier came for the parade and discovered—once again—that it was not a frequenting-together. It is not a celebration but a production. The Factory hums.

The poor live in New York for welfare. Some preach to caged dolls. Rich people live in New York for glamour. One of them straddles a tree branch, shaking and alone. "Glamour" is a Scotch term for "delusive charm." Two thousand years ago, Rome's glamour brought to the imperial capital rich and poor in the hundreds of thousands. The slaves had been brought here, abducted from their homes. Most slaveholders had ab-

ducted themselves. They'd left their country estates where greener strands had linked them to their possessions; where the system, though far from fair, had at least retained some saving mutuality. An overlord had related to his servitors through traditions transacted your-face-to-my-face. They had offered him the spitted calf. He had offered them the protective sword. These ceremonies had celebrated the very localness of their locality. When the local magnate left for the capital he left his anchorage for prestigious limbo.

In Rome he saw Caesar's face no more than he saw his slave's. All he could see was power, abasement, suspicion, and strategy. Invidious abstractions began to manipulate him and drove him against his peers. So the great Romans glistened against each other, courted Caesar's pleasure without ever finding their own, strove, groped, thrashed about in opulence vainly, without surcease. Rome's slaves were rootless, driven lackeys kissing the feet of rootless, driven parasites. Time had grown very late.

Caesar could reign only by making Rome's lateness bearable to Romans. His Coliseum was his people's cocaine. Its fanfares called the populace to the day's high. Everything that thrilled, resounded, titillated, tranced, was pushed into the arena. In the end nothing satisfied. Hunger could not be deafened. Nothing fed the famine screeching from that sea of throats. And so He appeared Who was truly bread. But if He had come to all at once, He would have come in vain. He would have been just another Caesar; another ikon blinding with universal glitter. He would not have relieved the need of hands to be touched, of eyes to be recognized within a circle no bigger than once cir-

cumscribed a campfire. He would have given nothing if He had given himself gigantically to the stadium's gigantic swarms. No: He gave Himself intimately. He fed a few hungry bleachers at a time. The apostles with whom He kept company formed a troop the size of a hunting band.

Christianity was born through the rebirth of the local. It was born in the *ecclesia*, Greek for "local assembly." From the roaring multitude, one small group after another would separate and tiptoe down into the catacombs. In the seclusion of the underground village, very late Romans became early Christians. They recovered their faces mutually. Your face restored mine; mine, yours. All wholeness must be small. The miracle came to pass through the *agape*, the love meal, shared in small conventicles, in hieratic caves not too unlike those where the running deer had been conjured. Here Christ's great coming could be ritualized. The old woman with the bird cage, the young woman in the tree, had they lived then, they might have met here. Here was announced the cleansing disaster, the Factory's destruction, that would make possible His Sabbath of Sabbaths.

✜

Forward—*voooom!* Our bus is on its way once more. The parade is over. The light is green. Naturally it is green too late. But in our bus's careening lurch, in this jolting and veering from one stop to another, there is more than haste to make up for lost time. There is anger. East of the park our driver has

become angrier than he was west at Sir Juan Wow! A logical progression, in a way.

Anger cumulates in our lives, saturates our culture. Anno Domini Zero we began with the imminence of Christ's Prime Time. The blaze of that expectation, that impatience, throws shadows into our dusty cubicles today. Our daily effort; our nightly let-down: they are an investment. They better add up to something. There has to be a pay-off in the end. There has to be the moment ahead when we will stretch out in some water-lapped warmth nobody can ever take away from us again. Only that moment is the way out of an endless maze of aggravations. Without that moment—wouldn't the maze be the vilest trap, unendurable, unthinkable? No, somewhere that grand poolside Sabbath has got to be waiting for us.

Its far-off glitter swells by contrast with the dulling of the immediate and near. The neighborhood is always running down. The day is always shot. But in the distance the Sabbath incandesces, taunting. The shine of it tickles our eyelids even as we sleep. We mustn't rest because any instant might be the one that's ripe; when we can make the leap to out there, to up there, to jackpot-land where the superstars are basking. Mean-time you can't slack off. You'd better keep working the maze. On your toes, baby, round the clock. The Factory can no longer be locked up.

My bus driver's lips move slightly, constantly, with silent curses. It's always the others that the Factory lets off easy. Not him. He's got to keep his goddamn shoulder to the wheel, even weekends when everybody else is having themselves a wing-ding, the Polish–Puerto Ricans parading their geek heads off,

gooking up his bus schedule, the West Side fatcats shopping themselves rich in the East Side, etc., etc. Each etc. bursts with another unfairness. The basic emotion of the late American is paranoia.

Like the rest of us, my bus driver is wasting his life at No. 9 Downing Street; while so close and yet so far, at No. 10, the smartasses are having champagne with the Queen. Out of some mysterious meanness the Sabbath always skips his house to bubble happily next door. The Sabbath even vanishes on him on his days off. The guys he liked to bowl with, they've moved out to the Island. The wife always wants to drag him to those sofa sales that always look so good on TV but that he can't afford. And when she drags him just the same, they've got to use the nigger subway because Junior grabbed the car. What will happen when his union gets him that thirty-five-hour week they've promised? He'll have gotten five hours more of the Sabbath that is not.

And yet this fight that's coming up between our driver's union and City Transportation—that's going to be his true holiday. Even the prospect makes his teeth flash as he slams the bus door shut at a mink-lapelled lady, her being just the kind that buys sofas by the bushel. The season of contract confrontation—those are the days when he can share and express and ceremonialize his feelings with his colleagues—his core feeling: anger. The strike is his celebrating, his frequenting-together, his *ecclesia*, his local assembly defending him against the imperial sonofabitch mass. It's his village altar where he renews his closeness with his buddies. He and they toil far apart while the buses roll and the Factory hums. But at con-

tract time the union local becomes their parish church. As the
strike bell tolls, they flock together to enact the only ritual they
can still enjoy—the typically contemporary ritual of resentment: the membership meeting with its congregational fervor,
the evangel of the negotiating committee, the antiphonal shouting, the solidarity of the resolutions passed, the comradeship
of the job action, the fraternal adventure of the walk-out, the
sociabilities of picketing, the sacrifice of no paycheck for the
cause, the deprivation now for the reward later—the faith that
is *us*, the Lucifer that's *them*.

A refrain runs through the seven o'clock news, on all channels: groups shaking their fists at the camera in an inexhausti-
ble series of various collective rancors. You just wait now; wait
till it's my bus driver's turn—his fists and his good buddies'.
There never was such shaking before. And once these fists of
theirs have hammered out their story on prime time, and those
bastard big shots *still* refuse to read it—okay, then that's it.
Then not a fucking wheel will turn—subway, surface, or anywhere. Then let's see the biggies put up their dukes. Let's
have a donnybrook, no holds barred, killer kung-fu, where the
whole goddamn city will go bust. Let's kick the Factory into
shambles. And *that* will be my bus driver's apocalypse.

✛

Meanwhile he's still late, of course. Not only late, but fouled
up, I see, by a lot of fresh kids, younger and richer than they
deserve. There's a crowd of them on 86th Street and Third

Avenue, by the Odeon Cinema. At least two hundred are lined up there before the box office, full of young punk energy and inherited boredom. They've formed a queue snaking right under the bus stop shelter and even into the gutter before meandering back onto the sidewalk. An usher shoos them where they belong, but after he leaves they spread right into the roadway again, out of sheer mischief. Do they care that the driver has to stop in the middle of the street? And get slapped with a ticket for impeding traffic? Of course they don't care. So why should he? He moves right up against them, braking at high speed, spraying up the puddles left from yesterday's rain. Good honest dirt splashes on their ritzy boots. They deserve it, too—spoiled smart-alecks, fooling and goofing on a movie line, while he's got to sweat to catch up with his schedule. He grins at them. They hoot at him. They flip joints at his windshield as he starts away.

Poor things. They are. He is. I am. We all—smart-alecks, bus driver and I—we're squirming against each other in the same bind. I'm staring at the Odeon Cinema as it dwindles in the rear window. That universal bind has crept onto the marquee where block letters spell it out in four words: THE FEDERAL RESERVE HEIST.

A fine title for a film because it voices a suspicion become traditional among us. We've been robbed. "Let us endure an hour," said A.E. Housman, "and see injustice done." A very central scam, a superior coup, has been brought off somewhere right under our noses and at our expense. Something big has been stolen. Let's not endure it. Let's not be poetic about it.

Let's rob it back. The bus driver, the smart-alecks and I—we resonate to the need to retrieve what's ours.

The classic movie plot echoes Yahweh's call to Abraham: go forth to the far shore of the river; go, search for the riches you deserve, which are withheld from you *here*, but which you can seize *there*. Take up the challenge of distance. Become the fighting stranger, become God's Cain. Prepare to be threatened, ambushed, rejected. Persist, survive, and the Lord gives you His pledge: you'll walk off with your prize in the sunset that greets the Sabbath.

Sheriff, underappreciated at home, has star pinned on him in new town. New sheriff stalks bad guys. New sheriff is cornered by bad guys. New sheriff outdraws bad guys. New sheriff lays them out in the dust. New sheriff is elected mayor. Or the same story in romantic costume. Boy, emotionally sterile with previous girls, meets new girl. Boy is defensively stiff. Girl acts defensively mean. Boy loses girl. Boy's vulnerability to loss charms her. Affections unlocked, boy "goes forth"—risks wild pass at girl. Boy wins girl.

This is the game plan of the Western faith inscribed in five daily showings on a hundred thousand silver screens. Of course, outside the theater reality has been getting out of hand. Here boy meets girl on a progressively darker street. He may bed her more easily and more baldly. But he loses her faster. Celebration has gone even from love. And so the boy's losing of the girl goes on and on. The winning recedes. Our time is late. Daily it grows later.

The movie industry has been trying to keep up with the lateness. Story conferences prune away at the nicey-nice fore-

play, at the celebration-become-corniness of preliminaries. Without the sense of face-to-face, all rituals, including the romantic, are good for snickers only. Prune that away. Put your money into late dramaturgy: pan in on the final crisis. Cut to the chase. Tune up the pouncing on the girl, the swooping down on the swag. Lay on the violence. Armageddon, swift and bloody, is what the caper film is all about. That's entertainment today—for the same reason that the man behind the bus wheel likes to entertain the idea of an all-out strike. Apocalyptic extravagance runs through our space-age dreams and daydreams. A growing number of American pop hits (a *New York Times* survey shows) present nuclear war as an ultimate fireworks that's inevitable and exciting. The Factory cannot be stopped unless we hold it up with some final machine gun. Fork over that Sabbath, Charlie. Before you know it, you'll be in itsy-bitsy little radioactive pieces.

Our bus driver leans to such fantasies. So do the kids. *The Federal Reserve Heist* will attract a Columbia sophomore especially if he has an upper-bracket allowance. His or his parents' checkbook can buy into a scene that has a lot going on. Yet he can't ever quite seem to get it together—into something to celebrate. There's an overload of activity, yes . . . but where is the action? Where the hell is the real fun? Somebody's copped it.

In word and spirit "festive" derives from "fane," or temple. When communality goes, so do the living insides of the temple. When we lose rite, we lose, sooner or later, spontaneity. We cannot improvise or exuberate in a vacuum. Our Columbia sophomore by the Odeon Cinema is young and therefore needs

to exuberate. But he stands in line on a very *pro*(outside) *fane*(temple) sidewalk, inching along in a very unfestive world. Where the fuck is the fun? His mischief at the bus shelter is bafflement stretched into aggression. He and the guys are having themselves a party. One thing about a party these days: if you want to enjoy yourself, you've got to know how to hack it. You've got to show 'em you know how to put that bus driver on.

Our sophomore knows. He has been educated in the aggressiveness discreetly animating our most common modern gathering: the party. The party exemplifies a frequenting-together that is a tournament. The more glamorous, exciting, the more pace-setting a party, the more rivalrous. No communal rites in this scene, only competitive norms; the kind, for example, that prescribe your phrasing when you want to maneuver away from your current conversational partner to a more strategically upscale constellation: "Be right back after I refresh my drink at the bar." The party is a jockeying of subgroups, all camouflaged in small-talk conviviality, all with a feral eye out for gains to be scored in sex or status from the clique in this corner, or the huddle in that. How do we know we've had a good time? When we've exploited every opening.

These commonplaces of hip socializing follow a pattern established in the Old Testament. The party consists of nomads from the other side of the river. Smiling, doing battle in leisure casuals, they are outsiders straining and drudging inward while goblets clink.

Our Columbia sophomore has seen the little sweat drops form on his father's forehead as the old man kisses away at cheeks. He's watched his mother pop Valiums to steady her

eyebrow pencil before the soirée at Regine's. As the Factory manager's kid he is susceptible to a suspicion he may never articulate to himself or to others but which will stain more and more of his moods: the suspicion that even those playing the Factory rules most cleverly will end up cheated. Cheated all the way. So let's do a job on those rules. An all-the-way job. Hey, let's pull a caper. At least, let's watch a caper movie.

There's a beautiful thing about the caper fantasy. The caper, again like the strike, features a campfire-sized camaraderie which has gradually grown extinct elsewhere, though our need for it remains exigent as ever. Cogwheels can't be pals. Faces petrify unless warmed by other human faces in human situations. There is no warmth, no *ecclesia* in working or studying or striving within the Factory. But there *is* warmth; there *is* ecclesia in working against it. There is family feeling. It's no semantic quirk that each Mafia unit ripping off the Factory calls itself a "family." The way to revive that long-gone gang of ours—is to become a gangster. Out of the nameless mass of the hyped and hassled rises a small, tough, knowing, mutually dedicated band of dudes sticking it out together. They're going to hassle the system back, man, all the way. All the way into the inmost vault with the best karats and out again into the getaway Ferrari.

The heat may track them down. So what? The gang has already stolen our Columbia boy's sympathy. Not merely the booty puts him on their side. It's the thoroughness and elegance of their rebellion. What if it were more than a dream? Maybe they've killed off the Factory for good. Maybe the whole country has been moved south of the border where there's *fiesta*

instead of Graduate School. Maybe after the big crunch it'll all be mellow. Now the big Sabbath can begin.

The Sabbath refuses to begin. Far from stopping, the Factory sledgehammers faster. My bus driver's distemper speeds his progress past trucks and double parkings. His impatience bears down on the gas pedal, vexation greases his reflexes. By the time he returns to the West Side he might be back on schedule. The apocalypt in him wants to disembowel the Factory. In the end, his fury—like yours and mine—only contributes to the product flow.

Item: the caper movie whose economics neatly reverse its story line. It couldn't entertain us so well if it didn't mock the values of the sweatshop to which we are yoked. Yet the profits from that mockery will pay for the expansion of just that sweatshop. The studio which made the hit will raise the net of the owning conglomerate by eight million. Smiles will light up the boardroom. The board, in turn, will spread the sunshine around into sundry areas financed by the umbrella company. There'll be more funding for more projects that will turn more faces into cogwheels, more conversations into computer printouts, more convivial street corners into automated shopping centers.

The board of directors is no conspiracy of villains. It only translates into large-scale methodical investment policy the compulsion which has, hitherto less methodically, stitched our culture together and which informs our very language. In the dictionary, "profit," "progress" and "proficient" are etymological cousins. In the boardroom they are a close-knit crackerjack team. After all, the board was elected to enrich

the stockholders by "developing" the world around them; that is, to process the world into more profitable, proficient and progressive units. The board would betray its mandate if it did otherwise. Therefore it uses the eight million earned by *The Federal Reserve Heist* to develop neighborly backyards into deadpan high-rises; chatty stoops into towering morgues; family stairs into elevators Muzak'd and TV-monitored and inhabited by lifeless masks of strangers.

Progress will be served. Progress will generate more sweat drops during cocktails, more Valiums at party time, more hunger of every hidden sort, more plain starvation in the tenements, more crack traded between garbage heaps, more with-it misery among the affluent young . . . and hence more of a ready market for the apocalyptic phantasmagorias shown five times a day, six bucks a ticket, at the Odeon Cinema.

In the darkness of the theater more audiences will applaud as the Federal Reserve gets heisted in yet another caper. The cash they'll pay to see the new film will help the Fed affiliates—banks, trusts, holding companies—heist the audience through devices much subtler than those seen on the screen. It's a perfect circle in which every asset becomes loot. Even the tax-sheltered chief executive turns into an ultimate loser, if only through his strung-out son. Since there is no longer any sense of belonging, nothing belongs to anybody anymore. Everything is up for grabs.

What we've been robbed of is much more than money. It's the precious possibility of the true Sabbath. Faster than ever the Factory hums. Once I could close it with my father.

✛

On Third Avenue a brontosaurus of a crane obstructs the street. Traffic must creep around it. Our bus has bogged down again. My fellow passengers don't much mind this time. Of course we have a whole new crop aboard. They've never been slowed down by the parade; they don't see the brontosaurus as delay piled on delay. But even veterans of this ride seem fascinated rather than vexed. All their faces have been pulled toward the side of the street where some machine has scooped out a hole the size of a lunar crater. It is so titanic and charismatic, this hole, that windows for viewing have been cut into the boardings that surround it. In front of them people actually line up, as though it were a free way of seeing *The Federal Reserve Heist*.

In a manner of speaking, it is. "Boy, that's going to be something," the man next to me says to the woman next to him. "But now they better fix up the bad side of the street."

Now "the bad side of the street" is a beautiful, slim art deco building with casements and a fine *bas relief* facade. It is also a carcass. Through its smashed windows sifts the dust of a gutted interior. Its entrance has been boarded up with torn-out room doors, and its walls peel with tattered posters.

I like the bad side of the street. First, it's not the side that makes me still later for my appointment with my daughter. Second, the "bad" house, even in its present straits, seems not only structurally hale but pleasing to the eye. Even as carrion

it looks better now than the monolith across the street will, after it has risen from that lunar chasm.

One hundredth of the financial verve which went into the funding of the new construction would have renovated the old house. One tenth of the municipal ingenuity—tax abatements, zoning variances or what have you—might have kept the old house alive. But the old house is of the here and now and therefore dross—garbage. The new house, being not yet, shines with preciousness. "The messianic idea," said Gershom Scholem, "has compelled a life lived in deferment." "Our life seems not present so much as prospective," said Emerson. "For more than three centuries," said Octavio Paz, "'American' designated a man who was defined not by what he had done, but by what he would do." "Americans love their country not as it is but as it will be," said the author of *Americans in Their Moral, Political and Social Relations*. He was an Englishman named Francis Grund, who traveled through the United States in the 1830's. In the 1980's Americans still love their country like that, but in more up-to-date, urgent language. Every politician's platform invokes the futurism of this love: "America is the world's greatest country as soon as we get rid of all the shit which holds us back now."

The shit is the disappointment in everything that exists already; in the results of everything we've tried for, so hard, so far. Everything that's fully built slides fast to the old bad side of the street. The greatness is tomorrow's landscape to be hammered out by piledrivers on the new, good side, in some better new neighborhood, in a new city or new state. Daily hundreds of thousands of living rooms roll away in moving vans, steered

by a messianic compass. The next stop has got to be the real thing. Or something a whole lot closer to it, for sure. Americans are the movingest people on earth.

The abandoned house on the wrong side of the street may have been architecturally comely and in "good" condition. Tenants resided here from the thirties on, at first with vitrines and cloisonné; later with conversation pits and Jackson Pollock lithographs; later still with op-art murals and Tiffany bud vases. People living here had enough money to reflect taste and fashion; that is, to furnish their rooms as display galleries for rat-race trophies, for the Factory's merit badges purchasable at Bloomingdale's, all discriminatingly nuanced, of course, adroitly decored, chicly arranged. The crosstown apartment tends to be an act of public relations, directed outward. It is not a familial site allowing those inside it to come closer to one another in ceremonies of intimacy.

And still each inhabitant must have been nagged by a certain hope: maybe he'll yet find what he has always found missing. He's worked so hard, maneuvered so assiduously, and still that something just won't happen. Couldn't he get it (together with a bit more prestige) by spending a little more? How about buying one of those "gracious luxury co-ops" like the ones planned across the street? He likes his apartment, of course; not as it is here, but as it will be, yonder. In Emersonian language he lives in it not presently but prospectively.

So he joins that pandemic vagabondage whose exploitation shoots wrecker's balls by the hundreds into the city's vitals. His disappointment is chronic. It's dynamic, too, because that hope of his keeps chafing inside it. This bruised, abused, stub-

born hope lies at the bottom of real estate speculation, urban politicking, demographic currents. His hope tells him that what he's had till now was just a dry run; just improvisation on the temporary side of the tracks. Wait till he crosses over and digs in. Just wait.

The future always makes a better neighborhood than the present. And on East 86th Street, on the blessed side of the street, the apparatus of the future towers glowingly. The workers flaunt their glossy hardhats like commodores' caps. Reverently the police usher all traffic around all construction machinery, even around the portable johns. Those are the same cops who ignore the litterbugs, the tidal trash, the turds left by dog walkers on the old bad side of the street.

Sixteen thousand years ago, the man who made the drawing in the cave lived in a moment so communally and ritually alive that it embraced many moments long gone and many more to come. The deer which he had hunted two suns ago and which he would hunt again; the deer his father had speared with other fathers, which his mother had skinned with other mothers, which his children would roast and his grandchildren eat . . . that deer flowed out of the charred tip of his drawing stick onto the wall into this instant now.

But then the hunter turned away from the gregarious chase and stooped, alone, to the plow. And any moment happening now declined into a mere, mean preliminary. I sweat now only so that I can feast later. I gorge now to gain strength so that I can plow more for a finer banquet still later. "Go forth into danger now, so that later the earth shall be thy footstool." Yah-

weh made official the servitor status of time present. Its inferiority became the premise of the Christian state.

"Americans love their country not as it is but as it will be." America, that quintessentially Western idea, is quintessentially Christian. Christ's later saints liked the world not as it was, but as it would be. As time passed after the Ascension, and the Savior delayed His coming, the devaluation of the Moment Now was divinely sealed. That Christ refrained from redescending showed how earth and earthly time remained unfit for His touch. The present was a mangy periphery in which iron rusted, lilies withered, flesh decayed, neighborhoods ran down. It was intrinsically unfulfilled, stunted; too far removed still from the exalted center beyond the horizon, behind a sun as yet invisible.

And so this agonizing insufficiency of the Now must be demolished, removed and rebuilt closer to the center of permanent redemption. The bad side of the street must be gutted on behalf of the good side. The Factory must be taken over, reassembled and relocated on more sacred ground. But the very reprocessing of the Factory was itself Factory work.

It was not work that could be done in the catacombs. The apostles ("the ones sent forth") must be messengers of His dealings to the Outer Now. And not just messengers but agents, even generals. They must fight His war in the squalor of that outer margin.

Fight they did. They left their pure small conventicles concealed below the crowd's grossness. They knew they could no longer shirk the Coliseum. They must engage the colossal. They went forth among the grandstands, purging the corrupted,

revealing to the besotted, preaching to the powerful. On their side was not only Jesus' ultimate supremacy, but the expendability of earth, indeed of all nature, vegetating as it did on the inferior rim of time. Earthly time, the fly-by-night present, was there to be stepped on, to leap up from . . . toward salvation. The earth was there to be ripped open and gouged deeply so that into the gashes could be driven the fundaments of His final temple. The expendability of earth sanctified Christian generalship. After they had erupted from their underground villages the apostles wore their halos like hardhats and marshaled themselves into the Counter Empire of the Church Triumphant. Quickly the *ecclesia* celebrating the moment became a troop obeying a future-driven hierarchy. The church triumphed as it abandoned *agape* for the bishopric, the love feast for the chain of command, the pastoral for the doctrinal, the charitable impulse for administrative strategy. The shepherds of its flocks hardened into the centurions of its legions. They subjugated Rome by becoming Rome.

They loved the world not as it was now, on the "bad" side, but as it would be later, after the battle, on the "good." Great wounds, demolitions, dislocations were—and are—surgery that must be suffered during the transformation from "bad" to "good." "We had to destroy the village in order to save it," said the U.S. officer in Vietnam. The statement summarizes our ethos. His civilian colleagues execute similar imperatives, recite similar catechisms, obey similar necessities at home, on East 86th Street, everywhere.

Those are the paradoxes of redemption. Somehow they don't console me for the slowness of my crosstown trip.

T WENTY MINUTES TO FOUR and I'm off the bus at last. At
York Avenue and 85th Street I jump off, jaywalk the
crossing to 85th, running about as fast as Christianity was Cae-
sarized. I was supposed to pick up my daughter at the slept-
over house at 3:00 p.m.

"Yessir," the doorman says.

"I'm going to Kahane's. Sixteen B."

"You expected?"

"Yes. I'm late."

"Go ahead. I'll announce yah. Yah gonna press it yourself?"
"Pardon?"

"We got computerized here. I can press that sixteen button
for yah from here."

"Oh. That's all right."

"That's for the strick Jewish gents in the house. So they
won't have to press the button Saturdays."

"I'll press it myself, thank you."

I should have known better. Elevators are no longer a handicraft in the 1980's. Now remote-control pressing is much more effective. I push the Up button with my own finger—and what happens? One elevator is out to lunch; no numbers light up on its indicator. The other diddles from the thirtieth to the thirty-first floor. Typical, when I'm late. I wait, brooding on all the typicalities involved here.

The typicality of the doorman, for example. He can't pronounce "strict" but has no difficulty whatsoever with "computerized." The further typicality of this being daughter's sleep-over building: with my encouragement daughter picked the girlfriend who happens to live here. I am a Jewish intellectual ruefully liberated from earlocks and phylacteries who likes his child to pal it up with an orthodox family. The typical ambivalence of covert de-assimilation.

And then we have the ambivalence typical of Judaism itself. On the one hand the Sabbath is its foundation, with the command not to move on the day when the Lord Himself stood still. Commit no action, the command says, don't even press a button that might propel you. Exclude during Sabbath services all prayers that are petitions, that is, requests for change from one state to another. Suspend for one day the Jewish burden. Forget the impetus to travel from the near shore to the far. Rest from the nomad's dynamism that is the Hebrew destiny. Observe the Sabbath by remaining local.

The Sabbath law, on the other hand, in no way diminishes the motion of the week's other six days. Here the chosen must move to the Lord's word to Abraham: depart, go forth and con-

quer. Extend yet further your control of the remote in all directions, stride on, reach out, grasp without cease.

A pair of contending orthodoxies. The scripture expresses both very early in the Old Testament. The Sabbath is so fundamental a decree that God pronounced it even before issuing the decalogue, even before Sinai. "Abide ye every man in his place," He said in Exodus 16:29. "Let no man go out of his place on the seventh day."

Only two chapters later, however, a drastic example of the reverse orthodoxy. In Exodus 18 a voice teaches the Hebrews a better, faster way of organizing their restlessness so that they might speed the journeys to which they are appointed. The teacher is Jethro, Moses' father-in-law. This Jethro business is so chilling under its surface solicitude, so disturbing, that I know it by heart.

"And Jethro, Moses' father-in-law, said to Moses: Why sittest thou alone and the people stand by thee from morning unto evening? And Moses said, Because the people come unto me to inquire of God. When they have a matter they come unto me, and I judge between one and another. And Moses' father-in-law said unto him, The thing that thou doest is not good. Thou wilt surely wear away, both thou and the people that is with thee; thou art not able to perform it thyself alone. Hearken now unto my voice. Thou shalt provide out of all the people able men, rulers of thousands, rulers of hundreds and rulers of fifties and rulers of tens: and let them judge the people at all seasons. . . . And Moses chose able men out of all Israel, and made them heads over the people, rulers of thousands, rulers of hundreds, rulers of fifties and rulers of tens. And they

judged the people at all seasons: the hard causes they brought to Moses, but every small matter they judged themselves."

I can't blame Moses' father-in-law for a delinquent elevator; it is still dawdling its way downward from the penthouse, floor by floor, down to my particular lateness. But Jethro does make me feel lonely as well as late. This troubledness of mine about Israel's conflicted orthodoxies: if I'd tried to bring the problem before Moses, surely I'd have been deflected to one of his sub-captains; to a ruler over fifties at best. It would not have been considered "a hard cause." Scarcely a matter relating to Israel's efficiency as a force traversing the wilderness. But Jethro's instruction had in itself resolved the conflict. Jethroan administration implemented the workday orthodoxy that says *Move on to conquer*; not the Sabbath orthodoxy that says *Stay and commune*.

Henceforth, when people came to the prophet to inquire of God, Moses would not have the time to answer in person. His captains would do it for him. They were the bureaucratic machine at the core of the mobile, puissant Factory. But of course they were *God's* bureaucrats. Their machine drove the chosen vehicle of Yahweh's call: drive on, ford the frontier river, and master the far shore.

In *Contrat Social* Rousseau found alienation in the very concept of governmental representation. "The People," he said, "are not and cannot be represented. . . . there is no intermediate possibility." In *Paths in Utopia* Martin Buber shakes his head over the difficulty of the idea of The State, "an institution in which a virtually unorganized mass allows its affairs to be conducted by 'representation.' . . . But what is representation?

Does not the worst defect of modern society lie precisely in everybody letting himself be represented *ad libitum*?" Now, Buber is my man in many ways, but on this I'd like to ask a counter-question. Why do you say "*modern* society"? Does that "defect" not date back to Jethro? Has it not continued and compounded ever since?

How Jethro troubles me on this late non-Sabbath Saturday in New York! He may be one of history's great insidious secrets. Long before becoming Israel's leader Moses took refuge with this same Jethro after slaying the Egyptian overseer. Already then Moses began to learn from Jethro, priest of the Kenites and father of the girl he took for his wife. Only during this sojourn did Moses' faith develop. The Bible records no prior religious thought, concept or encounter in the prophet's life. God spoke to him for the first time—from the burning bush— when he was keeping Jethro's flock. It was through Jethro that Moses was fired with the Lord's command to bring Israel out of Egypt, to make his people wander and struggle toward a remote Zion.

But who was this Jethro of the Kenites? His tribe's name harbors a clue: Jethro of the Cain-ites. He descended from Cain. In other words, he carried forward the Cainite aspect of Israel's mission, which is not much discussed in Jewish lore except, perhaps, through adumbrations of the mystics. In the cabala, reports Gershom Scholem, our foremost scholar in that field, "paradoxically many of the great figures of Jewish history are represented as stemming from the root of Cain . . . and as the messianic time approaches . . . the numbers of such souls

increase. . . . In the early cabala . . . Moses and Jethro are considered reincarnations of Abel and Cain."

Scholem does not explore the reasons behind this fact. To me they go to the crux of Jewishness—and don't seem so paradoxical at all. Cain was the arch-striver and loner, the armed vagabond among men, surviving through his very guilt, destined to beat iron into lethal blades and to build cities in far-off places. He heralded Israel's role as the striving roamer among nations, formidable-against-odds, failing God and yet preserved by Him.

Cain broke the bond with Abel. Unfettered, freed from brotherhood, he increased his power through mobility. Guilt sharpened his reflexes. Jethro did the same. He advised Moses to break the your-face-to-my-face bond of commonalty. Turn your villages into regiments, he said. Villages are for staying local and for communing. Regiments march and conquer. We will have an army organized with rulers over tens and rulers over hundreds, with sergeants and colonels, and we shall go forth out of the desert unto other nations: to storm their walls and to build our cities over the ashes of theirs. We may fail God because of the blood that shall mark our path, but in our failure He will preserve us.

Cain, with the crownlike brand on his forehead, lived on in Pharaoh and continued in Jethro and in the later Moses. He went on in David, in Solomon, in Rome's Augustus. But he came truly into his own when Christianity took possession of the earth.

It was Christ's promise of the *real* time to come, bringing *real* goodness, that gave theological resonance to the impulse

which had first moved Abel's brother. After Christ the way was cleared for Cainites much grander than Jethro.

Is the earth not temporary? Dross? Therefore it can and should be lacerated by the plow, tilled, gouged, striven with, beaten down and uprooted. Are men not fallible and brittle flesh? Therefore they can and should be expended like tin soldiers. Aren't all physical things inferior to the soul? Therefore they can and should be squashed, re-kneaded and manipulated toward the higher end. No present place is satisfactory. Therefore present places should be flung away, abandoned for future places elsewhere. In its burning insufficiency the world cries out for the strength that dominates, obliterates, sweeps on. It is the only strength that can jolt the world into regeneration.

The unity of dominion which the infidel Caesars sought to establish over diverse subject peoples—that unity the Caesar of the Faith found. His name was Constantine. Only after Christ did Rome's sundry nations become ecumenically unredeemed and thus ready for stringently efficient domination. Constantine, the first Christian Emperor, perfected the most centralized despotism in Roman history. He conquered in the name of the cross. In the spirit of Cain he reigned. He cast uncounted villages into the crucible of salvation, to lift them out again as uniform regiments.

Out of the Factory's travail the new faith was born. Soon it developed new techniques with which to tolerate yet harder labor. For a while its machines worked men even more fiercely after they had been baptized in the Holy Spirit.

✣

I'm late. By the time I reach the Kahanes' sixteenth-floor
apartment, most of the family has already left for the synagogue. Only young Amanda comes running to the door, together with daughter who has slept over. They toss me a hello,
pursue each other back into the living room, scramble out of
the apartment toward the elevator, a double screaming blur:
daughter holding a candle, Amanda clutching a box. Their
screams sound too fierce to be just fun.

"I'll only let you smell it if you come to shul!"

"I can smell it anyway!"

"No, you can't!"

"Yes, I do! I smell it!"

What is "it"? It must be the spice box filled with cloves,
used in the *havdalah* ceremonies with which the Sabbath ends
in shul, that is, in the synagogue. The youngest child often
brings it, and this youngest child, the sleep-over friend, holds
it out to daughter's nose. Daughter pounces, friend escapes, to
the violent, panting laughter of both.

The chase is suspended during the elevator ride. Amanda
muffles the box, its mystique, its smell, under her jacket until
we reach the ground floor. Here the game re-explodes—a
stomp past the doorman onto the sidewalk, out of sight. Two
minutes and three blocks later it's over. Amanda has vanished
into the synagogue. Daughter leans next to the entrance, still
holding the candle. Her breath is high, her little mouth pulled
down.

"Amanda wanted to know what party I'm going to! Amanda's so nosy!"

But the problem is not merely Amanda's nosiness but daughter's elbow. She rubs it near the abrasion, where red glimmers through a bit of broken skin.

"You fell!"

She nods. Sharp little pre-sobbing sniffs come from her nose. She throws the candle on the ground. "I didn't tell Amanda about my party, so she didn't tell me why the candle's funny. She's tit-for-tat!"

I pick up the candle. "Is that why you think it's funny? Because it's got two wicks instead of one?"

She nods, glowers at her wound.

"I suppose Amanda gave you the candle?"

"Yeah, so I'd go to the synagogue with her. So who cares!"

"You can still join her."

I say that though I know that she can't. To us the Sabbath doors won't open anymore. The Factory never closes, not for the likes of her and me.

"There's a reason," I say, "why the candle is funny with those two wicks."

"I don't care. I'm bleeding. I can't go the party anyway."

"All you've got is a little scratch." I give her the candle. From the Aux Chachkas bag I pull daughter's T-shirt with the Male Chauvinist Centaur. "The shirt will cover it."

"It'll make the shirt bloody."

"That nick will crust in a minute. Let's sit over there."

I steer her across the street to a space with benches. It's another construction site, but here the builder seems to have run out of money after the house had been razed. The lot is

now half wilderness, half improvised-park; daughter lets herself be walked toward it, raw-eyed, fingering the two wicks of her funny candle, trying to be too busy for tears. As my part of the anti-crying effort I feed the conversation.

"Okay, I'll tell you anyway why two wicks to your candle. They stand for creation and redemption. I mean, how the world was born, how it will be saved and how both will merge in a holy flame."

No answer.

"I guess that's a little heavy. Let's see. Look at it this way. You could light one wick remembering how your friendship was created, I mean yours and Amanda's, how you two got to know each other. And you could light the other wick in honor of how the friendship is going to be saved after all. And the common flame shows how you two are together even though the going can get pretty hot!"

Again no answer. But, after ten seconds, a question:

"How come you know so much about Jewish things?"

"How come?" I say. "How come. Well, I guess Jewish things don't come natural to me. Not the way they did, say, to my Grandpa. So I don't practice them. So at least I study up on them."

"Can I have a match, please?"

"Be careful."

She walks past the benches, careful, remote. Slowly she climbs up a small pyramid of rusted steel girders. Perhaps it reminds her of the monkey bars she's outgrown. Perhaps she's retreating toward the childhood of our race, looking for the lost Sabbath. We're a pair of the same kind. With my quasi-sermon

I must have been trying to stir up the rabbi I never got to be. I have no congregation, not even in her. She doesn't ask me: "Why don't we go to the synagogue? Why doesn't it come natural anymore?" She doesn't ask: "What is this redemption business? Why for Pete's sakes does God have to save the world He Himself has created?"

No, daughter doesn't discuss heavy stuff with me. That's how it is in the crosstown world: things that matter must be worked out alone. They are no longer sharable. Sharing, like staining glass windows, is a skill long lost in the Factory din. Our family, being modern, is a legal concept, a mutual self-help team, an intermittent attempt at love, an island in anonymity—but not really a closeness cradled in a communal network. We have no rhythm of rituals to replenish it.

Which is why I stand here, alone, on broken concrete. Up there, daughter perches on the rusty pyramid. She has lit her two-wick candle. She is trying, I imagine, to exorcise two hurts; the one on her elbow; and the other, less talkable and hardly conscious, that has to do with longing for the synagogue. With her little twin-flamed torch she looks pagan. And perhaps she should. When the synagogue was invented, after the destruction of the first temple, it served the aching pagan in the Jew.

He always existed, that pagan in the Jew, and he always ached. A direct line runs from Baal to shul. Four thousand years ago Yahweh imposed an exalted task on his Hebrews; to survive it, they needed a respite sanctioned by Him. And Yahweh, the Storm God, the Desert God, God of the Eternal and Infinite, did allow the Sabbath in which His chosen ones could

catch their breath. Apart from that, however, he granted them no pause. Under the Lord's sky lay arid vastness, dune after dune of unredemption, to be ransomed by the sword of His chosen soldiers. *Onward!* was his command. On, capture the horizon, break the wall of the next city, raze the sanctuary of infidels beyond the border. On, to the next rise in the growth curve, a bigger share of the market, a better price-earnings ratio. On, to the glamour-challenge of a penthouse party, on to the jacks tournaments of far-away Fifth Avenue. Impossible is un-American and anti-Factory.

This was the God Who was unmercifully one and Who brooked nothing less than atonement—at-one-ment—from His worshipers. Only incessant zeal would satisfy Him. The desert was faceless boundlessness. What else is the crosstown city? The Desert God was and is an imperious abstraction who drove bark-shod warriors to battles as He now drives the horn-rimmed ambitious through their office politics.

In Baal the pagans worshiped Yahweh's opposite. Baal's secret was that he was not Baal but baalim. In contrast to the austere, relentless One, he could become manifest in the sensuous many. Israel, toiling under a single harness, found herself seduced by the relief offered in the baalim's manifold. Nature served as Yahweh's battlefield: one total made for total conquest. But under baalim, nature could be celebrated in its diversities, almost tree by tree. To Canaan's heathens almost every distinctive natural object was another mode of Baal. This tall cedar. That mossy boulder. This hill of olives. Each was a fertility spirit to be blessed and worshiped on the spot without the mandate of distant conquest. Its celebrators could root and

revel in the local. "Up, make us gods!" the Hebrews cried at the foot of Mount Sinai when they could no longer bear the imminence of the One God of Whom they would not be able to partake, Who could be neither shared nor seen, Who permitted only prayer across the abyss dividing divine from carnal.

Therefore they made gods at the foot of Sinai. They fashioned the Baalish your-face-to-my-face thing before which "they rose up to play," eating and drinking and dancing together, a thing touchable as gold, the Calf.

Moses burned the Calf in vain. It was remade, reburned, remade, reburned for many generations. For some eight hundred years after Moses at Sinai, Israel went a-whoring after baalim in the "high places" of the land. Not that the Jews abandoned their one Yahweh. He was as unabandonable as their outsiderdom. He was the edge of Israel's sword, the gleam of its righteousness, its ever rampant hope. "I will make kings and nations out of thee," He had said to Abraham, and His word remained a drum in the Hebrews' ears. They worshiped Yahweh so they could be His chosen people. But the baalim made bearable their chosenness. They needed a place, a patch, a knoll, needed many a foothold down here to sustain the sweep of the one universal Godhead above.

And so, during the long conquest of Canaan, the baalim's smoke rose from the hills. Pagan smoke kept rising out of Israel during the rule of the Judges, through the splendors of David and Solomon. It kept rising despite the thunder of Jeremiah. It rose against the interdictions of Hosea, Amos, Elijah and Elisha. Only after the Babylonian captivity did it stop. By then the great temple was broken together with the

unbounded dream, the dream of kings and nations. For the first time the Hebrews recognized limit. They no longer needed Baalish solace against infinity. In its stead they created what daughter now misses, drying her little wound and burning her two-wick candle—they created the synagogue. The synagogue offered precisely the soul-nourishing small focus, the village-scaled your-face-to-my-face warmth which Baal-worshipers had given each other around the altars of the hill-god.

The synagogue incarnated every form of neighborliness. It was and has been school ("shul"), meeting house, study room, library, community hub. Here God's great word was localized into chapters to be absorbed by the congregation piece by piece. A different part of the Torah was discussed in groups small enough to make each worshiper a participant in—not a gawker at—the divine process.

As Christianity centralized the church around the Pope, Judaism decentralized. After Masada the idea of the Messiah receded from Jewish thought. What remained close and grew even closer was the synagogue, which did what the roots of the word suggest: it brought together. It did not send forth for conquistadorial glory, as the imperial temple had so often. It brought together fructifyingly. Here the Torah was measured out in segments of campfire dimensions. The sacred scrolls became Baal's equivalent in each Jewish place, high or low. And interpretations and elaborations of the law of the Torah, known collectively as Talmud, enveloped the Jew as woods do a hamlet. It was a forest forever in new leaf, brushing against every moment of Jewish life. For a long time each Talmudic comment planted another in the next generation, reflecting a

new age while preserving the experience of the old. Most important, the Talmud was un-monolithic and anti-central; not a slab of absolutist decrees but a transcript, edited and annotated, of informal talk among the learned. The talkers were rabbis in the early centuries after Christ, acting like small-town elders. They debated cunningly; digressed leisurely; speculated; wondered aloud; meandered through anecdote, through allegory, through many a homey aside—before finally arriving at a legal conclusion. They took on the law's high majesty and filtered it through the daily and ordinary down to man's littleness. How does God's great Sabbath command express itself in the barnyard—is an egg laid on the seventh day of the week the "work" of a hen, and therefore not fit for eating? Or: the duty, implied in the Torah, to thank God for blessings like food—should it be extended to the saying of a benediction at the sight of an attractive woman?

The Talmud reawakened the sacredness of the commonplace. Fenced about by the law, the Jewish unit changed from regiment back into a community stabilized by a village common. Israel learned how to be a parish, and was saved by being parochial. Outside the Talmud's fence, empires flared and died. Within, the Jew was sheltered from conflagrations. Solomon had built his temple for imperial throngs; it had fallen. The synagogue survived with its minyan of ten.

Most of the unrest that pushed toward the universal now passed from Hebrew to gentile. Great Christianized Constantine and his greatness-wracked successors on the throne kept straining for supremacy. Great landed magnates strained to be yet greater; they absorbed smaller farms and turned peas-

ants into paupers. The paupers left their hillside gods for a
new grand promise heard in the big city. They became the
Christ-prone proletariat of Rome, of Byzantium. Jesus' word
spread fastest through labyrinths of brick. It was pre-eminently
an urban evangel inspiriting the uprooted. Here was better,
hotter news than all the gnostic mysteries which also promised
an insider's path to the pinnacle somewhere in the numinous
mist. To be saved by the universal, you must shed your particular earthliness, your hinterland identity. You must cut
yourself off from the clay that bore you. "Woman, what do I
have to do with thee?" Hadn't Christ said those very words to
His own mother, a woman from the hick town of Nazareth? "If
any man hateth not his father and mother he cannot be my
disciple." Had Christ not said that, too? This voice, as heard
by later Christians, was absolute and absolutist. It rejected
roots and closeness. Only ultimates mattered by the time the
last of the gospels, John's, spoke in tones that overrode all
others: "I am the light of the world."

After John, the Christianized Roman became a metropolitan
hipster. He had gotten the final lowdown, the inside word, the
logos, behind all far-ranging confusions of existence. He was
privy to the secret in the center, the one that controlled all the
vast peripheries. Being hip to the universe, his interest and
knowledge lay in universals, not in the small potatoes of the
ecclesia. To him the pagans were those of the *pagus*, Latin for
"country district." *Pagan* smelled of the idolatry of local
yokels, those ignorant of the suffering, saving, cosmic godhead. *Pagan* meant those rubes from the naïve clan-centered
cults who got great kicks out of little immediacies. Heathens
drew their name—and their excitement— from the heather.

✢

Today daughter's friend Amanda may feel like a garlicky pagan beyond the pale: daughter, not she, is going to the hip glitter of some party. Jealousy may have been behind all that spice-chest teasing. Daughter, on the other hand, may envy Amanda the heart-warmth of shul, so much cozier than the penthouse anxiety ahead of us.

Of course "us" includes myself. Though no longer a wor-shiper of Yahweh, I am still, helplessly, subject to His command. "Get thee out of thy kindred," He commands me, as He once commanded Abraham. "Get away from that small-time world, that puny spice-chest provinciality. Travel elsewhere, travail upward, drive yourself farther, try something riskier, richer, go take your daughter to her party on Fifth Avenue where important parents of chic children are converging, where you might come closer to being Sir Frederic Wow!"

I have no nook, no shul as shelter against this dictate. It is bred into my reflexes. But I do enjoy a reprieve here in this weed-green building site that failed to become a building. A hot dog stand has opened on the lot. So has another stand with the sequined legend ZODIAK ZEKE. Behind it, a man with pink-tinted sideburns sells wax seraphim, voodoo shapes, astrological posters, even OTB tip sheets embellished by griffins. Two men in business suits slow down for a minute, go on with a headshake: "Back to the Dark Ages, man . . ."

Man, if you were only right. A dash of the Dark Ages might foul up nicely some of Yahweh's imperatives. They set my

blood hustling all too well. I could use a little disrepair in the engine driving me. Hooray for breakdowns! The breakdown of whatever corporate golem was to raise a skyscraper here produced this little surcease of an almost-park. The breakdown of the Roman Empire produced the surcease misnamed Dark Ages. Man's empire always falls to the benefit of men. The phrase "Dark Ages" itself reeks of the imperial obsession pumped into our language. Why call those ages dark? Because they left no trace of grandiosity. Early feudal times were livably local.

"Feudalism" derives from "fee"—originally "fehu," the Germanic word for "cow." Cattle were the most convenient unit of local property. For a fee of so many cows the local lord protected the local village. All the great blazonry of knighthood began as a bargain struck across grass between a herdsman and a swordsman. Of course the swordsman lived by his blade. But his combat was only with his peers, much of it ceremonialized harmlessly into jousts. The "real" wars of the Dark Ages inflicted scratches compared to the slaughter of armageddons before and after. Domains were small enough for every face to know most others. A knowledge that is peace, inward or out.

The Dark Ages also humanized God once more. In the early medieval parish the Christians found their New Testament synagogue. Christ no longer towered over all earth with otherworldly majesty. (In *Mont-Saint-Michel and Chartres* Henry Adams marvels at the humanity of the Gothic Jesus.) Beneficently He sent His agents down as angels or local saints. They resembled pagan djinns, crypto-baalim, each with a local mis-

sion, shielding this valley or guarding that plain. Here was St. Florian with his bucket, putting out a barn fire; there, haloed Gabriel gentling a child away from a cliff.

Sure, a slew of Holy Roman Emperors, be they Saxon, Salian or Hohenstaufen, made solemn noise about their suzerainty. But the crown was high theory. Life's daily facts were practiced under roofs grouped within earshot of a single church bell. The village tucked itself around the steeple or nestled against the manor. Traffic between men was intimate, eye-to-eye; between overlord and vassal; between vassal and serf. Gone was the Cainite bureaucracy, geared toward remoteness and its conquest. Gone was the regiment, restored into a village. Gone—for a while.

In this crevice of history some of the blessings of nearness were possible again. People could "frequent together." The saint no less than the demon lived breath-close. A scowl would come down from the skies. An ambush might wait in the forest. But every surprise wore a human countenance. The noble (that is, the known one) knew every villein of the village. Therefore villeins had not yet become villainous, nor churls—another early name for peasant—churlish.

This quasi-greensward here, on Second Avenue and 81st Street; what if it were not just a crosstown fortuity; not a brief happenstance in my life but a steady resource? What if I could escape from the Factory into the past—the direction of all true escapes? If I could make a break for it with all the other park-dwellers here, like Zodiak Zeke and daughter with her double-wick candle and the senior citizens with their magic OTB sheets, the kids with their eagles that only look like kites? Is

there no way to pull loose from the trap in which, possessed by tomorrow, I am dispossessed of today? Why can't I lean against some tenth-century oak and cup my fingers around *this* moment and sip the blue between the clouds?

✛

"COME BE MY TOY FRIEND! . . . COME TO ABE'S TOYMANIA! . . ." The calls come from a little Lady Go-divalette, blonde mane, pink bodystocking, with megaphone and rouged pretty-face, astride a golden donkey. Her donkey consists of two men suited up in sequined hind and forelegs. Mr. Forelegs brays rather hilariously between Godiva's calls. Down comes daughter from the girder pile, throws away her burned-down candle, runs after the apparition on the gilded ass. "COME BE MY TOY FRIEND! . . . COME TO ABE'S TOYMANIA! . . . COME ALONG! . . ."

I follow daughter and there, around the corner, is Abe's Toymania store. The donkey, bearing Godiva, trots through the open door; just past the threshold, it burps silver coins. Everybody rushes inside, daughter and thus myself included. Of course all those pieces of eight turn out to be chocolate flakes gussied up in tin foil. But Abe's Toymania is wholly spacey, unmarred by anything as bourgeois as a teddybear. It's kid fun with a kink, and it works. Daughter is lost in the tyrannosaurus playing the electric guitar, in the dumb-mugger-doll who can shoot himself in the foot, and especially in the disco-crusader—or that's what he looks like to me. Crank up this

horseback creature by the tail of his charger and he shakes
with Saturday Night Fever—spurred boots jigging, hooves
dancing, cross-emblazoned shield gyrating.

"Oh, Daddy, let's buy Viv that one for the party!"

"For this party, today?"

"I think it's her birthday."

"There's no birthday mention on the invitation."

"I think her parents don't want to make a fuss."

"You think," I say. "Let's go."

"I'm sure it's her birthday, Daddy! Her best friends know. If
you don't bring a present it shows you're not a best friend."

"Did you see the price tag on that crusader?"

"Oh, Daddy! Then let's look for something cheaper, please!"

I should simply pull her out of the store. Somehow I don't. I
let her loose on the Discount Crown Jewels Department.

She browses among rubber diadems and Styrofoam tiaras.
They are weapons with which to do party infighting ahead. We
reach for storybook props of long ago to guide us through a
future made of boredom and of boobytraps. Even in Silicon
Valley children yawn at microchips—they want to hear about
the rabbit and the prince. Why must I have my own computer?
Because I crave a fairy godmother I can take home and hook
up. Her programmed miracles will defend me against the wilderness bristling with other people's terminals. At last there'll
be one terminal that's *my* tutelary spirit. Scratch any sci-fi
wonderland: out oozes the hope of primordial Eden.

Actually such hope was played on by little Godiva on her
golden ass. That's what drew us into Abe's store. It lured
daughter down from her medieval perch. She is, of course, no

more temptation-proof than were the grown-ups of the Middle Ages.

By the eleventh century people needed to be re-enchanted. Europe was still a patchwork of farms, steeples, cobbles, castles and many holy candles burning. But holiness receded as prosperity grew together with the frustrations that can't help ripening in the agro-factory. Communities distended into areas too large to remain communal. Economics became more widely networked; transportation more accomplished; politics more ambitious. Human recognition shrank. The cultivator of wheat could no longer know the miller who ground his grain two changes of horse away. The miller, expanding his output, had little time to see the many bakers using his flour. All these people had in common was their count, who had no knowledge of them as men needing his protection. They were part of his base from which he jockeyed for a dukedom. Once more the centrifuge of power flung people apart. It became difficult again for my face to frequent together with yours. The fuller the belly of the knight, and the heavier the paunch of the plower, the more insistent their search for a satisfaction which the richest harvest could no longer bring. Such satisfaction, so perversely withheld, must be recaptured elsewhere. A marvelous suspicion settled on Europe. Somewhere in the distance a thrill lay waiting by which the soul could cleanse itself; some novel feat that would revive pristine contentment; some sacred adventure; some apocalyptic retrieval.

"*Deus vult,*" said Pope Urban, summoning Christendom to the first crusade. "The Lord wants it." Did He? It was not in response to His will but to His remoteness that the Western

armies began tramping eastwards. The crusades were yet another quest for the God that keeps absconding. By the eleventh century the redemptive heart of Him, His Sabbath essence, had begun to move away again. It had returned to Jerusalem, where Moslems kept It hostage.

Like the disco-equestrian in the toy store, the crusaders were wound up with Saturday Night Fever. They shook with the world's fever for the Sabbath that was so precious and fugitive. Now the infidels had abducted the Sabbath in the form of the Holy City. They must be dislodged and destroyed. For the second time in history Jerusalem became the prize of deliverance on which the faithful marched.

The first time around, a couple of thousand years earlier, David had said: This is my capital; the fulfillment of Sinai's covenant is here. A man of *Realpolitik*, he chose adroitly. The Hebrews had controlled most of Palestine for over two centuries, yet Jerusalem remained "the city of a stranger," as we read in Judges 19:12—an alien stronghold of the Jebusites. Just for that reason none of the twelve Jewish tribes could claim it after David's conquest. It was an ideal national center and the perfect dwelling place for the federal God Yahweh. Here Solomon could "raise a levy out of all Israel"; from here the royal attempt was made to fuse twelve tribes into one Zion.

This capital carved out of a hitherto foreign jungle—this Brasilia of Canaan—became in time the nostalgic jewel of the Jewish imagination; the heart of the heartland from which we've been exiled into our many Babylons. *If I forget thee, O Brasilia!* . . .

Two millennia later the city meant to rid Israel of its tribal

texture re-entered history on a similar errand. It triggered the crusades that rent the local fabric of the West. A dream mobilized the Occident: Jerusalem regained. In the end it was conquered only to be lost for good. Lost, too, was Christ's *ecclesia* as it had been reborn in the medieval village. God's alleged will swept up villagers by the hundreds of thousands into nomad hordes plundering their way toward the Land that had been Promised yet again.

When the trumpets grew still and the blood dried, Christendom found itself not saved but increasingly secularized. A new famine was abroad. No food from above could assuage it. Therefore people needed to devour all the more things below. The peasant, torn from his parish, grabbed for the gold of the town. A tantalization by sumptuous exotica, by spices and houris, overtook the yeoman from the Midi, the farmer from Navarre. Turbulence of this sort could be controlled—or manipulated—on a large scale only. Power escalated from the baronial to the royal range. What did the manor matter now? Or the village? Only an ignorant rube turned to his valley saint for help. Knighthood and chivalry became sentimental jokes. Parsifal began to look like Don Quixote. There *had* to be a prize, a plum, a marvel, that wasn't just quixotic, but bigger, more solid and more real.

The energies of disorientation overran the Occident. They pushed on toward the crosstown desert. The Factory shifted into high gear. *Brrr*.

✛

"Daddy, is Divine Comedy like a Coke?"
"Say that again?"

"Or like a soda? See, these are for sipping."

Daughter is holding up a bundle of straws. Each one consists of a snake-headed black coil at the bottom, a fiery red middle and a snow-white straight rod at the top with lateral bars near the mouth end. Serpent, flame and cross. Inferno, purgatory and heaven compressed into ten inches of plastic tube. *"Divine Comedy Straws,"* says the card on the counter. "$3.69 for twelve, plus one free per dozen." Compulsive symbolizer that I am, I may be wrong about its metaphoric intentions, but it's certainly a stunt of a sipping straw.

"I wonder if they had a baker's dozen back in Dante's time," I say. "Dante's the man who wrote a long poem called *The Divine Comedy.*"

"Was that a long time ago? Like ancient?"

"In a way."

"'Cause the invitations say ancient and the straws cost less than the disco-knight and we could buy a dozen for Viv and the free one for me? Please, Daddy?"

I give her four dollar bills. "I guess Dante is ancient enough for Viv."

A kiss from daughter and she runs off. Why did I agree? Because the straws are a nice conceit and cheap for their showiness. Because they let me get off a crack at Viv—a party intimidates less if you smirk at it in advance. Probably because I hoped for that tomboy kiss, little lips pushing headlong into my cheek, the kind of kiss of which there'll be no more when daughter reaches the age of premeditation. Last not least, I agreed because I have a mama's boy's weakness for Dante.

"*Homo sapiens,*" a psychoanalyst wrote, "is a nidicolous animal." That is, a being reared in the nidus, or nest. He is nest-reared and, consciously or not, nest-needy all his life. He needs the communal, eye-to-eye, your-face-to-my-face warmth of the nook in whose absence the gentlest breeze turns frosty. Art likes to accost this goose-pimpling nest-needing child in us. Much of our poetry is about exploring home, or pressing against its walls, or losing it altogether. In the Middle Ages we had a home, at least for a while. Dante, quintessentially medieval, charted heaven and hell with an imagination as at home on earth as in spheres above or below. There is a snugness to the grandeur of *The Divine Comedy*. Inferno, purgatory and paradise are stable, changeless chambers of the divine household. There we dwell together, kissed or punished by God according to our deserts, all under the one roof of His justice. In its medieval sense "comedy" meant a narrative with a happy ending.

Dante was the last major sensibility of the West to apprehend a happily domestic universe. He illuminated the interior of a mansion. Those who came after him poked lanterns into a maze. They were likely to light up not the company of men, but each man scrabbling by himself; each of us a bit of brevity stranded in long, long riddles.

The longest riddle is the chasm beyond which God resides, ineffable, immeasurable, infinite. On this side of the brink we squirm, we little sacks of blood. That was the vista opening before postmedieval eyes—a contrast which grew more exigent with every generation. The little sack began to covet infinity with an ebullience left over from the Middle Ages. But this

ebullience did not long retain the bounce of nestlings a-tumble
with others *in* their nest. It turned into excitement over the
worlds outside. Renaissance man, fevering, was an individual
infected and inflamed with the immense. Immensity was his
genius, his virus, his contagion.

What gorgeous disease of the strutting sick! Renaissance
artists gave it awed elbow room. These painters dilated the
canvas by inventing perspective. They unfurled a sense of distance dazzlingly unbounded. So many walls had been leveled
by the crusades that the eye careened through brand-new vastness. Was it a vast vacuum? Not if you could make it shine
with your talent. Certainly not if you could make it glow with
your power.

Aut Caesar aut nihil, read the motto and metaphysical pun
of that Renaissance virtuoso Cesare Borgia. "Either king," he
said, "or nothing." "The painter strives with nature," said
Leonardo da Vinci, competing with the Creator. "I want to
work miracles." "The pope cannot live long," wrote Emperor
Maximilian to his daughter. "I want to be pope." One reign at
a time was not enough.

Less and less able to commune, Renaissance egos were
more interested in what made them supreme than in what they
had in common. Good deeds—the "works" through which
Christians justified themselves—blurred. Goodness must be
defined by communal norms, and they were moldering. It was
time for Martin Luther to broadcast to the West the central
warning of the Reformation: you may no longer earn God's
favor by any action that is outward, communally palpable to

your fellow men. His favor will be given only through the private, inward exertion of your spirit, known as faith.

Of course Paul had already said that, addressing the straits of the early Christians. And even before Paul, during a yet earlier crisis, with Israel about to break into the shards of exile, Jeremiah had seen Yahweh's law written into His worshipers' "inward parts," independent of the outer witness or practice of commonalty. This had been the beginning of the end of God as a collective tribal experience. Now the possibility had been broached that He would make Himself available to *individuals* into which the tribe was shattering. Two thousand years after Jeremiah, fifteen hundred years after Paul, Luther faced yet another social disarray. He raised the point to a commanding dogma.

Protestant faith was a compact between one being and the One God. It bypassed the enfeebled community. Gregarious your-face-to-my-face rituals took on the sound of mumbo-jumbo. The *Hoc est corpus meum* of the priest at mass jangled into the *hocus-pocus* of the trickster. Luther shrugged at sacraments; they were, after all, communal transactions. He tolerated the Lord's Supper only at the price of de-communalization. The wafer turns into Christ's body not because the parson performs the divine office before the congregation. Not at all. The Lord becomes corporeally present only because He has promised to be so present—a promise whose substance must be constructed by the faith of each person separately. If I, by myself, do my believing well enough, everything will turn out fine in the end, for me. Luther's creed is the masterpiece of the solitary soul.

Gone, the present-minded sociability of the *ecclesia*. Now

we are all separate, redemption-bent wrestlers in the mud. The world is a free-for-all of mutually wary, dirty maneuverers, every fellow out to make *his* messianic killing in the future. The Lutheran faith spiritualizes the solitude of the entrepreneur; spiritualizes competitiveness that is asocial, toilsome, risk-taking, payoff-obsessed.

The vocation to which his God has called the entrepreneur is the dollar. Of course the dollar, like the wafer of the Eucharist, is a physically flimsy token. Yet at the altar a sliver turns into the Lord's body just as at the check-out counter the dollar bill transubstantiates into my loaf of bread. Both wafer and dollar are earnests of exchangeability requiring belief on the part of all exchangers. For the entrepreneur money comes alive during his weekday calculations the way the Lord comes alive to him at Sunday mass: through faith in a promise. Credo supports credit. The credit system pledging redemption of my bonds twenty years hence rests on the credo affirming the eventual redemption of my soul. Right now I must lay about me without mercy in the lovelessness of the marketplace. But one day I'll be a "philanthropist," rich enough to do as the word says—namely to love men. God's dollar will raise me unto love. His grace, cleansing me of the sins of the workaday jungle, will be generated through the booty I forage there. Grace emitted freely, automatically—like quarterly interest on bonds—will issue from capital to be accumulated in Him through my present dogged, drudging faith. In view of the reward ahead, present troubles must be shouldered, present transgressions will be forgiven, present goods (however opu-

lent) are at best preliminary. Fulfillment you can touch now is nothing. Only the promise is real.

I remember a sentence from an advertisement in the *New York Times* for a get-rich book called *Nothing Down*. It said: "Stop frittering away your money on possessions; instead use it to make more money." These words are the breviary of the Factory faith. They hallow the future and keep it pure of the strain, the stink, the deprivation of today. They are the words that energize capital investment by starving our souls and our senses. They are the words that made us modern.

✣

By the time we reach Third Avenue and 86th, it is five minutes past two. At this rate we'll get to Viv's at twenty after the hour. There is such a thing as half-assed unpunctuality. Twenty minutes late is sloppy, but forty is true insouciance. Why not let daughter inaugurate her Medici straw at a sidewalk café?

She slurps her malted happily. My ginger ale would taste better if I could keep my eyes closed. I know this block and don't care to look at what happened to it. Now it is a successful piece of real estate. Once it was a neighborhood: a Sicilian shoemaker, a tailor from the Abruzzi, a bakery with Neapolitan pastries, too sweet but wonderfully aromatic. Then the demolition crew drove up. Tailor, shoemaker, baker vanished into Wop limbo. But—presto!—the ethnic reappears in plastic. It pays much more rent and bedizens half the ground floor of the Miami-style high-rise. Here is one of your franchise operations

with an Italian bistro gimmick. Here's your fast food, paper-plate travesty of a Mama-and-Papa trattoria. Here, where I sit with daughter, is the terrace of the Cafe Ristorante Refresco flavored with vinyl fishnets. The poster showing Vesuvius has been printed in Korea, the pizza smells of Times Square, the *gondoliere* serving us sounds like a bronchitic actor out of work. *Garçon,* what's the damage? Lay *l'addition* on us. *Ciao!*

But no point getting angry. Why can't I view the Cafe Refresco as just another instance of miscarried nostalgia? After all, we've been nostalgic ever since we became modern. That's when we began to consummate our new individualism by abandoning home. That's also when, quite logically, the old hearth grew cold—and we couldn't stand to see it. The frigid nestless present which thrusts us forward to salvation-to-come also drives us back to consolations of the past.

Nostalgia means the pain caused by the absence of home. Since the Renaissance the search has been on for a cure. We've been trying to stake out new homesteads in the New World. We hoped to pile up snugness in taller buildings. But the more modern our remedies against the malaise, and the sicker our souls for homes of old, the greater our longing for classic serenity, Greek comeliness, Roman virtue. Even as Renaissance men explored the future, they went antiquing. They scavenged old traditions because they lacked sufficient community to gestate a live one of their own. The philosopher found his inspiration in Aristotle, the rhetorician in Cicero. Yes, novel looms drove weavers' hands faster than ever before, but ancient myth and classical allusion fed the imagery of poets, painters, sculptors. (What industrial emblems entered

the arts during the Industrial Revolution? I know of no sonnet celebrating the automatic fly shuttle.) Centuries passed, each grimier than the last; the rural took on the appeal of the classic. Hamlets in the hinterland shone with the charm, the freshness, the cohesion missed in the scrabbling pomp of court or capital. It was another nostalgic vogue. The bucolic became deliciously quaint just as new centralizing techniques ground it underfoot. During the years before the French Revolution when (in de Tocqueville's words) "local freedoms died out, local squires withered or departed for Paris . . . and villages were left to the tender mercies of the central government"—in those years Marie Antoinette played village shepherdess at the Petit Trianon. Bourbon courtiers luxuriated in the very rusticity that court policy was rendering passé.

A few decades later the full fury of steel mill and textile factory fell upon the nineteenth century. That was the season for the romantics to poeticize ye landscapes of old. Yet often they didn't exalt unselfconscious nature so much as the self-glorifying natural force. Wordsworth's skylark, for example, with his strong song, his "soul as strong as a mountain river," who is "laughing and scorning" at his "banqueting place in the sky." This paean to blithe careless power made an aria out of the very absoluteness of individual aspiration; it abetted the élan with which that newest high flier among men, the industrialist, could soar above all drab social considerations, to *his* fulfillment in the counting house. Over the last romantic lea settled soot flung by the heedlessness of the "free" enterpriser.

So it goes. Our nostalgic impulse is processed into grist for the mill grinding up what we are nostalgic for. So it went with

black gospel music. With its communal call-and-response, its intimacy between preacher and congregation, it was a your-face-to-my-face village rite. Such harmonies are not possible among the individualists of the power class—those too much at war with infinity and with each other. Such harmonies survive only in a parish far beyond the pale. Only here the nidicolous has not been overwhelmed by lust for the universal. Only here the finite can be celebrated to a holy beat. The fervor, the joy of *"He's got the whole world*—clap! clap!—*in his hands . . ."* can be heard only in the nonindustrial nigger sabbath separating one industrial work week from another. The nigger sabbath remained vital to the degree that white expectancies were excluded from its future. It remained immune to tomorrow's extortions. Unlike their boss, niggers could therefore smile at the blue of today's sky. Weekdays they sweated—but not the devious insomniac sweat of premeditation. And when the tambourine sounded by the altar Sundays, they attained a state whose ease would have tantalized Strether, Henry James's hero in *The Ambassadors*: they became "unclocked." Of course Strether never came near enough to the cleaners of his stable to know that they were oppressed—and he, deprived.

The stress-worn brahmins of today are "into" this un-clockedness. Their grandparents ogled it in the Cotton Club, their parents said "Pops" when they meant Louis Armstrong, and Michael Jackson videos are major with their children. They all want to buy the glee, the bounce born of (or descended from) pariahs. Black spontaneity has proved highly marketable, first as jazz, later as rock and roll. The nigger revved up Elvis Presley's hips. All the gregarious vitality of the

ghetto evangel was wired to the electric guitar; was adroitly distorted into the white punk's howl; was impresario'd into Madison Square Garden; echoed from a million jukeboxes as the roar of the loutish, unmoored, wounded self; blared from the megaspeakers of the Rolling Stones—and just stunned and blinded the little Harlem parishes to pieces.

✠

At 86th Street and Lexington we're suddenly not going any place. Three policemen stop daughter and me together with the whole sidewalk crowd. A patrol car, parked athwart the roadway, has halted traffic.

"Stay where you are, folks. Bomb Squad ahead. Just checking out a tip."

The message effervesces among us. I consider, then reject, the idea of a detour via another street. That would mean doubling back through the crush that has built up behind us. We are stuck, but not stolidly stuck. This is not the sullen stasis of the bus stop crowd. On this spot we're not just humdrum victims of some routine frustration. No, we're all fleshing out an excitement together. In other words, we've stumbled into a communing. Around me heads are shaking in a sort of vivacious shock. Opinions are shared about that Near Eastern consulate a block away, about some informer who must have phoned the cops, about things getting really out of hand. People are unburdening themselves warmly to fellow members of a club that will last for a few minutes before decomposing into

strangers again. But while it exists, so does an aura of relief. For some minutes we won't be each other's obstacles in the races we must run. Some *force majeure* has given us respite from the need to reach a certain place at a certain time. It takes an emergency to lift New Yorkers out of the rush of their daily crises.

I elbow my way to the curb. A huge banner lies in the gutter, some of its words blocked by the policemen standing on them.

STUDENTS FOR . . . BETRAY . . . ARAB NATION . . .

A phalanx of cops dissolves to show three young men spread-eagled against a patrol car, being frisked. The youth in the middle—that's the one who fascinates me. A good barber must have trimmed his little black beard. He wears a snow-white Bedouin headcloth. And somehow he still doesn't convey "Arab fanatic" to me. Maybe it's his mouth, pulled down at both corners into a peculiarly affecting curve. I know what he reminds me of—daughter. Daughter, after she'd fallen, at the end of the chase that left her standing alone outside the synagogue. He even wears white sneakers like her. A middle-class kid hot and heavy after something lost for good.

I should invent a name for him. Perhaps I could speculate about him better if I thought of a name to which his head might turn. Abdul. Three generations ago Abdul's ancestors were never frisked in some remote gutter before a crowd of strangers. Abdul's great-grandfather must have been a peasant among his kind, a fellah among fellaheen, part of the clan of his wadi. The wadi nurtured him, the clan gave him his bearings. His purposes, desires, exaltations—even his indigence

and miseries—were all sustained in a matrix of known faces moving through a known landscape. But in the next generation—did his son jump or was he pushed? Did he jump for the life of excitement and riches in the city as sung by radio, rumor, and all the other songs of progress? Or was he pushed because some refinery took over the wadi? Whatever the motive, I wouldn't be surprised if the son migrated to a porter's job in Cairo which gained him a bicycle and the chance to put *his* son through high school. Nor would I be surprised if that high-schooled son, Abdul's father, opened, say, a restaurant whose profits bought first a motor bike, then a refrigerator-freezer, then a Volkswagen, then a digital watch, then those other boons and trophies adding up to the gorgeously over-applianced urban minus where true satisfaction always escapes into whatever amenity is still priced out of reach.

Abdul's father, in brief, possessed more but enjoyed less than any of his forebears in the wadi. The family hegira had not borne fruit which blesses the tongue. Understandably he wanted to make sure that at least *his* son would be so blessed; would reach a truly rewarding altitude. Therefore he used his life savings to elevate this son to the Prince of Alienation known as the Foreign Student.

The Prince, Abdul, is before me now, being frisked by cops. Compared to his illiterate ancestors he has all the advantages, except the your-face-to-my-face emotion through which privilege turns into true pleasure. For who or what is Abdul now? His species is not organic but financial. He is a receiver of money orders from another continent. He is a senior in electrical engineering who can afford Maxwell's Plum twice a week. Forty thousand dollars plus per year in your chosen pro-

fession: yes, that might be a prospect to celebrate. But where is the muezzin's voice to convoke the celebration—that is, the frequenting-together?

No muezzin calls on 86th Street. An Arab knows himself through the gestures, symbols, and protocols of his clan. His very name welds him into the clan's generations: Abdul al-Omar al-Hassan al-Ahmed. But how much of a son can Abdul be to Omar? Sonship needs nurturing by daily contact within a nidus. Where the nidus of Abdul's clan used to be, a fractionating tower stands that cracks petroleum molecules and human families. Six thousand miles away Abdul, straddled against the cop car in his Adidas sneakers, isn't even Abdul— certainly not the way his great-grandfather Ahmed *was* Ahmed. But Abdul must be *some*thing. His humanity clamors for bounding and belonging. And so with the vengeance of the affluently parched, with the wrath of educated frustration, he becomes an Egyptian nationalist. He burns to resurrect in the nation what has been lost in the dead village. Tunisian students who have benefited most from the modernization of their country (reports the *New York Times*) "are now among the most implacable enemies" of the modernizing government. Prosperous scions of royal Egyptian families (says an article in the *Atlantic Monthly*), many of them holders of science degrees, are "righteous and fiercely single-minded" in the determination to turn Egypt into a great and pure Islamic state. Modern nationalism is the furious nest search of the middle-class young.

The first systematic outbreak of that fury was the French Revolution. To re-cite de Tocqueville on France before the deluge: "Local freedoms died out, local squires withered or departed for Paris . . . and villages were left to the tender mercies

of the central government." One provincial off to Paris was young Maximilien Robespierre, who left Arras for law school at the Sorbonne. There he began a career prototypical of the zealotry of the dislocated "foreign student." The evil done by all the withering and departing was avenged by the Robespierres. Not by peasants in the field, who still had some roots to clutch. Not by mill hands, all of whose energies went into surviving. The revolution recruited its ardor from the keen estrangement of the middle class. Almost overnight the bourgeoisie mustered formidable battalions. But just because it had no communal nerve it could not develop an idiom native to its insurgency. It fell back on the Renaissance method of scavenging older traditions. French burghers (alias The People) charged the palace with phrases and facsimiles of the Roman Republic. Today Arab nationalists clothe their fury in the jellabas of traditional Islam.

The revolution was not only revenge. It was hope: an attempt to revive the commonalty that had fragmented. Sansculottes would mount a barricade together as if it were a mystic village common. To the famished and alienated, *la patrie* represented the new nidus of convivial plenty where every singer of the *Marseillaise* found answering, nourishing faces in those who joined him. *"Allons enfants"* and "Workers of the world, unite!" and "Fighters for Egypt, close ranks!" are manifestos between whose lines runs a nostalgic whisper. The revolution is an old fantasy refurbished with the ideals of the young. A mirage of comrades, arms linked, swaying and humming around the same campfire.

Yet such love, such concord, can only breathe in a frame small enough for your eyes to know mine. And the people-come-to-power, whether they be the Awakened Nation, the

Reborn Religion, or the Risen Class, are a storm that blows smallness away. The old regime will not be ripe for rebellion until its center grows sufficiently rigid, massive, top-heavy. Only a force equally massive and centered will supplant it. No tyrant can be guillotined before he grows his huge head. Look for a rebel who is goaded—and therefore conditioned—by hugeness to bring off the decapitation. This rebel's principles oppose the tyrant's, of course; yet he can't help implementing them in terms as tyrannously sweeping. To undo the cosmic sins of the past, the revolution must universalize the future. It may dream of small felicities, but it has neither experience nor patience with them. Sooner or later it dissolves everything— county, valley, township, guild—into the republic. Communal idiosyncrasy is devoured by managerial expeditiousness.

We burst into the throne room, an exuberant band of insurgents. To stay there we become corporate bureaucrats. The country's freedom, we discover, needs to be shored up from border to border. Provincial concerns or the quirks of groups must not hamper us in our higher purpose. And so we administer particularities away. We smooth communications, commerce, transportation; like ice they close over hamlets that drowned. Our new government speeds the trend of the old. It levels the land still better.

Before long, the red banners become fuel for a gray machine; an engine that standardizes, franchises, spins out distribution patterns; processes the nation into a market accessible to the Factory's sales department. In the end, the overthrow of the *ancien régime* served to make the *nouveaux riches* richer faster. By plucking Marie Antoinette out of Versailles, the Jacobins did brute spadework for the steel monopoly.

An old story, and sad. It always starts with not knowing one another anymore. The Pharaoh yoking Moses' Jews "knew them not" the way an earlier Pharaoh had known earlier Jews. Yet after the revolution of the exodus, Moses followed Jethro the Cainite's advice: he decided not to know the Hebrews your-face-to-my-face anymore in order to command them more efficiently. It followed that the history of Israel liberated was strife, schism, jealousy. This sequence, expressed in Canaan with swords and chariots, was repeated some three thousand years later in France with muskets and sabers. Exiled villagers formed a Jethroan regiment as they marched on the castle. Regiments jelled into an army. And the army trampled underfoot remnants of surviving village life.

The revolution betrays the revolutionaries simply by succeeding. But comrades will not blame the cause that stirred them. Hence they must blame each other. Who embezzled our ideals? Who stole the brotherliness, the nidus, that was to be the prize of our upheaval? We sowed (to paraphrase Marx) Fraternity, Equality, Liberty. We harvested Infantry, Artillery, Cavalry. What devil did that? Who killed the *ecclesia* in which we were to celebrate together? Well, the Trotskyites did it. The Stalinists. The other, fake liberation front. The Gang of Four. The Robespierre clique. The Abdul faction.

A secularized messiah, the revolution looms at its most luminously pure before the coming, while the Bastille is still unstormed. The revolutionary stands before its ramparts as a sort of lay apocalypt. He sees time in terms of past evil, imminent battle, and future radiance. But even after the ordained war has been won—and the victory corrupted—the term "revolution" retains its power as modern evangel. It remains a ve-

hicle of communal hope, the Holy Ghost that keeps tomorrow sacred, a phantom whose sacral glow might outlast the rainbow of the growth curve. That's why the moldiest of South American juntas will fasten on the word. Any alliance of CIA bravos and plantation owners will call itself Partido Revolucionario. There are echoes of Sabbath in the phrase. You can hear it even through the Factory clangor.

✛

"Daddy, I'll go in, too! I'll say I'm looking for the restroom!"

Daughter's thumb jabs at the restaurant. We're still at 86th and Lex.

"You can't wait till we get to your friend's house?"

"That's not the idea!" She is whispering. "That's just pretend, so I can follow him in there!"

"'Him'?"

She pulls my ear down to her mouth.

"MICK!"

"So?"

"Oh, Daddy! I'll ask for two autographs. If I give one to Viv we can be three hours late! Please!"

At that level of intensity my "no" would start a twenty-four-hour sulk.

"Well, it's your party. All right."

She vanishes. I stand waiting at the same corner. Actually I'm trying to crack somebody's incognito myself. I mean the woman who is the only other person left from the bomb-scare crowd. She is photographing the gutter. But what intrigues me

is not just her eccentricity, which has a professional gloss to it (she keeps shooting with an expensive camera very oddly angled pictures of the street) Nor is it just her getup: big, smartly askew cap flopping over face, jeans stuffed into big floppy boots, heavy constructivist pendant dangling over Marimekko blouse. The most interesting thing about this woman is the suspicion that I know her from very different circumstances.

"Hello," I say, at last. "Aren't you—didn't you approve my Visa Card application at Manufacturers Hanover last week?"

She stares at me, very interrupted.

"At the Seventy-Ninth Street Branch, Seventy-Ninth and Amsterdam?"

"Oh," she says. "Probably. That's just my living. *This* is what I'm into. Excuse me."

She turns away, for a cunning reason, as I see. A fragment of the Egyptian students' placard still lies in the gutter. Close by a garbage truck has stopped. From its rear hangs a soiled rag, just over the letters LONG LIVE . . . An eloquent juxtaposition, a perfect moment for her to aim her Nikon. But she bends forward with a busyness that's a shade too theatrical. It asks me not to bother her when she is riding so high and so artfully in her true element.

"Of course you are excused."

Even as I say it I'm ashamed of my irony. I hope she hasn't heard me because I spoke so low. I have no right to dislike her. The fact is that she is doing photographically right now what I've been doing all along on this crosstown trip, in terms of cerebration. She is reducing Abdul's placard, and the social wound it represents, to a detail of her own subjective insightfulness. Haven't I similarly reduced the streets?

I should be able to understand her unpatronizingly. I am not. In my mind I call her, cattily, Ms. Nikon. We are simply not colleagues to one another, any of us who try to struggle "creatively" out of America's middle-class quicksands. Abdul may be under arrest, but even in his cell he'll be less lonely than the likes of Ms. Nikon. His nationalism can be exercised in unison with others. The spark of communality (the vision of Egypt as one vast wadi) still flickers inside him. But Ms. Nikon is too hip for that. She must reject her withered roots in order to reinvent herself better.

Abdul proclaimed his background through his beard and jellaba Ms. Nikon wouldn't be caught dead with her mother's mink stole, not to speak of her grandmother's silver-fox neckpiece. Ms. Nikon's background consists of the square prisses who sent her to business school instead of to Bard College and who expected her to be a good Jew and an early wife. What were the high points of her parental nidus? Dad's turn to host the golf dinner, Mom's bridge game (a joust heavily armed with heart-shaped gold brooches), the Pan Am–packaged Chanukah-at-Acapulco, the dais seat at the B'nai Brith fundraiser, the rock band (once actually a warm-up to The Who) at the Bas Mitzvah. None of the family's principal ceremonies worked inwardly, your-face-to-my-face, among its own members. They were outward gestures performed for the world at large. So conducted, family life constitutes a form of politics that won't stop at the bedroom or the dinner table. Politics, Henry Adams said, is hatred systematized. No wonder Ms. Nikon dragged her family background around with her as a millstone against which years of analysis had to be deployed before the shrink finally freed her.

Or did he? Ms. Nikon still continues her parents' concept of

life-as-public-relations, more currently known as lifestyle. There she is, bangs, sunglasses, mask makeup, all projecting laconic chic. It's a style that neutralizes all ethnic or religious implications. She has quarantined her persona from its source. With her background discarded as a sort of impurity, she can feel freer to be "into" something that is truly *her*. The mystique of the self-made millionaire has been extended to the self-made self.

Ms. Nikon's excision of her origins will unleash her utter originality. Right now she already distills a very personal statement from a torn placard in the gutter. As the instructor of her Seminar in Advanced Camera Strategies at the New School might put it: she is pulling that placard out of the mundane flow of history in order to integrate it into a visual and moral syntax all her own. She's not just photographing something seen by others. She is conceptualizing a sight altogether new. "I do not render the visible," said Paul Klee. "I render visible."

For Klee, as for Ms. Nikon, objective reality is as passé as Mom and Dad at Acapulco; a space-age cliché, emotionally sterile, culturally stale. There is no point in reproducing it. But the artist's subjective pressure whose heat melts (or renders) the truth out of surface platitudes—that is the modernist weapon of art.

Five hundred years ago reality had not yet flattened into triteness. Many of us who might have been content to be carpenters then feel the call to be neo-abstractionists today. Once, most carpenters could fashion a table which our contemporary jargon would term "esthetically valid." It was a table whose finish reflected the particular temper of its maker's skill. Just as important, the response to this particularity could be watched by the table maker in the table buyer's face. Now the furniture

industry demands only steady stupor from the lackeys along the assembly belts. Nor would they be roused if they were told the numbers of the credit cards purchasing their products.

That, as we all know, is how it is. What we'll never guess is how much "it" skews the soul. The highest-tech plant cannot automate humanness away. Somewhere, somehow, a lackey still longs to express the mode of his being to other beings in some frame of mutuality. Even his promotion won't cure his need. As boss, *his* boss will be the bottom line. And the bottom line will make him work his underlings impersonally, the way his underlings work the machines. If he treated them as faces, he'd be slacking off. His pay will be better than theirs, but his reward as arid. The carpenter could stroke a table that was all his. What can the Vice President, Manufacturing, stroke? The latest squiggle in the productivity chart. It is good but it doesn't make him as happy as it should, probably (he thinks) because it could be better still. Yet the better the squiggle, the less it will be his, the more it will be the bottom line's.

What used to be any craftsman's workaday satisfaction is now restricted to the sphere of art. Today only the artist can say to the world: "Look. This work is wholly mine. How do you feel about it?" The middle class is the owning class, yet nothing is wholly theirs. Hence their obsession with "creativity." Ms. Nikon can't exist meaningfully unless she is "creative." But just as the modern believer must confront his god alone, so Ms. Nikon, as an artist, has to depend on an inspiration that is stringently unsociable. Who are the dramatis personae of her world? Manipulative stereotypes like her parents or those wimps scheming around the watercooler at Manufacturers Hanover Trust. What surrounds her? Kitsch and knives-in-the-back.

How exact some significance from the banality of such a jungle? By uncompromising perceptiveness that is uniquely hers.

She must not indulge in any mode too readily shared by others. In the modernist canon the too-accessible ranks with the facile, at best. The Renaissance, for all its gilding of the ego, retained enough communality to let its talents avail themselves of popular iconography—*vide* Leonardo da Vinci availing himself of the Last Supper. But would Ms. Nikon ever consider the Passover meal as a visual theme? The signs and symbols of her milieu repel rather than attract her imagination. They are "bourgeois." Her esthetic juices flow not with but against the world's grain from a wellspring deep within her psyche. Here she keeps insulated the smithy of her soul that must forge the uncreated conscience of her race.

I have, of course, just paraphrased the crescendo sentence of *A Portrait of the Artist as a Young Man*. It resounds in my ear every time I see a Ms. Nikon (who might well be, in drag, the solitude and presumption of my own unfulfillment). This smithy in the soul must "render visible." It must draw its fuel not from the sodden conscienceless outside but from within. To tone up her inwardness Ms. Nikon uses every modality that will massage the self. Is she narcissistic? Of course. Narcissism helps her defend and ornament her creative isolation. Punctually she attends her aerobics class; it sculpts her true figure out of the flab imposed by the office chair. Herbal ointments restore the natural sheen of her skin. Swami Ski Siramshee helps her tap depths silted up with weekday pettiness. And of course the seminar in Advanced Camera Strategies encourages her to pursue the full, reckless potential of *her* vision.

Once upon a time her luckier ancestors found in the Sab-

bath what the week's toil was for. They discovered the reward by celebrating with their kind. Ms. Nikon has no kind. She's a nonpareil—at least a latent nonpareil—or she's not at all. Each weekend she must wring singularity out of her skull; ply her camera; tax her inventiveness; perspire through aerobics; transcendentalize with the swami; hunt nuances at the seminar . . . a tireless flagellant, one of the millions of upscale martyrs to yet another solipsist refinement of the American Dream. *Click!* goes her shutter on 86th Street. The Factory works overtime. It will not be stopped.

⁂

"Daddy!"

Daughter emerges from the restaurant, waving two scrawled-on paper napkins. Three men overtake her: two beefy types bracketing slim Mick in the middle. People clot around them, staring. Beefy on the left hails a taxi. Beefy on the right shakes his head at Ms. Nikon's camera. Though she's aiming it in a different direction, he steps between her and slim Mick boarding a cab. Ms. Nikon scowls. A camera artist like her—mistaken for a paparazzo! She stalks off. Vanishes. People walk on. The sidewalk hurry of hundreds washes the scene away. Only the placard remains in the gutter.

"I got two!" daughter exults. "Two Mick autographs! One for Viv, the bigger one for me! Let's go!"

We go, daughter doing a frolicsome imitation of a rock star's androgynous strut. "They won't believe me!" she exults. "He was eating yucko apple pie!"

Something in me wants to run after Ms. Nikon. To make up for my nasty ruminations about her, I want to tell her that she is indeed a paparazzo, but a metaphysical one: she's out to produce pregnant candids from the sterile flux. I might also tell her (if it's any consolation) that even the tabloids' paparazzi— especially adepts that catch Mick *in flagrante* with apple pie— are a guild akin to the painters of church murals five hundred years ago. Those muralists rendered visible to the faithful earthly glimpses of the divine. The groupies of today practice a faith which also needs accessible pictures of halos.

Daughter is an example. Look at her, still jerking along parodistically in Mick's gait, still intoxicated with her idol's outlandishness. Here, in the full flower of ambivalence, is a fan, that is, a fanatic; that is, one from the fane, or temple—one inspired by deity. Fans form a club to simulate an *ecclesia,* a minyan, a parish; a communal shelter they long for but cannot find in the desacralized barrens. The celebrity, then, enables his fans to celebrate, i.e., to frequent together, the way the fatherland joins patriots shoulder-to-shoulder, or the way the revolution sets comrades embracing.

We applaud the star. Our ovation voices a communality of pleasure; indeed, clapping my hands in rhythm with others, being fellow-partaker with them of the same good—all that contributes to the euphoria of applause. Similarly we gossip about the star and thus create a social linkage as pleasurable and important. Applauding alone is silly. Gossiping by myself is impossible. In fact, the history of the word "gossip" leads to its collective origins. It derives from "God's sibb"—"sibb" being the Gothic word for the clan that gathers at the godly rite of baptism to exchange family news around the crib. Around

the birth of a new star crystallizes an ad hoc kinship group of applauders and gossipers.

To be gossip-worthy the god/star needs to be two things: great *and* wounded. His greatness sweeps me out of my isolation and brings my face together with others by turning us all toward him. His wound connects him to our mortality. That's why Osiris was drowned, Adonis gored, Jesus crucified, Balder hanged, and the Phrygian Dionysus torn to pieces.

"What's he really like?" we keep asking about the superstar. In the question hides our hope that he'll giggle when tickled, stumble when drunk, bleed when nailed to the cross, just like you or me. Over ancient Egypt reigned Ra, the Sun God, in ever perfect impervious eternity. But by the end of the Middle Kingdom Ra lost his box-office appeal, so to speak, to Osiris, whose anguish pulsed through his timelessness.

All our successful theology deals with the charisma of vulnerability. It explains what God is really like backstage, without His makeup. In that sense the Gospel according to St. Mark offers the lonely and excluded the same consolation as the *National Enquirer*. The Old Testament reveals Yahweh in human, all too human detail: see Him howling, raging, hurting, even repenting. To a tremulous Israel His quiverings made His supremacy that much more effective. In the New Testament, Jesus' self-proclamation, serene and sovereign, "I am the light . . ." (John 8:12), gains poignancy through His creaturely despair: "My God, my God, why hast thou forsaken me?" (Mark 15:34).

It is the sore on the Godhead which enthralls the faithful and bedevils His interpreters. Christ had no sooner come and gone than generations of Christologists from Marcion to Origen to Arius anathemized each other over how much of Him was sheer

God, absolute, immaculate, unmitigated; and how much of Him flesh, fraying and fevering. At last the issue was settled by the Ecumenical Council at Chalcedon in A.D. 451. It held that Christ partook fully and equally of two natures, human and divine, "without confusion, without change, without division, without separation." This Chalcedonian summation of What He Is Really Like became the motto of the Judeo-Christian Factory. He is superchief, top boss, whose transcendence thrills us; He is the grease monkey under the next machine, sweating our sweat, groaning with our aggravation. The Chalcedonian formula defines the Superstar who walks funny and eats yucko pie.

Frank Sinatra's paradigmatic fame rests on such duality. He transports his fans in the manner of the ultimate media god; yet "without confusion or change" he also phosphoresces with the corruptions of the flesh. Gregory Peck will never be a legend. Humphrey Bogart was born to be one. The charismatic stigma makes the difference.

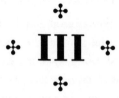

III

AFTER 2:30 P.M. SATURDAYS (the sign says) the garage door in Viv's building will be locked. And so it is. We are more than three quarters of an hour late for the party. We are also too late for my plan: to use the garage as change cabin in which to slip into our "come anciently" T-shirts.

Suddenly the door opens, emits a car that almost runs us over, stops—and brings us news that we are early. Behind the wheel Kevin says it's that last-minute contingent of kids being flown in for the party from Washington, where Viv spent her first school years—those extra kids caught the kitchen short of kiwi for the fruit dessert, so why don't we change shirts in the car and zip with him, Kevin, to the Emporium? That's the nearest place with genuine New Zealand imported kiwi—it'll take only a couple of minutes zinging back and forth, the whole party's behind schedule anyway, some snafu with the shuttle, the Washington bunch still on the way from La Guardia—so hop in, guys!

We hop in. Anyone familiar with Viv's family knows Kevin. The super's son, he is the money crowd's errand boy and troubleshooter par excellence, always dashingly on the go; but never until today did I realize how fast. He's whirling the wheel, swiveling us around corners, beating red lights, lighting himself a Kent, switching cassettes from punk to raga and throwing me about so with his veerings that it takes me awhile to find the armhole of my FIRST GRAFFITI T-shirt. Of course daughter is lighter, younger, and more native to speed, less subject to centrifugality. She changes much faster and flashes her Mick autograph at Kevin.

"Hey, all right!" he says, whizzing along. "But sell it quick. Like, when I was relief disc jockey at Fort Lee Danceteria, would you believe Olivia Newton You Know Who comes by. So naturally I grab an auto. Same night I could have sold it for ten. Today I couldn't even get five. That whole rock thing sucks. Up and down like a rollercoaster. I had such a great group all set, even a name, 'The Kevinauts' like 'Astronauts.' But then I look at the *Variety* newspaper. Boing-boing-boing, one group going bust after another. I got off that trip just in time. If I was a Beatle starting out today—forget it. Straight down the tube. You gotta choose your field right. See, my enthusiasm, that's my biggest problem. Not catching the bad vibes in time. Like, politics, I was bartending that fundraiser up at Mount Kisco, man, that was a hundred-bucks-per-pizza scene, imagine, the Senior Senator of New York State, he gives me his office number, I mean, that was Cloud Nine till I hear a little birdie saying, 'Cool it, man. No way.' I mean, who the hell ever wins that hassle? Say you make governor. The bigger

you are, the more you get trashed. They'll sic some dirt on you, don't worry, even if you're a stupid saint. The hell with the White House, gimme a million. You know what's for me? The commodity exchange, copper futures. Tremendous profit leverage on minimum investment. My friend Jay, he's a runner on the floor there, and Jay's one baby that keeps his eyes open. When the time is right we'll start a copper combo. Of course you need capital. That's where Viv's dad comes in. That's a swinging gentleman. He'll get me a lifeguard job at Southampton. Heiress Beach. Also, at the party today, I can serve canapés if I want to. Viv's older sister, she'll have girlfriends dropping by. Real heavy-bread chicks, man. Best way to get money is to marry it, right? I'm only half-kidding. Or maybe not marry, just, you know, connect. Here we are. Okay. This is the credit card. It's Viv's mom's. Could you kindly get thirty kiwis while I stay here double-parked?"

Unquote, Kevin the super's son of 15 East 83rd. I climb out of the car, impressed not only by the momentum with which he catapulted us here but also by his perspectives and ambitions. Kevin is such a different breed from Bernie, the son of the super of my American youth up in Washington Heights.

Unlike this zooming Tri-State-Area Kevin, Bernie found his métier in the world and underworld of our block. Bernie could change the basement into a bowling alley and any laundry room into a love nest; he even knew how to make snooty Irma of apartment 14C go almost all the way in the least usher-patroled part of our Loew's balcony, and how to tell Al, the soda jerk at Glick's, the kind of joke that got you a jumbo malted for the price of regular.

All that would be wimp stuff to Kevin. He's about the same age as the Bernie I remember but a long generation further away from the hearth—that is, from anything local that he could accept as his way of life. Would he see a shred of his future on his block? Or look for real fun there? Man, he'd be grossed out by the provinciality of the notion. Kevin lives in the Big Apple, not on any mere street. Nothing in his experience suggests that once a block was a homey kingdom you stroked into existence with your sneakers' soles as you strolled through it with the guys; that you kept leaning against its walls with a fond back and a leisured eye; that stickball yells and stoopball thuds were affirmations of belonging.

On the crosstown block, strolling, hanging-out, playing, are territorial enjoyments that have become extinct. They are buried in the same archaeological layer with the candy-store bunch, the newsstand wiseacres and other final practitioners of your-face-to-my-face. This fossil neighborhood lies under the grid of highways constituting the city today, along whose macadam Kevin hustles. He works the newest, most hopped-up Factory shift that can't bother with buddies on the block. If Kevin is on his way to a friend, it's to Jay down in Soho, his future partner-in-millionairedom. Kevin's reference point isn't any dinky little patch of asphalt but a vista of far-flung summits constantly conjured by the media: network specials, coast-to-coast finalists, top-forty favorites, national news conferences, the Fortune Five Hundred, anchorman ratings, golden records, World Series statistics, championship interviews, bestselling paperbacks, investment leaders. . . . In a framework so rigorously cosmic, what is the block to Kevin?

Once more I think what I've thought so often before on this crosstown trip. Humanity had it better earlier. Of course some men live in anachronistic nooks where "Hi there" still sounds better without a body mike. For example, the ghetto precinct of Sir Juan Wow! is still sufficiently disadvantaged to think turf instead of thinking world-wide. Another exception is Kevin's own father, the building superintendent. Kevin Senior still has a resort in the corner bar. By ambling a couple of hundred yards Kevin Senior finds what Junior never reaches no matter how long he races toward it at radar-trap speed. At McAllister's Pub, Senior enjoys some your-face-to-my-face, at least after the second round of Budweisers. That's when his crowd, warmed by ritual jokes and teasing, choruses their famous off-key, off-color variation of "My Darling Clementine." Lapped by such nidicolous music, a super in charge of a shack like 15 East 83rd is something of a class sonofabitch.

"Being recognized has its advantages," Al Pacino once confessed to columnist Liz Smith. "The whole city is like one big neighborhood block." And so Kevin Junior, to gain what Senior already possesses, must become a movie star or the President or Rockefeller. If he fails, he'll be less than his father and lower than Sir Juan Wow! He simply has no more neighborhood in which to be anybody. Consequently he must be Somebody to the whole world. For him fame is not a matter of arrogance but of moral survival. Anonymity amounts to humiliation. It's the sort of disgrace of which his father is ignorant, having been spared his son's fame-conditioning in his own youth.

"God," said a hermetic philosopher, "is that sphere whose

center is everywhere and whose circumference is nowhere." No presently existing circumference or other boundary is real for Kevin; no city block or landmark with visible and therefore limiting horizons; no "high places" of baalim around which to join the revels of fellow worshipers. No, Kevin wouldn't be part of any such boondocks crowd. He is the center—or rather he will be. His geography is Yahweh's universal future. Just wait—he'll hit the bull's eye of the whole scene pretty soon. Wherever he's barreling along on his hundred-and-fifty horse-power, there's his Big Timer's tomorrow just ahead, while all around, right and left, the square old provincial present blurs away into invisibility. Today consists of just some sleazeball outskirts. Tomorrow is IT, where you can do the essence of YOUR thing.

In zoologist's parlance the butterfly is the "imago" of the caterpillar; that is, its future and final and real image which for now is still shrouded in a purely prefatory guise. Is Kevin going to stay a caterpillar forever? Like hell. His future is a splendor that's compulsory, not optional. No maybe about it. He'd *better* wind up some sort of top honcho. This mandate dangles before him down that rushing windshield like a Play-boy Club key. He travels in stringent Pauline expectancy. The freeways thunder and screech with numberless caterpillars' impatiences like his.

The planet used to be quieter. Once upon a time comparatively few people stomped after supremacy. At first only one man—Pharaoh—incarnated the idea. Later Israel assumed it under the stewardship of Yahweh. Still later it became known as the Divine Right of Kings. The claim to

supremacy incandesced Renaissance genius and quattrocento prince. It unloosed the collective surges of nationalisms. But not until the last hundred years did supremacy cravings filter down to a workaday level and make the young-man-in-the-street feel pre-presidential. So nobody much says hello to him when he's coming out of his own house? Never mind, he'll show them. He'll build himself a capital-I Image that will compel capital-R Recognition up and down and all over. They don't know him now? They'll say they knew him when!

This means that he—and millions like him—must hack his way out of the log-cabin lonesomeness toward the big chair at the top of the board room table or toward the Marine Band awaiting him with "Hail to the Chief" on the White House lawn. He's sure he's got the stuff—just needs to get past those jealous killers. Meritocracy is an endless throne room, bloody and noisy with the fratricide of a nation of crown princes. Though you are the super's son, you were born the heir apparent. Therefore it's your fault—not the system's—if you don't seize the one scepter in this melee of millions of graspers. Kevin is fairly new to the fray and he has it tougher than combatants before him. His predecessors in absolute ambition, say a royal bastard pretending to the crown, could command a repertoire of historic gestures, an established style, a heraldic dramaturgy. Kevin must invent the character of the supremacy he claims with little help other than his dentist's copies of *Business Week* and *People* magazine. And so he grabs helter-skelter for every possible plume in his future.

"Hey, sir, please!" he calls after me, as daughter and I walk from the car to the Emporium. "When you pass the Beach Boy

Boutique, could you see if they're running any barbell specials this week?"

✜

Of course they have barbell specials at the Beach Boy Boutique, right next to the poster of Mr. Hawaii of the impossible biceps. The Stag Party (as the men's clothing department is billed) swings with Superguy Casuals; supersellers at extra discounts solicit from the Bookworm's World; the Mall Kitchen offers Royal Buckingham stemware. Under the fluorescent glitter superlatives lie in state, sexily embalmed for a long shelf life. In the Produce Pavilion there must be particles of the grocery from Bernie's old block, ground-up, freeze-dried, reconstituted, tinseled. Other aisles are other taxidermic mosaics of other disemboweled neighborhood stores. It's a brightly glazed death that encompasses the continents—florists on Long Island, done in by shopping-center price wars; failed farmer's markets in Bavaria; obsolete souks in Samarkand.

My New Zealand kiwis are arrayed here between mirrors that multiply them into exotic infinity; so are tabouli salad dishes from Tangier and reindeer *flanken* from Norway. Around the corner wait Hong Kong's combed cotton shirts along with wool scarves woven in the Hebrides and miniature rugs handhooked by Tunisian children. A few decades ago all these were primarily local wares sold by the corner store to neighborhood customers, your-face-to-my-face. Now they are export specialties packaged for connoisseurs of all latitudes. Everything

merges into sale-priced galactic dust, and over it washes hi-fi disco Muzak, the new music of the spheres.

Oh for Kevin's grandfather's village in Maine and for the General Store therein! How well it accomplished the reverse of the Emporium—and how healingly! Its customers were the guests of the storekeeper in a parlor not particularly centered around a cash register. Together they cut the big world down to cracker-barrel size and gave each hunk of new-fangled big-deal news a homespun cast. Here the rag was chewed person-to-person, back and forth across the chipped counter until the whole ornery earth took on folks-sized trappings and everybody moseyed on home pretty much on top of things.

By contrast, the Emporium gives each small tissue-need a global orchestration. Dry skin can be treated here by a Parisian moisturizer in hourglass jars or llama suet from the Andes in mauve tubes. You enter thirsty, to buy seltzer. You stay, hypnotized by bottled fjord water and Chilean pomegranate juice.

The Emporium is a centerfold vision of the peculiarly puritan wantonness we've been trained to find desirable: staged, painted, expertly inflated opulence purged of organic connections. It's the ultra-fuckable ass all a-quiver with foam rubber stuffing. No green shoots are left on the AAA radishes here; no stems on the Riviera cherries. You'd never guess from the waxed shine of the peppers that they sprang from the magic dullness of dirt. There is no such thing as a heifer grazing on a meadow. There is only a parsley-laced landscape of filet mignon.

A fairyland beyond the nitrogen cycle, the Emporium will

stimulate yens rather than satisfy needs. It ministers to the gourmet consumer. And the gourmet consumer is someone the totality of whose senses have been starved on behalf of a few selected, doctored and distended appetites. The boy who picks himself a pear by climbing the green breeze of a tree feels at home on the earth. But the boy who asks if the Coyennes du Comice have arrived yet from the pear orchards of Provence?

The Coyennes du Comice boy will always long somehow for the happy bough he never knew; that whisper of numinous benevolence our ancestors could hear coming out of the very blueness of the sky. Even veteran worldlings need some scientifically respectable analogue to what Christians call grace: God's largess poured out freely toward men. It blesses tree climbers more often than epicures.

But the Emporium offers something next to grace, in its own characteristic way, of course. It features a Tobler Swiss Chocolate Economy Bar Special, two for a dollar fifty, today only. Sales like that are the management's largess poured out freely toward its customers—a touch of love from on high. Against my own will it warms my heart far beyond the thirty-two cents saved on each bar. It shows that The Force is with me, after all, even here in the lonesome abundance of the Emporium where people talk less to each other than in a Presbyterian church. Being lonesome, we are acquisitive. Often greed becomes a form of loneliness—the loneliness of those who covet in objects what they can no longer find in friends. Since the your-face-to-my-face spirit is gone, we turn "materialistic" out of privation. We pounce on the sale in chocolates because we can no longer trust the sweetness of Bob's smile.

Carrying my basket of kiwis, I'm waylaid by the reference counter of the Bookworm's World. At ten percent off (today only) the *Pocket Oxford Dictionary* looks quite seductive. Does it contain the word "palatine"? If it passes that test I'll put it in my basket. In my loneliness I shop for what grace I can find.

✠

On line at the checkout counter: my search through P words is interrupted by daughter, running.

"Daddy! I found the smartest doll!"

But it's a doll that seems less smart than sick with a rash all over its bare little chest.

"Just watch, Daddy. You put this hospital coat on it, like this—and then you take off the coat again . . . and no more measles! See? All gone!"

I look at the marvel.

"Let me figure this out," I say. "Well, the 'measles' are just an outer skin on top of her regular skin and it sticks to the gown when you pull it off. Yeah, that's clever."

"Can I have it? It's ten percent cheaper, only today!"

"We spent enough this afternoon."

"But it's ten percent cheaper only today!"

"All right."

A growled acquiescence. Ten-year-old daughter can cure toy pustules, but no divine largess will relieve me of liver spots that one day will dot the face in my mirror. The weight of my decaying sags heavy at the Emporium, where fish gleam for-

ever fresh in the deep-freeze display. The radishes, shorn of green, mock all waxings and wanings of soil-bound life. Flown in from the antipodes, the strawberries defy the seasons. In this ingeniously artificed Eden I'm a lot dumber than a $10.95 doll. I'm worse than dumb. I'm guilty. Guilty of impermanence. Out of sheer criminal negligence I haven't been able to find a hospital gown that will peel off my measles now, let alone the smudges of rigor mortis later. My body erodes only because I don't trouble to stay fit, to get a by-pass job on time, to keep the right diet with the right vitamin/mineral/hormone mix. Only delinquents let their flesh fail. Only losers die these days.

"These days" go back awhile. They started with the middle-class chagrin at lapses in the human apparatus, which seemed to be much more unconscionable than, say, those of the steam engine. In *Erewhon*, Samuel Butler's Victorian send-up of modernity, the judges of that dubious utopia punished you with five months of hard labor for catching a cold. For pneumonia you could draw thirty years. Did Gustav Mahler read Samuel Butler? "Sickness is a lack of talent," said the genius with hemorrhoids and heart trouble. His symphonies cry out the angst of an age in which it just won't do anymore to be perishable.

Today I can be Somebody only if I am supreme. But what is supremacy without permanence? A sort of brutal joke. The higher a man's pinnacle, the more grotesque his tumble into the grave. As he plummets an ikon turns into Humpty-Dumpty. That's why dead rulers receive state funerals. Guns go off to mask the *flump!* of a mortifying pratfall.

Here is a prospect achievers don't like to contemplate, my-self included. But it's there and it keeps on being there while the arthritic chairman boards the Concorde or the young teller runs for the 8:05. The prospect looms below our daily busyness and its injustice provokes our retaliation, though we may not even know we are retaliating. Biology has manufactured us as gimcrack gadgets that obsolesce virtually overnight; our intol-erable death is the simple routine of its ongoing life. Therefore we construct a counter-biology of machines. We pollute the water of the spring that will flow long after we've gone; we pave over the earth that will inter us; we smash the atom outlasting our distintegration; we deploy fission, fusion, whatever is new-est in the arsenal of our laboratories. Nature's endurance con-sists of an endless chain of brevities like ours. We've been sentenced to death by the natural course of events. Perhaps we feel less helpless by sentencing nature.

If time is going to run us through—all right, then we'll gore space with rockets. Our arteries are powerless against the years. Very well, we'll let our red-shift spectroscopes go to town on light-years of vastness beyond the Crab Nebula. The giant telescope and the space probe are, besides their more obvious functions, spearheads of our counter-offensive. A long time ago, when death had not yet degenerated, we didn't have to work so hard against it. Death simply isn't what it used to be. Before the Factory, dying was part of the Orphic circle from which we borrowed our breath. It was a passage along a curve that passed into and out of the ever-burying, ever-pregnant earth. A gregarious passage, at that. In some Alpine villages the dead are still buried in coffins so porous they turn

quite fast into the valley's new soil. The vestments and chants escorting a corpse to the grave mark less the end of an individual than an overture to flowers. Such rites allow our temporariness to be embraced by the continuity of nature.

Where members of the nidus live your-face-to-my-face, past and future are on friendlier footing. The front line between life and death becomes less eerie, more companionable through genuine ceremonials, that is, true frequentings-together. But all that has withered with the withering of community. Now each of us is on his own above the earth as well as below. Horatio Alger's boy must make it all the way to the top, pushing the boulder of his career up the mountain. His solitude on the peak enhances his triumph. But the commensurate solitude of the grave that is to follow? No, he can't tolerate that. It simply isn't part of the forward-looking entrepreneurial spirit.

In this scenario getting old smacks of backwardness; falling sick is an embarrassment; "passing away" stands as euphemism for an obscene gaffe. Death is life's dirty secret. I've been programmed to accumulate forever; not to share and dwindle; certainly not to crumble into other creatures' thriving. How can I possibly be destined to give up my substance to worms? What kind of welfare state is the nitrogen cycle? Is there no tax lawyer in the bios?

As the premise of my being locks into the paycheck ahead, as more and more of my satisfactions hinge on the future, the scandal of my mortality deepens. The Factory has lavished on what is to come all the pleasure, the ease, the fun withheld from what is now. To earn all that, I must be my own do-it-myself messiah. I punch in, launch into my travails, take on

danger and drudgery for the sake of the wealth that awaits me. But look! Can that be? I wrinkle, I calcify even faster than I toil. What is to come will be my physiological bankruptcy. Each gray hair betrays another failure in self-redemption.

I'm guilty of knowing no better than the stupidly wilting grass. I hate being so brief. I hate the Emporium, where every corner brims with goods that could sate a dozen consumer lives. If I'm lucky I'll have all of one. *Timor mortis conturbat me.*

✠

On a day like today, after brooding like this, I feel more cheated than usual at the check-out counter. Almost instinctively I cheat back. The kiwis cost Viv's family twenty-eight dollars on their credit card. With tax, I paid eleven dollars ninety for the measles doll. The *Pocket Oxford Dictionary* is free. It's a discreet little lump in my trouser pocket.

"Come on," I say to daughter. "Let's get back to the car."

Kevin is double-parked on the other side of the street. Daughter's hand in mine, I scuttle through the bilious honks of drivers. Never mind them. Nobody will run us down. Nothing can hurt us. From the ten-percent-off bit of shoplifting in my pocket sprouts, quite unexpectedly, a sense of armored triumph, of indestructibility, of getting away with it for good. By suspending my conscience I seem to have rid myself of my hated transience. It's as though I've reached a position for a

trade-off with Him: I'll stop monkeying with His law only if He'll stop monkeying with my life.

On some such unarticulated rationale the crime statistics soar. The fact is that mortality and morality are yoked together. Adam became mortal only after he was subjected to the moral. Before the fall he was an ageless innocent in Eden, the carefree painter of cave-wall deer. After the fall, he turned into the Hebrew outsider, naked to judgment, to ambition, to conscience, to decay. In stealing that dictionary I was really giving back a piece of fruit: the apple on the tree whose bittersweet made us taste, all at once, good-versus-evil *and* life-against-death.

And so I'm jaywalking right now, back toward Eden, away from the God Who revealed that our flesh must suffer sinful perdition. Away from the Lord of the life-death chasm Who declared corpses unclean. I'm crossing against a red light that's been glaring into our eyes ever since we've left one another's nearness.

Is it my fault that we are now more apt to collide than to embrace? Is it my fault that His handiwork has evolved into a titanic demolition derby? That traffic lights must flash across all continents to keep His creatures from crashing into one another? Each hurtles alone and separate in carapaced, unmoored, incurable speed. Each has abandoned the comity which was once local and your-face-to-my-face. To prevent fratricide among the doomed, the decalogue had to be imposed by an Enforcer as invisible as a radar-trap cop. Directed at men strange to one another, His rule enjoined from the *outside* what had earlier been implicit *inside* through tribal usage and

custom. Earlier, in tribal times, hostility was often ritualized away by confrontations ceremonial, not lethal. Then the tribe faded; so did its preventive mores. Morality became necessary as the next best thing.

Ethics is one of the arts of alienation. Once fellowship worked spontaneously among people enjoying an intimate hunting-band knowledge of each other. Now fellowship needs to be pounded into us with crushing eloquence from an awesome altitude. Once we sensed ourselves children of a particular corner of the earth that will reclaim us; once burial ceremonialized a natural transformation. Now the biological law of death is writ on stone as adamant and foreign as that on which the moral law of the commandments was hammered.

I cannot soften such stone. That was done—almost—by the Son of Him Who hardened it. Jesus promised to take the fall out of Adam. What's more, the Son of God rose Himself beyond all moral/mortal rigors. He broke the moral code (the "curse of the law," as Paul put it in Galatians), violating the Sabbath habitually. He overrode the biological law of death by dying only to live again in the selfsame form. He was the Christ, so called because He had been anointed with the chrism—a salve distilling divine lawlessness. The orientalist Robertson Smith tells us that the chrism descends from the fat of human sacrifice. "Thou shalt not kill," said the Father's law. The Son gleamed with the symbol of the killing. Why can't I glow a little with my puny theft?

✣

Why can't I glow a little while longer? The question abides after daughter and I have gotten back into Kevin's car. During the ride to Viv's party my villain's high is fading fast. Nobody helps me keep it alive. Things are too quiet. Nobody talks. Of course daughter is busy, putting on and pulling off the doll's sickness. Up front, at the wheel, Kevin maintains an un-Kevin-like silence. But in the rearview mirror his eyes keep veering in my direction. Maybe he has spied that peccant lump in my pocket, the stolen little dictionary. I'm still exhilarated by its stolenness, but he no doubt despises me for being such a small-time crook.

I ought to find some way of explaining the modesty of my haul. Kevin, I ought to say (in language that will reach him)— Kevin, I'm sorry that's no Federal Reserve heist in my pocket, but even a paltry robbery can massage the robber's soul. It might even be his equivalent of encounter therapy. Through his offense the offender establishes himself as someone who matters to others. Just ask his victims. He has choked some responsive gasp out of all the heedlessness teeming around him. His deed affirms his presence—he has kicked a dent into the universe. The shock in his victim's face signals not only recognition of his existence but an obeisance to his particular style of existing. After all, his crime is very specifically *his*, fashioned by the idiosyncrasy of his impulse. The life of the predator is much less rote-like than that of his prey, and that's

why actors of greater dash or at least superior pungency portray him in the movies. It's not just loot that a robber garners. His robbery also earns him keen relationships. An energy field has developed of which he, the perpetrator, is the proprietor. Around him revolve detectives, clues, fears, speculations. He is less outside, less helpless and passive before the norms of ethics and death.

By making the Emporium my victim, I've personalized it. I've etched a bit of my spirit into that glittering chill. Crime is often a perverse try to desecularize the desert.

Actually it's through such attempts that the anti-hero becomes heroic in Western tradition. That, too, I ought to explain to Kevin. Kevin, I ought to say, I wish that little dictionary I copped were bigger. A college-sized one might detail the origin of the word "evil" down to its Old High German root "ubil," meaning "over there," "beyond the limit." You see, Kevin, the evolution of that term capsules the biography of the Judeo-Christian ethos.

It is evil, it is iniquitous, to go beyond. The Hebrews, or Ibhrim, etymologically "those from beyond the river," were superb bards of iniquity. It was a Jewish commonplace, noted Robert Graves, that Israel's worst day was not the destruction of the temple but the translation of the sacred book from Hebrew into the Greek of the Septuagint. The Bible, "which contained records of evil deeds done by their ancestors and reminders of God's punishment for continual backsliding, it was thought, should never have been divulged to Israel's enemies." Our scripture is one great song about man's brazenness and the Whirlwind's wrath. It sings about the enterprising

nomads who roved beyond the safely plausible and invested
their faith (the ultimate risk capital) in a God Who lives
beyond the visible. The Bible is about the chutzpah of believing Him and the consequent hubris of defying Him. Only those
strong enough to imagine His transcendent presence have the
strength to transcend His commands. Because they are chosen
they are also stiff-necked. God sears them with lightning that
shines like a halo. They have done evil in the sight of the
Lord. Yet their punishment marks them as His people. They
have gone beyond.

The cabala's principal reinterpretation of Genesis reflects a
similar paradox. At first there was only the limitless purity of
God. Then He created the universe by making room inside
Himself for it and for its flaws. The cosmos is an impurity, a
nomad-like incursion into the Godhead. Therefore denizens of
creation must sooner or later atone for having invaded the
good, pure spirituality of the Eternal with their bodily, time-
corrupted evil. Their going-beyond satisfies one part of the divine intention. The other part demands that their beyondness
be flogged with "the rod of His anger" to become worthy of
redemption.

This demand drives the Factory. Its machines hum to the
dynamics and dithyrambs of evil. The imminence of punishment daunts the workers and chains them to the wheel. At the
same time the Factory creed mythicizes the evil-doer in the
front office who advances our destinies along their foreordained
orbit. A big shot *has* to be a first-class sonofabitch. How else
would he get things done? "O happy fault!" exclaimed St. Au-
gustine over Adam's original sin because it engendered the re-

demptive sacrifice of Christ. "O truly needful sin!" intones the Catholic blessing of the Paschal candle. "God has assigned all men to disobedience," announced Paul, "so that He may have mercy upon them." Thus the pits of the fatal apple were the first seeds of our ethos. After Adam came other dark sowers. Cain, the brother-killer, founded our cities. Moses' trespasses kept him from entering the Promised Land the Hebrews would not have reached without his leadership. Adultery marked David's greatness, glorious Solomon knelt before idols. So it went, down to Roland, the first Christian hero of the Middle Ages: his arrogance earned him his fame. He refused to blow his horn until it was too late for Charlemagne to save him and the faithful from the infidels.

Though Judeo-Christianity did not invent guilt, guilt did become the undersong of its elite. Our compact with God is textured with prohibitions, yet transgressors have enacted our history. This tension, this potent ambivalence animates a faith right for uprooted aspirers, from Abraham pushing out of Ur, to the farm boy set to shake up Fifth Avenue. It is a faith serving a Godhead high up and far away; a faith in which everyday things are no longer holy or face-to-face near; in which the earth is remote, sinful, temporary, rapable, ripe for death and conquest, rife with taboo and lootable riches. A faith where the present is profane hostage to the sacred future. It is for us valorous venturous sinners that the Savior will come.

Meanwhile God's grace speaks through the restlessness and ruthlessness of His worshipers. "Happy shall he be," sings the psalmist of the Lord Whose commandment was not to kill, "happy shall he be that dashes the little children of Babylon

against the stones." The more closely I model myself on His supremely vengeful and wilful image, the greater my impatience with communal modes like ritual or compassion. Most of the successful devout are Low Church in denomination or in mood.

"No law can be sacred to me but that of my own nature," wrote the Reverend Ralph Waldo Emerson not too long before he proposed discontinuance of the Lord's Supper. "Our acts our angels are," he quoted Beaumont and Fletcher approvingly. On a planet bereft of the sacral, the only power left lives in *my* muscle, *my* mettle, *my* vision, *my* vindication, *my* initiative, *my* decision, *my* deeds. Only *my* uplifted arm can pluck vitality from that oversoul or hew sense into existence. For Emerson, the upwardly mobile Yankee metaphysician, such reasoning led to a sparkling, sequined existentialism. Kierkegaard, the Dane, had similar thoughts in the same decade of the same century. But the book in which he set them down was called *Fear and Trembling*. By the 1840's the fling of the lone self with experience had darkened in Europe. On the younger, dewier side of the Atlantic, Emerson and Whitman continued to rhapsodize.

✣

How can I get any of this across to Kevin? Something has happened to him. The way he is now, he'd be impervious to my point, however lucidly put—or to any other argument, for that matter. He seems different from the fireball who shot us over to

the Emporium. He's no longer even staring at me in the rear-view mirror—if he ever was. This changed Kevin is driving back to Viv's house with a slowness that's remarkable. His car rounds corners in such drowsy smooth leisure that daughter can practice her jacks in the backseat space between us.

The new Kevin doesn't talk or seem ready to listen; just lolls by the wheel; steers with one hand; whistles softly. And his whistling reminds me of something I can't quite place. His free hand lies palm open on the back of the front seat. For a moment I wonder whether he wants the sales slip from the kiwi purchase. Perhaps, after I give it to him, he'll resume his speed.

"Okay, Kevin, here's the receipt."

Indifferent, he waves it away.

"Say," he muses dreamily, "you mind keeping that slip and givin' it to Viv's folks?"

"All right."

"The kiwis, too? Mind givin' it to 'em?"

I'm surprised.

"You mean you're not coming up to the apartment?"

A shoulder shrug, a headshake, both absentminded. Both out of character. I feel I should remind him of his plans.

"Didn't you want to check out those heiresses at the party, Kevin?"

"Yeah, maybe later." He half-yawns. "I was just thinking, my Uncle Tim's stamps. Nice little collection he left me. I never really looked through it. About time I did." And resumes whistling.

Peculiar. To the earlier Kevin nothing little could have been

"nice." A stamp collection would have meant zilch to him, except perhaps as a portfolio of negotiables, a base to be expanded by trading and to be cashed in for a grander venture. But "just looking through" a "nice little" collection? Instead of prospecting for the main chance in a penthouse? Is that our Kevin?

He reaches out with his free hand and drops it on the radio knob of the dashboard. The ululations of some punkette stop. His whistling starts again, more clearly profiled. Suddenly its familiarity comes home. It has the tone of *switching off*. Decades ago, my father whistled in that tone while switching off the machines in our factory, every Saturday afternoon.

Those pistons, gears, transmission belts had fevered all week on behalf of weeks, and weeks, and many more weeks ahead. The products stamped out by the presses must bring money to pay for more advanced engines next month, a second factory floor next year, my university education ten years away. The future was a chronic war fought daily, morning, noon, and night.

But since this was the Sabbath we had arrived at a truce. Our tomorrowness could be put to rest while the afternoon lasted. For a while we were released into today. We could taste the here; touch the now. During this reprieve we did not have to keep and keep and keep collecting more stamps. Our eyes could take in the collection as it was, relish its colors, savor its watermarks.

And why shouldn't Kevin whistle himself toward such peace? Strivers more rabid than he have been haunted by it. The hope for absolute ease sustains the thrust for absolute con-

trol. In his table talk Adolf Hitler liked to dream ahead to puttering in the little garden he'd plant by his little house in Linz, *after* the universal establishment of the New Order. Henry Ford, whose cars juggernauted millions of villages to pieces, made a fetish—as well as a museum—out of Greenfield Village, its early American calm and purity. Karl Marx saw the proletariat as the militant agent of its own salvation. But after its triumph in the class struggle and after the alertness demanded during the subsequent socialist phase—after all that would come the utter relaxation of the final, post-socialist era; the dictatorship of the previously downtrodden would dissolve spontaneously into smiles; the workers of the world could bask in the lotus land of unpoliced communism. More than six hundred years before the founding of Marx's Internationale, Joachim of Floris beguiled thousands with the prophecy of similar deliverance. Joachim forecast an arduous path for Christendom that would lead at last into a perfect, churchless, effortless paradise of believers.

Something like my father's "switching-off" whistle must have sounded through all these visions. None of us are quite deaf to it. Our life—an ambitious, constrained, onerous, horizon-ridden life in which we are not comfortingly near to one another nor in sacred proximity to nature—such a life is time's fool, and time must have a stop. The hour hand rounds and rounds the circle of our frustrations. Night after night my bed bristles with the failures of the day. I cannot even feel the softness of my pillow . . . but tomorrow evening I'll luxuriate in it, carefree, after success has ransomed me. Year after year

I keep wriggling out of a restrictive "was" into a "will be" that never quite manages to set me free and never, never "is."

It's a tantalization. It has beset us ever since we started to push the plow. Henry James's clock-hounded Strether has a long line of predecessors, not least among them Faust. The bait Mephistopheles dangles is non-Faustian: a moment so fair, Goethe's hero will be content to live wholly within it instead of tensing to master what comes next. For the bliss of that instant he is ready to barter his soul. Yet even at the end, the instant remains a promise in the distance. Never does it touch him into a happy pagan letting-go. Amidst celestial hurrahs, he retains his striver's soul and dies a Christian, piously unfulfilled.

"What are you called?" said the first of the prophets to the Lord when He first revealed Himself. Moses asked that question of the bush that burned unconsumed because it burned outside time. "I AM THAT I AM" came the answer, spoken from an instant lasting forever, a divine dimension, an eternal present tense. Now the Hebrew consonants of "I AM THAT I AM" are J H V H. Vowels may be woven between them to form "YAHWEH." Though a holy name, the word is only a phonetic mask over the yet holier Thing so named, as Jewish mystics know. They know that "Yahweh" is a guise through which the Holiest manifests Itself as It wrings us through the throes of history. Only the semblance spelled "Yahweh" thunders at Israel and plucks His people out of their turpitude to hurl them at the receding perfection of the future. *"Shema Ysroel!"* echoes His exacting roar. Yet deep inside that clamor there abides, silently, "I AM THAT I AM." Here dwells the heart-of-hearts of the Godhead, the cabala's *en sof*, best described as

the wellspring of the infinite, the immeasurable serenity of an emptiness. Here the messiah has come before Adam stirred. Here no prayer is necessary; no moral or mortal ardor. The cosmic sabbath suffuses *en sof* with an absence of effort that is absolute and majestic. As one singular single second it overflows the millennia.

Cabalists discern in *en sof* the Godhead's most pristine principle: a pre-Genesis purity unstained by the pressures of creation. It remains forever free of what wracks us daily. Here all temporal machinery, all clocked elsewhereness, has been switched off. *En sof* rests in the wishless essence of Its own being, immune to the turmoil of "becoming." It is what It is. Alpha courses in Its omega. Cause and effect do not exist in *en sof*, nor does the tension between them, nor the chasm dividing past from future, nor the Faustian strain between desirer and the thing desired. *En sof* is the nothing comprehending everything, an unwilled, unopposed ineffability.

"I AM THAT I AM" speaks from the radiance of the vacuum in which the bush is burning. But "I AM THAT I AM" could also be the voice of *Abgescheidenheit*, a medieval German term meaning "disinterest." Meister Eckhart, Christianity's key mystic, uses it to convey detachment from all time-linked volition. To Eckhart *Abgescheidenheit* represents a good more fundamental than humility or love: unless I am detached, I will tailor my humbleness to some ulterior purpose and degrade my love into strategy. But *Abgescheidenheit* is not just man's culminating virtue. It is also God's own ultimate Sabbath. His innermost kernel is empty; pure of everything that dominates, threatens, decrees, or transforms. It is a supernal zero that

eternally encircles and embraces creation as it is, without the slightest pressure for change. This zero of Eckhart's mirrors the cabala's *en sof*. Only my unconditional detachment—my *Abgescheidenheit*—will achieve continuity with the unconditional detachment of *en sof*. In no other way can creature harmonize with creator.

An intertwining of detachments? Yes. The paradox of that union also illumines the "emptiness" of the Buddhist *sunyata*, the beatitude of *nirvana*, the *satori* of Zen, the Stoic stance, Schopenhauer's sanctuary from the torments of the will, the Sufi "valley of poverty and of nothingness," and, last but not least, the ground from which Kierkegaard's "knight of resignation" leaps toward faith.

✣

Of course it's Kevin who set me thinking of the "knight of resignation." That is, the new Kevin. He seems so oddly content to let others overtake him. We've stopped before an intersection, though the light has not yet changed from yellow to red. He leans back, resigned to letting less patient traffic move past us. Could this be Kierkegaard's apprentice lounging behind the Chevy's wheel? Is he learning that the first step of the mystic is to stand still? It's the only way not to fall behind in a race of losers.

During our village days everybody won his share of the bounty. We ran with—not against—each other in the joint hunt. Mysticism was not necessary as a solace, nor did it need

to be cultivated as an esoteric discipline. Not while all of us still knew each other and together celebrated the mystical that we heard breathing quite normally through the pores of the everyday.

But village distended and tautened into empire. We found ourselves running on a racecourse unmerciful, anonymous, far border to far border. Contestants were strangers who groaned in defeat and collapsed in victory. It was a lifelong marathon. To escape the imperial compulsion, some of us devised an occult exit. Yet no mystic I know has found his way back to the village or the villager's health. For that social bloom my face must inspirit yours with nearness. The mystic is not sociable. He arrives in history only after men have come to maintain a civilized distance from one another while at the same time tuning up their hunger for the prize beyond the moon. Separately each feels the pull, the vehemence and vertigo of a translunar itch. The air is electric between the individual's precariousness and the universe's conquerability. No mystic will be able to undo that voltage; however, the mystical experience can reverse its direction. I am no longer anxious to absorb the worlds around me. On the contrary, I am anxious to be absorbed. "The soul," wrote St. John of the Cross, "feels as if placed in a vast and profound solitude, to which no created thing has access, in an immense and boundless desert the more delicious the more solitary . . ."

The mystical and the imperial self must both deal with the same confrontation: a one-to-one encounter between ego and infinity. In vain, ego burns to annex, or at least to control, all perspectives. The longer it survives, the more vain its fevering.

It will choke on its fierceness and must suppurate as it swells. To cure the disease you must use its energies against itself. The mystic is ambitious to transform ambition into surrender. Instead of grasping endlessly, he desires dissolution into the endless.

I rush through the world only to compound my lateness. Yet the moment I summon enough power to switch off the "I" that runs, my hard cold heavy hurry will thaw and lighten into the flowing of a zero, will find release as ripples of that flow. And the flow always arrives on time.

Gautama Buddha, a king's son, a princely rover, charioted through all the bafflements of his realm until he stopped under Bodhi tree. He sat down. He switched off. Cravings departed. Enlightenment came. A little less than two thousand years later, on the other side of the globe, Meister Eckhart grew up during the Great Interregnum of the thirteenth century. The last Hohenstaufen emperor lay dead, the first Habsburg was not yet crowned. Through the gap spilled a livid rapids in the wake of the crusades. Claimants for primacy chased each other across the rubble of hamlets and counties down to the brink. Only Meister Eckhart's *Abgescheidenheit* could switch all that off.

In the later Middle Ages the cabala matured as Jews were harried from exile to exile with a severity unknown in earlier medieval times. On a deeper level of restlessness, secularization drove Jewish minds past rites and ordinances with which the Talmud gave daily life the cohesion of a nidus. Growing worldly, they lost a world; yet many found it again by contemplating *en sof* of the cabala. They switched off to receive the passive, blissful, reconciled suchness of the universe, the zero that is the palace of God's final reality.

True, from the Jewish perspective the mystic view seems to imply a schizoid Godhead. With His columns of fire, His serpents, behemoths and avenging angels, His clouds of locusts and His Whirlwind, the Lord of Hosts of the Old Testament fountains forth. At the heart of such miraculous flamboyance—the languor of a zero? Is that possible? Yes. The contrast is theologically viable; Yahweh's rabbinate has never ex-communicated the cabalists of *en sof*. The contrast may even be indispensable. On His surface the Almighty displays the window-rattling theater of His power even as He draws His ultimate persuasiveness from the quiet at His core. His exterior turbulence mesmerizes and rouses the knife-clutching nomad in me, prods all my martial, fearful hungers. At the same time I am haunted by intimations of surcease issuing from His inner oblivion. It promises messianic ease. It offers the Sabbath of Sabbaths. It beckons to me from the lee side of His tempests. In the deepest nook of my soul I do not hope for the glorious congestion that offers all I could ever crave. No. I hope for the haven that will allow me to stop craving.

The intuition of such repose grew a garden even in Adolf Hitler's mind. In these pastures the bush burns fresh and green, safe forever from the rampant furnace of the Factory. Beyond Armageddon, on the dulcet side of the apocalypse, the lion can lie down with the lamb. There grow those lilies in the field that need not toil nor spin yet are arrayed in the very sweetness of our dreams.

‡

"Move it!"

A voice bellows from behind our car. We are just four

blocks away from Viv's building. Kevin, who dozed through the changing of the light, moves. We shoot forward so rapidly that the glove compartment, not quite closed, falls open. Inside, a pill bottle with the lid screwed on askew. For quite a few seconds Kevin leaves it exposed to my view. In the rearview mirror his eyes blink at me, lazy-lidded, filmed over with lethargy. With a torpor somehow superior and knowing. "While you were in the Emporium," he says, "I did a little shoppin' of my own."

"Where?" Daughter looks up from her search for a lost jack. "What'd you buy?"

"Oh, Kevin just bought himself some aspirin for a headache," I say quickly.

Daughter points at her $10.95 doll. "Bet *she*'ll need some aspirin for her headache."

"Silly!" I tousle daughter's hair, pull her face sidewards, so she won't see the glove compartment. "New dolls don't get headaches."

"Bet this one'll get a party headache. She's weak from the measles."

"Come on, she'll have a great time at the party! She'll love the jacks tournament."

"She'll hate it when I lose."

Kevin finally slams shut the glove compartment.

"You'll see, Daddy, she'll get a real bad headache at Viv's. Can't you buy her some doll aspirin?"

"No, you little stupid, I can't." I smile, stroking daughter, though I don't feel a smile inside and though I *do* feel like buying aspirins—the kind in the glove compartment. I feel

like taking Kevin aside and slipping him a few bucks for a couple of his goodies. Then I could retire to any of the five and a half bathrooms in Viv's apartment to swallow the stuff. Once it's entered into my bloodstream it will protect with its chemical calm. No need to care or fret about any party, even a penthouse one with Egyptian conceits. I'd sail through it and go home after an adventure. I could find my home *in* the adventure and thereby follow a patriarchal pattern. I would repeat, in a minor key, Abraham's journey out of Ur. It would be a miniature re-experience of the original Hebrew quest. I would go beyond—again; violate bounds; do a little forbidden trafficking in controlled substances; risk something just a bit "far out"; engage the possibility, however remote, of danger in the form of a drug bust; and, having dabbled in the thrill of daring, nibble on its fruit by swallowing the downer. After passing through the jeopardy of my private apocalypse, I'd reach that zone of balm which, for a while, would relieve me of the future, its worry and ferment. After chancing a modest Armageddon within time, I'd partake of a few tablets' worth of timelessness.

I'm not going to do any of that. That smidgeon of *en sof* in my system, that midget messiah, would only last a few hours. Then I would excrete Him and It. The future would have me by the throat again, even more tightly this time. Maybe I'd have to work harder, write faster, thinner words to support a habit. Only your near face can save mine naturally. But my eyes can't find the salvation of yours.

"Let's go," I say to daughter.

The car slows, stops before Viv's house. No opiate or

goofball can stop the Factory. It whirs on and on, in me and through me toward the mirage of payday. It surrounds every hour with its assembly lines and has the globe for a flywheel. It claims all my strength and demands all my alertness. The hour has come to make the scene, to pull our act together, to take the old plunge. For what purpose? Why ask the question when there's no time to pursue the answer? The party is twenty-three floors up, and to work it the work force must put itself in working order.

Daughter hides the measles doll in my Aux Chachkas bag; clutches her jacks pouch; smooths the *Divine Comedy* straws into a prettier, more gift-looking bundle. "You think Viv will like 'em?" she asks. I nod. I think: will it look odd, to enter carrying kiwi fruit like an errand boy? What kind of joke will take the edge off the meniality? I smooth my FIRST GRAFFITI shirt. We come anciently, but we have lost our ancestors' gift. The crosstown journey is over, the Factory whirs on. *"Where is our sabbath?"* I want to cry as we leave the car. *"Who stole my father's sabbath?"*

NOTES

p. 10   "is seen by us to be true . . .": Quoted in Rene Dubos, *So Human an Animal* (New York: Charles Scribner's Sons, 1968), p. 124.

p. 13   "Man is a creature . . .": Conversation with the author, February 9, 1987.

p. 13   "does not reside in the rationalized perfection . . .": Quoted in the *New York Times*, September 3, 1985.

p. 13   "When a plant starts edging . . .": Quoted in the *Atlantic Monthly*, December 1982, p. 100.

p. 13   "local political parties . . .": Quoted in the *New York Times*, March 27, 1984.

p. 17   "We can affirm that the idea . . .": W. Robertson Smith, *The Religion of the Ancient Semites* (New York: Schocken Books, 1972), p. 245.

p. 18   "the childlike spirit . . .": Joseph Campbell, *The Masks of God: Primitive Mythology* (New York: Penguin Books, 1979), p. 350.

p. 18   "the horrendous myths and rites . . .": Mircea Eliade, *A History of Religious Ideas* (Chicago: University of Chicago Press, 1978), pp. 38–39.

p. 19   "He tried to immortalize his name . . .": Quoted in Louis Ginzberg, *The Legends of the Jews* (New York: Simon & Schuster, 1961), p. 60.

p. 22   "The King of Upper and of Lower Egypt . . .": Quoted in Chester G. Starr, *A History of the Ancient World*, 2d ed. (New York: Oxford University Press, 1974), p. 59.

p. 24   "Every city is the natural enemy . . .": Quoted in Lewis Mumford, *The City in History* (New York: Harcourt, Brace & World, 1961), p. 51.

p. 44   First flag a placenta: Homer W. Smith, *Man and His Gods* (New York: Grosset & Dunlap, 1952), p. 16.

p. 53   "Let us endure an hour . . .": A. E. Housman, "Be Still, My Soul, Be Still."

p. 55   Nuclear war as ultimate fireworks: *New York Times*, January 17, 1985.

p. 61   "The messianic idea had compelled . . .": Gershom Scholem, *The Messianic Idea in Judaism* (New York: Schocken Books, 1972), p. 35.

p. 61   "Our life seems not present . . .": Ralph Waldo Emerson, "Experience."

p. 61   "For more than three centuries . . .": Octavio Paz, "A Literature of Foundations," *Triquarterly* 13–14 (1968–69): 9.

p. 61   "Americans love their country . . .": Quoted in Rene Dubos, *A God Within* (New York: Charles Scribner's Sons, 1972), p. 104.

p. 70   "The People are not and cannot be . . .": Quoted in Ernst Fischer, *The Necessity of Art* (London: Penguin Books, 1978), p. 81.

p. 70   "an institution in which a virtually unorganized mass . . .": Martin Buber, *Paths in Utopia* (Boston: Beacon Press, 1950), p. 133.

p. 71   "paradoxically many of the great figures . . .": Gershom Scholem, *Kabbalah* (New York: Quadrangle/New York Times Books, 1974), pp. 163, 348.

p. 92   "*Homo sapiens* is a nidicolous animal": Rene Spitz, *The First Year* (Madison, Conn.: International University Press, 1960), p. 3.

p. 98   "local freedoms died out . . .": Alexis de Tocqueville, *The Old Régime and the French Revolution*, trans. Stuart Gilbert (Garden City: Doubleday Anchor Books, 1955), p. 125.

p. 103 Tunisian students: John B. Oakes, "Youth's Threat to Tunisia," *New York Times*, April 13, 1984.

p. 103 Scions of royal Egyptian families: *Atlantic Monthly*, January 1982, p. 23.

p. 110 "I do not render the visible . . .": Epigraph, *Paul Klee— The Late Years* (New York: Serge Sabarsky Gallery, 1977).

p. 121 "Being recognized has its advantages . . .": Quoted by Liz Smith, *Daily News*, March 25, 1982.

p. 133 "chrism descends from . . .": W. Robertson Smith, *The Religion of the Ancient Semites* (New York: Schocken Books, 1972), pp. 383–84.

p. 135 "which contained records of evil deeds . . .": Robert Graves and Raphael Patai, *Hebrew Myths: The Book of Genesis* (New York: McGraw-Hill, 1964), p. 233.

p. 138 "No law can be sacred to me . . .": Ralph Waldo Emerson, "Self-Reliance."

p. 145 "The soul feels as if placed . . .": Quoted in William James, *The Varieties of Religious Experience* (New York: New American Library, 1958), p. 313.

WITHDRAWN

DATE DUE

GAYLORD			PRINTED IN U.S.A.